What Alice
Forgot

What Alice Forgot

Liane Moriarty

AMY EINHORN BOOKS
Published by G. P. Putnam's Sons
a member of
Penguin Group (USA) Inc.
New York

æ

AMY EINHORN BOOKS
Published by G. P. Putnam's Sons
Publishers Since 1838
Published by the Penguin Group
Penguin Group (USA) Inc., 375 Hudson Street, New York, New York
10014, USA • Penguin Group (Canada), 90 Eglinton Avenue East, Suite 700, Toronto, Ontario
M4P 2Y3, Canada (a division of Pearson Penguin Canada Inc.) • Penguin Books Ltd, 80 Strand,
London WC2R 0RL, England • Penguin Ireland, 25 St Stephen's Green, Dublin 2, Ireland
(a division of Penguin Books Ltd) • Penguin Group (Australia), 250 Camberwell Road,
Camberwell, Victoria 3124, Australia (a division of Pearson Australia Group Pty Ltd) • Penguin
Books India Pvt Ltd, 11 Community Centre, Panchsheel Park, New Delhi–110 017, India • Penguin
Group (NZ), 67 Apollo Drive, Rosedale, North Shore 0632, New Zealand (a division of
Pearson New Zealand Ltd) • Penguin Books (South Africa) (Pty) Ltd,
24 Sturdee Avenue, Rosebank, Johannesburg 2196, South Africa

Penguin Books Ltd, Registered Offices: 80 Strand, London WC2R 0RL, England

Copyright © 2009 by Liane Moriarty
First edition: Pan Macmillan Australia 2009
First American edition: Amy Einhorn Books 2011
All rights reserved. No part of this book may be reproduced, scanned, or distributed in any printed or
electronic form without permission. Please do not participate in or encourage piracy of copyrighted
materials in violation of the author's rights. Purchase only authorized editions.
Published simultaneously in Canada

Library of Congress Cataloging-in-Publication Data

Moriarty, Liane.
What Alice forgot / Liane Moriarty.—1st American ed.
p.   cm.
"First edition: Pan Macmillan Australia 2009"—T.p. verso.
ISBN 978-0-399-15718-9
1. Memory disorders—Fiction.   2. Amnesiacs—Family relationships—Fiction.   3. Life change
events—Fiction.   4. Australia—Fiction.   5. Domestic fiction.   I. Title.
PR9619.4.M67W48   2011   2011002904
823'.92—dc22

Printed in the United States of America
1 3 5 7 9 10 8 6 4 2

BOOK DESIGN BY NICOLE LAROCHE

For Adam

Chapter 1

She was floating, arms outspread, water lapping her body, breathing in a summery fragrance of salt and coconut. There was a pleasantly satisfied breakfast taste in her mouth of bacon and coffee and possibly croissants. She lifted her chin and the morning sun shone so brightly on the water, she had to squint through spangles of light to see her feet in front of her. Her toenails were each painted a different color. Red. Gold. Purple. Funny. The nail polish hadn't been applied very well. Blobby and messy. Someone else was floating in the water right next to her. Someone she liked a lot, who made her laugh, with toenails painted the same way. The other person waggled multicolored toes at her companionably, and she was filled with sleepy contentment. Somewhere in the distance, a man's voice shouted, "Marco?" and a chorus of children's voices cried back, "Polo!" The man called out again, "Marco, Marco, Marco?" and the voices answered, "Polo, Polo, Polo!" A child laughed; a long, gurgling giggle, like a stream of soap bubbles. A voice said quietly and insistently in her ear, "Alice?" and she tipped back her head and let the cool water slide silently over her face.

Tiny dots of light danced before her eyes.

Was it a dream or a memory?

"I don't know!" said a frightened voice. "I didn't see it happen!"

No need to get your knickers in a knot.

The dream or memory or whatever it was dissolved and vanished like a reflection on water, and instead fragments of thought began to drift through her head, as if she were waking up from a long, deep sleep, late on a Sunday morning.

Is cream cheese considered a soft cheese?

It's not a hard cheese.

It's not . . .

. . . hard at all.

So, logically, you would think . . .

. . . something.

Something logical.

Lavender is lovely.

Logically lovely.

Must prune back the lavender!

I can smell lavender.

No, I can't.

Yes, I can.

That's when she noticed the pain in her head for the first time. It hurt on one side, a lot, as if someone had given her a good solid thwack with a baseball bat.

Her thoughts sharpened. What was this pain in the head all about? Nobody had warned her about pain in her head. She had a whole list of peculiar symptoms to be prepared for: heartburn, a taste like aluminum foil in your mouth, dizziness, extreme tiredness—but nothing about a hammering ache at the side of your head. That one should really have been mentioned, because it was very painful. Of course, if she couldn't handle a run-of-the-mill *headache*, well then . . .

The scent of lavender seemed to be coming and going, like a gentle breeze.

She let herself drift again.

The best thing would be to fall back asleep and return to that lovely dream with the water and the multicolored toenails.

Actually, maybe someone had mentioned headaches and she forgot? Yes, they had! Headaches, for heaven's sake! Really bad ones. Fabulous.

So much to remember. No soft cheeses or smoked salmon or sushi because of the risk of that disease she never even knew existed. *Listeria.* Something to do with bacteria. Hurts the baby. That's why you weren't allowed to eat leftovers. One bite of a leftover chicken drumstick could kill the baby. The brutal responsibilities of parenthood.

For now, she would just go back to sleep. That was the best thing.

Listeria.

Wisteria.

The wisteria over the side fence is going to look stunning if it ever gets around to flowering.

Listeria, wisteria.

Ha. Funny words.

She smiled, but her head really did hurt a lot. She was trying to be brave.

"Alice? Can you hear me?"

The lavender smell got stronger again. A bit sickly sweet.

Cream cheese is a spreadable cheese. Not too soft, not too hard, just right. Like the baby bear's bed.

"Her eyelids are fluttering. Like she's dreaming."

It was no use. She couldn't get back to sleep, even though she felt exhausted, as if she could sleep forever. Were all pregnant women walking around with aching heads like this? Was the idea to toughen them up for labor pains? When she got up, she would check it out in one of the baby books.

She always forgot how pain was so upsetting. Cruel. It hurt your feelings.

You just wanted it to stop, please, right now. Epidurals were the way to go. One epidural for my headache, please. Thank you.

"Alice, try and open your eyes."

Was cream cheese even *cheese*? You didn't put a dollop of cream cheese on a cheese platter. Maybe cheese didn't actually mean cheese in the context of cream cheese. She wouldn't ask the doctor about it, just in case it's an embarrassing "Oh, Alice" mistake.

She couldn't get comfortable. The mattress felt like cold concrete. If she wriggled over, she could nudge Nick with her foot until he sleepily rolled over and pulled her to him in a big warm bear hug. Her human hot water bottle.

Where was Nick? Had he already got up? Maybe he was making her a cup of tea.

"Don't try and move, Alice. Just stay still and open your eyes, sweetie."

Elisabeth would know about the cream cheese. She'd snort in her big-sisterly way and be precise. Mum wouldn't have a clue. She'd be stricken. She'd say, "Oh dear, oh no! I'm sure I ate soft cheeses when I was pregnant with you girls! They didn't know about that sort of thing back then." She'd talk on and on and worry that Alice had accidentally broken a rule. Mum believed in rules. So did Alice actually.

Frannie wouldn't know but she'd research it, proudly, using her new computer, in the same way that she used to help Alice and Elisabeth find information for school projects in her *Encyclopedia Britannica*.

Her head really did hurt.

Presumably this was only the squidgiest fraction of how much labor would hurt. So that was just great.

It was not as if she'd actually *eaten* any cream cheese that she could remember.

"Alice? *Alice!*"

She didn't even really like cream cheese.

"Has someone called an ambulance?"

There was that smell of lavender again.

Once, when they were undoing their seat belts, Nick said (in answer to some fishing-for-compliments thing she'd just said), "Don't be ridiculous, you goose, you know I'm bloody besotted with you."

She opened the car door and felt sunshine on her legs and smelled the lavender she'd planted by the front door.

Bloody besotted.

It was a moment of lavender-scented bliss, after grocery shopping.

"It's coming. I called triple zero! That's the first time in my life I've ever called triple zero! I felt all self-conscious. I nearly called 911 like an American. I actually punched in the nine. There's proof I watch too much television."

"I hope it's not, like, serious. I mean, I couldn't, like, get sued or anything, could I?"

Was that talkback radio she could hear? She hated talkback radio. The callers were always appalled by something. Alice said once that she'd never been appalled by anything. Elisabeth said that was appalling.

"Alice, can you hear me? Can you hear me, Alice?"

Sultana, can you hear me? Can you hear me, Sultana?

Every night, before they went to sleep, Nick talked to the baby through an empty toilet roll pressed to Alice's stomach. He'd heard this idea on some radio show. They said that way the baby would learn to recognize the father's voice as well as the mother's.

"Ahoy!" he'd call. "Can you hear me, Sultana? This is your father speaking!" They'd read that the baby was the size of a sultana by now. So that's what they called it. Only in private, of course; they were cool parents-to-be. No sappiness in public.

The Sultana said it was fine, thanks, Dad, bit bored at times, but doing okay. Apparently he wished his mum would stop eating all that boring green shit and have a pizza for a change. "Enough with the rabbit food!" he demanded.

It seemed the Sultana was most likely to be a boy. He just seemed to have a masculine personality. The little rogue. They both agreed on this.

Alice would lie back and look at the top of Nick's head. There were a few shiny silvery strands. She didn't know if he knew about them, so she didn't mention them. He was thirty-two. The silver strands made her eyes blur. All those wacky pregnancy hormones.

Alice never talked out loud to the baby. She spoke to it in her mind, shyly, when she was in the bath (not too hot—so many rules). "Hey there, Baby," she'd think to herself, and then she'd be so overwhelmed by the wonder of it she'd splash the water with the flats of her palms like a kid thinking about Christmas. She was turning thirty soon, with a terrifying mortgage and a husband and a baby on the way, but she didn't feel that different from when she was fifteen.

Except, there were no moments of bliss after grocery shopping when she was fifteen. She hadn't met Nick yet. Her heart still had to be broken a few times before he could turn up and superglue it together with words like "besotted."

"Alice? Are you okay? Please open your eyes."

It was a woman's voice. Too loud and strident to ignore. It dragged her up into consciousness and wouldn't let her go.

It was a voice that gave Alice a familiar irritated itch of a feeling, like too-tight stockings.

This person did not belong in her bedroom.

She rolled her head to one side. *"Ow!"*

She opened her eyes.

There was a blur of unrecognizable colors and shapes. She couldn't even see the bedside cabinet to reach for her glasses. Her eyes must be getting worse.

She blinked, and blinked again, and then, like a sharpening telescope, everything came into focus. She was looking at someone's knees. How funny.

Knobbly pale knees.

She lifted her chin a fraction.

"There you are!"

It was Jane Turner of all people, from work, kneeling next to her. Her face was flushed and she had strands of sweaty hair pasted to her forehead. Her eyes looked tired. She had a soft, pudgy neck Alice had never noticed before. She was wearing a T-shirt with huge sweat marks and shorts and her arms were thin and white with dark freckles. Alice had never seen so much of Jane's body before. It was embarrassing. Poor old Jane.

"Listeria, wisteria," said Alice, to be humorous.

"You're delirious," said Jane. "Don't try and sit up."

"Hmmph," said Alice. "Don't want to sit up." She had a feeling she wasn't in bed; she seemed to be lying flat on her back on a cool laminated floor. Was she drunk? Had she forgotten she was pregnant and got *deliriously drunk*?

Her obstetrician was an urbane man who wore a bow tie and had a round face disconcertingly similar to that of one of Alice's ex-boyfriends. He said he didn't have a problem with "say, an aperitif followed by one glass of wine with dinner." Alice thought an aperitif must be a particular brand of drink. ("Oh, *Alice*," said Elisabeth.) Nick explained that an aperitif was a predinner drink. Nick came from an aperitif-drinking family. Alice came from a family with one dusty bottle of Baileys sitting hopefully in the back of the pantry behind the tins of spaghetti. In spite of what the obstetrician said, she'd only had a half a glass of champagne since she'd done the pregnancy test and she felt guilty about that even though everybody kept saying it was fine.

"Where am I?" asked Alice, terrified of the answer. Was she in some seedy nightclub? How could she explain to Nick that she forgot she was pregnant?

"You're at the gym," said Jane. "You fell and knocked yourself out. Gave me an absolute heart attack, although I was sort of grateful for the excuse to stop."

The gym? Alice didn't go to gyms. Had she woken up *drunk* in a *gym*?

"You lost your balance," said a sharp, jolly voice. "It was quite a fall!

Gave us all a shock, you silly sausage! We've called an ambulance, so don't you worry, we've got professional help on the way!"

Kneeling next to Jane was a thin, coffee-tanned girl with a bleached-blond ponytail, shiny Lycra shorts, and a cropped red top with the words SPIN CRAZY emblazoned across it. Alice felt instant dislike for her. She didn't like being called a silly sausage. It offended her dignity. One of Alice's faults, according to her sister Elisabeth, was a tendency to take herself too seriously.

"Did I faint?" asked Alice hopefully. Pregnant women fainted. She had never fainted in her life, although she spent most of fourth grade practicing, in the hope that she could be one of those lucky girls who fainted during church and had to be carried out, draped across the muscly arms of their PE teacher, Mr. Gillespie.

"It's just that I'm *pregnant*," she said. Let her see who she was calling a silly sausage.

Jane's mouth dropped. "Jesus, Alice, you are not!"

Spin Crazy Girl pursed her mouth as if she'd caught Alice out being naughty. "Oh dear, sweetie, I did ask at the beginning of the class if anyone was pregnant. I would have put you up front near the fan. You shouldn't have been so shy."

Alice's head thumped. Nothing anybody said was making sense.

"Pregnant," said Jane. "At this time. What a disaster."

"It is not!" Alice put a protective hand to her stomach, so the Sultana wouldn't hear and be offended. Their financial situation was none of Jane's business. People were meant to be delighted when you announced a pregnancy.

"I mean, what are you going to *do*?" asked Jane.

For heaven's sake! "Do? What do you mean, what am I going to do? I'm going to have a baby." She sniffed. "You smell of lavender. I knew I could smell lavender." Her sense of smell had been extra strong because of the pregnancy.

"It's my deodorant." Jane really didn't look like herself. Her eyes didn't look right. It was quite noticeable. Maybe she needed to start using some sort of eye cream.

"Are you all right, Jane?"

Jane snorted. "I'm fine. Worry about yourself, woman. You're the pregnant one knocking yourself out."

The baby! She'd been selfishly thinking about her sore head when she should have been worrying about the poor little Sultana. What sort of a mother was she going to be?

She said, "I hope I didn't hurt the baby when I fell."

"Oh, babies are pretty tough, I wouldn't worry about that."

It was another woman's voice. For the first time Alice looked up and realized a crowd of red-faced, middle-aged women in sports gear surrounded her. Some of them were leaning forward, staring at her with avid road-accident interest, while others had their hands on their hips and were chatting to one another as if they were at a party. They seemed to be in a small, fluorescent-lit room. She could hear tinny music somewhere in the distance, clanking metal sounds, and a sudden burst of loud masculine laughter. As she lifted her head, she saw that the room was filled with stationary bikes, all crammed together and facing the same direction.

"Although, you shouldn't really be doing exercise that gets your heart rate up too high if you're pregnant," said another woman.

"But I don't do *any* exercise," said Alice. "I should do more exercise."

"You, my girl, couldn't do any more exercise if you tried," said Jane.

"I don't know what you're talking about." She looked around at the strange faces surrounding her. This was all so . . . silly. "I don't know where I am."

"She's probably got a concussion," said somebody excitedly. "Concussed people are dazed and disoriented."

Spin Crazy Girl looked frightened and stroked Alice's arm. "Oh dear, sweetie, YOU MIGHT BE JUST A LITTLE BIT CONCUSSED," she yelled.

"Yes, but I don't think that makes her deaf," said Jane tersely. She lowered her voice and bent her head toward Alice. "Everything is fine. You're at the gym, you were doing your Friday spin class, the one you've been wanting to drag me along to for ages, remember? Can't quite see the attraction, actually. Anyway, you must have got dizzy, or fainted or something, because one minute you were riding like a madwoman and next thing you were crashing to the floor. You're going to be fine. More importantly, why didn't you tell me you were pregnant?"

"What's a Friday spin class?" asked Alice.

"Oh, this is *bad*," said Jane excitedly.

"The ambulance is here!" someone said.

Spin Crazy Girl became goofy with relief. She bounded to her feet and shooed at the ladies like an energetic housewife with a broom. "Right, gang, let's give them some space, shall we?"

Jane stayed kneeling on the floor next to Alice, patting her distractedly on the shoulder. Then she stopped patting. "Oh, my. Why do you get all the fun?"

Alice twisted her head and saw two handsome men in blue overalls striding toward them, carrying first aid equipment. Embarrassed, she struggled to sit up.

"Stay there, honey," called out the taller one.

"He looks just like George Clooney," breathed Jane in her ear. He did, too. Alice couldn't help but feel cheerier. It seemed she'd woken up in an episode of *ER*.

"Hey, there." George Clooney squatted down next to them, big hands resting between his knees. "What's your name?"

"Jane," said Jane. "Oh. Her name is Alice."

"What's your full name, Alice?" George gently took her wrist and pushed two fingers against her pulse.

"Alice Mary Love."

"Had a bit of a fall did you, Alice?"

"Apparently I did. I don't remember it." Alice felt teary and special, as she generally did when she talked to any health professional, even a chemist. She blamed her mother for making too much of a fuss over her when she was sick as a child. She and Elisabeth were both terrible hypochondriacs.

"Do you know where you are?" asked George.

"Not really," said Alice. "Apparently I'm in a *gym*."

"She fell off her bike during the spin class." Jane adjusted her bra strap beneath her top. "I saw it happen. I'm pretty sure she fainted. Her head smashed against the handlebars of the bike next to her. She's been unconscious for about ten minutes."

Spin Crazy Girl reappeared, ponytail swinging, and Alice stared up at her smooth long legs and hard flat stomach. It looked like a pretend stomach. "She can't have had her feet strapped to the pedals properly. I *do* make a point of reminding everyone about that at the beginning of the class. It's a safety issue," said Spin Crazy Girl to George Clooney in the confidential tone of one professional talking to another. "Also, I really don't recommend spin classes to pregnant women. I *did* ask if anyone was pregnant."

"Don't worry, we'll sue if necessary," said Jane quietly to Alice.

"How many weeks are you, Alice?" asked George.

Alice went to answer and to her surprise found a blank space in her head.

"Thirteen," she said, after a second. "I mean, fourteen. Fourteen weeks." They'd had the twelve-week ultrasound at least two weeks ago. The Sultana had done a peculiar little jump, like a disco dance move, as if someone had poked it in the back, and afterward Nick and Alice had kept trying to replicate the movement for people. Everyone had been polite and said it was remarkable.

She put a hand to her stomach again and for the first time she noticed what she was wearing. Sneakers and white socks. Black shorts and a yellow sleeveless top with a shiny gold-foil sticker stuck to her top. It seemed to be a picture of a dinosaur with a balloon coming out of its mouth saying, "ROCK ON." Rock on?

"Where did these clothes come from?" she asked Jane accusingly. "These aren't my clothes."

Jane raised a meaningful eyebrow at George.

"There's a dinosaur stuck to my shirt," said Alice, awestruck.

"What day of the week is it today, Alice?" asked George.

"Friday," answered Alice. She was cheating, because Jane had told her they were doing a "Friday spin class." Whatever that was.

"Remember what you had for breakfast?" George gently examined the side of her head while he talked. The other paramedic strapped a blood-pressure monitor to her upper arm and pumped it up.

"Peanut butter on toast?"

That was what she generally had for breakfast. It seemed a safe bet.

"He doesn't actually *know* what you had for breakfast," said Jane. "He's trying to see if you *remember* what you had for breakfast."

The blood-pressure monitor squeezed hard around Alice's arm.

George sat back on his haunches and said, "Humor me, Alice, and tell me the name of our illustrious prime minister."

"John Howard," answered Alice obediently. She hoped there wouldn't be any more questions about politics. It wasn't her forte. She could never get appalled enough.

Jane made a strange explosive sound of derision and mirth.

"Oh. Ah. But he's still the prime minister, isn't he?" Alice was mortified. People were going to tease her about this for years to come. Oh, *Alice*, you don't know the prime minister! Had she missed an election? "But I'm sure he's the prime minister."

"And what year is it?" George didn't seem too concerned.

"It's 1998," Alice answered promptly. She felt confident about that one. The baby would be born next year, in 1999.

Jane pressed her hand over her mouth. George went to speak, but Jane interrupted him. She put her hand on Alice's shoulder and stared at her intently. Her eyes were wide with excitement. Tiny balls of mascara hovered on the ends of her eyelashes. The combination of her lavender deodorant and garlic breath was quite overpowering.

"How old are you, Alice?"

"I'm twenty-nine, *Jane*." Alice was irritated by Jane's dramatic tone. What was she getting at? "Same age as you."

Jane sat back up and looked at George Clooney triumphantly.

She said, "I just got an invitation to her fortieth birthday."

That was the day Alice Mary Love went to the gym and carelessly misplaced a decade of her life.

Chapter 2

J ane said of course she would have come to the hospital with her but she had to be in court at two o'clock.

"What are you going to court for?" asked Alice, who was perfectly happy not to have Jane come to the hospital. That was quite enough of Jane for one day. *"An invitation to her fortieth birthday."* What exactly did she mean by that?

Jane smiled oddly and didn't answer Alice's question about court. "I'll call someone to be there at the hospital waiting for you."

"Not someone." Alice watched the paramedics set up a stretcher for her. It looked a bit flimsy. "Nick."

"Yes, of *course*, I'll call *Nick*." Jane enunciated her words carefully, as if she were acting in a children's pantomime.

"Actually, I'm sure I can walk," Alice said to George Clooney. She never liked the idea of being lifted by people, even Nick, who was pretty strong. She worried about her weight. What if the paramedics grunted and grimaced like furniture removalists when they lifted the stretcher? "I feel fine. Just my head."

"You're suffering from a pretty serious concussion there," said George. "We can't muck around with head injuries."

"Come on now, our favorite part of the job is carrying attractive women around on stretchers," said the other paramedic. "Don't deprive us."

"Yes, don't deprive them, Alice," said Jane. "Your brain is damaged. You think you're twenty-nine."

What did that mean, exactly?

Alice lay back and allowed the two men to efficiently lift her onto the stretcher. As her head rolled to one side, the pain made her dizzy.

"Oh, here's her bag." Jane picked up a rucksack from the side of the room and squashed it next to Alice.

"That's not mine," said Alice.

"Yes it is."

Alice stared at the red canvas bag. There was a row of three shiny dinosaur stickers like the one on her shirt stuck across the top flap. She wondered if she was about to be sick.

The two paramedics lifted up the stretcher. They didn't seem to have a problem carrying it. She guessed it was their job to lift all-sized people.

"Work!" said Alice in a sudden panic. "You'd better call work for me. Why aren't we at work if it's a Friday?"

"Well, I really don't know! Why aren't *we* at work?" repeated Jane in that pantomime voice again. "But don't you worry a thing about it, I'll call 'Nick,' and then I'll call 'work.' So by work I assume you mean, ah, ABR Bricks?"

"Yes, Jane, I do," said Alice carefully. They'd been working at ABR for three years now. Could the poor girl have some sort of mental illness?

Alice said, "You'd better let Sue know I won't be in today."

"Sue," repeated Jane slowly. "And by Sue, I take it you mean Sue Mason."

"Yes, Jane. Sue Mason." (Definitely loopy.)

Sue Mason was their boss. She was a stickler for punctuality and medical certificates and appropriate work attire. Alice couldn't wait for her maternity leave to start so she could get out of the place.

"Get better soon, Alice!" Spin Crazy Girl called out from the front of the room, her voice amplified by a microphone strapped to her head. She was sitting astride a bike up on a small raised platform, facing the class. There was a television screen flickering above her head and a huge rotating fan next to her. All of the women except for Jane had climbed back onto their bikes and were pedaling slowly, their eyes fixed on some invisible horizon. As Alice's stretcher reached the door, there was a burst of loud throbbing music and the lights in the room suddenly went out, plunging them into darkness. "Let's go, team!" shouted Spin Crazy Girl. "We've got to make up for lost time! Where were we?"

"Stuck behind a semi-trailer halfway up the mountain!" shouted one of the women.

"That's right! Let's push it up a notch! Push it, push it, push it . . . and *out of the saddle*!"

The women's bottoms lifted simultaneously in the air as they stood up on their pedals, their strong legs pumping like pistons.

Goodness, thought Alice.

Jane propped a heavy glass door open with her foot, and Alice clutched the sides of the stretcher, worried that they'd have to turn her on an angle, like a sofa, but the paramedics carried her smoothly through.

"You'll be fine," said Jane, giving one of Alice's sneakers a jaunty pat.

The glass door closed, and the music's volume was suddenly reduced to the sound of a distant party. Alice could see Jane's face through the glass, watching them go. She was pinching her lower lip together with her finger and thumb, so she looked like a fish.

She must remember every moment of this freaky day to tell Nick. He'd think it was hilarious. Yes, this whole day was quite a hoot.

Now she was being carried through another, much larger, blue-carpeted room, with rows of complicated-looking machinery being operated by men and women who all seemed to be straining to lift, pull, or push things that were far too heavy for them. The place had the studious, muted feel of a library. Nobody stopped what they were doing as the stretcher went by. Only their eyes followed with blank, impersonal interest, as if she were a news event on TV.

"Alice!"

A man stepped off a treadmill, pushing his headphones down from his ears and onto his shoulders. "What happened to you?"

His face—bright red and beaded with sweat—meant nothing to her. Alice stared up at him, groping for something polite to say. It was surreal, making conversation with a stranger while lying flat on her back on a stretcher. She was in one of those dreams where she turned up at a cocktail party in her pajamas.

"Fell off her bike and got a bit of a bump on the noggin," George Clooney answered for her, sounding not at all medical.

"Oh no!" The man smeared a towel across his forehead. "Just what you need, with the big day coming up!"

Alice attempted to pull a rueful face about the big day coming up. Perhaps he was one of Nick's colleagues and it was some work function she was meant to know about?

"Well, that'll teach you to be such a gym addict, eh, Alice?"

"Ho," said Alice. She wasn't sure what she'd been trying to say, but that's what it came out as: "Ho."

As the paramedics kept walking, the man climbed back onto his treadmill and started running, calling out after her, "Take care, Alice! I'll get Maggie to call!" He held up his thumb and little finger to his ear.

Alice closed her eyes. Her stomach churned.

"You doing okay there, Alice?" asked George Clooney.

Alice opened her eyes. "I feel a bit sick," she said.

"That's to be expected."

They stopped in front of a lift.

"I really don't know where I am," she reminded George. She felt like it was worth mentioning again.

"Don't worry about it for now," said George.

The lift doors hissed open and a woman with sleek bobbed hair stepped out. "Alice! Are you okay? What happened?" She had one of those "How now, brown cow" accents. "What a coincidence! I was just *thinking* about you! I was going to call you about the—ahh, the little incident—at school, Chloe told me about it, you poor thing! Oh dear, this is all you need! What with tomorrow night, and the big day coming up!"

As she kept talking, the paramedics maneuvered the stretcher into the lift and pressed the "G" button. The doors slid shut on the woman lifting a pretend phone to her ear just like the treadmill guy, while at the same time a voice cried out, "Is that *Alice Love* I just saw on that stretcher?"

George said, "You know a lot of people."

"No," said Alice. "No, I really don't."

She thought about Jane saying, *"I just got an invitation to her fortieth birthday."*

She turned her head and was sick all over George Clooney's nice, shiny black shoes.

Elisabeth's Homework for Dr. Hodges

It was just toward the end of the lunch break when I got the call. I only had five minutes before I was back on and I should have been in the bathroom checking I didn't have food between my teeth. She said, "Elisabeth, oh, hi, it's Jane, I've got a problem here," as if there was only one Jane in the whole world (you would think somebody named Jane would be in the habit of giving their last name) and I was thinking Jane, Jane, a Jane with a problem, and then I realized it was Jane Turner. Alice's Jane.

She said that Alice had fallen over at the gym during her spin class.

So there I was with 143 people all sitting back behind their tables, pouring their ice water, eating their mints, looking expectantly at the podium with pens poised, who had each paid $2,950 to see me speak, or $2,500 if they took advantage of the Early Bird discount.

That's how much people pay me to teach them how to write a successful direct-mail campaign. I know! That nasty commercial world out there is entirely foreign to you, isn't it, Dr. Hodges? I could tell you were just politely nodding your head when I tried to explain my job. I'm sure it has never occurred to you that those letters and brochures you receive in the mail are actually written by real people. Real people like me. I bet you have a "NO JUNK MAIL" sticker on your letterbox. Don't worry. I won't hold it against you.

Anyway, it wasn't exactly the most convenient time for me to go rushing off to see my sister because she'd had a *gym* accident (some of us have jobs; some of us don't have time to go to the gym in the middle of the day). Especially when I wasn't talking to her since the banana muffins incident. I know we talked at length about trying to see her actions from a more "rational perspective," but I'm still not talking to her. (Of course she doesn't actually KNOW I'm not talking to her, but allow me my childish satisfaction.)

I said to Jane (somewhat irritably and self-importantly, I admit), "Is it serious?" For some reason it never occurred to me that it really could be serious.

Jane said, "She thinks it's 1998 and she's twenty-nine and we're still working together at ABR Bricks, so it's seriously weird, that's for sure."

Then she said, "Oh, and I assume you know she's pregnant?"

I am deeply ashamed of my reaction. All I can say, Dr. Hodges, is that it was as involuntary and unstoppable as a huge hay-fevery sneeze.

It was a feeling of trembly rage and it went from my stomach to my head in a WHOOSH, and I said, "I'm sorry, Jane, I have to go now," and hung up.

George Clooney was very nice about his shoes. Alice was appalled and tried to climb out of the stretcher so she could somehow help clean them, if she could have just found a tissue from somewhere, perhaps in that strange canvas bag, but both paramedics got stern with her and insisted that she stay still.

Her stomach felt better when she was buckled into the back of the ambulance. The chunky clean white plastic all around her was reassuring; everything felt sensible and sterile.

It seemed to be quite a sedate trip to the hospital, like catching a cab. As far as Alice could tell, they weren't screeching through the streets, flashing their lights at other cars to get out of the way.

"So I guess I'm not dying, then?" she asked George. The other guy was driving and George Clooney was in the back with Alice. He had hairy eyebrows, she noticed. Nick had big bushy eyebrows, too. Late one night Alice had tried to pluck them for him and he'd yelled so loud, she was worried Mrs. Bergen from next door would do her neighborhood-watch duty and call the police.

"You'll be back at the gym in no time," answered George.

"I don't go to the gym," said Alice. "I don't believe in gyms."

"I'm with you." George smiled and patted her arm.

She watched bits of billboards and office buildings and sky flash by through the ambulance window behind George's head.

Okay, so this was all very silly. It was only the "bump on the noggin" that was making everything seem strange. This was just a longer, more intense version of that funny, dreamlike feeling you got when you woke up on holiday and couldn't think where you were. There was no need to panic. This was *interesting*! She just needed to focus.

"What time is it?" she asked George determinedly.

"Nearly lunchtime," he said, glancing at his watch.

Right. Lunchtime. Lunchtime on a Friday.

She said, "Why did you ask what I had for breakfast before?"

"It's one of those standard questions we ask people with head injuries. We're trying to ascertain your mental state."

So presumably if she could remember what she had for breakfast, everything else would fall into place.

Breakfast. This morning. Oh, come on now. She must be able to remember.

The *idea* of a weekday breakfast was clear in her mind. It was two pieces of toast popping up in tandem from the toaster and the kettle bubbling crossly and the morning light slanting across the kitchen floor, just in front of the fridge, lighting up the big brown splotch on the linoleum, which looked like it could be scrubbed away in a jiffy, but most certainly couldn't. It was glancing up at the railway clock Nick's mother had given them as a housewarming present, with the fervent hope that it might be earlier than she thought (it was always later). It was the crackly background sound of ABC morning radio—worried, intense voices talking about world issues. Nick listened and sometimes said things like "You've got to be kidding," and Alice let the voices wash over her and tried to pretend she was still asleep.

She and Nick were not morning people. They liked this about each other, having both been in previous relationships with intolerably cheery morning people. They spoke in short, terse sentences and sometimes it was a game, exaggerating their grumpiness, and sometimes it wasn't, and that was fine, because they knew their real selves would be back that evening after work.

She tried to think of a *specific* breakfast memory.

There was that chilly morning when they were halfway through painting the kitchen. It was raining hard outside and there was a strong smell of paint fumes tickling her nostrils as they silently ate peanut butter on toast sitting on the floor, because all the furniture was covered with drop sheets. Alice was still in her nightie, but she'd put a cardigan on over the top of it, and she was wearing Nick's old football socks pulled up to her knees. Nick was shaved, and dressed, except for his tie. The night before he'd told her about a really important scary presentation he had to give to the Shiny-headed Twerp, the Motherfucking Megatron, and the Big Kahuna all at the same time. Alice, who was terrified of public speaking, had felt her own stomach clench in sympathy. That morning Nick took a sip of his tea, put down his mug, opened his mouth to bite the toast, and dropped it onto his favorite blue-striped shirt. It stuck right to the front of his shirt. Their eyes met in mutual shock. Nick slowly peeled off the toast to reveal a big greasy rectangle of peanut butter. He said, in the tone of a man who has just been fatally shot, "That was my only clean shirt," and then he took the piece of toast and slammed it against his forehead.

Alice said, "No it's not. I took a load while you were at squash last night." They didn't have a washing machine yet and they were taking all their clothes to the laundry down the road. Nick took the squished-up toast off his face and said, "You didn't," and she said, "I did," and he crawled through tins of paint and put both hands on her face and gave her a long, tender, peanut-buttery kiss.

But that wasn't this morning's breakfast. That was months ago, or weeks ago, or something. The kitchen was finished. She hadn't been pregnant then either. She was still drinking coffee.

There were a few breakfasts in a row where they were on a health kick and they had yogurt with fruit. When was that? The health kick didn't last very long, even though they were pretty gung ho about it in the beginning.

There were breakfasts when Nick was away for work. She ate her toast in bed when he was away, relishing the romantic pain of missing him, as if he were a sailor or a soldier. It was like enjoying feeling hungry when you knew you'd be having a huge dinner.

There was that breakfast where they had a fight—faces ugly, eyes blazing, doors slamming—about running out of milk. That wasn't so nice. (That breakfast definitely wasn't this morning. She remembered how they forgave each other that night while they were watching Nick's youngest sister acting a tiny part in a stupendously long postmodern play that neither of them could understand. "By the way, I forgive you," Nick had leaned over and whispered in her ear, and she'd whispered back, "Excuse me, *I* forgive *you*," and a woman in front had turned around and hissed, "Shhh! Both of you!" like an angry schoolteacher and they'd got the giggles so badly, they ended up having to leave the theater, clambering past knees and getting into terrible trouble afterward from Nick's sister.)

There was a breakfast where she'd grumpily read out possible baby names from a book while he'd grumpily said yes or no. That was nice, because they were definitely both only pretending to be grumpy that morning. "I can't believe they let us *name* a person," Nick had said. "It feels like something only the King of the Land should be able to do." "Or the Queen of the Kingdom," Alice said. "Oh, they'd never let a *woman* name a person," said Nick. "Obviously."

Did *that* happen this morning? No. That was . . . some time. Not this morning.

She had absolutely no idea what she'd eaten for breakfast that morning.

She confessed to George Clooney, "I just said I had peanut butter on toast because that's my normal breakfast. I can't actually remember anything about breakfast at all."

"That's fine, Alice," he answered. "I don't think I can remember what I had for breakfast myself."

"Oh." Well, so much for ascertaining her mental state! Did George actually know what he was doing?

"Maybe you've got concussion, too," said Alice. George laughed dutifully. He seemed to be losing interest in her. Maybe he was hoping his next patient would be more interesting. He probably liked using those heart defibrillator thingummies. Alice would if she were a paramedic.

One Sunday, when Nick had a hangover and she was trying to convince him to go to the beach with her and he was lying on the couch with his eyes closed, ignoring her, she said, "Oh, no, he's flatlining!" and rubbed two spatulas together before pressing them to his chest, yelling, "Clear!" Nick obligingly gave a realistic spasm right on cue. He still wouldn't move, until she cried, "He's not breathing! We've got to intubate him—*now*!" and tried to shove a straw down his throat.

The ambulance pulled up at a traffic light and Alice shifted slightly. Everything felt wrong about her body. She felt an overwhelming tiredness deep in her bones, as if she could sleep forever, but at the same time a jittery, twitchy energy making her want to get up and achieve something. It must be the pregnancy. Everyone said your body didn't feel like yours anymore.

She lowered her chin to look again at the strange, damp clothes she was wearing. They didn't even look like something she'd choose. She never wore yellow. The panicky feeling rose up again and she looked away and back up at the ambulance ceiling.

The thing was, she couldn't remember what she had for dinner last night either. Nothing. It wasn't even on the tip of her tongue.

Her chicken thing with the beans? Nick's favorite lamb curry? She had no idea.

Of course, weekdays always tended to mulch together anyway. She would try to remember what she did last weekend.

A tangled jumble of memories from various weekends poured into her head as if from an upturned laundry basket. Sitting on the grass in the park, reading the paper. Picnics. Walking around garden centers, arguing about plants. Working on the house. Always, always working on the house. Movies. Dinners. Coffee with Elisabeth. Sunday-morning sex, followed by sleep, followed by croissants from the Vietnamese bakery. Friends' birthdays. An occasional wedding. Trips away. Things with Nick's family.

Somehow she knew that none of them had happened last weekend. She couldn't tell when they'd happened. A short time ago or a long time ago. They'd just happened.

The problem was that she couldn't attach herself to a "today" or a "yesterday" or even a "last week." She was floating helplessly above the calendar like an escaped balloon.

An image came into her head of a gray cloudy sky filled with bunches of pink balloons tied together with white ribbon like bouquets. The balloon bouquets were being whipped ferociously about by an angry wind, and she felt a great wrench of sadness.

The feeling disappeared like a wave of nausea.

Goodness. What was *that* all about?

She longed for Nick. He would be able to fix everything. He would tell her exactly what they ate for dinner last night and what they did on the weekend.

Hopefully he would be waiting for her at the hospital. He might have already bought flowers for her. He probably had. She hoped he hadn't because it was far too extravagant.

Of course, really, she hoped he had. She'd been in an *ambulance*. She sort of deserved them.

The ambulance came to a stop and George leapt to his feet, ducking down so as not to bump his head.

"We're here, Alice! How are you feeling? You look like you've been thinking deeply profound thoughts."

He pushed the lever to open the back door of the ambulance and sunlight flooded in, making her blink.

"I never asked your name," said Alice.

"Kevin," answered George apologetically, as if he knew it would be a disappointment.

Elisabeth's Homework for Dr. Hodges

The truth is that sometimes my work gives me a little "rush," Dr. Hodges. I'm embarrassed to admit it. Not a huge rush. But a definite shot of adrenaline. When the lights go dim and the audience goes quiet and it's just me up there alone on the stage and my assistant Layla gives me her dead-serious "OK" signal as if this is a NASA space launch we're running. The spotlight like sunshine on my face, and all I can hear is the clinking of water glasses and maybe a respectfully restrained cough or two. I like that clean, crisp, no-nonsense smell of hotel function rooms and the chilly air-conditioned air. It clears out my head. And when I speak the microphone smooths out my voice, giving it authority.

But then again, other times, I walk onto the stage and I feel like there is some weight pressing on the back of my neck, making my head droop and my back hunch, like an old crone. I want to put my mouth close to the microphone and say, "What is the point of all this, ladies and gentlemen? You all seem like nice enough people, so help me out and tell me, what is the point?"

Actually, I do know the point.

The point is they're helping pay the mortgage. They're each making a contribution to our groceries and our electricity and our water and our Visa. They're all generously chipping in for the syringes and the shapeless hospital gowns and that last anaesthetist with the kind, doggy eyes who held my hand and said, "Go to sleep now, darling." Anyway, I digress. You want me to digress. You want me to just write and write whatever comes to my mind. I wonder if you find me boring. You always look gently interested, but maybe you have days where I walk in the office looking all needy, bursting to tell you all the pathetic details of my life, and you just long to put your elbows on your desk and your chin in your hands and say, "What is the point of all this, Elisabeth?" and then you remember that the point is that I am paying for *your* Visa, mortgage, grocery bills . . . and so the world goes around.

You mentioned the other day that a feeling of pointlessness is a sign of depression, but you see there, I don't have depression, because I do see the point. Money is the point.

After I hung up on Jane, the phone rang again immediately (presumably her—thinking we'd been cut off) and I turned it off mid-ring. A man walking by said, "Sometimes you wonder if we'd all be better off without these damned things!" and I said, "Damned right!" (I have never said "Damned right!" in my life before; it just popped bizarrely into my head. I like it. I might say it our next session and see if you blink) and he said, "Congratulations, by the way. I've been to a lot of these sorts of workshops before and I've never heard anyone speak such good sense!"

He was flirting with me. It happens sometimes. It must be the microphone and the bright lights. It's funny because I always think it must be obvious to any man that all my sexuality has been sucked out of me. I feel like a piece of dried fruit. Yes, that's it. I AM A DRIED APRICOT, Dr. Hodges. Not one of those nice, soft, juicy ones, but a hard, shriveled, tasteless dried apricot that hurts your jaw.

I took a few deep breaths of bracing air-conditioned air and clipped the microphone back onto my jacket. I was in such a frenzy to get back onstage, I was actually trembling. I feel like I may have become temporarily deranged for a while this afternoon, Dr. Hodges. We can discuss this at our next session.

Or maybe temporary insanity is just an excuse for inexcusable behavior. Maybe I'll be too ashamed to tell you that somebody called to say my only sister had been in an accident and I hung up on her. I package myself for you. I want to sound damaged, so you feel there is something useful for you to do, but at the same time I want you to think I'm a nice person, Dr. Hodges. A nice damaged person.

I strode onto that stage like a rock star—and I started talking about "visualizing your prospect" and I was on fire. I had them laughing. I had them competing with each other to yell out answers to me, and the whole time we were visualizing the prospect I was visualizing my little sister.

I was thinking, head injuries can be pretty serious.

I was thinking, Nick is away and this is not really Jane's responsibility.

And finally I thought: Alice was pregnant with Madison in 1998.

Chapter 3

Nick wasn't waiting at the hospital with flowers for Alice. Nobody was waiting for her, which made her feel slightly heroic.

Her two paramedics disappeared as if they'd never existed. She couldn't recall them actually saying goodbye, so she didn't get to say thank you.

The hospital was all flurries of activity, followed by periods of waiting alone on a stretcher in a small white box of a room, staring at the ceiling.

A doctor appeared and shone a tiny pencil-thin torch in her eyes and asked her to follow his fingers back and forth. A nurse with stunning green eyes that matched her hospital uniform stood at the end of her stretcher with a clipboard asking about health insurance and allergies and next of kin. Alice complimented her on her green eyes and the nurse said they were colored contacts and Alice said, "Oh," and felt duped.

An icepack was applied to what the green-eyed nurse described as an "ostrich egg" on the back of her head, and she was given two white tablets in a tiny plastic cup for the pain, but Alice explained the pain wasn't that bad and she didn't want to take anything because she was pregnant.

People kept asking her questions, in voices that were too loud, as if she were asleep, even though she was looking right at them. Did she remember falling over? Did she remember the trip in the ambulance? Did she know what day of the week it was? Did she know what date it was?

"Nineteen ninety-eight?" A harried-looking doctor peered down at her through glasses with red plastic rims. "Are you quite sure about that?"

"Yes," said Alice. "I know it's 1998 because my baby is due on August eight, 1999. Eighth of the eighth, ninety-nine. Easy to remember."

"Because, you see, it's actually 2008," said the doctor.

"Well, that's not possible," explained Alice as nicely as she could. Maybe this doctor was one of those brilliant people who were hopeless with normal stuff like dates.

"And why isn't it possible?"

"Because we haven't had the new millennium yet," said Alice cleverly. "Apparently all the power is going to fail because of some computer bug."

She felt proud of knowing that fact; it was sort of current affair–ish.

"I think you might be confused. You don't remember the new millennium? Those great fireworks on the harbor bridge?"

"No," said Alice. "I don't remember any fireworks." Please stop it, she wanted to say. This isn't funny, and I'm just being brave about the pain in my head. It really does hurt.

She remembered Nick saying one night, "Do you realize that on New Year's Eve of the new millennium we will have a toddler?" He was holding a sledgehammer in both hands because he was about to knock down a wall.

Alice had lowered the camera she was holding to photograph the end of the wall. "That's true," she'd said, amazed and terrified by the thought. A toddler: an actual miniature person, created by them, belonging to them, separate from them.

"Yep, guess we'll have to get a babysitter for the little bugger," Nick had said with elaborate nonchalance. Then he'd joyfully swung the hammer and Alice had clicked the camera as a shower of pink plaster fragments rained down all over them.

"Maybe I should get an ultrasound to check that my baby is okay after the fall," said Alice firmly to the doctor. This was how Elisabeth would be in a situation like this. Alice always thought "What would Elisabeth do?" whenever she needed to be assertive.

"How many weeks pregnant are you?" asked the doctor.

"Fourteen," said Alice, but there was that strange space in her mind again, as if she wasn't absolutely sure that was correct.

"Or you could at least check the heartbeat," said Alice in her Elisabeth voice.

"Mmmm." The doctor pushed her glasses back up her nose.

A memory of a woman's voice with a gentle American accent came into Alice's head.

"I'm sorry, but there is no heartbeat."

She remembered it so clearly. The tiny pause after the "sorry."

"I'm sorry, but there is no heartbeat."

Who was that? Who said that? Did it really happen? Tears welled in Alice's eyes, and she thought again of those bouquets of pink balloons whipped by the wind in a gray sky. Had she seen those balloons in some long-forgotten movie? Some extremely sad movie? She felt another wave of extraordinary feeling rise in her chest. It was just like in the ambulance. It was a feeling of grief and rage. She imagined herself sobbing, wailing, digging her fingernails into her own flesh (and she'd never behaved like that in her whole life). And just when she thought the feeling would sweep her away, it dissolved into nothing. It was the strangest thing.

"How many children do you have?" asked the doctor. She had pulled up Alice's T-shirt and pushed down her shorts to feel her abdomen.

Alice blinked to make the tears go away. "None. This is my first pregnancy."

The doctor stopped and looked at her. "That looks very much like a cesarean scar to me."

Alice lifted her head awkwardly and saw that the doctor was pointing a nicely shaped fingernail low down on Alice's stomach. She squinted and saw what looked like a very pale, purple line just above the top of her pubic hair.

"I don't know what that is," said Alice, mortified. She thought of the solemn expression on her mother's face when she used to tell Elisabeth and Alice, "You must never show your private lady's parts to anyone." Nick fell about laughing the first time he heard that. Why hadn't he noticed that funny scar? He'd spent enough time examining her private lady's parts.

"Your uterus doesn't seem to be enlarged for fourteen weeks," commented the doctor.

Alice looked again at her stomach and saw that it was actually looking pretty flat. Skinny-person flat, which would normally be an unexpected bonus, except that she was having a baby. Nick had started to chuckle gleefully whenever she wore something that showed the round bulge of her stomach.

"Are you sure you're that far along?" said the doctor.

Alice stared at her flat stomach—very flat!—and didn't say anything. She was filled with confusion and fear and excruciating embarrassment. It occurred to her that her breasts—which had become so heavy and tingly and overtly *breasty*—felt like they had gone back to their normal humble, unobtrusive state. She didn't feel pregnant. She certainly didn't feel like herself, but she didn't feel pregnant.

(What was that scar? She thought of those stories of people drugging you and removing your organs to sell. Had she gone to the gym, got deliriously drunk, and someone had taken the opportunity to help themselves to her organs?)

"Maybe I'm not fourteen weeks," she said to the doctor. "Maybe I've got that wrong. I can't seem to get anything straight in my head. My husband will be here soon. He'll explain everything."

"Well, you just relax and try not to worry for now." The doctor readjusted Alice's clothes with gentle pats. "First we're going to get you a CT scan and see if you've done anything serious to yourself, but I think you'll find things will start to fall into place soon. Do you remember your obstetrician's name? I could give him or her a call and check how far along you are. I don't want to upset you if we can't find the heartbeat because you're not far enough along to hear it."

I'm sorry, but there is no heartbeat.

It was such a clear memory. It felt like it really happened.

Alice said, "Dr. Sam Chapple. He's at Chatswood."

"Okay, good. Don't worry. It's perfectly normal to feel confused after a serious head injury."

The doctor smiled sympathetically and left the room. Alice watched her go and then lifted up her shirt again to look at her stomach. In addition to being flatter, her stomach had feathery silver lines up and down the sides. Stretch marks. Awestruck, she ran her fingertips over them. Was this really her stomach?

A cesarean scar, the doctor had said (unless she'd got it wrong, of course. Maybe it wasn't a cesarean scar at all, just a perfectly normal . . . scar. Of some sort).

But if she was right, that would mean some doctor (her own Dr. Chapple?) had sliced through her skin with a scalpel and lifted a bloody squawling baby straight out of her stomach and she didn't remember any of it.

Could a bump on the head really knock out such a significant event from her memory? Wasn't that a bit *excessive*?

She thought of times when she'd been watching a movie with Nick and had fallen asleep halfway through with her head on his lap. She hated it because she would wake up sticky-mouthed to see the lives of the movie characters had moved on and the couple who hated each other were now sharing an umbrella under the Eiffel Tower.

"You had your baby," she said tentatively to herself. "Remember?"

This was absurd. Surely she wasn't about to slap herself on the side of the head and say, "Oh, the *baby*, of course I had the baby! Fancy that slipping my mind."

How could she have forgotten her baby growing and kicking and rolling inside her? If she'd already had the baby, that meant she'd already been to the prenatal classes with Nick. It meant she'd bought her first maternity clothes. It meant they'd painted the nursery. It meant they'd been shopping for a crib and a pram and nappies and a stroller and a changing table.

It meant there *was* a baby.

She sat up, her hands pressed to her stomach.

So where was it? Who was looking after it? Who was feeding it?

This was far bigger than a normal "Oh, Alice" mix-up. This was huge. This was terrifying.

For God's sake, where was Nick? Actually, she was going to be just a bit snappy with him when he finally turned up, even if he did have a good excuse.

The nurse with the green eyes came back into the room and said, "How are you feeling?"

"Fine, thank you," said Alice automatically.

"Do you remember why you're here and what happened to you?"

This constant re-asking of questions was presumably to check her mental state. Alice thought about yelling, *ACTUALLY, I'M GOING OUT OF MY MIND!* but she didn't want to make the nurse feel uncomfortable. Crazy behavior made people feel awkward.

Instead, she said to the nurse, "Can you tell me what year it is?" She spoke quickly in case the doctor with the glasses came back in and caught her checking up on her facts behind her back.

"It's 2008."

"It's definitely 2008?"

"It's definitely second of May, 2008. Mother's Day next weekend!"

Mother's Day! It would be Alice's first-ever Mother's Day.

Except, if it was 2008, it wasn't her first Mother's Day at all.

If it was 2008, the Sultana was ten years old. He wasn't a sultana at all.

He would have progressed from sultana to raisin to peach to tennis ball to basketball to . . . baby.

Alice felt an inappropriate gale of laughter catch in her throat.

Her baby was ten years old.

Elisabeth's Homework for Dr. Hodges

Much to Layla's horror, I stopped halfway through "Visualizing the Prospect" and switched over to the "Idea Olympics." I'm sure you'll be fascinated to hear, Dr. Hodges, that this is the part where I get them to look under their tables and find their "Mystery Product." Everybody gets pretty excited about this and they dive under the tables. It's amazing how so many different people can come out with EXACTLY the same jokes. It reinforces this feeling I have that the years are rolling by but nothing is changing. I am the perfect example of the phrase: Going nowhere fast.

While all my students were writing down ideas on butcher paper for how to market their Mystery Products, I tried to call Jane back. Only of course now Jane had switched her phone off, so I loudly said "Fuck it" and saw Layla give a tiny, tight smile. I had offended her by changing the agenda, as if the agenda didn't matter, when the agenda is her life.

I explained to her that my sister had been in an accident and I didn't know what hospital she was at and I needed somebody to pick up her kids from school. Layla said, "Okay, but when are you going to finish the rest of the 'Visualizing the Prospect' segment?" (I guess that sort of dedication is good in an employee, but isn't it a bit pathological, Dr. Hodges? What's your expert opinion?)

I called Mum next and got her voice mail, too. Oh for the days before Mum got a life. It seems only a short time ago that I would have called Frannie first. She was always so calm in a crisis. But Frannie decided to stop driving when she moved into the retirement village. (I still find that weirdly upsetting. She was such a good driver.)

I called the school and got put on hold listening to a recorded message about family values. I called Alice's gym to find out if they knew which hospital she'd been taken to and got put on hold listening to a message about sensible nutrition.

Finally, I called my husband, Ben.

He answered on the first ring, listened to me babble, and said, "I'll take care of it."

Look, *Grey's Anatomy* starts in ten minutes. This journal writing must not impact on my nightly TV gorge. I don't care what Ben says, without the narcotic effects of TV, I might have gone truly insane a long time ago.

Chapter 4

pparently Alice's CT scan was "unremarkable," which had made her feel ashamed of her mediocrity. It reminded her of her school reports with every single box ticked "Satisfactory" and comments like "A quiet student. Needs to contribute more in class." They may as well have just come right out and written across the front: "So boring, we don't actually know who she is." Elisabeth's reports had some boxes ticked "Outstanding" and others ticked "Below Standard" and comments like "Can be a little disruptive." Alice had yearned to be a little disruptive, but she couldn't work out how you got started.

"We're concerned about your memory loss, so we're going to keep you overnight for observation," said the doctor with the red plastic glasses.

"Oh, okay, thank you." Alice self-consciously smoothed her hair back, imagining a row of doctors and nurses with clipboards sitting next to her bed, watching her sleep. (She sometimes snored.)

The doctor hugged her own clipboard to her chest and looked at her brightly, as if she felt like a chat.

Oh. Gosh. Alice searched around for interesting topics of conversation and finally said, "So, did you ring my obstetrician? Dr. Chapple? Of course, you might not have had a chance . . ." She didn't want the doctor to snarl, "Sorry, I was busy saving somebody's life."

The doctor looked thoughtful. "I did, actually. It seems Sam Chapple retired three years ago." Alice couldn't believe that Dr. Chapple was no longer sitting in his big leather chair, carefully noting down answers to his courteous questions in beautiful copperplate writing on white index cards. She really needed to get this . . . this *problem* sorted out once and for all. Pronto! Quick sticks! As Frannie would say. Was Frannie still alive in 2008? Grandmothers died. It was to be expected. You weren't even allowed to be that upset about it. Please don't let Frannie have died. Please don't let anyone have died. "Nobody else in our family will die," Elisabeth had promised when she was ten and Alice was nine. "Because it wouldn't be fair." Alice had believed every single word Elisabeth had said when they were little.

Maybe Elisabeth had died? Or Nick? Or Mum? Or the baby? (*I'm sorry, but there is no heartbeat.*)

For the first time in years, Alice had that feeling she used to get when she was little, after their dad died, that someone else she loved was about to die. She longed to gather everybody she loved and stow them safely under her bed with her favorite dolls. Sometimes the stress would become so overwhelming she would forget how to breathe and Elisabeth would have to bring her a brown paper bag to breathe into.

"I might need a bag," Alice said to the doctor.

"A bag?"

Ridiculous. She wasn't a child who hyperventilated at the thought of people dying.

"I had a bag," she said to the doctor. "A red backpack with stickers on it. Do you know what happened to it?"

The doctor looked vaguely irritated by this administrative question but then she said, "Oh, yes. Over here. Would you like it?" She picked up the strange backpack from a shelf at the side of the room and Alice looked at it apprehensively.

The doctor handed it to her and said, "Well, you just rest up and someone will be along to take you up to a ward soon. I'm sorry there is so much waiting. That's hospitals for you." She gave her a motherly pat on the shoulder and quickly left the room, suddenly in a hurry, as if she'd remembered another patient who was waiting.

Alice ran her fingers over the three shiny dinosaur stickers on the flap of the backpack. They each had speech bubbles saying either "DINOSAURS RULE!" or "DINOSAURS ROCK!" She looked down at the sticker on her shirt and peeled it off. It was a definite match. She stuck it back on her shirt (she felt that she should for some reason) and waited for a feeling or a memory.

Did these belong to the Sultana? Her mind skittered away from the idea, like a frightened animal. She didn't want to know. She didn't *want* a ready-grown baby. She wanted her own little future baby back.

This could not be happening to her. *But it is, so get a grip, Alice.* She began to open the bag and her fingernails caught her attention. She held up her hands in front of her. Her nails were beautifully shaped and long and painted a very pale, beige color. Normally they were ragged and broken and rimmed with dirt from gardening or painting or whatever other renovation job they were doing at the time. The only other time they'd looked like that was for her wedding when she'd got her manicure. She'd spent the whole honeymoon flapping her hands at Nick, saying, "Look, I'm a *lady*."

Apart from that, her hands still looked like her hands. Actually, they looked quite nice.

They were bare, she noticed. No jewelry. It was a little unusual that she wasn't at least wearing her wedding ring, but perhaps she'd been in a rush when she was getting ready for her "spin class."

She held up her left hand and saw that there was a thin white indentation from her wedding ring that hadn't been there before. It gave her a disconnected feeling, like when she'd seen the feathery marks on her stomach. Her mind thought everything was still the same, but her body was telling her that time had marched on without her.

Time. She put her hands to her face. If she was supposedly sending out *"invitations to her fortieth-birthday party,"* if she was . . . *thirty-nine*—she mentally choked and gasped for air at the thought—then her face must be different. Older. There was a mirror over a basin in the front corner of the room. She could see the reflection of her feet, in their short white socks; one of the flurry of nurses had taken off the strange sneakers (chunky, rubbery things) and put them on the floor next to the bed. Alice could just hop out of the bed and walk over and look at herself.

Presumably it was against strict hospital regulations to get out of bed. She had a head injury. She might faint and hit her head again. Nobody had told her not to get out of bed, but they probably thought it was obvious.

She should look in the mirror. But she didn't want to see. She didn't want to know. She didn't want this to be real. Besides, she was *busy* at the moment. She had to look through the bag. Quickly, she undid the buckles of the backpack and shoved her hand in. She pulled out . . . a towel.

A plain, innocuous, clean blue bath towel. Alice looked at it and felt nothing but embarrassment. She was fossicking through somebody else's private stuff. Jane Turner had obviously picked up someone else's bag and insisted it was hers without really looking at it. It was just like Jane. So bossy and impatient.

Well.

Alice examined her beautifully manicured fingernails again. She put her hand in the bag again and pulled out a plastic bag, folded flat. She opened it and emptied it onto her lap.

A woman's clothes. Underwear. A red dress. A cream-colored cardigan with a single large wooden button. Knee-high beige boots. Small jewelry case.

The underwear was creamy lace-edged satin. Alice's underwear tended to be flippant and faded; jolly seahorses on her pants and purple cotton bras that clipped at the front.

She held the dress up in front of her and saw that it was beautiful. A simple design of silky fabric with tiny cream flowers. The cream of the cardigan matched the cream of the flowers on the dress exactly.

She checked the label on the dress. An S for small. It wouldn't fit her. She was a medium at best. It couldn't be hers. She folded the clothes back up and opened the jewelry case, lifting out a fine gold necklace with a big topaz stone. The stone was too big for her taste, but she dangled it over the dress and agreed that it was an excellent match. Well done, whoever you are.

The other piece of jewelry was Alice's gold Tiffany charm bracelet.

Alice said, "Fancy meeting you here." She picked up the bracelet and laid it across her wrist and felt comforted, as if Nick had finally arrived.

Nick had bought this bracelet for her the day after they found out she was pregnant with the Sultana. He shouldn't have spent that much because they were experiencing what Nick called "severe fiscal stress," due to the fact that every single thing they did to the house ended up costing more than planned, but Nick said it could go on the balance sheet under "extraordinary items" (whatever that meant) because it was extraordinary that they were having a baby.

The Sultana had been conceived on a Wednesday night, which just didn't seem exciting enough a night for such a momentous event, and the sex hadn't even been that passionate or romantic. It was just that there had been nothing much on TV and Nick had yawned and said, "We should paint the hallway," and Alice had said, "Oh, let's just have sex," and Nick had yawned again and said, "Mmmm. Okay." And then they'd discovered there weren't any condoms in the chest of drawers next to the bed, but by then the action was under way and neither of them could be bothered to get up and find one in the bathroom, and besides which it was a *Wednesday* and it was only *once* and, well, they were married. They were allowed to get pregnant, so therefore it wasn't really likely. The next day Alice discovered there actually had been a condom in the back of the drawer if she'd bothered to stretch her fingers just a bit further but by then it was too late. The Sultana had already started doing what it needed to do to become a person.

The day after they did the eight positive pregnancy tests (just in case the first seven were wrong) Nick had come home from work and handed her a small gift-wrapped box with a card that said "For the mother of my child," and inside was the bracelet.

To be honest, she loved that bracelet even more than she loved her engagement ring.

Of course, to be *really* honest, she didn't actually love her engagement ring at all. She sort of hated it.

Not a single person in the world knew this. It was her only real secret, so it was a pity it wasn't juicier. The ring was an Edwardian antique that had belonged to Nick's grandmother. Alice had never met Granny Love, but she had apparently been formidable but adorable (she sounded dreadful). Nick's four sisters, whom Nick called "the Flakes" because of their undeniably flaky tendencies, were crazy about that ring and there had been a lot of bitter remarks when Granny Love left the ring to Nick in her will. One or another of the Flakes was always grabbing Alice's left hand and sniffing, "You just can't *get* jewelry like that anymore!"

Alice thought it was ugly. It was a big emerald set in the middle of a cluster of diamonds to look like a flower. It reminded her of a hibiscus for some reason and she'd never been a fan of the hibiscus, but what did she know, because every other girl in the world seemed to think the ring was *divine*, and apparently it was worth a small fortune.

And that was the other problem. This was the most expensive piece of jewelry Alice had ever owned, and Alice lost things. Constantly. She was always retracing her steps, emptying out garbage bins and calling up train stations, restaurants, and grocery stores to see if they had her purse or her sunglasses or her umbrella.

"Oh *no*," said Elisabeth when she heard that Alice's ring was an irreplaceable family heirloom. "You'll just have to—I don't know—get it surgically attached to your finger?"

Most of the time, except for special events or if she was seeing the Flakes, Alice just didn't wear the ring. She wore her plain gold wedding band, or nothing at all. She'd never really been a jewelry sort of person anyway.

However, she loved the gold Tiffany bracelet. Unlike the ring, it seemed to represent all the wonderful things that had happened over the last few years—Nick, the baby, the house.

Now she fastened the bracelet around her wrist, laid her head back against the white hospital pillow, and held the backpack close to her stomach. The thought crossed her mind that there were probably a million bracelets just like this one around and it could just as easily belong to somebody else. It wasn't like she recognized anything else in the bag, but she knew it was hers.

She was starting to get angry with herself. *Come on, now! Remember!* Furious, she shoved her hand back in the rucksack and pulled out a black purse. It was a long, luxurious rectangle of black leather. Alice turned it back and forth in her hands. "Gucci," it said, in tiny discreet letters. Goodness. She opened the purse and the first thing she saw was her own face staring back at her from a driver's license.

Her own face. Her own name. Her own address.

Well, here was the proof that the bag belonged to her.

The photo was typically blurry, but she could see she was wearing a white shirt and what looked like long black beads. Long beads? Had she become the sort of person who wore long beads? Her hair was cut in a bob just above her shoulders and it seemed to have been colored very blond. She'd cut her hair! Nick had once made her promise to never cut her hair. Alice had thought that exquisitely romantic, although Elisabeth had made gagging sounds when she told her and said, "You can't promise to still have a fourteen-year-old's hairstyle when you're forty."

When you're forty.

Oh.

Alice put a hand up to the back of her head. She'd been vaguely aware that her hair was pulled back in a ponytail before; she hadn't realized that it was actually more of a pigtail. She pulled out the elastic band and ran her fingers through her hair. It was even shorter than in the driver's-license photograph. She wondered if Nick liked it. In a minute, she would have to be brave and face herself in the mirror.

Of course, she was still pretty busy at the moment. No hurry.

She put the license back in the wallet and began to rifle through it. There were various credit and ATM cards with her name embossed on the front, including a gold American Express card. Wasn't a gold Amex just a status symbol for the sort of person who drives a BMW? Library card. Health Fund card.

A plain white business card for a Michael Boyle, "Registered Physiotherapist." The address was in Melbourne. She flipped it over and saw a handwritten message on the back.

Alice,

We're all settled and doing OK. I think of you often and "happier times." Call anytime.

M. xxx

She dropped the card in her lap. What did this Michael Boyle mean when he presumptuously referred to "happier times"? She didn't want to have had happier times with a physiotherapist in Melbourne. He sounded awful. She imagined a balding, paunchy type with soft hands and moist lips.

Where the bloody hell was Nick?

Perhaps Jane had forgotten to call him. She'd been acting so strangely at the gym. Alice should just phone him herself and explain that this was pretty serious and she really needed him to leave work right now. Why hadn't she thought of that before? Suddenly she was desperate to get herself a phone and hear Nick's lovely, familiar voice. She had a strange feeling as if it had been ages since she'd spoken to him.

She looked feverishly around the small room and of course—there was no phone. There was nothing in the room at all, except for the basin, the mirror, and a sign about how to wash your hands correctly.

A mobile phone! That's what she needed. She'd only recently got her first one. It was an old one belonging to Nick's father and it worked fine, except that it had to be held together with an elastic band. Something told her that she would probably have a more expensive phone by now, and when she opened the zippered pocket at the front of the bag, she saw she was right; there was a tiny, sleek, shiny, silver phone sitting right there as if she'd known it would be. (Had she? She couldn't tell.)

There was also a leather-bound day planner, which Alice opened quickly, just to confirm that it was indeed 2008, noting with sick wonder that her own handwriting filled the pages. "2008," it said in no-doubt-about-it black letters at the top of each page: 2008, 2008, 2008 . . .

She stopped flipping the pages and picked up the shiny phone, breathing shallowly, as if a huge metal bar had been plonked across her chest.

Could she even work this strange phone? She was hopeless at working out how to use new appliances, but her elegantly manicured fingers seemed to know what to do, pushing the silver buttons on either side of the phone so it snapped open. She punched in the number for Nick's direct line and held the phone up to her ear. It rang. *Please answer, please answer.* She felt like she would burst into sobs of relief at the sound of his voice.

"Hello. Sales Department!"

It was a young girl's voice, frothy with good humor. Someone in the background was roaring with laughter.

Alice said, "Is Nick there at the moment? Nick Love?"

There was a slight pause. When the girl spoke again, she sounded as though she had just been sternly reprimanded. The laughter in the background stopped abruptly. "I'm sorry, you've come through to the wrong extension, but I could put you through to Mr. Love's personal assistant if you like."

Alice paused, diverted by the fact that Nick had a "personal assistant." How posh.

The girl continued, as if Alice had argued with her: "Mr. Love is actually in Portugal this week, so his PA would be the best person to help you."

Portugal! She said, "What's he doing in Portugal?"

"Well, it's some sort of international conference, I think," said the girl uncertainly. "But if I could just put you through—"

Portugal, and a personal assistant. He must have got a promotion. They'd have to have champagne!

Alice said (cunningly!), "Um, could you remind me of Mr. Love's position with the company?"

"He's our general manager," said the girl in an everyone-in-the-world-knows-that tone.

Good grief.

Nick had the Motherfucking Megatron's job.

That was more than one promotion. That was a giant superhero leap up the corporate ladder. Alice was filled with giggly pride at the thought of *Nick* strutting about the office, telling people what to do. Wouldn't people just laugh at him?

"I'm putting you through to his PA now," said the girl firmly. The phone clicked and began to ring again.

Another female voice answered smoothly. "Mr. Love's office, this is Annabelle, how can I help you?"

"Oh," said Alice. "This is Nick's wife, ah, Mr. Love's wife. I was trying to get hold of him, but, ummm . . ."

The woman's voice turned razor sharp. "Hello, Alice. How are you today?"

"Well, actually . . ."

"As you're aware, Nick isn't back in Sydney until Sunday morning. Obviously if there is something that absolutely can't wait, I can try to get a message through to him but I'd really prefer not to disturb him. His schedule is frantic."

"Oh." Why was this woman being so mean? She obviously knew her. What could Alice have done to make her dislike her so much?

"So, can it wait or not, Alice?" She wasn't imagining it; this was real live hatred she was hearing. The pain in Alice's head got worse. She wanted to say, "Hey, lady, I'm in hospital. I came here in an *ambulance*!"

"I wish you wouldn't let people stomp all over you," Elisabeth was always telling her. Sometimes, long after Alice had forgotten the incident, Elisabeth would say, "I was up all last night thinking about what that woman in the chemist's said to you. I can't believe you just *took it*—you've got no backbone!" Alice would drop to the floor, all jelly-like, to demonstrate her lack of backbone, and Elisabeth would say, "Oh for God's sake."

The problem was, Alice needed more warning when it came to being assertive. These sorts of situations were so unexpected. She needed hours to really think things through. Were they really being nasty, or was she just being sensitive? What if they'd just found out they had a terminal disease that morning and were entitled to be in a bad mood? She was about to mumble something pleading and pathetic to Nick's PA when, against her will, her body began an unfamiliar sequence of actions. Her back straightened. Her chin lifted. Her stomach muscles clenched. She spoke and didn't recognize her own voice. It was taut and tart and decidedly snooty. "No, it can't wait," she said. "It is urgent. There has been an *accident*. Please ask Nick to call me as soon as possible."

Alice couldn't have been more surprised if she'd found herself doing a triple backflip.

The woman answered, "Fine, Alice, I'll see what I can do." Her contempt was still palpable.

"I'd appreciate it."

Alice hung up and said, with the phone still to her ear, "Cow. Bitch. *Slut.*" She spat the words out of the side of her mouth, like poisonous pellets.

She swallowed. Now that was even more surprising; she sounded like a tattooed girl who quite liked the occasional catfight.

The mobile rang in her hand, making her jump.

It must be Nick, she thought, awash with relief. Once again, her fingers knew what to do. She pressed the button with the green phone symbol and said, "Nick?"

A child's voice she'd never heard before said crossly, "Mum?"

Chapter 5

Frannie's Letter to Phil

Dearest Phil,

I'm a little riled up today.

You'll remember I mentioned I'd taken on the role of running the Social Committee. Well, for the last few months I've been arranging a Family Talent Night. It's next Wednesday. Children, grandchildren, and so forth will be performing a variety of acts. Should be a fun night! In all honesty it will probably be excruciating, but it will be a diversion from our arthritis if nothing else.

(I was thinking today about the musical we organized together. Oklahoma! 1972? 1973? You kissed me backstage and that sly little Frank Neary caught us. The news spread like wildfire: "Mr. Peyton and Miss Jeffrey are a couple. The school principal and the maths coordinator! Ooh, scandal! It just made everything even more delicious, didn't it?)

Anyway, today we had a new resident turn up at the Social Committee meeting. I can't recall his name. (See? Shocking memory!)

I'll call him Mr. Mustache because that's his most defining feature: a comically large white mustache. It gives him the look of a retired used-car salesman. Or perhaps a seedy Santa Claus.

Anyway, Mr. Mustache was full of suggestions.

We're serving tea, coffee, sandwiches, pikelets, and scones on the Family Talent Night. Standard fare for a function at a retirement village. Mr. Mustache piped up and suggested we set up a cocktail bar. Said he once spent a year bartending on some Caribbean island and that he could make a cocktail "guaranteed to blow my socks off." I'm not joking, Phil. This is the way he talks.

I tried to explain about liquor licenses, but he was already on to a new topic. He said he knew a young girl who wasn't exactly a family member, but would she still be allowed to perform? Of course, I said. He said that was wonderful because she did a very entertaining "pole dancing" act. All the men slapped their knees, roaring with laughter. (You wouldn't have laughed, would you?)

Even some of the women were laughing. Rita was laughing like a loon. She has dementia, so I guess I can excuse her—but still, you'd think she'd retain a modicum of decency!

It was the strangest thing. I felt the most absurdly embarrassing desire to burst into tears. All at once, I was straight back in my very first classroom out of teacher's college. There was a very handsome boy in my class (I can still see where he sat—second row from the back) who was always cracking jokes and making everyone laugh. Did I ever tell you about him? He made me feel so humorless and stodgy. Like an old maid. (And I was twenty years old, for heaven's sake!)

You never made me feel—

Barb just phoned.

Alice has had a nasty fall during her gym class (she seems to spend half her life at that gym) and she's in hospital.

I'm in a fluster.
I'll finish this later.

"Mum?" the child spoke again, impatiently. Alice couldn't tell if it was a boy or a girl. It was just an average kid's voice. Breathy, rushed, a touch snuffly. Kind of adorable. She hardly ever spoke to children on the phone, except for an occasional stilted birthday chat with one of Nick's nephews or nieces, and she was always struck by the sweetness of their kidlike voices. They seemed so much bigger and scarier and dirtier in the flesh.

Her hand was sweaty. She took a firm grip of the phone, licked her lips, and said hoarsely, "Hello?"

"Mum! It's *me!*" The kid's voice bubbled up and out of the phone, as if he or she were yelling straight in her ear. "Why did you think it would be Dad? Is he calling you from Portugal? Oh! If you speak to him, can you please tell him that the name of the Xbox game I want is Lost Planet, Extreme Condition, okay? Got it? 'Cause I think I told him the wrong name. Okay, Mum, this is pretty important, so you might need to write this down. Do you want me to talk slowly? *Lost. Planet. Extreme. Condition.* Anyway, where are you? We've got swimming and you *know* I hate being late because then I get stuck with the stupid paddleboard. Oh, there's Uncle Ben! Is he taking us swimming today? Okay! Cool! Why didn't you tell us? HI, UNCLE BEN! Okay, gotta go, see you, Mum."

There was a scraping sound, a thud, and the sounds of children shouting in the distance. A man's voice said, "Gidday, champ," and then the line was cut off.

Alice dropped the phone in her lap and stared straight ahead at the open doorway. Had she just had a *conversation* with the Sultana?

She didn't even know the baby's name. They were still arguing over the names. Nick wanted "Tom"—a "good honest name for a man"—and Alice wanted "Ethan"—a sexy, successful name. Or if the Sultana surprised them

by being a girl, Alice wanted "Madeline" and Nick wanted "Addison"—
because apparently girls didn't need "good honest names."

Alice thought, I could not be mother to a child and not know his name.
This is simply not possible. It is beyond the realms of possibility.

Maybe it was a wrong number! The child had mentioned an "Uncle
Ben." There was no "Ben" in Alice's family. She didn't know a single Ben.
She wasn't sure she'd ever even met a Ben. She searched her mind and all
she could dredge up was a huge bearded neon-sign designer she'd once met
while helping Nick's older sister, Dora (possibly the flakiest of the Flakes),
at her "Psychic Arts" shop, and in fact his name could just as easily have
been Bill or Brad.

The problem was that the kid had asked, "Why did you think it would
be Dad?" when she'd said "Nick." Also, he knew Nick was in Portugal.

It was beyond the realms of possibility, yet, on the other hand, it seemed
sort of conclusive. She closed her eyes briefly and opened them again, trying
to visualize a ten-year-old son. How tall would he be? What color eyes?
What color hair?

Part of her wanted to scream with the sheer terror of this situation, and
part of her wanted to roar with laughter because it was so ridiculous. An
impossible joke. A hilarious story she would be telling for years—"And *then*,
I ring Nick and this woman tells me he's in Portugal! And I'm thinking,
Portugal!?"

She picked up the phone gingerly, as if it were an explosive device, and
considered calling somebody else: Elisabeth? Mum? Frannie?

No. She didn't want any more strange voices telling her things she didn't
know about the people she loved.

Her body felt weak and heavy. She would do nothing. Nothing at all.
Eventually something would happen; somebody would come. The doctors
would fix her head and everything would be okay. She began shoving things
back into the rucksack. As she picked up the leather-bound diary, a photo
fell out.

It was a photo of three children in school uniforms. It was obviously a posed shot because they were sitting in a row on a step with their elbows on their knees and their chins in their hands. There were two girls and a boy.

The boy was in the middle. He had messy white-blond hair, ears that stuck out, and a turned-up nose. He had tipped his head to one side and clenched his teeth together in a grotesque grimace that Alice knew was meant to be a smile. She knew this because she must have seen at least a hundred photos of her sister pulling an identical face. "Why do I do that?" Elisabeth would say sadly when she saw the photo.

On the boy's left side was a girl who looked older. She was a chunky, stolid-looking girl with a long face and straight brown hair in a ponytail that had fallen over one shoulder. She was slumped forward in a way that clearly said, "I do not want to sit in this ridiculous position." Her mouth was compressed in a straight line and she was looking grimly off to the right of the camera. She had a nasty graze on one chunky knee, and both her shoelaces were undone. There was nothing remotely familiar about her.

To the boy's right was a little girl with blond curls bunched together in fat pigtails on either side of her head. She was smiling ecstatically with a dimple denting her cherubic cheeks. There was something stuck to both the shirt collars of her uniform; Alice held the photo up closer. They were shiny dinosaur stickers just like the one on Alice's own shirt.

Alice turned the photo over and saw there was a typewritten label stuck to the back. It said:

Children (left to right): Olivia Love (Kindergarten), Tom Love (Yr4B), Madison Love (Yr5M)

Parent: Alice Love

Number of copies ordered: 4

Alice turned the photo back over and looked again at the three children. *I have never seen you before in my life.*

There was a distant buzzing sound in her ears; she could feel herself breathing short, shallow breaths, her chest rising and falling quickly as if she were at high altitude. (Oh, it was so *funny*! So, I'm looking at this photo, right, of three kids? And it's my own children! And *I don't even recognize them*! Hilarious!)

Another nurse Alice hadn't seen before came into the room, glanced briefly at Alice, and picked up the clipboard at the end of her stretcher. "I'm so sorry we're still keeping you waiting. The powers that be assure me it should only be a few more minutes and we'll have a bed free for you. How are you feeling?"

Alice put crazily trembling fingertips to her head. "The thing is, I don't actually remember the last ten years of my life." There was a quiver of hysteria in her voice.

"I think we might try and organize a nice cup of tea and sandwiches for you." The nurse looked at the photo lying in Alice's lap and said, "Your kids?"

"Apparently," said Alice, and gave a little laugh that turned into a sob, and the taste of tears in her mouth felt so familiar, and the thought came into her head, *Stop it! I'm so sick, sick, sick of crying*, but what did that mean, because she hadn't cried like this since she was little, and anyway she couldn't stop even if she wanted.

Chapter 6

Elisabeth's Homework for Dr. Hodges

In the afternoon tea break I called Ben on his mobile and he said, over a babble of noise that sounded like twenty kids, not three, that he'd picked up the children from school and he was driving them to their swimming lessons now. He said he'd been informed it was impossible to miss even one swimming lesson because Olivia had just become a crocodile or a platypus or something and I heard Olivia's gurgling laugh as she shouted, "A DOLPHIN, silly billy!" I could also hear Tom, who must have been in the front next to Ben, saying monotonously, "You are now five kilometers OVER the speed limit, you are now four kilometers OVER the speed limit, you are now two kilometers UNDER the speed limit."

Ben sounded stressed, but happy. Happier than I've heard him in weeks. Picking up the children and driving them to swimming is not something Alice would normally ask (trust) us to do and I knew that Ben was probably exhilarated by the responsibility. I imagined how people glancing over at traffic lights would see a standard dad (maybe a bit bigger and bushier than average) with his three kids.

If I think too much about this, it will hurt a great deal, so I won't.

Ben told me that Tom had just spoken on the mobile to Alice and according to Tom she didn't say anything about falling over at the gym and she sounded "just like Mum except maybe ten to fifteen percent grumpier than usual." I think he's learning percentages at school right now.

Weirdly, I'd never even thought of just ringing Alice's mobile myself. So I immediately dialed her number.

When she answered, she sounded so strange that I didn't recognize her voice and thought that a nurse must have picked up the phone. I said, "Oh, sorry, I was just trying to reach Alice Love," and then I realized it was Alice and she was sobbing, "Oh, Libby, thank God it's you!" She sounded terrible, hysterical really, babbling about a photo and dinosaur stickers and a red dress that couldn't possibly fit her but was really beautiful and being deliriously drunk in a gym and why was Nick in Portugal and she didn't know if she was pregnant or not and she thought it was 1998 but everybody else said it was 2008. It gave me a fright. I can't remember when I last saw or heard Alice cry (or call me Libby). Even though she has had so much to cry about over the past year, she doesn't cry in front of me, and there is such a horrible polite restraint in all our conversations recently, with both of us putting on these oh-so-reasonable voices.

It actually felt sort of good to hear Alice cry. It felt real. It's been such a long time since she needed me, and that used to be such an important part of my identity, being the big sister who shielded Alice from the world. (I should save my money and analyze myself, Dr. Hodges.)

So I told her not to worry, that I was coming straight there and we would sort everything out and I went straight back onstage and said that there had been a family emergency and that I had to leave but that my very capable assistant Layla would be taking over and when I looked at Layla to see her reaction, she was pink and radiant, as if she'd just got religion. So that was OK.

Of course the hospital would have to be Royal North Shore.

I always feel as though I have swallowed something huge when I drive into that car park. It's shaped like an anchor, this thing I've swallowed, and it goes straight down my throat and stretches out on either side of my belly.

Another thing: the sky always seems so huge, like a big empty shell. Why is that? I must always look up as I'm driving in, or maybe it's something to do with me feeling tiny and useless, or maybe it's just simple geography for heaven's sake, and the road goes up before it dips down into the car park.

I'm here for Alice, I reminded myself when I got out of the car.

But everywhere I looked I could see old versions of Ben and me. We haunt the place. If you ever go there, Dr. Hodges, keep an eye out for us. There we'll be, shuffling down the pathway along the side of the hospital back toward the car park on a sunny ice-cold day, me in that unflattering hippie skirt that I keep wearing because it doesn't need ironing, and I'm holding Ben's hand, letting him lead me, looking at the ground and chanting my mantra, "Don't think about it. Don't think about it. Don't think about it." You'll see us standing at the reception desk filling in forms and Ben is close behind me, rubbing my lower back in tiny circles and I feel like the circles are somehow keeping me breathing, in, out, in, out, like a ventilator. There we are, squashed into the back of the lift with an excited family, their arms overflowing with flowers and "It's a girl!" balloons. We both have our arms wrapped protectively around our stomachs in exactly the same way, as if we're hugging ourselves close, so all that joy can't hurt us.

You told me the other week that this doesn't define me, but it *does*, Dr. Hodges, it just does.

As I walked along the echoey corridors (clop, clop, clop, went my heels, and the *smell*, well, you probably know that horrible boiled-potato smell, Dr. Hodges, the way it floods your sinuses with memories of every other hospital visit), I ignored the badly dressed ghosts of hospital visits past and concentrated on Alice and wondered if she was still thinking it was 1998, and if so, what that would be like. The only thing I could compare it to was the one time when I was a teenager and got horribly drunk at a twenty-first party and stood up and gave a long, loving toast to the birthday boy, whom I had never met before that night. The next day, I didn't remember a thing about it, nothing, not even shadowy snippets. Apparently I used the word "paucity" in my speech, and that disturbed me, because I didn't think my sober self had ever said that word out loud before and I wasn't even entirely sure what it meant. I never got drunk like that again. I'm too much of a control freak to have other people falling about laughing while they describe my own actions to me.

If I couldn't stand losing two hours of my memory, what would it be like to lose ten years?

As I looked for Alice's ward number, I had a sudden memory of Mum and Frannie and me, giddy with excitement, just like that family in the lift, practically running through the corridors of another hospital looking for Alice's room when Madison was born. We happened to see Nick in the distance, walking along ahead of us, and we all shrieked, "Nick!" and he turned around and while he waited for us to catch up, he ran around in circles on the spot, and did a two-fisted punch in the air like Rocky, and Frannie said fondly, "He's such a card!" and I was dating that patronizing town planner at the time and I decided right then and there to break up with him, because Frannie would never call him a card.

If Alice had really lost every memory of the last ten years, I thought, then she would have no memory of that day, or of Madison as a baby. She wouldn't remember how we all shared a tin of Quality Street chocolates while the pediatrician came in to check Madison. He flipped her this way and that, and held her in one palm with casual expertise, like a basketballer spinning a ball, and Alice and Nick blurted out in unison, "Careful!" and we all laughed and the pediatrician smiled and said, "Your daughter gets ten out of ten, an A-plus." We all applauded and "whoo-hoo'd" Madison for her first-ever good mark, while he wrapped her back up in her white blanket, a neat packet of fish-and-chips, and ceremonially presented her to Alice.

I was just starting to consider the enormity of all the things that had happened to Alice over the last ten years when I found her ward number, and as I glanced through the door, I saw her in the first curtained-off cubicle, propped up against pillows, her hands resting on her lap and her eyes staring straight ahead. There was no color to her. She was wearing a white hospital gown, lying against a white pillow with a white gauze bandage wrapped around her head, and even her face was dead white. It was strange to see her so still; Alice is all about sharp, quick movement. She's texting on her mobile, jangling her car keys, grabbing one of the kids by the elbow and saying something stern in their ear. She's fingernail-tapping busy, busy, busy.

(Ten years ago she was nothing like that. She and Nick slept till noon every Sunday morning. "How will they *ever* find time to renovate that enormous house!" clucked Mum and Frannie and me, like elderly aunts.)

She didn't see me at first and as I walked up to her, her eyes flickered, and they looked so big and blue in her pale face, but more importantly, she was looking at me in a different, but familiar, way. I don't know how to describe it, except that the strange thought came into my head, "You're back."

You want to know the first thing she said to me, Dr. Hodges?

She said, "Oh Libby, what *happened* to you?"

I told you, it defines me.

Alice had finally been moved up to a ward and given a hospital gown and a remote for the television and a white chest of drawers. A lady wheeling a trolley brought her a cup of weak tea and four tiny triangular curried-egg sandwiches. The nurse was right; the tea and sandwiches had made her feel better, except they hadn't done anything about the huge gaping crevasse in her memory.

When she'd heard Elisabeth's voice on the mobile phone, it was just like each time she'd called home on that disastrous trip around Europe when she was nineteen and trying to pretend she had a different personality—an adventurous, extroverted sort of personality; the sort of person who *loves* exploring cathedrals and ruins all day on her own and talking to drunk boys from Brisbane in youth hostels at night—when really she was homesick and lonely and often bored, and couldn't make head or tail of the train timetables. The sound of Elisabeth's voice, loud and clear in a strange phone box on the other side of the world, always made Alice's knees buckle with relief, and she'd press her forehead against the glass and think, *That's right; I am a real person.*

"My sister is coming right now," she told the nurse when she hung up, as if giving her credentials as a proper person with a family; a family she recognized.

Although, when Elisabeth first walked toward her bed, she actually didn't recognize her. She vaguely assumed that this woman in the cream suit with the glasses and the swinging shoulder-length hair must be a hospital administrator coming to do something administrative, but then something about the woman's straight-backed "I'll take you on" posture, something essentially Elisabeth, gave her away.

It was a shock, because it seemed that overnight Elisabeth had put on a lot of weight. She'd always had a strong, lithe, athletic-looking body, because of her rowing and her jogging and whatever else it was she was always so busy doing. Now she wasn't fat but definitely larger, softer, and bustier; a puffed-out version of herself, as if someone had blown her up like a plastic pool toy. She won't like that, thought Alice. Elisabeth had always been so amusingly moralistic about fattening food, refusing an offer of pavlova as if it were crack cocaine. Once, when Nick, Alice, and Elisabeth went away for a weekend together, Elisabeth spent ages at the breakfast table studying the "nutritional information" panel on the side of a container of yogurt, warning them darkly, "You have to be *really* careful with yogurt." Whenever Nick and Alice ate yogurt after that, one of them would always shout, "Careful!"

As she got closer and the bright light over Alice's bed lit up her face, Alice saw fine spidery lines etched around Elisabeth's mouth and on either side of her eyes behind the elegant spectacles. Elisabeth had large, pale blue eyes with dark lashes, like Alice, inherited from their father; eyes that attracted compliments, but now they seemed smaller and paler, as if the color had begun to wash out.

There was something bruised and wary and worn out about those washed-out eyes, as if she'd just been badly defeated in a fight she'd expected to win.

Alice felt a surge of worry; something terrible must have happened.

But when she asked, Elisabeth said, "What do you mean what happened to *me*?" so briskly and spiritedly that Alice doubted herself.

Elisabeth pulled over a plastic chair and sat down. Alice caught a glimpse of her skirt pulling unflatteringly across her stomach and quickly looked away; it made her want to cry.

Elisabeth said, "You're the one in hospital. The question is what happened to *you*?"

Alice felt herself slip into the role of irrepressible, hopeless Alice. "It's completely bizarre. It's like a dream. Apparently, I fell over at the gym. Me, at the gym! I know! According to Jane Turner I was doing something called my 'Friday spin class.'" She could be silly now, because Elisabeth was here to be sensible.

Elisabeth stared at her with such grim, frightened concentration that Alice felt her silly grin drift away.

She reached out for the photo she'd left sitting on the chest of drawers next to her bed and handed it to Elisabeth, saying in a small, polite voice, "Are these my . . ." She felt more foolish than she'd ever felt in her life. "Are these my children?"

Elisabeth took the photo, glanced at it, and something complicated crossed her face, a barely perceptible tremor, and vanished. She smiled carefully and said, "Yes, Alice."

Alice took a deep, shaky breath and closed her eyes. "I've never seen them before."

She heard Elisabeth take a deep breath herself. "It's just temporary, I'm sure. You probably just need to rest, to relax and—"

"What are they like?" Alice opened her eyes. "Those children. Are they . . . nice?"

Elisabeth said in a stronger voice, "They're wonderful, Alice."

Alice said, "Am I a good mother? Do I look after them all right? What do I feed them? They're so big!"

"Your children are your life, Alice," said Elisabeth. "You'll remember for yourself soon. It will all come back. Just—"

"I could cook them sausages, I guess," said Alice, cheering up at the thought. "Kids love sausages."

Elisabeth stared. "You would never feed them sausages."

"I thought I was pregnant," said Alice. "But they did a blood test and told me I'm definitely not. I don't feel like I am, but I can't believe I'm not. I can't believe it."

"No. Well, I don't think you would be pregnant—"

"*Three* kids!" said Alice. "We're only going to have two."

"Olivia was an accident," said Elisabeth stiffly, as if she disapproved.

"None of this seems real," said Alice. "I'm like Alice in Wonderland. Remember how much I hated that book? Because nothing made sense. You didn't like it either. We liked things to make sense."

"I can imagine it must feel *really* strange, but it's not going to last, it's all going to come back to you any minute. You must have hit your head quite . . . severely."

"Yes. Very severely." Alice picked up the photo again. "So this little girl. This little girl is the oldest, so she must be my first baby, right? So we had a girl?"

"Yes, you did."

"We thought it was a boy."

"I remember that."

"And labor! I went through labor three times? What was my labor like? I'm so nervous about it. I mean, I *was* . . ."

"I think you had a pretty easy time with Madison, but there were complications with Olivia—" Elisabeth fidgeted in her plastic seat. "Look, Alice, I think I should go and try to talk to one of your doctors. I'm finding this really hard. It's weird. It's really . . . scary."

Alice reached out for Elisabeth's arm in a panic. She couldn't stand to be alone again. "No, no, don't go. Someone will be around soon. They keep coming and checking on me. Hey, Libby, I called Nick at work and they told me he was in Portugal! Portugal! What's he doing there? I left a message with some horrible secretary. I stood up to her. You'd be proud of me! I showed backbone. My backbone was like *steel*."

"Good for you," said Elisabeth. She looked as if she'd just eaten something that disagreed with her.

"But he still hasn't called me back," sighed Alice.

Elisabeth's Homework for Dr. Hodges

It was only when she started talking about Nick being in Portugal that the obvious hit me, and it seemed even more shocking than when she asked me whether her children were "nice."

She really has forgotten everything.

Even Gina.

Chapter 7

S o, you *seriously* don't remember anything, not a single thing, since 1998?" Elisabeth shifted the plastic chair in closer toward Alice's bed and leaned toward her, as if it was time to get to the bottom of this. "Nothing at all?"

"Well, I've been having some funny snippets of things come into my mind," said Alice. "But none of them make sense."

"Okay, so tell me about them," urged Elisabeth. Her face was closer now to Alice and the lines on either side of her mouth were even deeper than Alice had first thought. Goodness. Involuntarily, Alice pressed her fingertips to her own skin; she still hadn't looked at herself in a mirror.

She said, "Well, when I first woke up, I was having this dream, and I couldn't tell if it was just a dream or something that really happened. I was swimming, and it was a beautiful summer's morning, and my toenails were all painted different colors. There was somebody else with me and their toenails were painted the same way. Hey, maybe the other person was you? I bet it was you!"

Elisabeth said, "No, that doesn't mean anything to me. What else?"

Alice thought about the bouquets of pink balloons bobbing about in the gray sky, but she didn't want to tell Elisabeth about that great tidal wave of grief that kept sweeping her away, and she wasn't all that keen on finding out what it meant.

Instead she said, "I remember an American lady saying, '*I'm sorry, but there is no heartbeat.*'"

"Oh," said Elisabeth.

Elisabeth's Homework for Dr. Hodges

I admit I found it oddly touching, flattering even, that of all the billions of memories significant enough to float to the surface of Alice's mind, that was one of them.

Alice has always been good at imitating accents and she did that woman's voice perfectly. The tone and the rhythm were exactly the way I remembered, and for a moment I was back there in that gloomy room, trying to understand. I haven't thought about it in such a long time.

Imagine, Dr. Hodges, if I could travel back in time to that day and whisper in my ear, "This is only the beginning, honey." Then I'd throw back my head and laugh a demented witchy laugh.

Actually you don't really like it when I do that sort of black, bitter humor thing, do you? I've noticed that you smile politely and sort of sadly, as if I'm making a fool of myself and you know exactly why, as if I'm a teenager who isn't in control of her own embarrassing emotions.

Anyway, I didn't want to talk about the American woman to Alice. Obviously. Especially not to *Alice*. I don't especially want to talk about it with you, either. Or think about it. Or write about it. It just happened. Like everything else.

Elisabeth smoothed the white blanket next to Alice's leg with the flat of her palm. Her face seemed to harden. She said, "Sorry, that doesn't mean anything to me, either. Not a thing."

Why did she sound angry? Alice felt as if she'd done something wrong but couldn't work out what; she felt stupidly clumsy, like a child trying to grasp something big and important that the grown-ups weren't telling her.

Elisabeth met Alice's eyes and gave her a half-smile and looked away again quickly.

A woman carrying flowers came into the ward, peered hopefully at Alice and Elisabeth, blinked dismissively, and walked past their curtained-off cubicle to the next one. They heard a disembodied voice squeal, "I was just thinking about you!"

"I should have brought you flowers," murmured Elisabeth.

Alice said suddenly, "You're married!"

"Pardon?"

Alice picked up Elisabeth's left hand. "You've got an engagement ring! It's gorgeous. That's exactly the sort of ring I would have got if we'd got to choose our own ring. Not that I don't love Granny Love's ring, of course."

Elisabeth said dryly, "You hate and despise Granny Love's ring, Alice."

"Oh. Did I tell you that? I don't remember telling you that."

"Years ago, I think you might have had too much to drink, that's why I don't understand why . . . well, anyway."

Alice said, "Well, are you going to keep me in suspense? Who did you marry? Was it that cute town planner?"

"*Dean?* No, I didn't marry Dean, and I only went out with him for five minutes. Also, he died. In a scuba diving accident. Tragic. Anyway, I married Ben. You don't remember Ben? He's looking after your children at the moment."

"Oh, that's nice of him, good," said Alice weakly, and felt sick again, because presumably a good mother would immediately have checked on who was looking after her children. The problem was that it still seemed preposterous that they existed. She pressed a hand to her flat stomach where there was no longer a baby and fought that feeling of vertigo. If she let herself think too much about this, she might start screaming and not be able to stop.

"Ben," said Alice, focusing on Elisabeth. "So you married someone called Ben." She remembered hearing that snuffly child say "Uncle Ben" on the phone. It was somehow worse when things clicked together, as if everything in the world made sense except for Alice.

She said, "It's funny, I was thinking earlier that the only Ben I knew was this huge neon-sign designer I met once at Nick's sister's shop. I always remembered that guy because he was so big and slow and silent, it was like a giant grizzly bear had been turned into a man."

Elisabeth burst out laughing, and the sound of her laugh (it was a full-throated, generous laugh that always made you want to say the funny thing again) and the way she tipped back her head made her seem like her proper self again.

"I don't get it." Alice smiled, ready to get it.

"That's the Ben I married. I met him at the opening of Dora's shop. We've been married eight years."

"Really?" Elisabeth married that huge grizzly neon-sign designer? She normally went for terribly witty, successful corporate types, who made Alice feel stupid. "But didn't he have a *beard*?"

Surely Elisabeth wouldn't have married someone with a beard.

Elisabeth shook with laughter. "Yep, he's still got it."

"And does he still design neon signs?"

"Yes, beautiful ones. My favorite is the one for Rob's Ribs and Rumps in Killara. It came in second in the annual Neon Design Awards last year."

Alice looked at her sharply, but she seemed perfectly serious.

She said, "So he's my brother-in-law. So I guess I . . . know him. I know him pretty well. Does Nick get on with him? Do we all go out together?"

Elisabeth paused and Alice couldn't read the expression on her face. Then she said, "Years ago, before Ben and I were married, when Madison was a toddler and you were just pregnant with Tom, we got a house together at Jervis Bay one Easter. It was right on Hyams Beach, you know—whitest sand in the world—and the weather was perfect, and Madison was so cute, we were all just in love with her. We played stupid card games like Cheat and one night Nick and Ben got drunk and danced to eighties music. Ben *never* dances. That might have been the only time I've seen him dance. They were being so stupid! We were just rolling around laughing so much, we woke Madison up and she got out of bed and danced with them in her pj's. Actually, that was a really special holiday. It makes me feel so nostalgic. I haven't thought about it for ages."

"I don't remember a thing about it," said Alice. It seemed so cruel that she couldn't remember a wonderful holiday, as if some other Alice had got to live her life in her place.

Elisabeth's tone changed abruptly. "It's amazing you don't remember Ben." There was something almost aggressive in her voice and she was looking sharply at Alice as if daring her to say something. "You saw him just yesterday. He came over to help you with your car. You baked him his favorite banana muffins. You had *quite* a chat."

"So," said Alice nervously. "We have a car now?"

"Mmmm. Yes you do, Alice."

"And I make banana muffins?"

Elisabeth smiled. "Low fat. High fiber. But surprisingly delicious."

Alice's mind jumped about feverishly, this way and that, until she felt dizzy, from those three strange children sitting in a row to banana muffins to a car (she didn't like cars: she liked buses, the ferry; also, she wasn't the best driver) to Elisabeth marrying a neon-sign designer called Ben.

She seized on a sudden hurtful thought. "Hey! You must have had a wedding without me!" Alice loved weddings. She would never forget a wedding.

Elisabeth said, "Alice, you were my matron of honor and Madison was flower girl. You had matching dresses the color of a Singapore orchid. You made a funny speech, and you and Nick made a spectacle of yourselves dancing to 'Come On Eileen.' You gave us a blender."

"Oh." Frustration welled up in her. "But I just can't believe I don't remember *any* of this. It doesn't even sound familiar!" She stuck her fingers though the holes in the blanket over her legs and bunched it together hard with both hands in a silly, childish movement. "There is so much . . . *stuff*!"

"Hey . . . hey, there." Elisabeth rubbed Alice's shoulder a bit too vigorously, as if she were a boxer, and looked around her feverishly for help. "You've got to let me go and find a doctor to talk about this."

She was a problem solver, Elisabeth. She always wanted to find a solution for you.

There was a burst of screechy female laughter from the cubicle next to them. "You *didn't*!" "I *did*!" Alice and Elisabeth raised their eyebrows at each other in mutual silent distaste and Alice was filled with soothing, sisterly affection.

She let go of the blanket and managed to put her hands sedately back in her lap. "Please don't go. A nurse will come along and check on me soon and you can talk to her. Just stay here and keep talking to me. I think that will cure me."

Elisabeth glanced at her watch and said, "I don't know about that," but she sat back in her chair.

Alice shifted herself against the pillows behind her back to get comfortable. She thought about asking more questions about the children in the photo (*three!*—the number was so unwieldy and impossible) but it was so surreal it was silly, like a movie that was so far-fetched you kept shifting in your seat and trying not to guffaw. It was better to ask about Elisabeth's life.

Elisabeth had her head bent, scratching at something invisible on her wrist. Alice looked again at the lines that seemed to pull her sister's mouth down into a sad sort of grimace. Was it just age? (Did her own mouth turn down like that, too? Soon she would look. Soon.) But it was more than that;

there was a deep, slumping sort of sadness about her. Was she not happy being married to that grizzly-bear man? (Was it possible to love a man with a beard? Childish. Of course it was possible. Even if it was a remarkably *bushy* beard.)

As Alice watched, Elisabeth's throat moved as she swallowed convulsively.

"What are you thinking about?" asked Alice.

Elisabeth started and looked up. "I don't know, nothing." She swallowed a yawn. "Sorry. I'm just tired. I only got a couple of hours' sleep last night."

"Ah," said Alice. She didn't need an explanation. She and Elisabeth had both suffered from bouts of terrible insomnia all their lives. They had inherited it from their mother. After their dad died, Alice and Elisabeth would often stay up right through the night with their mother, sitting in their dressing gowns in a row on the couch, watching videos and drinking cocoa, and then they'd sleep the next day away, while sunlight streamed through the muffled, sleeping house.

"How has my insomnia been lately?" asked Alice.

"I don't know actually. I don't know if you still get it."

"You don't know?" Alice was baffled. They always kept each other up to date with their insomnia battles. "But don't we—don't we talk?"

"Of course we talk, but I guess you're pretty busy, with the kids and everything, so our conversations are maybe a bit rushed."

"Busy," repeated Alice. She didn't like the sound of that at all. She had always had a slight mistrust of busy people; the sort of people who described themselves as *"Flat-out! Frantic!"* What was the hurry? Why didn't they slow down? Just what exactly were they so busy doing?

"Well," she said, and felt unaccountably awkward. It felt like things weren't exactly right between herself and Elisabeth. There seemed to be a sort of stilted, friendly politeness, as if they were good friends who didn't see each other so often anymore.

She would ask Nick about it. It was one of the best things about him; he liked to talk about people, study them, and work them out. He was interested in the complexities of relationships. Also, he loved Elisabeth, and when he made fun of her, or complained about her (because she could at times be profoundly annoying), he did it in just the right brotherly way so that Alice didn't feel she had to defend her.

Alice looked at Elisabeth's beautifully cut cream suit (both their wardrobes seemed to have improved in 2008) and said, "Are you still working at the catalogue place? The Treasure Chest?"

Elisabeth had a job writing the text for a huge monthly mail-order catalogue called *The Treasure Chest*. She had to find clever, persuasive things to say about hundreds and hundreds of products, anything from banana-flavored lip gloss to an instant egg poacher to a waterproof radio you could play in the shower. She got a lot of free stuff to give away, which was nice, and every month when the catalogue came out, everyone in the family read out their favorite lines to Elisabeth. Frannie kept every issue of *The Treasure Chest* on proud display and made her friends read it when they came to visit.

"Oh, that feels like such a long time ago," said Elisabeth. She looked at Alice and shook her head slightly, as if she'd never seen anything quite like it. "You're like a time traveler. You really are."

"So I guess you don't work there anymore?" Alice felt irritable. This was going to get tiring if everyone looked at her with awe each time she asked a simple question. How much could have changed in ten years? It seemed like everything.

"*The Treasure Chest* is a website now," said Elisabeth. "And I stopped working there about six years ago. I worked for an agency for about four years, and then two years ago I started running these training seminars on how to write direct mail. Or junk mail, as most people would call it. They're quite—well, they're quite successful, actually, as strange as that may seem. Anyway, it pays the bills. I was running one today when I got the call from Jane about you."

"So it's your own business?"

"Yes."

"Wow! That's so impressive. You're a success story. I always knew you would be a success story. Can I come along and watch you?"

"Come along and watch? Watch *me*?" Elisabeth snorted.

"Oh. I guess I've already done that, have I?"

Elisabeth said, "No, Alice, you've never shown the slightest interest in coming along to one of my seminars." Her voice had that sharp edge again.

"Oh," said Alice, confused. "That seems . . . well, I wonder why not?"

Elisabeth sighed. "You're just really busy, Alice. That's all."

There was that "busy" word again.

"And also, I think you find my whole choice of career maybe a bit—tacky."

"Tacky? I said that? I said that about you? I would never say that!" Alice was horrified. Had she turned into a nasty person who judged people by their choice of a career? She'd always been proud of Elisabeth. She was the smart one, the one who was going places, while Alice stayed safely put.

Elisabeth said, "No, no, you never actually said that. You probably don't even think it. Just forget I said that."

Maybe, thought Alice fearfully, the other Alice who has been living my life for the last ten years isn't very nice.

Alice said, "Well, what about me? What do I do for a job?"

Alice had worked as an administrative assistant in the pay office at ABR. She didn't love it or hate it, it was just a job. She wasn't especially interested in a career. "You're such a domestic goddess. You're like a 1950s housewife," Elisabeth had once said to her, when Alice admitted that she'd just spent the most blissful day gardening, making new curtains for the kitchen, and baking a chocolate cake for Nick.

"You don't work." Elisabeth gave her an inscrutable look.

"Oh, well, that sounds good!" said Alice happily.

"You're very busy, though." What was it with that word? "You do a lot of stuff at the school."

"The school? What school?"

"The children's school."

Oh. Them. The three scary little strangers.

"Frannie," said Alice suddenly. "What about Frannie? She hasn't—got sick or anything, has she?" She didn't want to even say the word "died."

"She's fine," said Elisabeth. "Full of beans."

The silver mobile phone sitting on the cabinet next to Alice's bed burst into life.

"It must be Nick at last!" Alice lunged for the phone.

"Oh!" Elisabeth jumped to her feet. "Let me talk to him first!"

"No way." Alice held the phone away from her, irritated. "Why?" Without waiting for an answer, she pressed the green button and held the phone to her ear.

"Hello?"

"Yeah, hi, it's me." It was Nick; Alice felt blissful relief running straight through her bloodstream like a shot of brandy.

"What's happened?" His voice was deeper, rougher than usual, as if he had a cold. "Is it one of the kids?"

So Nick knew about "the kids," too. Everyone knew about the kids.

Elisabeth was jumping up and down, waving her arms about, gesturing for the phone. Alice poked her tongue out at her.

"No, it's me," said Alice. There was so much to tell him, she didn't know where to start. "I fell over at the, ah, gym, with Jane Turner, and hit my head. I was unconscious. They had to call an ambulance—oh, and I was sick in the lift all over this guy's shoes, so embarrassing! And wait till I tell you about this bike-riding class! So funny. Hey, you're in Portugal, I can't believe you're in Portugal, what's it like?"

There was so much to tell him, she felt like she hadn't seen him in years. When he got back from Portugal, they would have to go out for dinner at that Mexican restaurant they liked and talk, talk, talk. They would have margaritas; she could drink again, now that she wasn't pregnant anymore. Oh, she *yearned* to be in that restaurant with him right now, sitting in a dark corner booth, his thumb caressing her palm.

There was silence on the other end of the phone. He must be in shock.

"But I'm not badly hurt!" Alice reassured him. "It's not serious. I'll be fine! I feel fine!"

He said, "Then why the *fuck* did I need to call you?"

Alice felt her head snap back as if she'd been hit. Nick had never, ever spoken to her like that before, not even when they were fighting. He was meant to fix the nightmare, not make it worse.

"Nick?" There was a tremor in her voice. She was going to be so mad with him later about this; her feelings were *extremely* hurt. "What's the matter?"

"Is there some sort of strategy to all this? Because I'm not getting it, and to be frank, I don't have time for it. You don't want to change any of the arrangements for the weekend, do you? Is that what it's about? Or, for Christ's sake, tell me it's not something to do with Christmas Day again. *Is* it?"

"Why are you talking to me like that?" said Alice. Her heart raced. This was more terrifying than anything that had happened to her today. "What did I do?"

"Oh, for God's sake, I don't have time for fucking games at the moment!"

He was shouting. He was actually shouting at her, and she was in *hospital*.

"Paprika," whispered Alice. "You have to wash your mouth out with paprika, Nick."

Elisabeth stood up. "Give it here," she ordered.

She removed the phone from Alice's trembling fingers, put the phone to her ear, and pressed a finger to her other ear. She turned her face away from Alice and dropped her chin. "Nick, it's Elisabeth. This is actually quite serious. She's had a bad head injury and she's lost her memory. She's forgotten everything since 1998. Do you understand what I'm saying? *Everything*."

Alice let her head fall back against the pillow and breathed shallow gasps of air. What did it mean?

Elisabeth paused, listening, her forehead furrowed. "Yes, yes, I understand, but she doesn't actually remember any of that."

Another pause.

"They're with Ben. He's taken them to their swimming lesson, and I guess we'll stay over with them tonight, and then—"

Pause. "Yes, okay, and then your mum can pick them up exactly as per the arrangements, and I'm sure by Sunday night Alice should be back on her feet and everything will be back to normal." Pause. "No, I haven't talked to a doctor yet, but I will soon." Pause. "Right. Okay, well do you want me to put Alice back on?"

Alice held out her hand for the phone—surely Nick would be himself again now—but Elisabeth said, "Oh. Okay. Well, bye, Nick."

She hung up.

Alice said, "He didn't want to talk to me? He actually didn't want to talk to me?" She could feel stabbing pains all over her body, a long witchy finger poking her cruelly.

Elisabeth clicked the phone shut and put her hand on Alice's arm. She said gently, "You'll remember soon. It's okay. It's just that you and Nick aren't together anymore."

Alice felt a sensation of everything around her plummeting toward the central point of Elisabeth's moving lips. She focused on those lips. Raspberry lipstick with a darker line around the edge. Elisabeth must use lip liner. Fancy that. She must *line her lips.*

What was she saying? She could not be saying—

"What?" said Alice.

Elisabeth said again, "You're getting divorced."

Well, fancy that.

Chapter 8

A lice had one glass of champagne with her bridesmaids while they were getting their makeup done, another half a glass in the limo, three and a quarter glasses at the wedding reception (including strawberries), and another glass sitting up with Nick on the king-size bed in their hotel room that night.

So she was somewhat sozzled, but that was no problem because she was the bride and it was her wedding day, and everyone had said she looked beautiful, and so this was a beautiful, romantic drunkenness that would probably not result in a hangover.

"Do you love and adore my wedding dress?" she asked Nick for what could have been the third time, as she ran her hand across its rich, lustrous fabric. It was called Ivory Silk Duchess Satin, and touching it gave her the same sensuously satisfied feeling as when she was a little girl and she used to run her finger over the plush pink lining of her music box, except this was even better because back then she really wanted to be *in* the music box, rolling around on pink satin. "I love my wedding dress. It sort of looks like golden, magical ice cream, doesn't it? Couldn't you just *eat* it?"

"Normally I'd tuck in," said Nick. "But I'm full of cake. I had three pieces. That was outstanding cake. Everybody will be talking about the cake at our wedding for years to come. Most wedding cake is boring, but our cake! I'm so proud of our cake. I didn't make the cake, but I'm proud of it."

It seemed Nick had drunk quite a bit of champagne, too.

Alice set her glass on the bedside table and lay down on her back with a rich rustle of fabric. Nick slid down beside her. He'd taken off his tie and undone the buttons of his white dinner shirt. He had the beginnings of a five-o'clock shadow and slightly bloodshot eyes, but his hair was still perfect with a ridgelike wave at the part. Alice touched it and pulled her hand back. "It feels like straw!"

"The sisters," explained Nick. "Armed with gel."

He stroked her hair and said, "That's a nice synthetic feel you've got going there, wife."

"Hairspray. A lot of hairspray, husband."

"Is that right, wife?"

"Yes it is, husband."

"How interesting, wife."

"Are we going to talk like this forever, husband?"

"No way, wife."

They looked up at the ceiling and said nothing.

"What about Ella's speech!" said Alice.

"I think it was meant to be touching."

"Ah."

"What about your Aunt Whatsie's dress!"

"I think it was meant to be, um . . . stylish."

"Ah."

They snickered quietly.

Alice rolled onto her side and said, "Imagine," and her eyes filled with tears. She always got emotional when she drank too much champagne. "Imagine if we never met."

"It was fated," said Nick. "So we would have met the next day."

"But I don't believe in fate!" whimpered Alice, reveling in the luxurious feeling of hot, wet tears rolling down her cheeks; those triple coats of mascara would be streaked all over her face. It seemed truly frightening that it was only by sheer chance that she had met Nick. It could so easily not have happened, and then she would have had a shadowy, half-alive existence, like some sort of woodland creature who never sees sunlight, never even *knowing* how much she could love and how much she could be loved. Elisabeth once said—very definitely and severely—that the right man didn't complete you, you have to find happiness yourself, and Alice nodded agreeably, while thinking to herself, "Oh, but yes he does."

"If we'd never met," continued Alice, "then today would just be like any other day and right now we'd be watching television in separate homes, and I'd be wearing *tracksuit pants* and, and . . . we wouldn't be going on honeymoon tomorrow." The full horror of what could have been struck her. "We'd be going to work! *Work*!"

"Come here, my darling inebriated bride." Nick pulled Alice to him, so that her head was resting beneath his shoulder and she breathed in the scent of his aftershave. It was much stronger than usual; he must have slapped on extra that morning, and the thought of him doing that was so unbearably sweet, it made her cry even harder. He said, "The important point here is this—wait for it, it's a very important and intelligent point—you ready?"

"Yes."

"We *did* meet."

"Yes," conceded Alice. "We did meet."

"So it all turned out okay."

"That's true," sniffed Alice. "It all turned out okay."

"It all turned out okay."

And then they had both fallen into a deep, exhausted sleep, with Alice's Ivory Silk Duchess Satin wedding dress swirled all over them, and a single red dot of confetti stuck to the side of Nick's face, which would leave a red circle that would stay there for the first three days of their honeymoon.

"We must have just had a bad argument," said Alice to Elisabeth. "We're not actually divorcing. We would never divorce."

That word—"divorce"—was so ugly; her lips pursed together like a fish on the second syllable. Dee-*vorce*. No. Not them. Never, ever them.

Nick's parents divorced when he was a child. He remembered everything about it. Whenever they heard about a couple divorcing—even a trashy, laughable celebrity couple—Nick always said, sadly, like an Irish grandma, "Ah, that's a shame." He believed in marriage. He felt that people gave up on their relationships too easily. He once said to Alice that if they were ever having troubles in their marriage, he would move heaven and earth to fix things. Alice couldn't take it seriously because heaven and earth wouldn't need to be moved; any troubles in their relationship could always be fixed with a few hours in separate rooms, a hug in the hallway, the quiet sliding of a chocolate bar under an elbow, or even just a gentle, meaningful poke in the ribs that meant "Let's stop fighting now."

Divorce was like a phobia for Nick, his only phobia! If this were true, then he would be devastated, crushed. The thing he feared most had happened. Her heart broke for him.

"Did we have a really bad argument about something?" Alice asked Elisabeth. She would get to the bottom of it, she would put a stop to it.

"I don't think it's just one argument. I guess it's probably a whole lot of little issues, but to be honest, you haven't really told me that much about it. You just rang me the day after Nick moved out and said—"

"He moved *out*? He actually moved out of the house?"

It was mind-boggling; she tried to visualize how it could actually happen, Nick throwing stuff into a suitcase, slamming the door behind him, a yellow taxicab waiting outside—it would have to be yellow, like an American cab, because this could not be real, this was a scene from a movie with a heart-wrenching soundtrack. This was not her life.

"Alice, you've been separated for six months, but you know, once you get your memory back, you'll realize it's okay, because you're fine with this. This is what you want. I asked you just last week. I said, 'Are you sure this is what you want?' and you said, 'Absolutely sure. This marriage was dead and buried a long time ago.'"

Liar, liar, pants on fire. That could not be true. That had to be a fabrication. Alice tried to keep the rage out of her voice. "You're just making that up to make me feel better, aren't you? I would never say that. 'Dead and buried!' That doesn't even sound like me! I don't talk like that. Please don't make stuff up. This is hard enough."

"Oh, *Alice*," said Elisabeth sadly. "I promise you, it's just your head injury, it's just . . . oh, hi there, hi!"

A nurse Alice hadn't seen before pulled back the curtain briskly on their cubicle and Elisabeth greeted her with obvious relief.

"How are you feeling?" The nurse pumped up the blood-pressure strap around Alice's arm once again.

"I'm fine," said Alice resignedly. She knew the drill now. Blood pressure. Pupils. Questions.

"Your blood pressure has soared from the last time I checked," commented the nurse, making a note on her chart.

My husband just yelled at me like I was his worst enemy. My lovely Nick. My Nick. I want to tell him about it, because he'd be so angry if he ever heard somebody speak to me like that. He's the first person I want to tell when somebody upsets me; my foot pressing on the accelerator, desperate to get home from work just to tell him, the moment I tell him, the moment his face lights up with fury on my behalf, it's better, it's fixed.

Nick, you will never believe how this man spoke to me. You will want to punch him in the nose when you hear. Except it's so strange, because it was you, Nick, you were the man.

"She's had a few shocks," said Elisabeth.

"We really need you to try and stay relaxed." The nurse leaned close and did something feathery-quick with her fingers to pull back Alice's eyelids while she shone her miniature torch into each pupil. The nurse's perfume reminded Alice of something—someone?—but of course the feeling vanished as soon as the nurse moved. Was this going to be her from now on—a permanent, irritating case of déjà vu like an itchy rash?

"Now I'm just going to ask you a few boring questions again. What's your name?"

"Alice Mary Love."

"And where are you and what are you doing here?"

"I'm at Royal North Shore Hospital because I hit my head at the gym."

"And what day is it?"

"It's Friday, 2 May . . . 2008."

"Good, excellent!" The nurse turned to Elisabeth, as if expecting her to be impressed. "We're just checking that her cognitive reasoning isn't affected by her injury."

Elisabeth blinked irritably. "Yes, okay, great, but she still thinks it's 1998."

Tattletale, thought Alice.

"I do not," she said. "I know it's 2008. I just said that."

"But she still doesn't remember anything *since* 1998. Or hardly anything. She doesn't remember her children. She doesn't remember her marriage breakup."

Her marriage breakup. Her marriage was something that could be sliced up like a pizza.

Alice closed her eyes and thought of Nick's face, creased from sleep, lying on the pillow next to hers on a Sunday morning. Sometimes in the morning his hair would be all spiked up in the middle of his head. "You've got a Mohawk," said Alice the first time she observed this phenomenon. "Of course," he said. "It's Sunday. Mohawk day." Even with his eyes closed, he knew when she was awake, lying there, looking at him, thinking hopefully that he might bring her a cup of tea in bed. "No," he would say, before she'd even asked. "Don't even think about it, woman." But he always got it for her.

Alice would give anything, anything at all, to be lying in bed right now with Nick, waiting for a cup of tea. Maybe he got sick of making her cups of tea? Was that it? Had she taken him for granted? Who did she think she was, some sort of princess, lying in bed waiting for cups of tea to be delivered, without even brushing her teeth? She wasn't pretty enough to get away with that sort of behavior. She should have jumped up before he woke, done her hair and makeup and made him pancakes and strawberries, wearing a long lacy nightgown. That was how you kept a marriage alive, for God's sake, it wasn't as if there wasn't enough advice around in every women's magazine she'd ever read. It was basic knowledge! She felt as though she'd been unforgivably negligent—careless! sloppy!—with the most precious, wonderful gift she'd ever received.

Alice could hear Elisabeth murmuring urgently to the nurse, asking if she could see the doctor, wanting to know what tests had been done. "How do you know she hasn't got some sort of *clot* in her brain?" Elisabeth's voice rose a bit hysterically, and Alice smiled to herself. Drama queen.

(Although, could there be a clot? A dark, ominous thing swooping about in her head like an evil bat? Yes, they really should look into that.)

Maybe Nick had got bored with her. Was that it? Once, when she was in high school, she overheard a girl saying, "Oh, Alice, she's okay, but she's a *nothing* sort of person."

A nothing sort of person. The girl had said it so casually, without malice, as if it were a fact, and at fourteen Alice had felt cold with the official confirmation of what she'd always believed. Yes, of course she was boring, she bored herself silly! Other people's personalities were so much more substantial. That same year, a boy at the bowling alley leaned in close with the sweet smell of Coke on his breath and said, "You've got a face like a pig." And that just confirmed something else she'd always suspected; her mother was wrong when she said her nose was as cute as a button; it wasn't a nose, it was a *snout*.

(The boy had a skinny, tiny-eyed face like a rat. She was twenty-five before it occurred to her that she could have insulted him back, but the rule of life was that the boys got to decide which girls were pretty; it didn't really matter how ugly they were themselves.)

Maybe Nick had been bringing her a cup of tea one morning and all of a sudden a veil lifted from his eyes and he thought, Hey, wait a second, how did I end up married to this lazy girl with her boring nothing personality and piglike face?

Oh Lord, were all those terrible insecurities really so fresh and close to the surface? She was grown up; she was twenty-nine! It was only recently that she'd been walking home from the hairdresser's, feeling gorgeous, and a gaggle of teenage girls walked by, and the sound of their strident giggles made her send a message back through time to her fourteen-year-old self: "Don't worry, it all works out. You get a personality, you get a job, you work out what to do with your hair, *and* you get a boy who thinks you're beautiful." She'd felt so *together*, as if all the teenage angst and the failed relationships before Nick had all been part of a perfectly acceptable plan that was leading to this moment, when she would be twenty-nine years old and everything would finally be just as it should be.

Thirty-nine. Not twenty-nine. She was thirty-nine. And that day with the teenagers must have been ten years ago.

Elisabeth came back in and sat back down next to Alice. "She's going to try and get the doctor to come around again. Apparently that's a very big deal, because you're just under observation now and the doctor is 'extremely busy,' but she's going to 'see what she can do.' So I think our chances are probably zero."

Alice said, "Please tell me it's not true. About Nick."

"Oh, Alice."

"Because I love him. I properly love him. I love him so much."

"You did love him."

"No, I *do*. Right now. I know I still do."

Elisabeth made a "tsk" sound that was full of sympathy, and lifted her hands in a hopeless sort of gesture. "When you get your memory back—"

"But we're so happy!" interrupted Alice frantically, trying to make Elisabeth see. "It's not even possible to be happier." Tears slid helplessly down the sides of her face and trickled ticklishly into her ears. "What happened? Did he fall in love with someone else? Is that it?"

Surely not. It was impossible. Nick's love for Alice was a fact. *A fact.* You were allowed to take facts for granted. Once, a friend was teasing Nick for agreeing to go with Alice to a musical (although he actually quite liked musicals). "I can see the thumbprint in between your eyes," the friend said, and Nick shrugged. "Mate, what can I do? I love her more than oxygen."

Sure, he'd been drinking a lot of beer, but he said that in a *pub*, when he was trying to be blokey. He loved her more than oxygen.

So, what—the boy didn't need oxygen anymore?

Elisabeth put the back of her hand to Alice's forehead and stroked her hair. "He didn't meet anyone else as far as I know, and you're right, you were happy together and you did have a wonderful, special relationship. I remember it. But things change. People change. It just happens. It's just life. The fact that you're getting a divorce doesn't change the fact that you had all those wonderful times. And I swear to you that once you get your memory back, you'll be fine with this."

"No." Alice shut her eyes. "No, I won't. I don't want to be fine with it."

As Elisabeth continued to stroke her forehead, Alice remembered the day from her childhood when she'd been dropped home after a birthday party still fizzing from winning the Simon Says competition. She was carrying a balloon and a basket made of shiny cardboard and filled with lollies. Elisabeth had met her at the front door and ordered, "Come with me."

Alice trotted along behind her, ready for whatever new game Elisabeth must have organized, and ready to share the lollies, but not the Freddo Frogs—she loved Freddo Frogs—and as they walked past the living room, her balloon bobbing along behind her, she noticed that it seemed to be full of strange grown-ups surrounding her mum, who was sitting on the couch with her head resting back on the couch at a strange angle (odd, but maybe she had a headache). Alice didn't call out to her because she didn't want to have to talk to all the strange grown-ups, and she followed Elisabeth down the hallway to her bedroom, where Elisabeth said, "I have to tell you something that is going to make you feel very bad, so I think you should get in your pajamas and get into bed and be ready for it so it won't hurt so much."

Alice didn't say, "What? What is it? Tell me now!" because she was six and nothing bad had ever happened to her, and besides which she always did what Elisabeth said. So she was perfectly happy to put on her pajamas while Elisabeth went to fill up a hot water bottle and put it in a pillowslip so it wouldn't burn. She also brought along a spoonful of honey, the Vicks VapoRub, and half an aspirin and a glass of water. These were all things their mother did when they were sick, and Alice loved being sick. Once Elisabeth had her tucked in bed and had rubbed the Vicks on her chest, she started stroking back the hair off Alice's forehead, just like their mum did when either of them had an especially bad stomachache, and Alice had closed her eyes and enjoyed all the good parts of being sick, without the actual sick feeling. Then Elisabeth said, "Now I have to tell you the bad thing. It's going to give you a bad, surprised feeling, so be ready for it, okay? You can suck your thumb if you want." Alice had opened her eyes and frowned, because she did not suck her thumb anymore, except for when she'd had an extremely bad day, and even then it was just the very tip, hardly the whole thumb. Then Elisabeth said, "Daddy has died."

Alice could never remember what happened next, or even how she felt on hearing the words. All she remembered was how Elisabeth had tried so hard to protect her from the "bad, surprised feeling." She was twenty-four before it occurred to her with a jolt of surprise that Elisabeth had been only a little girl herself that day. She'd phoned her to talk about it, to thank her, and the funny thing was that Elisabeth had an entirely different set of memories about when their dad died and didn't even remember putting Alice to bed.

Of course, there was also the time Elisabeth had thrown a pair of nail scissors at her, which got impaled in the back of her neck. But still . . .

Now Alice opened her eyes and said to Elisabeth, "You're such a good big sister."

Elisabeth took her hand away and said flatly, "No I'm not."

Neither of them said anything for a few seconds, and then Alice said,

"Are *you* happy, Libby? Because you seem . . ." Desperately unhappy, she wanted to say.

"I'm fine."

Elisabeth seemed to be thinking of things to say and then discarding them. "Just be your proper self!" Alice wanted to scream.

Finally Elisabeth said, "I guess maybe our lives haven't turned out quite the way we envisaged they would when we were thirty."

A voice interrupted them. "At last! I found you! I thought I'd never find you!"

There was a woman standing at the end of the bed, her face hidden for a moment as she ceremoniously held up a large bunch of yellow tulips.

She lowered the tulips and revealed her face. Alice blinked and blinked again in disbelief.

Chapter 9

M um?" said Alice.

It was Alice's mother standing at the end of her bed, but this was an extraordinarily different Barb Jones from the one Alice knew.

For a start (and there were so many possible places to start), her hair was no longer short and brown, the humble nunlike hairstyle that she'd had for as long as Alice could remember. Instead, it was a rich mahogany color and long, falling past her shoulders, with two strands pulled back on either side of her face (so her pixie ears stuck out comically) and pinned at the top with a huge, jaunty tropical silk flower. Her mother, her unassuming, fade-into-the-background mother who normally wore only an apologetic smear of the mildest pink Avon lipstick, was wearing what could only be described as theatrical makeup. Her lips were the same mahogany as her hair, her eyelids were purple, her cheeks were bright, her foundation was thick and too dark, and were those, surely not, *false eyelashes*? She was wearing a halter-neck, glittery sequined top, pulled in tight at the waist with a big black belt, and a full scarlet skirt. Alice lifted her chin and saw the outfit was completed with fishnet stockings and high, strappy shoes.

Her mother said, "Are you all right, darling? I always said those spin classes were too hard on your joints, and now look what's happened."

"Are you going to a fancy-dress party?" asked Alice with sudden inspiration. That would explain it, although even that would be amazing.

"Oh, no, silly, we were doing a demonstration at the school when Elisabeth left the message—I came straight here without stopping to change. I do get a few stares, but I'm used to that now! Anyway, enough of that, tell me what happened and what the doctors are saying. You're as white as a sheet." Her mother sat on the side of the bed and patted her leg. Sparkly bracelets slid up and down her arm. Was Mum *tanned*? Did Mum have *cleavage*?

"A demonstration of what?" asked Alice. She couldn't take her eyes off this exotic creature. It was Mum, but not Mum. Unlike Elisabeth, she didn't have any new wrinkles; in fact, that thick layer of makeup smoothed out her face so she seemed younger.

Elisabeth said, "Alice has lost a huge chunk of her memory, Mum. She doesn't remember anything since 1998."

"Oh," said Barb. "I don't like the sound of that at all. I *knew* she looked too pale. You must have concussion, I suppose. Don't fall asleep! You have to stay awake after a concussion. Whatever you do, Alice darling, you *must not fall asleep*!"

"That's a myth," said Elisabeth. "They don't advise that anymore."

"Well, I don't know about that actually, because I think I read something in the *Reader's Digest* quite recently about a little boy, a boy called Andy, and he hit his head riding one of those mini-bikes out in the bush, which is exactly what happened to Sandra's grandson, and I can tell you, I would not be letting Tom on one of those, Alice, even though I bet the little devil would love it, because they're terribly dangerous, even if you do wear a helmet, which this little boy, this Andy, was not, I think it was Andy, it could have been Arnie, although that's a funny, old-fashioned name you don't hear much these days—"

"Mum?" Alice interrupted, knowing there was no way out of the Andy/Arnie labyrinth. Her mother had always been a pathological chatterbox, although normally, when she was out in public like this, she would lower her voice in irritating deference to those around her, so you'd always be saying "Speak *up*, Mum!" If somebody she hadn't known intimately for at least twenty years turned up, her chatter would stop instantly mid-sentence, like a switched-off radio, and she would duck her head, avoid all eye contact, and smile an infuriatingly humble smile. She was so shy that when Alice and Elisabeth were at school, she became literally sick with nerves before their parent-teacher nights and would come home white and trembly with exhaustion, barely able to remember a word any of the teachers had said, as if the point of it had just been to show up, not to actually listen, which always drove Elisabeth insane, because she wanted to hear all the nice things the teachers said about her. (Alice didn't care because she knew most of her teachers probably didn't know who she was, because she suffered from the same shyness.)

Now Alice's mother was talking at a normal volume (actually, even a little louder than strictly necessary) and she wasn't darting cautious looks around to make sure any important strangers weren't about to turn up. Also, she seemed to have developed a new way of holding her head, her chin jutting and her neck strained, like a peacock. It reminded Alice of somebody, somebody she was sure she *hadn't* forgotten, somebody she knew perfectly well, although she couldn't temporarily name that person.

"But I still don't understand why you're dressed like that, Mum," said Alice. "You look . . . incredible."

Elisabeth's Homework for Dr. Hodges

I was thinking to myself, "Please don't mention Roger's name, Mum. She can't take another shock. Her brain might explode.

"Well, as I said, darling, Roger and I were doing a salsa-dancing demonstration up at the school when Elisabeth left the message. I got such a shock when I heard—"

"Did you say salsa dancing?"

"You can't possibly have forgotten our salsa dancing! I'll tell you why, because you actually described our last performance as unforgettable. It was just last Wednesday night! We had Olivia up on the floor with us, of course we couldn't convince Madison and Tom to have a go, or *you* for that matter, Roger was quite disappointed, but I tried to explain—"

"Roger?" said Alice. "Who is Roger?"

Elisabeth's Homework for Dr. Hodges

Who was I kidding? It's not like she ever goes more than five minutes without mentioning Roger's name.

"Yes, Roger, of course. Now, you can't have forgotten *Roger*. Can you?" Her mother looked frightened and said to Elisabeth, "This is quite serious, isn't it. I knew she looked too pale. She is literally bleached of color."

Alice was trying to think of other names that sounded like Roger. Rod? Robert? Her mother had a habit of getting people's names just slightly wrong, so that Jamie became Johnny, Susan became Susannah, and so on.

"The only Roger I know is Nick's dad," said Alice, with a little laugh because Nick's dad was a little laughable.

Her mother stared at her. She looked like a doll with those spiky black eyelashes. "Well, that's the Roger I'm talking about, darling. My husband Roger."

"Your *husband?*"

"Oh, give me strength," sighed Elisabeth.

Alice turned to her. "Mum married *Roger?*"

"I'm afraid so."

"But . . . Roger? Really?"

"Yep. Really."

So here was another wedding that the other Alice had attended in her place, but this was a wedding Alice couldn't even begin to envisage.

For one thing, her mother had always refused to consider the possibility of *dating* other men. "Oh, I'm too old for all that," she'd say. "You need to be young and pretty to date! And besides, you only have one love of your life, and that was your father. How could any man ever measure up to him?" And although Elisabeth and Alice had continually tried to convince her that she was still young and attractive, and that Dad would never have expected her to mourn him forever, Alice had been secretly proud of her mother's devotion. It was sort of beautiful and moving, even though it was also annoying because it meant Alice and Elisabeth were responsible for her entire social life.

So okay, fine, she'd overcome her fear of dating (and probably that's what it had been, rather than eternal devotion), but to marry Nick's father of all people?

"But why?" said Alice helplessly. "Why would you marry Roger?"

That's right, she thought, it's *Roger* who has that peacock way of holding his head.

Barb widened her eyes and pursed her lips together coyly, with an expression that was so bizarrely unlike her that Alice had to avert her eyes as if she'd interrupted her mother doing something perverse and sexual.

She said, "I fell madly in love with him, you remember, of course you remember, it all started at Madison's christening, when Roger mentioned to me that he was thinking of taking up salsa dancing and would I be interested, and he didn't actually give me a chance to say no, he just seemed to be under the impression that I was coming along, and I didn't want to let him down, it seemed so rude, and even though I was in a state about it, and I actually thought about making an appointment to see Dr. Holden for a prescription for something to calm my nerves, and you girls got so cranky about that, as if I was going to become a *crack cocaine* addict or something, for heaven's sakes, just a little Valium was all I was thinking, which apparently just gives you a lovely floaty feeling, but I couldn't get an appointment, typical of course, that new receptionist is so snooty, I do wonder what happened to that lovely Kathy—"

"How long have you been married for?" Alice interrupted. The terror of not knowing the facts of her own life gripped her again. She was on one of those amusement park rides that slammed you left, then right, then turned the whole world upside down, giving you unfamiliar glimpses of familiar things. Alice hated amusement park rides.

"Well, it's coming up to five years. You remember the wedding, Alice, of course you do. Madison was flower girl. She looked so adorable in that yellow dress, she looks so nice in yellow, not many people do, I've bought her a yellow top for Christmas, but whether she'll wear it or not is another matter—"

"Mum," said Elisabeth tersely. "Alice doesn't even remember *Madison*. The last thing she remembers is being pregnant with her."

"She doesn't remember Madison," repeated Barbara in a hushed voice. She took a deep breath and put on a nervous, merry voice as if to jolly Alice out of all this silliness. "Well, I can understand you wanting to forget Madison at this *particular* moment, the little grumble-bum, although I'm sure she'll snap out of it soon, but of course, you remember Tom and darling Olivia, don't you? Well, I can't believe I'm asking the question. Of course you do. You can't forget your own children! That would be . . . unthinkable."

There was a tremor of fear in her voice that Alice found strangely comforting. Yes, Mum, this is scary. Yes, this is unthinkable.

"Mum," said Elisabeth again. "Please try and get your head around this. She doesn't remember *anything* since 1998."

"Nothing?"

"I'm sure it's just temporary."

"Oh! Of course. Temporary!"

Her mother lapsed into silence and ran a fingernail around the edge of her thickly lipsticked mouth.

Alice tried out this new fact in her mind: *My mother married my husband's father.*

It was as unforgettable a fact as *I have three children* and *My husband whom I adore has moved out of our house,* but somehow she'd forgotten it.

None of it could be true. It must all be an absolutely huge, elaborate practical joke. It must be an incredibly realistic dream. A vivid hallucination. A nightmare that kept going and going.

Roger! What could have possessed her sweet, cautious mother to "fall madly in love" (Mum never said extravagant things like "madly in love") with someone like Roger? Roger with his overpowering aftershave, his radio-announcer voice, and his habit of saying "methinks" and "mayhaps"? Roger, who after a few drinks at family parties would pin Alice in a corner and treat her to a monologue all about himself and his eternal fascination with the intricacies of his own personality. "Am I an athletic person? Yes, definitely. Am I an intellectual? Okay, maybe not in the strictest la-di-da Ph.D. sense of the word. But put it another way, am I an *intelligent* person? The answer would have to be yes; I've got a Ph.D. from the University of Real Life, Alice. You may well ask, am I a spiritual person? Methinks the answer would have to be yes, most certainly."

Alice would be nodding helplessly, taking shallow breaths so she didn't feel sick from the scent of his aftershave, until Nick would appear, saying, "Methinks the lady needs a drink, Dad."

And what about Nick? What would he think about this development? He had such a weird, fragile relationship with his father. He imitated him mercilessly behind his back and there was something close to hatred in his voice when Nick spoke about the way his dad had treated his mother during their divorce, but at the same time Alice noticed that whenever he was in Roger's company, his voice would become deeper, his shoulders squarer, and he would often casually bring up some big deal he'd negotiated at work, or some other accomplishment that Alice didn't even know about, as if deep down he still wanted his dad's approval, even though he would have denied this vehemently, angrily even.

Alice couldn't think what his reaction would be to this news. And didn't it mean she and Nick were *related*? He was her stepbrother! Her first thought was that she and Nick would have laughed themselves silly over that, turned it into a stupid game, made lecherous remarks about incest, and pretended they were Greg and Marcia Brady. But maybe it hadn't been funny at all. He might have been angry on behalf of his mother, even though his mother seemed to treat her ex-husband like a bumbling distant uncle.

And what about Nick's sisters, the Flakes? Oh God, the Flakes. Nick's nutty sisters were now her stepsisters. There was no way they would have reacted calmly to this news; they didn't react calmly to anything—they fainted, they sobbed, they stopped talking to each other, they were offended by the most innocuous comments. There was always at least one sister in the middle of a crisis. Alice had never realized family life could be so dramatic until she met Nick's family, with all those sisters, in-laws, boyfriends, aunties, and cousins by the dozen. Her own quiet, polite, mini-sized family had seemed boring and sedate in comparison.

Alice said, "Is this why Nick and I are . . . ? Because he's upset about his dad marrying Mum?"

"Of course not!" Her mother was reenergized. "This divorce is a terrible mystery to all of us, but it's certainly got nothing to do with Roger and me! Roger would be devastated to hear you even thought about such a thing. Of course Roger does have his own theories about the divorce—"

Elisabeth cut in, "Mum and Roger got together years ago. You and Nick were a bit funny about it at the time, and the Flakes were all in hysterics of course, but it settled down and nobody thinks twice about it now. I promise you, Alice, all these things that seem so shocking aren't really that shocking. When you get your memory back, you'll be laughing at yourself."

Alice did not want to get back a self who thought there was nothing shocking about the fact that she and Nick were divorcing; she couldn't believe how casually her mother had referred to "the divorce," as if it were something solid and real, as if it were a *thing*.

"Well, I'm not getting a divorce anymore, actually," said Alice. "There is no divorce."

"Oh!" Her mother clasped her hands together rapturously, as if in prayer. "Oh, but that's wonderful—"

"Mum!" Elisabeth said. "You must promise not to say one word about that to Roger or anybody else. She doesn't know what she's saying."

"I do so," said Alice. She felt a bit drunk. "You can tell the whole world, Mum. Tell Roger. Tell the Flakes. Tell our three children. There is no divorce. Nick and I will work out whatever this thing is."

"Wonderful!" cried Barb. "I'm so happy!"

"You will not think this is wonderful when you get your memory back," said Elisabeth. "You've got legal proceedings going on. Jane Turner will have heart failure if you start doing this."

"Jane Turner?" said Alice. "What's Jane Turner got to do with the price of fish?"

"Jane is your lawyer," said Elisabeth.

"A lawyer? She's not a lawyer." A memory flitted into Alice's head of some guy losing an argument with Jane at work and saying, "You should have been a lawyer," and Jane had said, "Yes, I'm perfectly aware of that."

"She got her law degree years ago and now she specializes in divorce," said Elisabeth. "She's helping you—ah, divorce Nick."

"Oh." How ridiculous, how *stupid*, that Jane Turner was helping her "divorce Nick." "A little Jane goes a very long way," Nick once said, and Alice agreed. How could Jane Turner have anything to do with their lives?

"You and Nick are in the middle of a custody battle," said Elisabeth. "It's really serious."

Custody battle. It sounded like "custardy" battle. Alice imagined herself and Nick flinging spoonfuls of sweet yellow custard at each other, laughing and shrieking and licking it off afterward.

Presumably a custody battle wasn't as much fun as a custardy battle.

"Well, that's off, too," pronounced Alice. (Why in the world would she want "custody" of three children she'd never met! She wanted Nick.) "We don't need a custody battle because we're not getting a divorce, and that's final."

"Hooray!" said her mother. "I'm so glad you've lost your memory. This accident is going to turn out to be a blessing in disguise."

"Well, there's only one tiny problem with all that, isn't there?" said Elisabeth.

"What?"

"Nick has still got his memory."

Chapter 10

N ick?" said Alice.

"Sorry, sweetie, it's just me again," said the nurse.

They were waking her every hour to check on her and shine the light in her pupils and ask the same questions over and over. "Alice Mary Love. Royal North Shore Hospital. Hurt my head," Alice mumbled. The nurse chuckled. "Well done. Sorry about this. Go back to sleep now."

Alice slept and dreamed of nurses waking her up. "Wake up! It's time for your salsa-dancing lesson!" said a nurse with a huge hat that was actually a profiterole cake. "I dreamed we were getting a divorce," said Alice to Nick. "And we had three children, and Mum married your dad, and Elisabeth was so sad." "Why the *fuck* would I care?" said Nick. Alice gasped and sucked her thumb. Nick peeled a piece of red confetti off his neck and showed it to her. He said, "Only joking!"

"Nick?" said Alice.

"I do not love you anymore because you still suck your thumb."

"But I don't!" Alice was so embarrassed she could die.

"What's your name?" shouted a nurse, but this was another one that couldn't be real because she was floating through the air, holding on to bouquets of pink balloons. Alice ignored her.

"Me again," said a nurse.

"Nick?" said Alice. "I've got a headache. Such a bad headache."

"No, it's not Nick. It's Sarah."

"You're not a real nurse. You're another dream nurse."

"Actually, I'm a real one. Can you open your eyes and tell me your name?"

Elisabeth's Homework for Dr. Hodges

Hi, me again, Dr. Hodges. It's 3:30 a.m. and sleep feels like something impossible and stupid that only other people do. I woke up thinking of Alice and how she said to me, "You're such a good big sister."

I'm not. I'm not at all.

We still care about each other, of course we do. It's not that. We'd never forget each other's birthdays. In fact, there's a weird sort of silent competition going on to see who can give the best present each year, as if we're always jostling for the role of most generous, thoughtful sister. We see each other pretty regularly. We still have a laugh. We're just the same as a million sisters. So I don't even know exactly what I'm talking about. It's just that it isn't the same as when we were younger. But that's just life, isn't it, Dr. Hodges? Relationships don't stay the same. There isn't *time*. Ask Alice! She converted to the role of busy North Shore Mum like it was a religion.

Maybe if I'd been more vigilant? Perhaps it was my responsibility as the older sister to keep us on track.

But the only way I've been able to get through the last seven years is by wrapping myself up like a package with a tighter and tighter string. It's so tight that if I'm talking about anything (other than how to write the perfect direct-mail package), I feel as though there is something constricting my throat, as if my mouth doesn't open wide enough for proper, unthinking conversation.

The problem is the rage. It's permanently simmering, even when I'm not aware of it. If I hurt myself unexpectedly, or drop a punnet of blueberries all over the kitchen floor, it bubbles over like boiling milk. You should have heard the primeval scream of rage when I banged my forehead against an open cupboard door the other day when I was unpacking the dishwasher. I sat on the kitchen floor with my back against the fridge and sobbed for twenty minutes. It's pretty embarrassing.

Before Alice and Nick split up, I sometimes felt there were unforgivable words hovering on the tip of my tongue whenever I spoke to Alice, words like: "You think the world begins and ends with you and your perfect little family and your perfect little life and you think stress is finding the perfectly color-coordinated cushions for your new $10,000 sofa."

And I feel like scribbling those things out because they're nasty and not even true. I don't think those things at all, but I could have said them, I could still say them, and if I did, those words would have been there in both our memories forever. So it was safer to say nothing and pretend, and she knew I was pretending and she pretended too, and then we forgot how to be real with each other.

That's why when she called me to say that Nick had moved out, it was as shocking as a death. I had no idea, no inkling they were having troubles. There was the indisputable evidence that we didn't share secrets anymore. I should have known what was going on in her life. She should have been asking me for wise, sisterly advice. But she didn't. So I've let her down as much as she let me down.

And that's why, when I got the news about Gina, I couldn't

think what the right thing was to do. Should I phone Alice? Should I drive straight over? Should I call and ask first? I couldn't think what Alice would want. I was worrying about the right etiquette, as if this was someone I didn't know very well. And OF COURSE I should have driven straight to her, for God's sake. What was wrong with me that I even had to think about it?

As we were walking out of the hospital, Mum said to me in a diffident, un-Mumlike voice, "I guess she doesn't remember anything about Gina, either, does she?" And I said, "I guess not." Neither of us knew what to say about that.

How do you find the thread that started it all and follow it all the way back through the tangles of phone calls and Christmases and kids' parties, right back to the beginning when we were just Alice and Libby Jones? Do you know, Dr. Hodges?

Anyway . . . maybe I should try and sleep.

No. Can't even fake a yawn.

Tomorrow I'm going to the hospital to pick up Alice and take her home. They're expecting to discharge her by 10. She just seemed to take it for granted that I would be the one to come and get her. If she were her normal self, she would be making a point of not relying on me. She only takes favors from other school mums, because they can be repaid with complicated playdate arrangements involving their children.

I wonder if she'll have her memory back by tomorrow. I wonder if she will feel embarrassed by the things she said this afternoon, especially about Nick. I wonder if that was her real self, or her old self, or just a confused, banged-on-the-head self. Deep down, is she devastated about the divorce? Was that a glimpse of what she's really feeling? I don't know. I just don't know.

The doctor I spoke to seems confident that she'll have her memory back by the morning. She was one of the nicer doctors I've met in my years of doctors. She actually looked me in the eyes and waited till I'd finished speaking before she spoke. But I could tell she was just focused on the fact that Alice's CT scan didn't show any sign of what she called "intracranial bleeding." She blinked a bit when I said Alice doesn't remember the existence of her own children, but she said people can have a wide variety of responses to concussion and that rest was the best thing. She said as her injury heals, her memory will come back. She seemed to be implying that they'd already gone above and beyond what they'd do in a normal concussion case by keeping her overnight for observation.

I felt strangely guilty leaving Alice there at the hospital. She seems so much younger. That's the thing about this I couldn't seem to get across to the doctor. It's not just Alice being confused. It's like I am *literally* talking to 29-year-old Alice. Even the way she talks is different. It's slower and softer and less careful. She's just saying whatever comes into her head.

"Did I have a thirtieth birthday party?" she asked me before we left and I couldn't for the life of me remember. But then on the way home in the car I remembered they had a BBQ. Alice had a big pregnant belly and they were right in the middle of renovations. There were ladders and paint tins and gaping holes in walls. I remember standing in the kitchen helping Alice and Nick put candles in the cake, when Alice said, "I think the baby has the hiccups." Nick pressed his hand to her stomach and then he grabbed my hand and held it over her stomach so I could feel the freaky fishy movements too. I have such a clear memory of both their faces turned to me, their eyes shiny, flushed with the excitement and wonder of it all. They both had flecks of blue paint in their eyebrows from painting the nursery. They were lovely. They were my favorite couple.

I used to secretly watch Nick listening to Alice when she told a story; that tender, proud look he got on his face, the way he laughed harder than anyone else when she said something funny or typically Alice. He got Alice, the way we did, or maybe even more so than us. He made her more confident, funnier, smarter. He brought out all the things that were there already and let her be fully herself, so she seemed to shine with this inner light. He loved her so much, he made her seem even more lovable.

(Does Ben love me like that? Yes. No. I don't know. Maybe in the beginning. All that shiny love stuff doesn't seem relevant anymore. That's for other younger, thinner, happier people, and besides which, it's not actually possible for a dried apricot to shine.)

I miss the old Nick and Alice. When I think of them standing in that kitchen, putting candles on the cake, it's like remembering people who I once knew, who moved to another country and didn't keep in touch.

At 4:30 a.m. Alice woke with a start and the thought clear in her head: *I never asked Elisabeth how many children she has.*

How could she not know the answer to that question? But more important, how could she have forgotten to *ask* it when she didn't know? She was a selfish, self-obsessed, shallow person. No wonder Nick wanted to divorce her. No wonder Elisabeth didn't look at her in the same way anymore.

She would ring Mum in the morning and check with her and then she would pretend that of course she hadn't forgotten the existence of Elisabeth's children (just her own) and say, "Oh, by the way, how is little thingummybob?"

Except she couldn't be sure Mum still had the same phone number anymore. She didn't even know where Mum lived. Had she moved into Roger's cream-and-chrome apartment with its harbor views? Or had Roger moved into Mum's house with the doilies and knickknacks and potted plants? Either possibility seemed ludicrous.

The girl in the cubicle next to her was snoring. It was a thin, whiny sound like a mosquito. Alice turned over on her front and pushed her face hard into the pillow, as if she were trying to suffocate herself.

She thought, *This is the worst thing that has ever happened to me.*

But actually, she couldn't even be sure of that.

Elisabeth's Homework for Dr. Hodges

After we left the hospital this afternoon, Mum and I went over to Alice's place to meet Ben and the kids. We all had pizza for dinner. (Thankfully Roger had a Rotary meeting; I was not in the mood for Roger. I can't think of anyone ever being in the mood for Roger, except for Mum, presumably, and Roger, of course.) We didn't tell the children that Alice had lost her memory. We just said she'd hit her head at the gym but she was going to be fine. Olivia clasped her hands together and said, "Darling Mummy! This is an absolute tragedy!" and I could see Ben's back shaking with suppressed laughter as he stood at the cutlery drawer. Madison curled her lip and said contemptuously, "So, does Dad know about this?" and then stomped up to her bedroom as if she already knew what the answer would be. Tom waited till Olivia was busy at the kitchen table with crayons and glitter making a huge get-well card for Alice before silently taking me by the hand and leading me into the living room. He sat me down and looked me straight in the eyes and said, "Okay, tell me the truth. Has Mum really got a brain tumor?" Before I could answer, he said, "Don't lie! I'm a human lie detector! If your eyes look up to the right, that means you're lying." I had to make a superhuman effort not to look up to the right.

It was sort of a fun night. I don't know why. A fun night at poor Alice's expense.

Oh, a yawn! A precious, proper yawn! I've got to go now, Dr. Hodges. It might be sleep.

———

As the sky began to lighten outside the hospital Alice fell into her deepest sleep of this long, strange, fragmented night. She dreamed of Nick sitting at a long pine table she'd never seen. He shook his head, picked up a coffee mug, and said, "It's always about Gina, isn't it? Gina, Gina, Gina." He drank from the coffee mug and Alice felt pure dislike; she turned away from him to wipe vigorously at a dried grease spot on a granite countertop.

In her sleep, Alice twitched so violently the bed moved.

She dreamed she was standing up in a small, darkened room, and Elisabeth was lying next to her, looking up at her with a frightened face, saying, "What does she mean there is no heartbeat?"

She dreamed of a giant rolling pin. She had to push it up a hill while thousands of people watched. It was important that she make it look easy.

"Good morning, sleepyhead!" said a nurse. Her bright, bubbly voice was like glass breaking.

Alice jumped and gasped for air as if she'd been holding her breath.

Chapter 11

Frannie's Letter to Phil

I'm back again, Phil.

It's six a.m. Still dark outside, and chilly. Brrrrr! I'm writing this in bed.

Barb called again last night to say that Alice is fine. They've done a CT scan apparently, whatever that is, and everything looks normal, although evidently Alice is suffering some memory loss. When she woke up, she thought she was still together with Nick!

Now Barb is celebrating because she thinks they'll get back together. She has become so irritatingly optimistic ever since she took up salsa dancing.

I think reconciliation is unlikely. Alice was here on Monday (which was lovely, although I do sometimes feel as though I'm a chore being crossed off her list, but perhaps that's unfair). I asked her about Nick and the most repellent expression crossed her face. She became quite ugly with hatred.

After she left, I was thinking about the first time Alice brought Nick

*around to meet me. They'd come straight from the beach, their feet
sandy, their hair still wet, smelling of the sea. They were sitting on the
couch chatting politely with me, not touching, or so it seemed, except
that I happened to glance down and I saw that their hands were lying
next to each other on the couch, and that Nick was caressing Alice's
little finger with his own. I remember being shocked by a feeling of
pure envy. I wanted to be Alice, young and lovely, feeling the secret
caress of a handsome boy's fingertip.*

*Isn't it strange and sad what time can do? What became of those
passionate young people?*

*But what do I know about marriage? It's a mystery to me. I assume
it's a matter of compromise. Negotiation. Give and take.*

*Actually, I remember seeing Alice and Nick, after another trip to
the beach, except by this time they had three children and there was
certainly no fingertip caressing. Something had obviously happened (to
do with Olivia, I think) and you could have cut the air with a knife.
They were talking to each other in those terrible, icily polite voices I've
noticed couples use in public when they're arguing.*

*Do you ever wonder, Phil, what sort of a marriage we would
have had?*

*Would we have fought? For example, you always said you didn't
mind that I had the more senior position, but perhaps that wasn't really
true and it would eventually have become a problem for us. They say
that men are defined by their work.*

*Do you know I've been writing to you now for over three decades?
That's longer than a lot of marriages. Longer than Alice's marriage.*

*May I share another quibble with you about that fellow? That Mr.
Mustache? Last night, I was in the dining room for dinner and he was
sitting at the same table. He asked if any of my own family were
performing at the Talent Night. I said that my "honorary
granddaughter" would be dancing.*

Mr. Mustache wanted to know what I meant by "honorary."

I briskly gave him the facts. I said that I had lived next door to a young family, and that when the father died suddenly of a heart attack the mother wasn't coping especially well and I stepped in to help out, as she had no other family. Eventually I became a sort of "pseudo" grandmother.

I didn't tell him how the shattered, white faces of those poor little girls are imprinted on my memory forever. I didn't tell him about the many days I had to drag their mother out of bed. (Once I got so frustrated, I actually pinched poor Barb, quite hard, on the arm. Isn't that dreadful! I was tough back then.)

Of course, I didn't tell him about you.

Mr. Mustache listened (I'll give him that. He really did listen.) and then he said, "I think you can drop the 'honorary.' Sounds like they really are your family."

Phil, I'm not sure why this bothered me so much. It was something about his tone. So definite. So presumptuous. I've only known the man five minutes and he's making remarks about my life. And he seemed to be implying that I was being overly pedantic.

Am I making too much of this? Am I pedantic?

I guess I've always taken secret pride in my pedantry.

Oh I can just imagine you snorting!

Must rush. I'm catching the minibus into the shops to buy a gift for Alice. I'll never get this letter finished at this rate!

Right! Time to get moving. A nice hot shower. Clothes. Hair. Makeup.

The last nurse had left and now a brisk, bossy voice in Alice's head was telling her what to do.

Too tired, replied Alice truculently. Her eyes were dry and stinging. *I've just had the worst night of my life. Also I should probably wait and ask a nurse.*

Rubbish! You'll feel more awake after your shower. You always do!

Do I?

Yes! And it's time to look in the mirror, for heaven's sake. You're only thirty-nine, not eighty-nine. How bad can it be?

What about a towel? I don't know which towel to use. There might be procedures.

You smell of sweat, Alice. From that gym class. You need a shower.

Alice sat up. She couldn't stand the thought of having any sort of body odor. It was the ultimate humiliation. She was horrified even when Nick casually mentioned she had garlicky breath the day after they'd eaten an especially garlicky dinner. She would clap a hand to her mouth and run to clean her teeth and spend the whole day chewing gum. Nick was bemused by the fuss. He couldn't care less if he smelled. After working all day on the house, he'd sniff cheerfully at his armpits like an ape and announce, "I stink!" as if it were a fine achievement.

Maybe Nick was divorcing her because she'd developed extremely bad breath.

She put a tentative hand to the tender lump on her head. The pain was still there, but it was definitely better, more like a memory of yesterday's pain.

But she didn't remember those children, and she didn't remember Nick moving out.

She slid her bare feet onto the cool floor and looked around her. The tulips her mother had given her were fat, gold bulbs against the white of the hospital room wall. She tried to imagine her mother dancing the salsa with Roger, their hips swiveling in unison. She could imagine Roger's hips swiveling all right, but Mum's? She was fascinated and repelled by the thought. She couldn't wait to talk to Nick about it.

Well.

She remembered his voice on the phone yesterday, thick with hatred. It had to be over something more than bad breath. If that had been the reason, he would have sounded compassionate and embarrassed.

Even with the memory of that phone call (the way he swore at her!), it still seemed impossible that Nick wasn't about to turn up any minute, breathless and rumpled, apologizing for the misunderstanding, hugging her to his chest. She couldn't feel properly upset about this talk of divorce because it was too stupid. This was *Nick*! Her Nick. As soon as she saw him again it would all be okay.

The rucksack with the dinosaur stickers was sitting in the cupboard next to her bed. She thought about that beautiful red dress; maybe she could squeeze into it.

She held the rucksack under one arm and prudishly clutched the hospital robe together behind her in one hand so as not to reveal her underpants, but there was no need. The curtains around the other girl's bed were pulled and she was still snoring her mosquito-whine snore.

Maybe as Alice had got older her snoring had got even worse and that's why Nick had left. She could get one of those horrible mouthguard things. That was easy to solve. Come on home, Nick.

She was so tired it felt like she was walking through wet concrete.

I think I should get back into bed.

Don't you dare get back into bed. You'll make them late for school again and you'll never hear the end of it.

Alice's chin jerked up with surprise. Where did that come from? She thought of the photo of the three children in their school uniforms. It must be Alice's responsibility to get them to school on time each day.

Maybe, just maybe, there was the tiniest, fleeting, corner-of-the-eye memory of pounding footsteps down a hallway, doors slamming, a horn tooting, a child wailing, a drilling feeling right in the center of her forehead. But as soon as she tried to grab hold of it, it vanished, as if she'd made it up.

It felt like she was facing straight ahead but just to the left and right of her were ten years' worth of memories, if only she could find a way to just turn her head to face them.

She went into the small bathroom that she and the snoring girl shared, switched on the fluorescent light, and locked the door behind her. She blinked in the all-enveloping brightness. Last night she'd managed to use the toilet and wash her hands without looking at her reflection in the mirror above the sink. There would be no more of that. Today was the day for clean, crisp action.

She undid the ties around her neck and back, let the robe fall to the floor, and stepped in front of the mirror.

She could see herself from the waist up.

Skinny, she thought, pressing her fingertips to the curve of her waist and then running them up and down her ribs. She could actually see her ribs. You're a skinny girl. Her stomach was hard and flat like that girl's at the gym. How did that happen?

Of course she'd always said that she should get fit and lose weight, without ever actually doing anything about it. It was something you were meant to say to your girlfriends at regular intervals to show you were a proper woman: "Oh God, I'm so fat!" When she was going out with Richard, the boyfriend before Nick, who would say "Heave 'em up!" when he watched her pull up her jeans over her thighs, that slight dissatisfaction with her body occasionally turned to self-hatred and she'd starve herself for a day before eating a packet of chocolate biscuits for dinner. But then she met Nick, who told her she was beautiful, and whenever he touched her, it was as if his touch were actually making her as beautiful as he seemed to believe she was. So why would she deny herself a second piece of mud cake or glass of champagne if Nick was there with the knife or the bottle poised, grinning evilly and saying "You only live once," as if every day were a celebration. Nick had a little boy's sweet tooth, and an appreciation of good food, fine wine, and beautiful weather; eating and drinking with Nick in hot sunshine was like sex. He made her feel like a well-fed, happy cat: plump, sleek, purring with sensual satisfaction.

Alice couldn't decide if she liked her flat new stomach or not. On the one hand, there was a distinct feeling of pride, like discovering a new skill. Look what I did! I've got a stomach like a supermodel! On the other hand, the feeling of hard bone under her skin gave her a slight feeling of revulsion, as if her flesh had been shaved away.

What did Nick think of this new skinny body? Perhaps he didn't care. *"So why the fuck did you ring me?"*

Her breasts were a lot smaller, she noted, and not quite as perky. Actually, they were awful, elongated and sagging like socks down toward her stomach. She held them up in her hands and let them drop again. Oh, yuck. She didn't like that at all. She missed her nice, round, cheerful, bobbing-about breasts.

Was it breast-feeding three children that had done this? And that would be perfectly fine if she had nostalgic memories of late nights sitting in a rocking chair with a downy-headed baby in her arms, except she *didn't*. She was looking forward to breast-feeding. It was meant to happen in her future, not in her past.

Okay, forget the breasts. The face. It was time for the face.

She took a step closer to the mirror and held her breath.

At first it was a relief, because it was still her own Alice face looking dopily back at her. She wasn't hideously deformed. She hadn't grown horns. In fact, she quite liked her thinner face. It seemed to have more definition and made her eyes look bigger. Her eyebrows were perfectly shaped and her eyelashes were dark. She didn't seem to have as many freckles. Her skin looked smooth and clear, although actually, there were quite a few funny, faint scratches on her face around her mouth and eyes. Maybe from when she fell over? She leaned in closer to examine them.

Oh.

They weren't scratches. They were wrinkles, just like Elisabeth's, maybe worse than Elisabeth's. There were two deep grooves in between her eyes. When she stopped frowning they didn't go away. There were little pouches of pink skin under her eyes, and Alice remembered how when she'd seen Jane yesterday she thought at first there was something wrong with her eyes. There had been nothing wrong with Jane; she was just ten years older.

She rubbed her fingertip over the fine scratchlike lines around her mouth and eyes as if she could just smear them away. They seemed wrong, as if they shouldn't be there; thank you anyway, but I don't think so, not for me, these don't belong on my face.

She gave up and stood back from the mirror so she couldn't see the wrinkles.

Her hair was still pulled back in the elastic band from the night before. She pulled it out and looked at it in the palm of her hand, amazed afresh that she didn't even recognize the black hair band and had no memory of putting it in her hair.

Her hair fell just above her shoulders. She must have had it cut, as she suspected. What brought on that decision, she wondered. The color was different, too. It was bordering on blond rather than brown; a dark ashy sort of blond. It was messy from her night of tossing and turning, but then she ran her fingers through it and saw that it was cut in an elegant shape that curved around the neck, making it seem longer. It wasn't her taste, but she had to admit it did suit her face better than any other haircut she'd had.

She'd grown up. That was it. A grown-up looked back at her. She just didn't feel that way.

Okay, then. This is you, Alice. This is who you are. A grown-up skinny mother of three in the middle of a nasty custard-throwing divorce.

She squinted her eyes and imagined her old self, her real self, staring back at her from the mirror. Long brown hair in no particular style, a rounder, softer face, perkier, bigger breasts, fatter (pretty fat) stomach, more freckles, no wrinkles to speak of—in love with Nick and pregnant with her first baby.

But that girl was gone. There was no point thinking about her.

Alice turned away from the mirror and, looking around the unfamiliar bathroom, she was overwhelmed with loneliness. She thought again of that silly solitary trip through Europe, brushing her teeth in strange bathrooms, staring at herself in speckled mirrors with a dizzy feeling of dissociation as she tried to work out who she really was without people who loved her to reflect back her personality. Now she wasn't in a strange country where people spoke a different language, but she was in a strange new world where everybody knew what was going on except for her. She was the foolish one making a goose of herself, saying the wrong thing, not knowing the rules.

She took a shaky breath.

This was only temporary. Soon she would have her memory back and life would go on as normal.

But did she *want* her memory back? Did she want to remember? What she really wanted was to hop in her time machine and go directly back to 1998.

Well. Bad luck. Deal with it, honey. Have a shower. Time for coffee and an egg-white omelette before the kids wake up.

"Before the kids wake up." The way this rather bossy, acerbic voice kept popping into her head was really freaking her out. And an "egg-white omelette"? What was that all about? Wouldn't it be entirely without flavor? She didn't fancy that at all for breakfast.

Or did she? She licked her lips experimentally. Egg-white omelette or peanut butter on toast? Both choices seemed simultaneously delicious and disgusting.

Well, it's hardly a matter of life and death, is it, Alice?

Oh shut up. No offense, but you sound like a bit of a bitch, Alice.

She went to the rucksack and pulled out the swish toiletries bag. Presumably she could rely on new Alice to have packed shampoo and conditioner. She rifled through chunky, expensive-looking jars and bottles (good Lord, wasn't this just a trip to the gym?) and found two slim, tall, dark bottles. They were brands she didn't recognize promising "salon-quality results."

As she stood under the shower and massaged the shampoo into her hair, the fragrant smell of peach filled her nostrils and it was so entirely familiar her knees buckled. *Of course, of course.* She made a sound like a strangled sob and remembered herself standing under a pounding shower, steam billowing, resting her forehead against a wall of blue tiles and howling silently while the bubbly lather from the peach-smelling shampoo slipped into her eyes. *I can't bear it. I can't . . . I can't . . .*

For a moment the memory was so real, it could have been happening right then, and then the next second it slithered away like the froth from her shampoo.

The smell of the shampoo remained intensely, ridiculously familiar, but she couldn't grab hold of another memory.

Oh, that feeling of hopeless grief and just wanting the pain to stop.

Am I remembering crying over Nick?

If these were the memories that were locked away in her head—memories of a perfectly wonderful marriage disintegrating, memories of clinging to a shower wall while she cried—did she really want them back?

She turned off the shower and dried herself with the towel from the rucksack. With the towel wrapped around her, she pulled the bottles and jars out of the toiletries bag and lined them up in front of her. What did she actually do with all that stuff?

Move it, move it.

Her hand moved instinctively toward a jar with a gold lid. She opened it to reveal a thick, creamy moisturizer. With rapid, efficient movements she briskly rubbed the moisturizer all over her face. Dab, dab, dab. Without stopping to think, she picked up a glass bottle of foundation, poured some onto a sponge, and began rubbing it all over her face. A part of her mind registered all this with astonishment. Foundation? She never wore foundation. She hardly ever bothered with makeup. But her hands were moving so fast, her head tilting this way and that as if she'd done this a million times before. Next came a shiny gold-colored stick that she rubbed into her cheeks. She snapped open jars, bottles, and containers. Mascara. Eyeliner. Lipstick.

Suddenly—it must have taken less than five minutes—she was finished and stowing all the bottles away in the toiletries bag. Without stopping, she unzipped a pocket on the side of the bag and wondered what she was looking for until she pulled out a portable hair dryer and a round brush. Oh, right, fair enough. Time to blow-dry your hair. She plugged it in and once again her hands moved without waiting for her to tell them what to do. The brush moved back and forth. The hair dryer roared hot air.

Okay, so once you leave here, you've got to—

Her mind went blank.

. . . you've got to . . .

Her hair was done.

She snapped off the hair dryer, pulled the plug out of the socket, twirled the cord round and round, and shoved it back into the bag and began to rustle again for something else. Good Lord. Why was she moving so *fast?* Where was the fire?

She pulled out the flat plastic bag with the clothes, shook it open, and pulled out the matching cream underwear and dress. The underwear felt smooth and luxurious against her skin and the bra lifted her breasts back to their former perky position. Surely this beautiful dress would not fit, but she was sliding it over her head, doing up the zipper at the side without having to look for it, and there were no bulges of unsightly fat because she didn't have them anymore.

Jewelry. She found the topaz necklace and Nick's bracelet and put them on. Shoes. She slid her feet into them.

She stopped and looked at the woman in the mirror and watched her bottom lip drop in awe.

She looked, well, she had to say that she looked pretty good. She turned side to side and observed herself over one shoulder.

An attractive, elegant, slim woman. The sort of woman she never thought it was possible for her to be. She had become one of *those* women, those *other* women, who had seemed too perfectly put together to be real.

Why did Nick want to leave her if she looked this damned good?

There was still something missing.

Perfume.

She found it in the zippered section at the front of the toiletries bag. She sprayed it on both wrists and suddenly she was leaning forward, grasping both sides of the basin to stop herself from falling. The scent was vanilla, mandarin, and roses. Her whole life was right there in that scent. She was being sucked into a massive swirling vortex of grief and fury and the ring, ring, ring of the phone and the rising whiny shriek of a child and the babble of the television and Nick sitting on the end of the bed, bent right over with his hands laced tightly around the back of his head.

"Excuse me?"

There was a knock on the bathroom door.

"Excuse me? Will you be much longer? It's just that I'm dying to go!"

Alice stood slowly back up. The color had drained from her face. Was she going to be sick again, like yesterday? No,

"Sorry!" she called out. "Won't be a second."

She put her hands in the sink and used the pink soap from the soap dispenser to scrub away hard at the perfume. As the straightforward, bracing smell of strawberry bubble gum mixed with disinfectant filled her nostrils, the vortex receded.

I don't remember.

I don't remember.

I won't remember.

Elisabeth's Homework for Dr. Hodges

She was dressed and waiting for me when I went to pick her up from the hospital. She had dark circles under very red eyes, but her hair was done and her makeup perfect as always.

She looked so much like her normal self that I was sure she must have her memory back and this strange interlude in our lives was all over.

I said, "Has it all come back to you now?" and she said, "Just about," and avoided my eyes and I thought she must have felt embarrassed about what she'd said about Nick. She said she'd been checked over by the doctor, and signed all the forms, and couldn't wait to get home to her own bed.

She didn't say much as we were leaving the hospital, and I

didn't either. When she finally went to speak, I thought for sure she would be talking about all the million things she had to do that weekend and the precious time she'd lost being in hospital. Instead she said, "How many children do you have?"

I said, *"Alice!"* and nearly swerved the car as I turned my head to look at her.

She said, "I'm sorry I didn't ask earlier, I think I was just in shock. I would have rung Mum to ask her but I wasn't sure whether she still had the same phone, and then I thought, What if Roger answers the phone?"

I said I thought she had her memory back, and she said, "Well, not exactly."

I started insisting that we go straight back to the hospital and asking did she lie to the doctor to get herself discharged, and she stuck her chin out (she looked just like Madison). She said if I took her back to the hospital, she would just say that she didn't know what I was talking about because her memory was perfect and then the hospital would have to decide which one was crazy and she bet they'd choose me and next thing they'd have me in a straitjacket.

I said I didn't think they used straitjackets anymore. (Do they, Dr. Hodges? Have you got an emergency one in your drawer, ready to whip out at a moment's notice?)

Alice folded her arms across her chest and writhed about as if she was in a straitjacket, saying, "Let me out! My sister is the nutter! I'm the sensible one!"

I was flabbergasted. She was being so . . . silly. So old Alice.

Next thing we were giggling like schoolkids. We laughed and laughed and I kept driving her toward her house because I didn't know what else to do. It was so strange, laughing like that with Alice. It was like tasting something delicious I hadn't eaten for years. I'd forgotten that drunken, euphoric feeling of being rocked with laughter. We both cry proper tears when we laugh hard enough. It's a family trait we inherited from our dad. How funny. I'd forgotten that too.

Eventually they stopped laughing and became quiet.

Alice wondered if Elisabeth would return to the subject of going back to the hospital, but she didn't say anything. Instead she wiped under each eye with a fingertip, sniffed, and reached over to turn on the car stereo. Alice steeled herself; Elisabeth enjoyed the sort of loud, angry, heavy metal music that normally appealed to teenage boys in hotted-up cars and made Alice's head ache. Instead, slow chords and a mellow female voice filled the car, as if they were in a smoky jazz bar. Elisabeth's taste in music had changed. Alice relaxed and looked out the window. The streets of Sydney looked pretty much as she remembered them. Had that coffee shop always been there? That block of units looked new, although it was entirely possible they'd been there for twenty years and she'd just never noticed them before.

There was an incredible lot of traffic, but all the cars looked the same. When she was little, she had assumed that by the year 2000 they'd be living in a space-age future complete with flying cars.

She glanced at Elisabeth's profile. She still had a leftover smile from their laughing fit.

Alice said, "Last night I dreamed again about that woman with the American accent, and this time I remembered you being there. Are you sure it doesn't mean anything to you?"

The leftover smile vanished from Elisabeth's face, and her cheeks, which had been puffed out and pink from laughing, seemed to collapse inward; Alice regretted saying anything.

Finally, Elisabeth said, "It was six years ago."

Elisabeth's Homework for Dr. Hodges

So I told her all about it, as if it was a story. Actually, all of a sudden I was desperate to tell her before she remembered for herself. Before she could write it off as a tiny, sad incident that had happened a long time ago.

This is what happened, Dr. Hodges. FYI.

Alice and I were both pregnant at the same time. Her baby was due exactly one week after mine.

Alice's third pregnancy was another accident of course, something complicated and typically Alice (typically old Alice; not the new and improved pedicured, manicured, peeled, waxed, and tinted Alice) to do with swapping brands of the pill.

My pregnancy was not an accident. The very idea of an "accidental pregnancy" seems so flippant and free. It makes me think of summer holidays, kissing for hours, smooth young skin, and . . . I don't know, piña bloody coladas. It feels like something that would always have been impossible for me, not just because of my stupid body, but because I don't have the right personality. I'm not whimsical enough. I don't get caught up in the moment. I want to say to people, "Why didn't you just use CONTRACEPTION?" Alice told me once that if she'd just stretched her fingertips a bit further she would have found the condom in her bedside drawer and Madison would never have been conceived. I found that immensely irritating because *how hard is it to stretch your fingertips, ALICE?*

Ben and I tried to get pregnant naturally for two years. We tried all the stuff people try. The temperature-taking, the charts, the acupuncture, the Chinese herbs, the holidays where we pretended not to think about it, the kits where you check your saliva under a microscope for the pretty fern pattern that meant you were ovulating.

The sex was still nice. It was before I became a dried apricot, you see, Dr. Hodges, and I was thin and fit. Although sometimes I would notice that Ben had the same grimly determined expression on his face as when he was trying to fix something tricky on his car with a wrench.

I was upset that we couldn't get pregnant, but I was still pretty upbeat, because I was an upbeat sort of person. I read a lot of self-help books back then. I even went along to weekend seminars and found the power within and hollered and hugged strangers. Oh yes, I was a believer. If someone gave me lemons, I made lemonade. I had inspirational quotes stuck on the noticeboards in front of my desk. This was my mountain and I was going to climb it. (I was a nerd.)

So we started IVF.

And we got pregnant on our very first cycle. That hardly ever happened! Well, we were ecstatic. We were giddy with happiness. Every time we looked at each other we laughed we were so happy. It was the proof of positive thinking! It was the miracle of modern science! We loved science. Good old science. We loved our doctor. We even loved those daily injections—they'd been no problem at all, didn't even hurt, weren't that scary! The medication hadn't really made me *that* moody and bloated. Actually, the whole process had just been interesting and fun!

I despise our old selves and at the same time I feel indulgently fond of them, because we didn't know any better (and, what, do I think everyone should lead their lives pessimistically, expecting the worst so they don't end up looking silly?). I can hardly bear to think of ourselves hugging and crying and making giggly phone calls, like we were in some inane sitcom. We actually discussed names. *Names!* I want to shout back through the years at myself, "Just because you're pregnant doesn't mean you get a baby, you idiots!"

There is a photo somewhere of Alice and me standing back-to-back with our hands pressed meaningfully to our stomachs. We look pretty. I'm not doing my stupid teeth-gritting fake smile and Alice hasn't got her eyes closed. We were thrilled when we found out our due dates were only days apart. "They could be born on the same day!" we said, pop-eyed by the coincidence. "They'll be like twins!" we cried. We were going to take photos of ourselves every month in the same position to record the progress of our bellies. It was so fucking sweet. (I'm sorry to swear, Dr. Hodges. I just wanted to sound cool and angry for a moment. A spoonful of paprika for me. That's what Mum used to give us when we swore as children, instead of washing our mouths out with soap and water, which she felt was unhygienic. I can never say "fuck" without tasting paprika. Ben laughs whenever I swear. I don't do it right. Neither does Alice. It's something to do with the paprika. I think we screw our faces up in preparation for the horrible taste.)

Alice came with me for my twelve-week ultrasound because Ben was away in Canberra at a car show. Madison was at preschool, but Tom was with us, sucking on a rusk in his stroller, sitting up very straight and alert and monitoring the world. I was completely besotted with Tom's laugh when he was a baby. I used to do this thing where I would keep my face completely straight and then, without warning, puff out my cheeks and shake my head from side to side like a dog. Tom thought it was hysterical. He'd watch me closely, his eyes dancing, and when I did my head-shaking thing, he'd fall straight back in his stroller and laugh with his whole body, slapping his knee in imitation of Nick's dad, because he thought that was a rule when you laughed. He had two tiny front teeth and the sound of his laugh was as delicious as chocolate.

Alice wheeled Tom into the room with us, parked the stroller in the corner, and I took off my skirt and lay down on the chair.

I wasn't taking all that much notice of the wispy-haired woman with the American accent who was rubbing cold jelly on my tummy and typing things into her computer, because I was making eye contact with Tom, ready to make him laugh again. Tom was looking straight back at me, his solid little body quivering all over with anticipation, and Alice was chatting to the wispy-haired woman about how they'd both rather the weather was cold than muggy, although not too cold of course.

The woman tapped away at the keyboard as she rubbed the plastic probe back and forth. I glanced briefly at the screen and saw my typed name in the right-hand corner over the top of the lunar landscape that apparently had something to do with my body. I was waiting for the woman to start pointing out the baby, but she was silent, tapping at her keyboard and frowning. Alice stared up at the television screen and chewed her nail. I looked back at Tom, widened my eyes, lifted my chin, and shook my head about.

Tom fell back in his stroller in an ecstasy of mirth, and the woman said, over the top of his laughter, "I'm sorry, but there is no heartbeat." She had a soft Southern accent, like Andie Mac-Dowell.

I didn't understand what she meant, because Ben and I had already heard the heartbeat when we went for our first visit to the obstetrician; it was a strange, eerie sound like the beat of a horse's hooves underwater and it didn't seem quite real, but it seemed to please Ben and my doctor, who both grinned proudly at me as if they were responsible for it. I thought the wispy-haired woman must mean that there was a problem with her machinery; something had broken down. I was about to say politely, "That's no problem," but then I looked over at Alice, and she must have understood right away because she'd curled her hand into a fist and pressed it against her mouth and when she turned around to look at me her eyes were red and watery. The woman touched me on the arm with her fingertips and said, "I'm so sorry," and it was slowly dawning on me that maybe something quite bad had happened. I looked back at Tom gnawing on his rusk and grinning, thinking, "She's going to do that crazy thing again soon!" and I smiled involuntarily back at him, and said, "What do you mean?"

Afterward, I felt guilty because I hadn't been concentrating on my own baby. I shouldn't have been playing with Tom when my poor little baby was trying to have a heartbeat. I felt that it must somehow have known I wasn't concentrating. I should have had my eyes fixed on that screen. I should have been helping it along, thinking: Beat. Beat. Beat.

I know this is irrational, Dr. Hodges. I'm never going to give you the professional satisfaction of hearing that story so you can point out it's irrational and pat yourself on the back for a good day's work at the office.

I know it's irrational, and I know there is nothing I could have done.

But I also know that a good mother would have been concentrating on her baby's heartbeat.

I never pulled that silly face for Tom again. I wonder if some part of his baby mind missed it. Poor little Tom. Poor little lost astronaut.

"Remember?" asked Elisabeth. "The woman with the wispy hair? Tom had rusk smeared all over his face. It was a really hot, humid day and you were wearing khaki pants and a white T-shirt. On the way home you had to stop and get petrol and when you came back to the car, both Tom and I were crying. You'd bought a Twix in the service station and you handed out pieces, and a man behind you waiting for the pump tooted his horn at us, and you put your head out the window and shouted at him. I was proud of you for shouting."

Alice tried to remember. She wanted to remember this. It seemed a betrayal of Elisabeth to have forgotten. She strained her mind with all her might, like a weight lifter, heaving to lift something huge that had lodged itself in her memory.

Scenes came into her head of a baby laughing in a stroller, Elisabeth crying in the car, a man angrily tooting his horn; but she couldn't tell if they were real memories or just her imagination painting pictures as Elisabeth talked. They didn't feel like real memories; they were insubstantial and shadowy, without context.

"You remember now?" said Elisabeth.

"Maybe a bit." She didn't want to disappoint her; she looked so hopeful.

"Well. Good. I guess."

Alice said, "I'm sorry."

"What for? It's not your fault. You didn't throw yourself headfirst at the floor at the gym."

"No, I mean, I'm sorry about your baby."

Chapter 12

A lice groped for the right thing to say next. The obvious thing to ask was, "Did you try to get pregnant again?" but that would be like saying, "So! Moving right along!"

She glanced over at Elisabeth. She had put on sunglasses, so Alice couldn't see her eyes, and was steering with one hand while she used the other hand to rub compulsively at something on the side of her face.

Alice looked away and saw that they were only a block away from the house. She and Nick had gone for so many walks around this area in the twilight, stopping to look at other people's houses to steal renovation ideas for their own. Was that really ten years ago? It didn't seem possible. The memory was so clear and ordinary it could have happened yesterday. Nick always said hello first to other neighborhood walkers. "Beautiful evening!" he would call out with a cheery lack of cool, and then he'd stop and chat, as if these people were old friends, while Alice stood there, smiling tightly, thinking, "Why are we bothering with these *strangers*?" But she was so proud of Nick's uninhibited sociability, the way he could walk straight into a party full of people they didn't know and stick his hand out to a stranger and say, "I'm Nick. This is my wife, Alice." It was as though he had an amazing skill, like playing a complicated musical instrument, that Alice could never hope to master. The best part was that she could coast along safely beside him at any social event, so that parties became glittery and giggly instead of excruciating torture, so much so that she wondered if she'd ever really been that shy in the first place. Even when he wasn't right by her side, she always knew that if the person talking to her drifted off, she wouldn't be stranded in the crowd; she could go and find Nick with a purposeful expression on her face, and he'd put an arm around her shoulder and draw her smoothly into the conversation.

Did she have to go to parties on her own again now?

She remembered that raw sensation she'd felt after previous relationships had ended. For months afterward, it had felt like she'd lost a layer of skin. If she'd felt like that after those meaningless boys, what would she feel like after breaking with Nick? She'd been so cozy in the cocoon of their relationship. She assumed she got to stay there forever.

Alice looked up from her lap, where she'd been fiddling with her bracelet, and saw they were turning into Rawson Street. As she watched the long line of leafy liquid ambers and the car ahead putting on its right-hand indicator to turn into King Street, she felt a sudden sense of horror. Her heart palpitated as if she'd woken up in the middle of a nightmare; something grabbed her throat and squeezed; pure fear rammed her hard against her seat.

She went to reach out for Elisabeth, to touch her arm to let her know that she might be dying, but she couldn't move. Elisabeth braked and looked left and right to turn onto King Street. Alice was having a heart attack right next to her and Elisabeth didn't even realize.

They turned the corner and Alice's heart began to slow. She could breathe again. She made a whooshing sound of relief as air filled her lungs once more.

Elisabeth glanced over at her. "You okay?"

Alice spoke, her voice high. "I felt really, really strange for a moment there."

"Dizzy? Because I can take you straight back to the hospital right now if you like. It's no problem."

"No, no, it's gone now. It was just—nothing, really."

The fear had vanished, leaving her weak and shaky as though she'd just stepped off an amusement park ride. What did these huge tidal waves of feeling mean? First there had been that unimaginable grief. Now it was terror.

As they drove down Alice and Nick's street, she saw a For Sale sign on the house directly opposite theirs. "Oh, are the Pritchetts selling?" she asked.

Elisabeth glanced at the sign and a strange, inscrutable expression crossed her face. "Um. I think they sold years ago. The family who bought it from them is selling it now. So, anyway—" She turned into Alice and Nick's driveway and pulled on the handbrake. "Home sweet home."

Alice looked out the window at her house and pressed her hand to her mouth. She threw open the car door and jumped out, the smooth white gravel driveway crunching beneath her shoes. White gravel! "Oh," she said ecstatically. "Look what we *did*!"

They first saw the house on a gloomy July day.

"Oh dear," they both said simultaneously when they pulled up in front of it, and then as they sat there in Nick's sister's car, gazing at it for a few seconds, they both made rising "ummm?" sounds, which meant, "But maybe it's got something?"

It was a ramshackle two-story Federation house with a sagging roof, blankets hanging in the windows instead of curtains, and an overgrown junkyard lawn. It looked sad and battered, but if you squinted your eyes, you could see the stately home it had once been.

The For Sale sign out front said POTENTIAL PLUS, and everyone knew what that meant.

"Too much work," said Nick.

"Far too much," agreed Alice, and they gave each other sidelong suspicious looks.

They got out of the car and stood shivering on the street, waiting for the real estate agent to arrive. The front door of the house creaked open and a bent old lady wearing a man's jumper over a checked skirt, long socks, and sneakers came shuffling up the footpath toward the letterbox.

"Oh *God,*" said Alice in agony. It was bad enough when you caught a glimpse of a harried middle-aged couple rushing out to their car to drive away before you went stomping through their house, making disparaging remarks about their choice of carpet. It broke Alice's heart when she saw the things they did to try to make their house sell—the fresh flowers, the kitchen counters with wet streaks from where they'd been vigorously wiped, the coffee plunger and cups placed just so on the living room table to make it look homey. Nick would snort cynically when people lit scented candles in the bathroom as if that's the way they always lived, but Alice was always touched by their hopefulness. "Don't go to all that effort to try and impress *me,*" she wanted to tell them. And now here was this ancient, trembly old lady. Where would she go on this freezing day while they looked at her house? Had she scrubbed the floors on arthritic knees for their appointment, when they probably wouldn't even buy it?

"Hi!" called out Nick, while Alice shrank behind him, saying, "Shhh!" He pulled her out from behind him, and because she didn't want to have a full-on wrestling match in public, she had no choice but to walk along beside him toward the old lady.

"We're meeting the real estate agent here in a few moments," explained Nick.

The old lady didn't smile. "Your appointment isn't until three."

"Oh, no," said Alice. There *was* something a bit familiar about the time three o'clock and she and Nick were always getting things like that wrong. ("God help you if you two ever have children," Nick's mother had said to them once.)

"Sorry about that," said Nick. "We'll go for a drive around the neighbor-hood. It looks beautiful."

"You may as well come in now," said the old lady. "I can do a better job of showing it to you than that smarmy weasel."

Without waiting for an answer, she turned around and started shuffling up the path toward the house.

Nick whispered in Alice's ear, "She's going to put us in cages and fatten us up before she eats us."

"Leave a trail of crumbs," whispered back Alice.

Shaking with repressed laughter, they obediently followed her.

There were two stately sandstone lions at the top of the veranda stairs, guarding the house. Their eyes seemed to follow Nick and Alice as they walked by.

"Raaaah!" whispered Nick to Alice, lifting his hand like a claw, and Alice said, "Shhhh."

Inside, the house was better and worse than they'd expected. There were soaring ceilings, ornate cornices and ceiling roses, original marble fireplaces; Nick quietly kicked back a corner of fraying old carpet to show Alice wide mahogany floorboards. At the same time there was a nose-tickling smell of damp and neglect, gaping holes in plaster, ancient moldy bathrooms, and a kitchen with 1950s linoleum and a stove that looked like it came from a museum.

The old lady sat them down in front of a single bar heater and brought them cups of tea and a plate of Scotch Finger biscuits, waving away Alice's desperate offers to help. It was excruciating to watch her walk. She finally sat down with a dusty black old photo album.

"This is what the house looked like fifty years ago," she said.

The photos were small and black-and-white, but you could still see that the house was once beautiful and proud, not the shrunken skeleton it had become.

The old lady pointed a yellowed fingernail at a photo of a young girl standing with her arms outspread in the front garden. "That was me on the day we moved in."

"You were so pretty," said Alice.

"Yes," said the old lady. "I didn't know it, of course. Just like you don't know how pretty you are."

"No she doesn't," agreed Nick solemnly, who was eating his third stale Scotch Finger as if he hadn't eaten for a month.

"I should be leaving this house to my children and grandchildren," said the old lady. "But my daughter died when she was thirty, and my son doesn't talk to me anymore, and so I'm putting it on the market. I want two hundred thousand for it."

Nick choked on his biscuit. The ad had listed it at over $300,000.

"The real estate agent will tell you I want a lot more, but I'm telling you if you offer that much, I'll accept. I know I can probably get more than that from an investor who will do it up quick-sticks and sell it on, but I was hoping a young couple might buy it and take their time restoring it and bring back the happy memories. We had a lot of happy memories here. Even though you probably can't feel them, they're here."

She spat out the words "happy memories" with slight disgust.

"It could be beautiful," continued the old lady as if she were reprimanding them. "It *should* be beautiful. Just a bit of a spit and polish."

Later in the car, they sat and looked at the house silently.

"Just a bit of a spit and polish," said Alice.

Nick laughed. "Yeah, gallons of spit and truckloads of polish."

"So what do you think?" asked Alice. "Should we forget it? We should just forget it, shouldn't we?"

"You go first. What do you think?"

"No, I want you to go first."

"Ladies first."

"Okay, fine," said Alice. She took a breath and looked at the house, imagining fresh paint, a mowed lawn, a toddler running around in circles. It was madness, of course. It would take them years to fix it all up. They didn't have the money. They were both working full-time. They didn't even own a car! They had agreed they would *not* buy a house that needed anything but superficial renovations.

She said, "I want it."

Nick said, "I want it, too."

Alice was in seventh heaven. Everywhere she looked there was something new and wonderful to see. The big square sandstone pavers leading up to the veranda (Nick's idea); the glossy white wooden window frames with glimpses of cream-colored curtains; the pink bougainvillea climbing froth-ily up the trellis at the side of the veranda (she could swear she'd only just thought of that idea the other day—"We'll have our breakfast there and pretend we're on a Greek island," she'd told Nick); even the *front door*, for heaven's sake—at some point they must have finally got around to stripping it back and painting it.

"We had a list," she said to Elisabeth. "Do you remember our list? It was three foolscap pages of things we needed to do to the house. There were ninety-three things on that list. It was called "The Impossible Dream." The last thing on that list was "white stone driveway." She bent down and picked up a smooth white stone and showed it to Elisabeth in the palm of her hand. Had they crossed everything off on that list? It was nothing short of a miracle. They'd achieved the Impossible Dream.

Elisabeth smiled tiredly. "You made a beautiful home—and wait till you see inside. I assume you've got your keys in your backpack there."

Without needing to think, Alice bent down and pulled out a fat jangle of keys from a zippered pocket at the side of the backpack. The key ring was a tiny hourglass; she knew where it would be, but she had never seen it before.

She and Elisabeth walked up onto the veranda. It was beautifully cool after the heat. Alice saw a set of cane chairs with blue cushions (she loved that shade of blue) and a half-empty glass of juice sitting on a round table with a mosaic top. Automatically, she went over and picked up the glass, hefting her backpack over her one shoulder; she kicked against something with her foot and saw it was a black-and-white soccer ball. It rolled away and hit the wheel of a child's scooter lying on its side, with shiny ribbons tied around the handles.

"Oh," she said in sudden panic. "The children. Are the children in there?"

"They're with Nick's mother. It's his weekend for the kids. Nick is back from Portugal tomorrow morning. So he'll drop them back to you Sunday night, as usual."

"As usual," repeated Alice faintly.

"Apparently that's your usual procedure," said Elisabeth apologetically.

"Right," said Alice.

Elisabeth took the glass of orange juice from Alice's unresisting fingers. "Shall we go inside? You probably need to lie down for a while. You still look so pale."

Alice looked around her. Something was missing.

"Where are George and Mildred?" she said.

"I don't know who George and Mildred are," said Elisabeth in a gentle, dealing-with crazy-person-here voice.

"That's what we called the sandstone lions." Alice gestured at the empty spot on the veranda. "The old lady left them for us. We love them."

"Oh. Yes, I think I remember them. I expect you got rid of them. Not quite the look for you, Alice."

Alice didn't understand what she meant. She and Nick would never have got rid of the lions. "Just off to the shops, George and Mildred," they'd say as they left the house. "You're in charge."

Nick would know. She would ask him. She turned around and lifted the keys to the door. The locks were new to her. There was a solid-looking gold dead bolt, but her fingers instantly found the right key, holding down the door handle and pushing with her shoulder against the door in a practiced, smooth movement. It was extraordinary the way her body knew how to do things—the mobile phone, the makeup, the lock—without her mind remembering her ever having done them before. She was about to comment on this to Elisabeth, but then she saw the hallway and she couldn't speak.

"Okay, listen to me, because I am a visionary," Nick had said standing in the musty, dark hallway in the first shell-shocked week after they'd moved into the house. (His mother had *cried* when she saw the house.) "Imagine sunlight flooding through this hallway because of the skylights we'll put here, here, and here. Imagine all this wallpaper gone and the walls painted something like a pale green. Imagine this carpet gone somewhere far, far away and the floorboards varnished and shiny in the sunlight. Imagine a hall table with flowers and letters on a silver tray, you know, as if they've been left there by the butler, and an umbrella stand and a *hat stand*. Imagine photos of our adorable children lined along the hallway—not those horrible portrait shots—but real photos of them at the beach or whatever or just picking their noses."

Alice had tried to imagine but she was suffering from a bad cold and one nostril was stinging so badly it was making her eyes water and they had two hundred and eleven dollars in the bank and twenty minutes ago they'd just discovered the house needed a new hot water system. All she could say was "We must have been out of our minds," and Nick's face had changed and he'd said, desperately, "Please don't, Alice."

And now here was the hallway exactly as he'd described it: the sunlight, the hall table, the floorboards shining liquid gold. There was even a funny old antique hat stand in the corner covered with straw hats and baseball caps and a few draped beach towels.

Alice walked slowly down the hallway, not stopping, only touching things with a vague caressing fingertip. She looked at the framed photos: a fat baby crawling on hands and knees in the grass, gazing huge-eyed up at the camera; a fair-haired toddler laughing uncontrollably next to a little girl in a Spider-Man suit with her hands on her hips; a skinny brown boy in baggy wet board shorts, caught ecstatically midair, bright-blue sky behind him, arms and legs flailing in every direction, droplets of water on the camera lens as he crashed down into unseen water. Every photo was another memory Alice didn't have.

The hallway led out to what had been the tiny living room where the old lady had given them tea and biscuits. Their plan had been to knock down three walls in this back area—it was Alice's idea; she'd drawn it up on the back of a Domino's Pizza napkin—so that it would create a huge open space where you could be cooking in the kitchen and see right out to the jacaranda tree in the back corner of the yard. "You're not the only visionary around here," she'd told Nick. And now here it was, almost exactly as she'd drawn it, but even better. She could see long, sleek marble countertops in the kitchen, a *huge* stainless-steel refrigerator, and complicated appliances.

Elisabeth walked into the kitchen—as if it were just an ordinary kitchen!—and poured the glass of orange juice down the sink.

Alice dropped her bag on the floor. There was no way this "divorce" talk could be serious. How could they be anything but blissfully happy living in this house?

"I can't believe it," she said to Elisabeth. "Oh look! I *knew* white shutters would be perfect on that back window. Nick wanted timber. Although, I see he won on the tiles. No, but I have to admit he was right. Oh, and we found a solution to the weird corner! Yes! Perfect! Oh, I don't know about those curtains."

"Alice," said Elisabeth. "Have you actually got *any* of your memory back?"

"Oh my God! Is that a pool out there? A swimming pool? An in-ground swimming pool? Are we rich, Libby? Is that what happened? Did we win the lottery?"

"What did you tell them at the hospital?"

"Would you *look* at the size of that television? It's like a movie screen."

She knew she was babbling, but she couldn't seem to stop.

"Alice," said Elisabeth.

Alice's legs felt wobbly. She went and sat down on the brown leather couch (expensive!) in front of the television. Something dug into her leg. She pulled out a tiny plastic toy, a figure of a murderous-looking man carrying a machine gun under one arm. She placed it carefully on the coffee table.

Elisabeth came and sat next to her. She handed her a sheet of folded paper. "Do you know who this is from?"

It was a handmade card with glitter stuck to the front and a drawing of a stick-figure woman with a turned-down mouth and a Band-Aid on her forehead. She opened it and read out loud, "Dear darling Mummy, get well soon, love from Olivia."

"It's from Olivia of course," said Alice, fingering the glitter.

"And do you remember Olivia?"

"Sort of."

She had no memory whatsoever of "Olivia," but her existence seemed indisputable.

"And what did you tell them at the hospital?"

Alice pressed her hand to the still tender spot at the back of her head. She said, "I told them that some things were a bit hazy, but I remembered most things. They gave me a referral for a neurologist and said if I kept having any significant problems to make an appointment. They said I should expect to feel totally back to normal within a week. Anyway, I think I actually do remember bits and pieces."

"Bits and pieces?"

The doorbell rang.

"Oh!" said Alice. "That's beautiful! I hated that old doorbell!"

Elisabeth lifted her eyebrows. "I'll get it." She paused. "Unless you want to get it."

Alice stared at her. Why shouldn't Elisabeth answer the door? "No, that's fine."

Elisabeth disappeared down the hallway and Alice laid her head back against the couch and closed her eyes. She tried to imagine what it would be like when Nick dropped the children off on the following night. Her natural instinct would be to throw her arms around him like she did when he'd been away. (She had a distinct feeling that she hadn't seen him in ages, as though he'd been away for weeks and weeks.) But what if he just stood there, without touching her back? Or what if he gently pushed her away? Or *shoved* her away? He would never do that. Why was she even thinking such a thing?

And "the children" would all be there. Milling about. Doing whatever kids do.

Alice whispered their names to herself.

Madison.

Tom.

Olivia.

Olivia was a pretty name.

Would she tell them? "Sorry, I know your face, I just can't quite place you." But she couldn't do that. It would be terrifying for a child to hear their mother didn't remember them. She'd have to pretend until her memory did come back, which it would, of course. Soon.

She'd have to try and talk to them in a natural voice. Not one of those jolly, fake voices people put on for children. Kids were smart. They'd see right through her. Oh heavens—what would she *say* to them? This felt worse than trying to think up appropriate conversation topics before going to one of Nick's scary work parties.

She heard voices coming down the hallway.

Elisabeth came in, followed by a man pushing a trolley piled with three cardboard boxes.

"Apparently they're glasses," said Elisabeth. "For tonight."

"Where do you want 'em?" grunted the man.

"Um," said Alice. For tonight?

"I guess just here in the kitchen," said Elisabeth. The man lifted the boxes onto the counter.

"Sign here," he said. Elisabeth signed. He ripped off a sheet of paper, handed it to her, and looked around him briefly. "Nice house," he said.

"Thank you!" Alice beamed.

There was a shout from down the hallway. "Alcohol delivery!"

"Alice," said Elisabeth. "I don't suppose you remember anything about hosting a party tonight?"

Chapter 13

Together, they flipped to the date in Alice's diary.

"Kindergarten Cocktail Party," read out Alice. "Seven p.m. What does that mean?"

"I'd say it means that it's all the parents from Olivia's class," said Elisabeth.

"And I'm hosting it?" said Alice. "Why would I host it?"

"I believe you host a lot of these sorts of things."

"You believe? Don't you know? Don't you come to all these 'things'?"

"Well, no. This is to do with the school," said Elisabeth. "It's all mothers. I'm not a mother."

Alice looked up from the diary and said, "You're not?"

Elisabeth seemed to flinch. "No, I'm not. I haven't had any luck in that regard. So, anyway"—she seemed desperate to get off of the subject—"what are you going to do about this party?"

But Alice didn't care about the party. There was no way she was going to host any "kindergarten cocktail party." She said, "So will you tell me what happened? Please? Did you try again to get pregnant after you had that miscarriage?"

Elisabeth's eyes slid away.

Frannie's Letter to Phil

So, the village minibus was pulling out of the driveway, and all of a sudden there was a commotion. It was Mr. Mustache, do you mind, running alongside the bus, rapping his knuckles on the window, shouting, "Wait for me!"

I thought there must have been some crisis, but no, he was just running late. He leapt aboard, all breathless and excited, as if we were off somewhere far more thrilling than the local shopping center. He announced to the entire bus that he'd been held up on the phone "placing a bet on the doggies." I think that means greyhound racing, Phil. Charming.

There were plenty of spare seats, but for some reason, he chose to plonk himself down next to me. It was uncomfortable. He's not a large man, but he did seem to take up a lot of room. I found I was pressing myself against the side of the bus, so our thighs didn't touch. Also, he was close enough that I could smell some sort of aftershave or cologne. I'm not saying it was unpleasant. It just seemed overly personal.

I said something about the weather but he ignored that and said, "How's that honorary family of yours?"

I found myself telling him about Alice's accident and how she didn't remember anything about her marriage breakdown. I told him how worried I was about the children. He told me a rather sad story about his own son, who had gone through a divorce, and how his daughter-in-law didn't let them see their grandchildren anymore. "It broke my wife's heart," he said. He told me that his wife had died two years ago and that he truly believed she would have lived longer if her grandchildren hadn't been taken from her.

When we got to the shopping center, I naturally assumed he would go off and do his own thing, but he cheerfully admitted he didn't have a thing to buy and he'd be happy to keep me company. I'd had enough of him by now but I couldn't think of a polite way to get rid of him.

So he followed me around while I bought talcum powder for Alice. I needed some new deodorant at the chemist's, but I was too embarrassed to buy it in front of him, as if deodorant could only be purchased in private. Isn't that the most ridiculous thing you ever heard?

Also, we couldn't seem to synchronize our walking. We kept bumping into each other and treading on each other's toes. It was driving me a little batty, to be honest. (I'm sure it was his fault, not mine. I'm perfectly able to walk alongside other people. You and I used to go on such long walks! Never a problem!)

At one point we saw a toddler sitting in one of those toy cars. The child was having a tantrum, screaming, "Just one more turn!" at his poor harassed mother. Next thing, Mr. Mustache took a coin from his wallet and leaned past the toddler and popped it in the slot to activate the ride. Of course, the toddler shrieked with delight, while the poor mother didn't know what to do.

We were having quite a spirited argument about this (I felt that he had rudely undermined the young mother's authority) when he suddenly got all excited by a pink neon sign advertising free iced doughnuts with your coffee. He insisted on buying me a cappuccino. For something to say, I told him about Ben and how he designs rather beautiful neon signs for a living, and that led to us talking about Elisabeth's problems.

He was very sympathetic to Elisabeth and, strangely, that made me want to argue with him. I said that babies weren't the be-all and end-all and that Elisabeth might do better to concentrate on her marriage and her lovely husband.

He asked whether I'd ever had a "lovely husband" myself.

I said no.

Then I got a little snappish and said that my doughnut was stale.
That was a fib. It was actually quite delicious.

Elisabeth's Homework for Dr. Hodges

It was surreal hearing Alice ask me if I tried again, so wide-eyed and respectful. I nearly laughed. I wondered if it was an act.

It's been a long time since I've thought properly about those early "losses," as you call them with a straight-mouthed grimace, as if you're constipated. I sort of hate that face you pull, Dr. Hodges. I bet your wife does, too. It always makes me think about what else I could be doing with the $150 I spend on you. I remember in one session you wanted me to start talking through the "early losses" (grimace, grimace), and I gave a dramatic sigh and said I didn't think I could, but really I was just so irritated by that expression on your face.

Mostly now I just think of my "losses" as bullet points on my medical history. If a doctor asks me for my history I can reel off every single procedure and test and crushing disappointment without even a tremor in my voice, as if they don't mean a thing, as if they happened to somebody else.

So I can say "second first-trimester miscarriage in April 2006" without blinking, and I don't even think about what it was like, or how it felt.

I want you to know that I've missed all of *Grey's Anatomy* now. I'm really working hard on this therapy. I wish you were grading me. You should give grades to your approval-seeking patients.

I remember how happy we were when we got pregnant again, because this time, for some reason, we managed a "natural" pregnancy.

That was to be my January baby, due on 17 January (the day after Ben's birthday; imagine if it was born on the same day! But no, shhhh, don't say that out loud). We kept the pregnancy a secret this time. We thought that telling everybody about the first baby had been our beginner's mistake. I imagined announcing my second pregnancy with calm, womanly confidence after I'd passed the first trimester. It seemed a more grown-up, safer way to handle things. "Oh no, not an IVF baby this time," I'd say casually. "A *natural* pregnancy." This time we didn't talk about names, and Ben didn't pat my stomach when he kissed me goodbye each morning. We said things like "*If* I'm still pregnant at Christmas" and lowered our voices to a whisper when we used the word "baby," as if getting our hopes up had been the mistake, as if we could trick the gods into not noticing us sneakily trying to have a baby.

This time Ben was there for the first ultrasound and we both dressed up carefully as if it was for a job interview, as if our clothes would make a difference. The woman doing it was young, Australian, and a little cranky. I was worried, but on the other hand I was faking it for the cameras, if you know what I mean. I was all twitchy nerves on the surface, but deep down part of me was enjoying observing my anguish: *Ooh, look at her digging her nails into her hands as she lies down, the poor, traumatized thing, when of COURSE there is going to be a heartbeat THIS time because this sort of thing doesn't happen twice!* I could already feel the huge rush of relief that would be released. I had tears of joy banked up, just waiting for me to push "go." I was ready to send a poignant message of love to my first baby, something along the lines of "I will never forget you, I will always hold you in my heart," and then it would be time to focus on this baby: our real baby. Alice's baby would only be a few months older. We could still call them twins.

The cranky girl said, "I'm sorry . . ."

Ben clenched his jaw hard and took a step back, as if someone had just threatened to hit him in a pub brawl and he was trying not to get involved.

I've heard so many professional "I'm sorry"s now, Dr. Hodges. I'm sorry. I'm sorry. I'm sorry. Yes, your colleagues in the medical profession are all very sorry. I wonder if one day you'll be the next to say, kindly and sadly, "I'm sorry but I can't cure you. You're a nutter. It might be time to look at other options, like transplanting somebody else's personality."

I was embarrassed that it had happened twice in almost exactly the same way. I felt as if I was wasting people's time, constantly turning up for ultrasounds of dead babies. What? You thought you had a real live baby in there? Don't be ridiculous. Not you. You're not a proper woman with these half-hearted, faintly ridiculous attempts to have a baby. There are women out there with proper swollen pregnant stomachs and live kicking babies.

Afterward, I felt it had been wrong not telling the family about the baby, because then I wanted them to know about the miscarriage, so that they knew the baby had existed. But when I told people, they seemed more interested in the fact that I'd kept the pregnancy a secret. They felt they'd been tricked. They said things like "Oh, I did wonder that day when you didn't drink at the Easter BBQ but you said you just didn't feel like drinking!" In other words, LIAR.

Ben's mother was offended. We had to take her out twice for a "buy one, get one free!" meal at the Black Stump before she forgave us. The point of it seemed to be that I'd hidden the pregnancy, not that I'd lost the baby. People weren't as upset as with the first one, and how could they be, when they'd only just heard it existed in the first place. I felt this ridiculous protective feeling for my January baby, as if nobody loved her, as if she wasn't as pretty or as smart as the first baby.

I know she was a girl. This time they sent off the "fetal material" for testing and told me it was a chromosomally normal female. They said they were sorry but they couldn't find any reason why

I'd lost the baby. They said there was a lot they didn't know about miscarriage, but according to the statistics I still had an excellent chance of having a healthy baby next time. Chin up. Try again.

A week after the D&C (such a chipper name for something so horrible; I never feel so desolate as I have after waking up in Recovery from a D&C) I went to visit Alice in hospital and see her new baby girl. Of course, Alice said I didn't need to go and Ben said he didn't want me to go, but I went. I don't know why but I was determined to do everything I normally would.

I went to the greeting card store and chose a card frosted with pink glitter saying "Congratulations on your darling little girl." I went to Pumpkin Patch and bought a tiny yellow dress with embroidered butterflies all over it. "It just makes you long to have a baby girl, doesn't it!" cooed the saleslady.

I wrapped up the dress in pink tissue paper and wrote on the card and I drove to the hospital and found a parking spot and walked through the corridors with the present under one arm and some trashy celebrity magazines for Alice under the other. The whole time I floated alongside myself, impressed. "You're doing fine. Well done. It will all be over soon and you can be home watching television."

Alice was on her own in the room, breast-feeding Olivia.

My own breasts still ached and burned. It's so mean-spirited of your body, the way it keeps acting like you're pregnant, even after the baby has been scraped out of your womb.

"Oh, *look* at her!" I said to Alice, ready to begin the new-baby patter.

I'm so good at it these days. Just last week I went to visit a friend who had given birth to her third child and, even if I say so myself, my performance was flawless. "Look at his tiny hands!" "Oh, her eyes/nose/mouth is just like yours!" "Of *course* I'd love a hold!" And, breathe. And, chat. And, smile. Don't think about it, don't think about it, don't think about it. There should be Oscars for that sort of thing.

But Alice didn't let me get started on my act.

As soon as she saw me, she held out the arm that wasn't holding the baby and her face crumpled and she said, "I wish it was me visiting you."

I sat on the bed with her and let her hug me. Alice's tears dripped straight onto Olivia's soft, tiny, bald head, but she kept right on sucking Alice's nipple, as if her life depended on it. She's always loved her food, that kid.

I'd forgotten all about that day until now—how much it meant to me that Alice cried so genuinely for me. It was like she was taking on some of my grief. I thought, It's okay, I can do this, I can get through it, I'll be fine.

I just didn't realize that "this" would keep on going and going and going.

Mmmm. I think we may have just had a mini-breakthrough in my journal-writing therapy. Although no need to get too big for your boots, Dr. Hodges. It wasn't like I'd *repressed* that memory with Alice. I just hadn't thought about it for a while, but still, bravo, maybe there is something in this, even though I've just missed what was promised to be an "explosive" episode of *Grey's Anatomy*.

I'd toughened up by the next "loss."

Elisabeth said, "You're not just pretending you don't remember, so you can make some sort of point, are you?"

Alice felt the same punched-in-the-stomach feeling as when Nick had yelled at her on the phone. He'd said something about her making a point, too. Had she become a person who had points to make?

"What sort of point?"

"Forget it. I was just being paranoid." Elisabeth stood up and walked into the kitchen. She stopped in front of the refrigerator. It was covered with magnets, notices, photos, and children's drawings. "I wonder if there is an invitation here for this party of yours."

Alice twisted on the couch to watch her. Her head ached.

"Libby. Please. What sort of point? I don't understand. Sometimes you talk to me like you—well, it's almost like you don't like me anymore."

"Ha!" Elisabeth picked up something off the fridge and brought it over to her. "Here's the invitation. There's another woman's name on it for the RSVPs. You should ring her and ask if she can change the party venue."

She went to hand it over, but Alice ignored it.

Elisabeth sighed. "Of course I still *like* you. Don't worry about it. There's nothing to worry about. Here—this woman's name is Kate Harper. Actually, I think I've heard you talk about her before. I think you're quite good friends with her."

She looked expectantly at Alice.

"I've never heard of her," said Alice dully.

"Okay, then," said Elisabeth. "Well, why don't I call her and you can go upstairs and lie down. You look like death warmed up."

Alice looked at Elisabeth's lined, anxious face.

Have I let you down? Have I lost you and Nick?

Chapter 14

Alice stood in the middle of her unfamiliar bedroom, looking for something—anything—that belonged to Nick. There was no sign of him. No pile of books or magazines on his bedside table. He liked bloodthirsty thrillers (they both did), war histories, and business magazines. No cylindrical piles of coins taken from the pockets of his trousers each day. No ties draped over the door handle. No giant dirty sneakers. Not even a lone crumpled T-shirt or sock.

They were both messy. Their clothes were normally tangled together on the floor in flamboyant embraces. Sometimes they purposely asked people over just to give themselves the incentive to clean up in a frantic rush before they arrived.

But the carpet (dark maroon—she had no memory of choosing it) was pristine, newly vacuumed.

She went to the wardrobe (they'd found it lying on its side outside someone's house for council pickup; it was autumn, like now; they brushed away a layer of crackly brown leaves to reveal patterned mahogany). It was filled with spaced-out good heavy hangers containing beautiful clothes that presumably belonged to Alice. Although it gave her fleeting pleasure to feel the lustrous fabrics as she flipped through the hangers, she longed to see just one of Nick's shirts. Even a boring white business shirt. She would wrap its sleeves around her like his arms. Bury her nose in the collar.

As she closed the cupboard door and slowly looked around the bedroom, she realized it smelled and felt essentially feminine. There was a white lacy duvet on the bed and a row of small shiny blue cushions. Alice thought the bed looked absolutely beautiful (actually it was her dream bed), but Nick would have said that all that prettiness would render him instantly impotent; so, fine, if that's what she wanted, he was just warning her. There was a Margaret Olley print hanging above the bed that Alice knew would have made Nick wince as if hit by a sudden attack of nausea. The dressing table had rows of different-colored glass bottles (*What exactly is the point?* Nick would have said) and a crystal vase containing a big bouquet of roses.

This was the bedroom she would have created for herself if she were living on her own. She'd always wanted to collect beautiful glass bottles and thought it was something she would never do.

Except for the roses. She remembered how the image of exactly those roses had popped into her mind while she was in the ambulance yesterday. She went over to the dressing table and studied them. Who gave her those? And why was she keeping them in her bedroom when she hated that sort of arrangement?

There was a small square card sitting next to the vase. Nick? Nick wanting her back and forgetting she didn't like roses? Nick *making a point* by sending her roses he knew she would hate?

Alice picked it up and read: *"Dear Alice, I hope we can do that again one day—next time in the sunshine? Dominick."*

Oh God. She was dating.

She plunked herself down on the end of the bed, holding the card between disbelieving fingers.

Dating was meant to be something from her past, not something from her future. She'd never enjoyed it that much anyway. The self-conscious, trapped feeling when you were sitting in the car together for the first time; the constant horrifying possibility of food caught in between your teeth; the sudden feeling of exhausted boredom when you realized it was your turn to come up with the next stilted topic of conversation. *So what do you like to do on the weekends?*

Oh, sure, yes, there was nothing better than when a date actually *worked*. She could remember the euphoria of those early dates with Nick. There was a night where they'd watched Australia Day fireworks from a bar in the Rocks. She was drinking a huge creamy cocktail, and Nick was telling a story about one of his sisters and he was so funny and so sexy and Alice's hair looked nice and her shoes weren't hurting and there were curls of shaved chocolate floating on top of her cocktail and Nick's hand massaging her lower back and she felt such an intense sensation of happiness it frightened her, because surely there was a price to pay for this sort of bliss. (And was this the price? All these years later? Nick swearing at her on the phone from the other side of the world. Had she finally been sent an exorbitant bill?)

A date with any man other than Nick would be boring and awkward and stupid. Dominick. What sort of a name was Dominick?

In a sudden rage, she took the card and tore it into tiny pieces. How could she betray Nick like that by keeping these flowers in her bedroom?

And then there was that other man—that physiotherapist from Melbourne—who had sent her the card with the mention of "happier times." Who was he? Was she already on to her *second* relationship after breaking up with Nick? Had she turned into a *hussy*? A point-making hussy who went to the gym and upset her beloved sister and hosted "Kindergarten Cocktail Parties"? She hated the person she'd become. The only good part was the clothes.

This all had to stop. She had to get Nick's coins and his socks and his sneakers back in her bedroom, and these roses gone.

She lay back on the bed. Elisabeth was downstairs phoning up that Kate Harper woman trying to get tonight's party canceled.

Alice crawled across the bed, pulled back the duvet, and got into crisp, clean sheets, still wearing her red dress.

She looked at the ceiling (plastered and painted, the water stains and cracks gone as if they'd never existed) and thought of that moment in the bathroom at the hospital when she had been going through that odd makeup routine and she had that rush of feeling after she smelled her perfume. It had seemed like she was about to fall headfirst into all her memories but then she'd deliberately resisted it, stepped back from the edge when she really should have let herself go. It would be far easier and less confusing if she could just remember what the hell was going on in her life. She sniffed at her wrist where she'd sprayed the perfume that had seemed so evocative of everything, but this time she experienced only a confused, choppy mass of half-remembered feelings; they were insubstantial and slippery, gone before she could even attempt to name them.

She woke to find Frannie sitting at the end of her bed, holding a gift.

"Hello, sleepyhead."

"Hello." Alice smiled with relief, because Frannie looked exactly as she should. She was wearing a familiar pale-pink buttoned-up blouse Alice had seen many times before, or at least one like it, and tailored gray pants. Her back was ramrod straight. She was like a little elf. She had short white hair tucked behind tiny ears, creamy white skin, and cat's eye glasses on a gold chain.

Alice said happily, "You haven't changed a bit. You look just the same."

"You mean as I did ten years ago?" Frannie adjusted her glasses on her nose. "I guess there was no room for any more wrinkles. Here." She handed her the present. "You probably won't like it, but I wanted to get you something."

Alice sat up in bed. "Of course I'll like it." She unwrapped a bottle of talcum powder. "Lovely." She twisted the lid, poured some into her palm and sniffed. The scent was simple and flowery and reminded her of nothing. "Thank you."

"How are you feeling?" asked Frannie. "You gave us all a fright."

"Fine," said Alice. "Confused. Sometimes I feel like I'm on the verge of remembering everything, and then other times it all feels like a huge practical joke and you're all just pretending I'm thirty-nine when you know perfectly well that I'm about to turn thirty."

"I know that feeling," said Frannie reflectively. "Just the other day I woke up and felt like I was nineteen. I went into the bathroom and saw an old lady staring back at me from the mirror and it really startled me. I thought, 'Who is that dreadful old crone?'"

"You're not a crone."

Frannie waved her hand at that dismissively. "Well, anyway, I think you're probably having a nervous breakdown." Alice looked appalled. "Don't look at me like that! People do have nervous breakdowns, and you've been under so much stress lately. What with this divorce—"

"Yes, about that. *Why* are we breaking up?" interrupted Alice. She couldn't bring herself to say the word "divorce" out loud. Frannie wouldn't try to hide anything from her. She would tell her straight.

But Frannie said, "I have absolutely no idea. That's between you and Nick. All I know is that you both seem very set on the idea. There doesn't seem any chance of reconciliation. So we've all just had to button our lips and accept it."

"But you must have an opinion. You always have an opinion!"

Frannie smiled. "Yes, I generally do, don't I? But in this case, I really don't know. You haven't confided in me. It's very sad for the children. Especially this awful fighting-over-custody business. I don't approve of that at *all*, as you know."

"I don't know. I don't remember."

"Oh. Well, I've made my opinions on the matter clear. Too clear, you might say."

Alice said, "Do you think I can get him back?"

"Who back? You mean Nick? But you don't want him back," said Frannie. "Actually you talked to me on Wednesday and said you'd just received roses from some new fellow called Dominick. You seemed very excited about it."

Alice looked with dislike at the roses. She said sourly, "I thought you said I was stressed."

Frannie said, "Well, yes, you're stressed, but you were happy about the roses."

Alice sighed. "How are *you*, Frannie? You're still living next door to Mum, right?"

"No, darling." Frannie patted Alice on the leg. "I moved myself into a retirement village five years ago. Just after your mother moved in with Roger."

"Oh." Alice paused to consider this news. "Do you like the retirement village? Is it fun?"

"Fun," said Frannie reflectively. "That's what's important these days, isn't it. Everything should be *fun* and lighthearted."

"Well, not everything, obviously."

"Do you think I have a sense of humor?" asked Frannie. She gave Alice a look that was surprisingly vulnerable.

"Of course you have a sense of humor!"

Although "sense of humor" weren't exactly the first words that came to mind when you thought of Frannie.

Frannie sighed and smiled. She wasn't an especially smiley lady, so when she smiled, it was like receiving a gift. "Thank you, darling. Tell me something, would you buy deodorant in front of a man? Or would you think that was too . . . personal?"

"What man?" said Alice.

"Any man!" said Frannie irritably.

"Well, I think I probably would. There's nothing especially personal about deodorant. Unless, I guess, you had to use some really heavy-duty one that would make him think you had some sort of rare and horrible perspiration disease."

"I can assure you, Alice, I don't need a 'heavy-duty' deodorant!" said Frannie, looking affronted.

"What's this about?" asked Alice.

"Nothing. Just a very silly friend of mine asked the question."

Was *Frannie* interested in some man? Alice knew that Frannie had lost a boyfriend during the Second World War, but as far as she was aware, there had never been anyone else in her life since, although there had been that time when they were teenagers and Elisabeth had seen a half-finished letter sitting on Frannie's desk. When Elisabeth asked who she was writing to, Frannie had apparently been so flustered, she had actually (Alice thought Elisabeth must be making this part up) *blushed*. She had said she was writing to "an old friend," but Elisabeth had been convinced from her reaction that it was a "secret lover." "Probably someone else's husband," Elisabeth had said, with a knowing, cynical look. "I expect they meet at motels in the middle of the day." Alice had been deeply shocked and wasn't able to look Frannie in the eye for weeks after.

"Come on, let's go downstairs," said Frannie. "Your mother is making lunch."

As they walked out of the room and down the hallway toward the stairs, Frannie said, "Walk alongside me, Alice."

"I am," said Alice.

"No. Properly. That's it! See! We can walk side by side, without tripping all over each other, can't we?"

"We sure can," said Alice, wondering if Frannie had gone a little senile in 2008.

As they reached the top of the stairs, Alice stopped abruptly at the sound of a deep, familiar male voice. "Alice, my dear! I was just coming up to collect you!"

"How are you, Roger?" Alice peered over the banister, horrified to see him at the bottom of the stairs. He was all out of context without Nick. He was a visitor you planned for (steeled yourself for), not someone who looked comfortably up at you from the bottom of your stairs, as if he belonged in your house.

"Never better," Roger called back. "It's you we're worried about!"

Frannie's eyes met Alice's and she lifted a wry eyebrow. She wasn't senile. She was still as sharp as a tack.

"Is she up, then?" Alice's mother emerged from the kitchen and looked up at them.

Alice walked behind Frannie down the stairs, glad to see that although she was behaving oddly, she didn't seem that much frailer than Alice remembered.

Barb and Roger stood at the bottom with their palms lifted, like ministers welcoming the congregation, identical weirdly evangelical expressions on their faces.

"Did you have a good sleep, Alice?" asked Barb, trying in vain to take Frannie's elbow. "Rest is the best thing for you, I'm sure. I suppose everything has come back to you now?" She didn't wait for an answer. "Are you hungry?"

Roger took Alice by the arm and led her into the dining area, behind Barb and Frannie, his fingertips solicitously pressed to the small of her back.

"Don't *hover*, Barbara!" snapped Frannie, as Barb fussed about the best seat for her at the long pine table.

Alice sat down next to her, anxious to escape the oily feel of Roger's fingertips. She watched in fascination at the relaxed way her mother tilted her head coquettishly up at him. Thankfully, she was no longer wearing the exotic salsa-dancing outfit from the day before, but she was wearing a rather low-cut T-shirt and capri pants, and her long hair was up in a jaunty ponytail.

"Now, I've made a nice tuna salad for our lunch. I chose that specifically for you, Alice, because fish is brain food. Roger and I have been taking fish oil every day, haven't we, darl?"

Darl. Her mother just called Roger "darl."

Roger didn't seem to have changed at all in the last ten years. He was still tanned and polished and pleased with himself. Had he had plastic surgery? Alice wouldn't put it past him. He was wearing a pink polo-necked shirt, with a gold chain nestled in graying chest hair. His shorts were just a little too tight, revealing muscular brown legs.

As Barb turned to go back toward the kitchen, Roger gave her a playful, not-at-all-discreet slap on the bottom. Appalled, Alice averted her eyes. (Roger, she remembered, owned a waterbed. "The ladies love it," he'd told Alice once.)

Frannie gave a low chuckle and laid her hand over Alice's in sympathy. Alice distracted herself by examining the long pine table in front of her. She'd dreamed about this table at the hospital. Nick was sitting at it, while she was cleaning the kitchen. He'd said something that made no sense. What was it?

Elisabeth came into the room, lifting her handbag over her shoulder. "I've got to go."

"Where are you going?" asked Alice desperately. She needed support to help her cope with Roger and her mother. "Are you coming back?"

Elisabeth gave her an odd look. "I'm meeting some people for lunch. I'll come back if you like."

"Who?" asked Alice, trying to keep her there for longer. "Who are you meeting?"

"Just some friends," said Elisabeth evasively. "Anyway, make sure you listen out for the phone because I've left three messages for that Kate Harper about tonight's party but she still hasn't called back." She looked at Alice. "You still seem very pale. I think you should go back to bed after lunch."

"Oh, I agree!" said their mother as she walked in from the kitchen, carrying a glass salad bowl. "I'm packing her straight off to bed after lunch, don't worry. We need to get her completely recovered before those little terrors are back."

Alice looked at the big glass salad bowl her mother was holding and for no particular reason the name "Gina" came into her head.

It's always about Gina. Gina, Gina, Gina. That's right. That's what she'd remembered, or dreamed, Nick saying as he sat at this table.

"Who is Gina?" asked Alice.

The room became extremely still and silent.

Finally Frannie cleared her throat. Roger looked at the floor and fiddled with the chain around his neck. Barb froze at the entrance from the kitchen and hugged the salad bowl to her stomach. Elisabeth chewed hard at her lip.

"Well, who is she?" said Alice.

Elisabeth's Homework for Dr. Hodges

One thing I've been thinking about a lot is how I would feel if I lost ten years of my memory, and what things would surprise me, or please me, or upset me about how my life had turned out.

I hadn't even met Ben ten years ago. So he would be a stranger. A big scary hairy stranger sharing my bed. How could I explain to my old self that I had accidentally fallen in love with a silent mountain of a man who designs neon signs for a living and whose most passionate interest is cars? Before I met Ben, I was one of those girls who was deliberately, prettily ignorant about cars. I described them by size and color. A big white car. A small blue car. Now I know makes and models. I watch the Grand Prix. Sometimes I even flick through his car magazines.

Do you like cars, Dr. Hodges? You seem more like an art galleries and opera sort of guy. I see you have a photo of your wife and two small children on your desk. I secretly look at this photo every session when you're writing out my receipt. I bet your wife had no trouble getting pregnant at all, did she? Do you ever thank your lucky stars you didn't end up with a reproductively challenged wife like me? Do you give that photo an affectionate look as I walk out of the room and think, Thank God my wife is a good breeder? Don't worry if you do. I'm sure it's innate, it's just biology, for a man to want a woman who can give him children. I raised this with Ben once. I said he must secretly resent me and I understood that. He got so angry. The angriest I've seen him. "Never say that again," he said. But I bet that's why he got so angry, because he knew it was true.

Before I met Ben, I used to go for witty successful types. I'd never been out with a man before who owned a toolbox. A proper big dirty well-used toolbox full of, you know, screwdrivers and stuff. It's embarrassing how aroused I became when I first saw Ben selecting a chunky oily wrench from that toolbox. My dad had a toolbox. So maybe I'd been subconsciously waiting for a man with a toolbox. I bet you don't have a toolbox, do you, Dr. Hodges? No. I didn't think so.

I used to think that one of my main prerequisites for a man was that he be good at dinner parties. Like Alice's Nick. But Ben is hopeless at dinner parties. He always seems too big for his chair. He gets this trapped expression. It's like I've brought along a big tame chimp. Sometimes he's OK if he happens to find another man (or woman—he's no chauvinist) who can talk about cars, but mostly he's miserable, and he breathes out gustily when we get in the car, as if he's been let out of jail.

It's funny. I had all those years of being driven mad by Mum and Alice and their fear of social events. "Oh, *no!*" they'd say tragically, and I would think someone had died, and it would turn out they'd been invited to some party or lunch where they'd only know one person, and then there would be all the strategizing about how to get out of it, and the drama of it all and the *sympathy* they'd pour on each other. "Oh, you poor thing! That would be awful! You absolutely must not go." I couldn't stand it, and yet I ended up marrying a man who also thinks socializing is something that's meant to be endured. Not that he's shy like they were. He doesn't get butterflies in his stomach or agonize over what people think of him. Actually I don't think he has any self-consciousness whatsoever. He is a man without vanity. He's just not a talker. He has no small talk ability whatsoever. (Whereas Mum and Alice, of course, were talkers, and they were actually interested in meeting other people. In reality they were more social than me. But their shyness stopped them from being the outgoing people they actually were. They were like athletes trapped in wheelchairs.)

As it turns out, Ben and I don't really go to many dinner parties anymore. I can't stand them. I've lost my ability to chat, too. I listen to people talk about their interesting, full lives. They're training for marathons, they're learning Japanese, they're taking the kids camping and renovating the bathroom. I had a life like that once, too. I was interesting and active and informed. But now my life is three things: work, television, IVF. I no longer have anecdotes. People say, "What have you been up to, Elisabeth?" and I have to stop myself from treating them to a complete medical update. I understand now why very sick people and the elderly have such a compulsion to tell you everything about their health. My infertility fills every corner of my mind.

How things have changed. Now I'm the one groaning when I hear someone's cheerful voice on the phone asking me if I'm free next Saturday, while Alice is hosting kindergarten cocktail parties and Mum is salsa-dancing three nights a week.

Alice can't believe she's got three children. I wouldn't be able to believe I had none. I never expected to have trouble getting pregnant. Of course, no one does. It hardly makes me unique. It's just that I *did* expect so many other different medical problems. Our dad died of a heart attack, so I've always been frightened by the slightest case of heartburn. I've had two grandparents on different sides of the family die of cancer, so I've been permanently on standby, waiting for the cancer cells to strike. For a long time

I was terrified I was about to be struck down by motor neuron disease for no other reason than the fact that I'd read a very moving article about a man who had it. He first noticed he had a problem when his feet started hurting on the golf course. Whenever I'd feel a twinge in my foot, I'd think, OK, here we go. I told Alice about the article and she started to worry about it, too. We'd take off our high heels and massage our sore feet and discuss how we'd cope with getting around in wheelchairs, while Nick rolled his eyes and said, "Are you two for *real*?"

Alice is the other reason I didn't expect infertility. We've always been so similar health-wise. We both get a dry, irritating cough every winter that takes exactly one month to go away. We have weak knees, bad eyesight, a slight dairy intolerance, and excellent teeth. When she had no problem getting pregnant, I thought that meant it would be the rule for me, too.

So it's Alice's fault that I never invested the appropriate time worrying about infertility. I never insured against it by worrying about it. I won't make that mistake again. Now every day I remember to worry that Ben will die in a car accident on his way to work. I make sure I worry at regular intervals about Alice's children—ticking off every terrible childhood disease: meningitis, leukemia. Before I go to sleep at night I worry that someone I love will die in the night. Every morning I worry that somebody I know will be killed in a terrorist attack that day. That means the terrorists have won, Ben tells me. He doesn't understand that I'm fighting off the terrorists by worrying about them. It's my own personal War on Terror.

That was a tiny joke, Dr. Hodges. Sometimes you don't seem to get my jokes. I don't know why I want you to laugh so badly. Ben finds me funny. He has this sudden bellow of appreciative laughter. He did, anyway—when I wasn't an obsessive bore with only one topic of conversation.

I guess it might be sensible to cover this "worrying" issue at one of our sessions because it's obviously just stupid superstition, and childish, too—as if I'm the center of the universe and what I think actually makes a difference. But I don't know, I can already guess all the sensible things you'd say, the perceptive questions you'd ask, trying to gently lead me to my own personal "Eureka!" moment. It all seems sort of pointless and dull. I'm not going to stop worrying. I like worrying. I come from a long line of worriers. It's in my blood.

I just want you to make it stop hurting, please, Dr. Hodges. That's why I'm paying you the big bucks. I just want to feel like me again.

I have wandered off from the point again. My point was that I've been imagining what it would be like if I lost memory. So, I hit my head, and I wake up and I discover it's 2008 and I've got fat and Alice has got thin and I'm married to this guy called Ben.

I wonder if I would fall in love with Ben all over again. That would be nice. I remember how it crept up so slowly on me, like that agonizingly slow old electric blanket which used to almost imperceptibly heat up my frosty sheets, second by second, until I'd think, "Hey, I haven't shivered in a while. Actually, I'm warm. I'm blissfully warm." That's how it was with Ben. I moved on from "I really shouldn't be leading this guy on when I have no interest" to "He's not that bad-looking really" to "I sort of enjoy being with him" to "Actually, I'm crazy about him."

I wonder if Ben would try to protect me from bad news, the way we've been skirting around certain subjects with Alice. He's a terrible liar. I'd say, "How many children have we got?" and he'd mumble, "Well, we haven't much luck there," and he'd scratch his chin and clear his throat and look away.

I would bossily insist on all the details, and eventually he'd just have to go ahead and say it.

Over the last seven years, you've had three IVF pregnancies and two natural pregnancies. None of those theoretical babies became real babies. The furthest you ever got was sixteen weeks and that one broke both our hearts so badly we thought we'd never recover. You've also been through eight failed IVF cycles. Yes, this has changed you. Yes, it has changed our marriage, and your relationships with your family and your friends. You are angry, bitter, and, frankly, you're often a bit strange. You are currently seeing a counselor after an embarrassing incident in a coffee shop. Yes, all this has cost a lot of money, but we really prefer not to go into the figures.

(Actually, Dr. Hodges, I've had six miscarriages. But Ben doesn't know this. I only got to five weeks, so it barely counted. Ben was away on a fishing trip with a friend, and I'd only done the pregnancy test the day before, and then the next day I started bleeding and that was that. He was so happy and dirty and sunburned when he came back from that trip, I couldn't tell him. It was just another lost little theoretical baby. Another tiny astronaut adrift in space.)

So, what would I say after Ben told me this long sorry story?

Well, this is the thing, Dr. Hodges, because I remember the old decisive, take-action, nerdy me and my first thought was that I would say something bracing along the lines of "if at first you don't succeed." After all, I was the woman who used to start each day by looking at a framed picture of a snow-capped mountain with a quote from Leonardo da Vinci: "Obstacles cannot crush me; every obstacle yields to stern resolve."

Good one, Leonardo.

But the more I think about it, the more I think that maybe I wouldn't say anything motivational at all.

It's quite possible that I might briskly slap my hands against my knees and say, "Sounds like it's time you gave up."

Chapter 15

It was Alice's mother who finally broke the silence. She said, "Gina was a friend of yours." She placed the salad bowl on the table without meeting Alice's eyes. "Actually, I think this bowl was a gift from Gina. That's probably why you thought of her."

Alice looked at the bowl and closed her eyes. She saw crumpled yellow paper. She tasted champagne. Possibly heard a peal of feminine laughter. Then nothing.

She opened her eyes again. Everyone was looking at her.

"Well, I really have to go," Elisabeth said, looking at her watch.

There was a flurry of relieved activity. "I think I've parked you in!" Roger said happily, pulling out a huge set of keys from his pocket and jumping to his feet.

"Don't forget to listen out for that call from Kate," said Elisabeth as she hurriedly backed out of the room. "Otherwise you're hosting a party tonight."

"I'll come and wave you off," Barb said as she and Roger followed Elisabeth down the hallway, obviously wanting to speak to her privately.

When it was just Alice and Frannie left alone, Alice picked a cherry tomato out of the salad and said, "So how do I know this Gina?"

"She lived across the road," said Frannie. "I think they moved in just before Olivia was born. You don't remember anything about her?"

"No. So she doesn't live across the road anymore?"

Frannie paused. She seemed to be struggling with the right thing to say. She said, "No. The family moved to Melbourne. Not that long ago."

Suddenly Alice got it.

Something went on between this Gina and Nick. It explained everything. That's why everybody had behaved so awkwardly.

Gina. Yes. The name was definitely associated with raw pain of some kind.

Why had she thought she was exempt from infidelity? It happened all the time. It was one of those tacky soap opera events that always seemed sort of vaguely comical when it happened to someone else but was earth-shakingly horrible when it happened to you.

Alice thought of poor Hillary Clinton. Imagine having the whole world know that your husband had cheated on you in such a *messy* way. You would have thought being president of the United States should have been a pretty *distracting* sort of job. It could happen to Nick.

After all, she realized with a shock, they'd been married for over ten years by now. Maybe Nick caught a slight case of the seven-year itch (which was practically a medical phenomenon, not really his fault), and then this awful manipulative woman took advantage of him, seduced him.

The bitch.

He was probably drunk. It probably just happened once. Maybe there was a party and Nick kissed her (quickly! hardly at all!) and Alice had over-reacted and Nick had apologized but Alice wouldn't budge (stupid!) and now they were getting a divorce because of it. It was all Alice's fault. And Gina's fault.

She must be very beautiful.

The thought of her beauty, and the thought of Nick finding her beautiful, hurt so sharply that she groaned out loud.

"Are you remembering?" asked Frannie anxiously.

"I think so." Alice massaged her forehead.

"Oh darling," said Frannie, and when Alice looked up and saw the utter sympathy on her grandmother's face, she knew it had been far more than just a kiss.

How could you, Nick? She wouldn't throw her arms around him on Sunday night. She would beat closed fists against his chest. How could he make her feel so safe in their relationship, so *smug*, so comfortable—and then maliciously rip it all away? Make her look like a fool?

Still, Hillary was prepared to stand by her man while his *semen stains on another woman's dress were analyzed*. Poor old Hillary.

It occurred to Alice that the whole Monica Lewinsky affair must be ten-year-old news now. She wondered if Hillary's marriage had survived.

The phone rang.

Alice stood up automatically and went to answer it.

"Hello?"

"Alice? Kate! I've just been doing a million things at once and I've only just now picked up your sister's messages! I was so *worried* when I saw you at the gym yesterday morning, I've been telling everybody, and I meant to call you, but I'm just run off my *feet* right now, as you well know, and then Melanie said she saw you laughing in a car at the traffic lights at Roseville, so I thought, Phew, she's okay! But now, your sister says you're possibly not well enough to host the party?"

Alice recognized the terribly cultured voice. It was the sleek blond woman she'd seen at the gym before she'd been sick all over George Clooney's shoes.

"Ah," said Alice.

"Of course, normally I'd say no problem! Have it here! In an instant! But what with the renovations, and Sam's mother staying with us, it's just literally, physically *impossible*. I mean, you don't have to do a thing tonight, you really don't, if you've still got a bit of a headache. I'll take care of everything. I have to admit I haven't been feeling that well myself, but I'll be all right, just a touch of the flu. Melanie said to me, 'You're a superwoman, Kate, how do you do it?' And I said, 'Well, no, Melanie, not a superwoman, just an *exhausted* woman trying to do what she can.' Sam says I just need to learn to say no and stop putting myself out for everyone, but I can't help it, I've always been that sort of person. Anyway, as I say, if your head is aching, I promise you can just put your feet up tonight, and we'll all rush around and bring you drinks. I mean, it's not like you have to cater or anything."

A strange inertia had crept over Alice as Kate spoke. Was this woman really her *friend*? Alice couldn't imagine wanting to talk to her for more than five minutes. She'd take Jane Turner's brisk snippiness any day over this woman's prissy sweetness with its razor-sharp edges.

She said, "Oh, okay, fine."

Who cared if hundreds of strange people turned up on her doorstep tonight? Her life was a nightmare and she may as well let it continue on its nightmarish way.

"We don't need to change it, then? Well, thank *goodness*. I knew I could rely on you! I had thought to myself your sister probably had it wrong. She's the bad-tempered career woman with all the infertility problems, isn't she? I guess she just has no inkling what a mother can do when she has to! All right, I must dash, and I'll look forward to seeing you tonight. All right! Bye!"

The line went dead. Alice slammed down the phone so hard, the cradle shook. How dare that horrible woman speak about Elisabeth like that? She thought about the way Elisabeth's face had caved in when she talked about the baby's heartbeat and she wanted to punch that woman's elegant nose.

"Is everything okay?" said Frannie.

But did that mean Alice had been complaining to Kate Harper about Elisabeth? "Alice?"

There was an old-lady quaver in Frannie's voice. Alice suddenly saw her as a stranger would: tiny and frail.

She pulled herself together. She was nearly thirty—whoops, forty—years old. She couldn't go and sob in her grandmother's lap anymore.

"Everything is fine," she said. "I told Kate Harper we could still have the party here."

"You did?" Her mother had walked back into the room, followed by Roger. "Are you sure you're up to it?"

"Oh sure," said Alice. "Sure. Why not?"

"She's remembering Gina," said Frannie.

"Oh, *darling*," said Barb, while Roger's face contorted into a horrendously mournful expression which was meant presumably to convey sympathy.

Apparently Roger had affairs when he was married to Nick's mother. "I'm afraid my ex-husband was something of a philanderer," Nick's mother had once told Alice with a delicate sigh, and Alice had been impressed at the way she could make even a cheating husband sound elegant and expensive.

Was Roger cheating on her mother now?

Maybe it wasn't so surprising that Nick had turned out to be a cheat, too. Wasn't there some old proverb about the orange not falling far from the tree? She should say that to Roger, look him straight in the eye and say sneeringly, "So, Roger, I see the orange doesn't fall far from the tree." But knowing her, she'd get it wrong and nobody would understand what she was trying to say. "What do you mean, darling?" her mother would say, brightly interested, spoiling the moment.

And actually, she had a funny feeling it was meant to be an apple, not an orange. The *apple* doesn't fall far from the tree. She felt a hysterical giggle rise in her throat. She was such an idiot. "Oh, *Alice*," they would all say.

"Alice?" said her mother. "Do you want a cup of tea? Or a painkiller?"

"Or a drink?" Roger furrowed his brow. "A brandy?"

"Oh, the last thing she needs is alcohol, Roger," snapped Frannie.

"I'm fine," said Alice.

She would think about all this later, when Roger wasn't there pulling his grotesquely sympathetic expressions.

She didn't care how much her world had changed. Apple or orange, Nick was absolutely nothing like his father.

Elisabeth's Homework for Dr. Hodges

Alice gave me such an imploring look, I almost considered cancel-ing my lunch, but it wasn't like I was leaving her *alone* with Roger-Dodger. That's what Ben calls him. It suits him.

Anyway, I didn't want to get into a conversation about Gina. My feelings about Gina are complex. Or maybe childish is a more appropriate word.

I was having lunch with the Infertiles.

We met about five years ago when I joined this "Infertility Sup-port Group." At first we were meeting at the community center and we had a facilitator, a professional like you, Dr. Hodges, who was there to keep us on track. The problem was that she kept trying to make us be positive. "Let's try and reframe that in a more positive light," she'd say. But we didn't want to be positive, thanks very much. We longed to say out loud all the bitter, negative, nasty things we kept in our heads. The medications, the hormones, and the relentless frustration of our lives make us bitchy, and you're not allowed to be bitchy in public or people won't like you. So we formed our own private group. Now we meet up once a month, at a swish restaurant, where we're not likely to come across Moth-ers' Groups and their circles of prams. We eat, we drink, and we bitch to our hearts' content—about doctors, family, friends—and most of all about the insensitivity of "Fertiles."

At first I resisted the idea of splitting the world into "Fertiles" and "Infertiles," as if we were in some science-fiction movie, but soon it became part of my new language. "What Fertiles can never understand . . ." we say to each other. Ben hates it when I say things like that. He doesn't really like the group, either, although he's never met them.

I'm making them sound awful, but they're not. Or maybe they are and I can't see it because I'm exactly the same. All I know is that sometimes it feels like lunch with those girls is the only thing that keeps me sane. And it's Mother's Day next Sunday. (As the television keeps loudly reminding me every two minutes.) That's the most painful day of the year for an Infertile. I always wake up feeling ashamed. Not sad so much. Just ashamed. Sort of stupid. It's a version of that feeling I had in high school when I was the only one in my class who didn't need to wear a bra. I'm not a proper woman, I'm not a *grown-up*.

Today we met at a restaurant in Manly right on the harbor. When I got there, they were all sitting outside in a dazzle of sun and water and blue sky, huddled over something in the middle of the table, their sunglasses pushed on top of their heads.

"Anne-Marie's pregnancy tests," said Kerry when she saw me. "We disapprove, of course, but see what you think."

Anne-Marie does this every time she does an IVF cycle. They tell you not to do a home pregnancy test after you've had an embryo transfer because the results are not conclusive. You might get a positive when you're not really pregnant because your body still has hormones left over from the "trigger injection" that mimic pregnancy, or you might get a negative just because it's too early to tell. The best thing is to wait for the blood test. I never do a pregnancy test because I like things to be conclusive and I'm a good girl, but Anne-Marie starts doing them the day after the transfer and admitted once that one day she did seven tests. We all have our own versions of this obsessive-compulsive behavior, so we don't scoff.

I squinted at Anne-Marie's tests. There were three, wrapped up in aluminum foil, as usual. They all looked negative to me, but there was no point telling her this. I said I thought I could maybe see a very faint pink line on one of them, and she said her husband had said he was sure they were all negative, and she'd yelled at him that he obviously wasn't trying. You have to want to see the second line, she'd told him, and they'd had a big fight. Anne-Marie has never had a successful IVF cycle and she's been trying for over ten years. Her doctors, her husband, her family are constantly campaigning for her to give up. She is only thirty, the youngest of us all, so she has time to ruin another decade of her life. Or maybe not, of course. That's the thing for all of us. The elusive happy ending could be just a cycle away.

Kerry (two years of IVF with donor eggs, one ectopic pregnancy that nearly killed her) said to Anne-Marie, "Elisabeth is ten days past transfer and I bet she hasn't even been tempted to do a test."

We all keep up to date with our IVF cycles by e-mail. Anne-Marie, Kerry, and I are all in the middle of cycles. The other three are in between, or just about to start.

To be honest, all the drama about Alice has meant that I haven't even been considering whether or not this cycle will work. In the early years, when I still believed in the power of the mind, I used to meditate each morning after a transfer. "Please stick around, little embryo," I'd chant. "Stick, stick, stick." I'd offer it bribes: *I'll take you to Disneyland when you're five. You'll never have to go to school if you don't feel up to it. If you would just please let me be your mother, please?*

But none of it seemed to make any difference. So now I just assume that it won't work, and that if it does work, I'll lose it anyway. This is meant to protect me, although it doesn't, because somehow the hope sneakily finds its way in. I'm never aware of the hope until it's gone, whooshed away like a rug pulled from under my feet, each time I hear another "I'm sorry."

The waiter came with our drinks and said, "Let me guess— you've left the kids with their dads and escaped for the day!"

Ah, the sweet innocence of the Fertiles. They assume any group of women of a certain age must surely be mothers.

"What's the point of looking like fucking mothers when we're fucking not," said Sarah, who is our newest recruit. She has only been through one IVF cycle, but she's already energetically bitter about infertility. She makes me realize I'm even jaded about being jaded. I admire the way she swears.

That sets us off on listing the ways we've been offended since we last met.

We had:

The boss who said, "Going through IVF is a choice, it's not like getting the flu, so, no, I can't sign your sick-leave form."

The aunt who said, "Just relax and have a massage, you're not getting pregnant because you're too tense." (Oh, there's always one of those.)

The brother who said (with screaming child in the background), "You've got such a romantic idea of having children. It's just bloody hard work."

The cousin who said sympathetically, "I know exactly what you're going through. I've been trying to finish this Ph.D. for six years."

"What about your sister?" Kerry said to me. "You said something in your last e-mail about something she'd done that had you infuriated."

"She's the supermum with three children, isn't she?" Anne-Marie's lip curled. "The one who doesn't need to work because she's got the rich husband."

They all looked at me avidly, ready to be disgusted with Alice, because, to be honest, Dr. Hodges, I've complained about her before.

But I thought about laughing with Alice on the way home from the hospital and the horrified, hurt expression on her face when she talked to Nick on the phone. I thought about how she'd said, "Don't you like me anymore?" and how when I'd left her today, her dress was all crumpled from her sleep and her hair was sticking up on one side. That was so typically old Alice, not to even look at herself in the mirror before she came downstairs. And I thought about how she'd cried at the hospital with me when Olivia was born, and how she'd said so innocently to us all today, "Who is Gina?"

I felt sick with shame, Dr. Hodges. I wanted to say to them, "Hey, that's my little sister you're talking about."

Instead I told them about how Alice had lost her memory and thought she was twenty-nine, and how it had made me think a lot about what my old self would say about this life I'm leading. I said I thought my younger self might think it was time to give up. Just to give up. Let it go. Walk away. No more injections. No more test tubes of warm blood. No more grief.

Of course they snapped to attention like good soldiers who know their duty.

"Never give up," they told me, and one by one they recounted horrendous stories of infertility and miscarriage that had all ended with healthy bouncing babies.

I listened and nodded and smiled and watched the seagulls squabbling.

I don't know, Dr. Hodges. I just don't know.

Over lunch, Roger took it upon himself to bring Alice up to date with his own interpretation of every historical event that had taken place over the last ten years, while her mother decided to simultaneously do the same thing with the personal lives of everyone she'd ever met.

"And then the U.S. invaded Iraq, because old matey, Saddam, was stockpiling weapons of mass destruction," intoned Roger.

"Except there were no weapons," interrupted Frannie.

"Well, who really knows for sure?"

"You *are* joking, Roger."

"And then Marianne Elton, oh, of course you remember her, she used to coach Elisabeth's netball team," said Barb. "Well, she married Jonathon Knox, that nice young plumber we had over that time when we had that problem with the toilets that very cold Easter, they had the wedding on some tropical island, so inconvenient for everyone, and the poor flower girl got badly sunburned, anyhow, two years ago they had a baby daughter called Madeline, which made Madeline very happy as you can imagine. I said, 'Well, I never expected my girls to name their children Barbara,' which I didn't, but Madeline is such a popular name now, anyhow, poor Madeline turned out . . ."

". . . and let me tell you, Alice, exactly what the government should have done straight after the Bali attacks . . ."

"Oh, and one of Felicity's boys was there in Bali!" said Barb, the personal world suddenly intersecting with the political. "He flew out *the day before*. Felicity thinks it means he's been chosen to do something great, but so far he doesn't seem to do anything much but visit Facebook, is that what it's called, Roger—Facebook?"

Frannie said, "Does any of this mean anything to you at all, Alice?"

Alice had only been listening with one part of her mind. She was busy thinking about the concept of forgiveness. It was such a lovely, generous idea when it wasn't linked to something awful that needed forgiving. Was she a forgiving person? She had no idea. She'd never been called upon to forgive something as big as infidelity. Anyway, did Nick *want* her forgiveness?

She said to Frannie, "I'm not exactly sure."

Some things that Roger had been saying had maybe seemed familiar, as if they were things she'd learned once at school and then forgotten. When he talked about terrorist attacks, she felt a reflexive feeling of horror, and maybe even some fleeting memories: a woman in a sun visor with a hand pressed to her mouth saying, "Oh my word, oh my word." But she couldn't remember where she was when she first heard about them, if she'd been with Nick, or alone, if she'd watched them on TV or heard about them on the radio. She also seemed to recognize some parts of her mother's stories. There was something familiar, for example, about the phrase "sunburned flower girl," like the punch line of a joke she'd heard before.

Frannie was saying, "Well, she's going to have to go back to the doctor. There's something not right here. Look at her. It's obvious."

"I doubt they can just transplant her memories back in her head," said Roger.

"Oh, I'm sorry, Roger, I didn't realize you had experience as a neurosurgeon," said Frannie.

"Who wants a nice piece of custard tart, then?" said Barb brightly.

Chapter 16

A lice was alone.

There had been a lot of intense debate about the wisdom of leaving her alone after lunch. Barb and Roger had their Saturday-afternoon advanced salsa-dancing class. They said they could *easily* miss it just this once, although, of course, it was an especially important class because they were rehearsing for the Family Talent Night at Frannie's retirement village, but really and truly, it would be no problem to miss it if Alice needed them there. Frannie had an important meeting at the retirement village—something to do with Christmas. She was chairing the meeting but she could *easily* call and ask Bev or maybe Dora to do it, although they were both nervy public speakers, and it was likely they'd be railroaded by this rather domineering new resident, but that would hardly be the end of the world; her granddaughter came first.

"I'll be fine," Alice had repeated over and over. "I'm nearly *forty* years old!" she'd added flippantly, but there must have been something strange about the way she'd said it because they'd all stared at her for a moment, and then a whole new round of offers to stay began.

"Elisabeth will be back any minute," she'd told them, shooing them out of the kitchen, down the hallway, and out the door. "Off you go! I'll be fine!"

And within minutes, they were packed into Roger's big shiny car, shadowy figures waving at her behind tinted windows, and the car was disappearing down the driveway, gravel flying.

"I'll be fine," Alice repeated quietly to herself.

She saw old Mrs. Bergen coming out of the house next door wearing a big Mexican hat and carrying a pair of gardening shears. She liked Mrs. Bergen. She was teaching her how to garden. She'd given Alice lots of advice about the problems with her lemon tree (she suggested Nick should give it the occasional "tinkle," which he had, with rather revolting enthusiasm) and was always bringing over cuttings from her own garden for Alice and gently pointing out what needed watering or pruning or weeding. Mrs. Bergen didn't like cooking much, so in return Alice took over Tupperware containers with leftover casseroles and pieces of quiche and carrot cake. Mrs. Bergen had already crocheted three sets of bootees for the baby and was starting on a matinee jacket and bonnet.

But that was all ten years ago.

So were those tiny items now faded and dusty in a cupboard somewhere?

Alice lifted her hand in affectionate greeting. Mrs. Bergen lowered her head and turned pointedly in the direction of her azaleas.

Oh.

There was no mistaking it. Mrs. Bergen had snubbed her.

Would sweet, chubby *Mrs. Bergen* yell and swear at her, as Nick had, if Alice went over to say hello? That would be like when the little girl's head spun around in *The Exorcist*.

Alice went back inside quickly and closed the door behind her, feeling an absurd desire to cry.

Maybe Mrs. Bergen was going senile and didn't recognize Alice anymore. That was a perfectly reasonable explanation. Yes, that would do. For now.

Once she got back her memory, everything would fall neatly into place. "Oh," she'd say. "Of course!"

Well. What next?

She wondered exactly what she did on these weekends when "Nick had the children." Did she like the break? Was she lonely? Did she long for the children to come back?

The sensible thing to do would be to explore the house for clues about her life. That way she'd be ready for when Nick came back tomorrow night. She should have a persuasive presentation prepared: Ten reasons why we should not be getting this divorce.

Maybe she would find something about Gina. Love letters to Nick? But presumably he would have taken those with him when he moved out.

Or perhaps she should be doing something for this party tonight? But what? The party seemed strangely irrelevant.

Actually, she didn't want to be in the house at all. Her stomach felt uncomfortably full from all that custard tart she'd eaten. "You want a *second* piece?" her mother had said with pleased surprise and Alice guessed that this was unusual for her.

She would go for a walk. That would clear her mind. It was a beautiful day. Why spend it indoors?

She went upstairs and then stopped in the hallway, looking at the other three bedroom doors. That must be where the children slept now. She and Nick had left them empty, except for the one they were going to use for the baby's nursery. They'd spent a lot of time in there, sitting cross-legged on the floor, planning and imagining. They'd picked the paint color: *Ocean Azure*. It would work even if the baby surprised them by being a girl (which she had—a girl!).

Alice tentatively pushed open the nursery door.

Well. What did she expect? Of course there was no white crib or change table, no rocking chair. It wasn't a nursery anymore.

Instead there was a single unmade bed, strewn with clothes and a bookshelf crammed with books, old empty bottles of perfume, and glass jars. The walls were almost entirely plastered with moody black-and-white pictures of European cities. Alice saw a tiny square of blue in between two posters. She went over and put her finger to it. *Ocean Azure.*

There was a desk against one wall. She saw a ring binder labeled *Madison Love.* The handwriting was familiar. It looked like Alice's own writing when she was in primary school. She noticed an open recipe book face down on the desk and picked it up. A recipe for lasagne. Wasn't Madison too little to be *cooking?* And for posters of European cities? Alice was still playing with dolls at that age. Her own daughter was making her nine-year-old self feel inferior.

She carefully placed the recipe book back down and tiptoed out of the room.

The next bedroom door was closed and there was a note pinned to it.

KEEP OUT. DO NOT ENTER WITHOUT PERMISSION. NO GIRLS ALLOWED. THE CONSEQUENCES WILL BE DEATH.

Goodness. Alice let go of the door handle and backed away. She was a girl, after all. This must be Tom's room. Maybe he had it booby-trapped. Little boys. How terrifying.

The next room was more welcoming. She had to push through beads hanging from the doorway. The bed was a little girl's dream: four-poster, with a purple gauze canopy. Fairy wings hung from a hook on the wall. There were tiny glass ornaments shaped like cupcakes, dozens of stuffed animals, a makeup mirror with lights around it, hair clips and ribbons, a music box, glittery bangles and long beads, a pink portable stereo, a dress-up box filled with clothes. Alice sat down and rifled through the dress-up box. She pulled out a familiar green summer dress and held it up in front of her. She'd bought it especially for her honeymoon. It was one of the most expensive dresses she'd ever owned. Dry-clean only. Now it had a brown stain on the neckline and a jagged hemline where someone had taken to it with a pair of scissors. Alice dropped the dress, her head swimming. There was a sickly-sweet scent in the room like strawberry lip gloss. Fresh air. She definitely needed air.

She went to her own bedroom and quickly found shorts and a T-shirt in the chest of drawers, and her sneakers and sunglasses still in the rucksack she'd brought back from the hospital. She hurried back downstairs and pulled off one of the baseball caps from the hat stand. It said PHILADEL-PHIA on the brim.

She left the house, locking the door behind her and noting with relief that Mrs. Bergen had gone back inside.

Which way? She turned to the left and took off at a brisk pace. A woman was approaching from the other direction, wheeling a stroller with a stern-faced baby who was sitting very straight-backed and solemn. As Alice got closer, the baby frowned up at her, while the woman smiled and said, "Not running today?"

"Not today." Alice smiled back and kept walking.

Running? Good heavens. She *hated* running. She remembered the way she and her friend Sophie used to shuffle around the oval in the high school, moaning and clutching their sides, while Mr. Gillespie called out, "Oh for God's sakes, you girls!"

Sophie! She would give Sophie a call when she got home. If she hadn't been confiding in Elisabeth, maybe Sophie knew more about what was going on with her and Nick.

She kept walking, seeing houses that had doubled in size, like cakes in the oven. Red-brick cottages had been transformed into smooth mushroom-colored mansions with pillars and turrets.

Actually, it was interesting, because she was walking quicker and quicker, sort of bouncing along the pavement, and the idea of running didn't seem that stupid at all. It seemed sort of . . . pleasant.

Was it a bad idea with a head injury? Probably a very bad idea. But maybe it would jar all those memories back into place.

She began to run.

Her arms and legs fell into a smooth rhythm; she began to breathe deep, slow breaths, in through the nostrils and out through the mouth. Oh, this felt good. It felt right. It felt like something she did.

At Rawson Street she turned left and picked up her pace. The fat red leaves of the liquid ambers trembled in the sunlight. A white car packed with teenagers screeched by, thudding with music. She passed a driveway where a group of kids were shrieking and brandishing water guns. Someone started up a lawn mower.

Up ahead, the white car with the teenagers pulled up at the corner.

A momentous feeling of panic exploded in her chest. It was happening again, just like in the car with Elisabeth. Her legs quivered so ridiculously she actually had to crouch down on the footpath, waiting for whatever it was to pass. A scream of horror was lodged in her throat. If she let it out, it would be very embarrassing.

She looked around, her hands on the ground to balance herself, her chest heaving, and saw that the children with the water pistols were still running back and forth, as if the world hadn't turned black and evil. She looked back at the end of the street where the white car was waiting for a break in the traffic.

It was something to do with a car pulling up at that corner.

She closed her eyes and saw the brake lights of a green four-wheel-drive. The number plate said: GINA 333.

Nothing else. She felt simultaneously hot and cold, as if she had the flu. For *God's sake*. Was she about to be sick again? All that custard tart. The children could clean it up with their water pistols.

A horn tooted. "Alice?"

Alice opened her eyes.

A car had pulled up on the other side of the road and a man was leaning out the window. He opened the car door and quickly crossed the street toward her.

"What happened?"

He stood in front of her and blocked out the sun. Alice squinted mutely up at him. She couldn't make out the features of his face. He seemed extremely tall.

He bent down beside her and touched her arm.

"Did you faint?"

She could see his face now. It was an ordinary, kind, thin, middle-aged sort of face, the unassuming face of a friendly newsagent who chatted to you about the weather.

"Come on. Up you get," he said, and lifted her by both elbows so she rose straight to her feet. "We'll get you home."

He led her across the street to the car and deposited her in the passenger seat. Alice couldn't decide what to say, so she didn't say anything. A voice from the back of the car said, "Did you fall over and hurt yourself?"

Alice turned and saw a little boy with liquid brown eyes staring at her anxiously.

She said, "I just felt a bit funny."

The man got back in the car and started the engine. "We were on our way over to your place and then Jasper spotted you. Were you going for a run?"

"Yes," said Alice. They stopped at the corner of Rawson and King. She thought of the car with the GINA number plate and felt nothing.

"I saw Neil Morris at the IGA this morning," said the man. "He said he saw you being carried out of the gym on a stretcher yesterday! I left a few messages for you, but I didn't . . ."

His voice drifted away.

"I fell over and hit my head during my 'spin class,'" said Alice. "I'm fine today, but I shouldn't have been running. It was stupid of me."

The little boy called Jasper giggled in the backseat. "You're not stupid! Sometimes my dad is stupid. Like today, he forgot three things and we had to keep stopping the car and he'd say, 'Boofhead!' It was pretty funny. Okay, first thing was his wallet. Second thing was his mobile phone. Third thing—ummm, okay, third thing—Dad, what was the third thing you forgot?"

They were pulling into Alice's driveway. They stopped the car and the little boy gave up on the third thing and threw open his car door and ran toward the veranda.

The man pulled on the handbrake and then turned to look at Alice with gentle concern. He put a hand on her shoulder. "Well, I think you'd better put your feet up while Jasper and I take care of those balloons."

Balloons. For the party, presumably.

"This is a bit awkward," began Alice.

The man smiled. He had a lovely smile. He said, "What is?"

Alice said, "I have absolutely no idea who you are."

(Although, in truth, there was something about the way he smiled and the feeling of his hand on her shoulder that was giving her an idea.)

The man's hand sprang back like an elastic band.

He said, "Alice! It's me. Dominick."

Frannie's Letter to Phil

Me again, Phil.

Barb and Roger took me for lunch at Alice's place today.

Physically she seems fine, but she is definitely not herself. She didn't remember Gina! It was disconcerting. Gina played such a big part in Alice's life. Almost too big a part.

Barb talked about it all the way home. "Sometimes I wish Alice had never met Gina," she fretted. "You can't change the past," pronounced Roger, and we were all quite overcome by his wisdom. He's a philosopher, that fellow.

It's not relevant now but I always thought that Gina did dominate Alice. (Alice does have a slight tendency toward hero worship.) I remember her making some comment about Alice's outfit at Olivia's birthday party last year. It was something along the lines of "Your such-and-such blouse looks nicer with that skirt." Alice went straight back upstairs and changed. I noticed Nick was watching the whole incident and didn't look too happy about it.

After Barb and Roger dropped me off, we had yet another Social

Committee meeting. This time we were discussing plans for this year's Christmas party. Mr. Mustache suggested a "Casino Night." People loved the idea! Can you think of anything less Christmassy, Phil?

He's the most aggravating man.

I will admit, however, that he did make a point of asking me whether Alice liked the talcum powder.

Elisabeth's Homework for Dr Hodges

A funny thing happened when I got home from lunch with the Infertiles. Not exactly ha-ha funny. Just stupid ironic funny.

Driving home after lunch, I kept thinking about "Giving Up." The idea grew stronger and stronger in my head. It suddenly seems quite obvious to me. I can't go through another miscarriage. I can't. The thought of it happening again gives me the feeling of a block of concrete dropping on my chest. I have had enough. I didn't know I'd had enough, but it turns out I have.

We used to keep setting those deadlines. No more after my fortieth birthday. No more after Christmas. But then each time we'd think, well, but what else is there to do? We'd traveled, we'd been to lots of parties, lots of movies and concerts, we'd slept in. We'd done all those things that people with children seem to miss so passionately. We didn't want those things anymore. We wanted a baby.

I remember thinking about how mothers were prepared to run into burning buildings to save their children's lives. I thought I should be able to go through a bit more suffering, a bit more inconvenience to *give* my children life. It made me feel noble. But now I realize I'm a crazy woman running into a burning house for children who don't exist. My children were never going to exist. They were always in my mind. That's what's so embarrassing about all this. Each time I sobbed for a lost baby, it was like sobbing over the end of a relationship when I'd never even gone out with the guy. My babies weren't babies. They were just microscopic clusters of cells that weren't ever going to be anything else. They were just my own desperate hopes. Dream babies.

And people have to give up on dreams. Aspiring ballet dancers have to accept that their bodies aren't right for ballet. Nobody even feels that sorry for them. Oh, well, think of another job. My body isn't right for babies. Bad luck.

At the pedestrian crossing I saw a pregnant woman, a woman pushing a pram, a woman holding a child's hand. And I actually felt nothing, Dr. Hodges. Nothing! That's a big thing for an Infertile—to see a pregnant woman and feel nothing. No knife-in-the-stomach feeling of bitterness. No ugly envy twisting my mouth.

So here's the funny thing.

I got home, and for once, Ben wasn't in the garage working on his car. He was sitting at the kitchen table with paperwork spread out all around him, and I noticed his eyes were a bit red and puffy.

He said, "I've been thinking."

I told him so had I, but he could go first.

He said he'd been thinking about what Alice had said last week and he'd decided she was one hundred percent right.

Oh, *Alice*.

Alice sat on the couch and watched Dominick using a helium tank to blow up blue and silver balloons. He and Jasper had finally got sick of breathing in the helium and talking in chipmunk voices. Jasper had laughed so hard at his dad squeakily singing "Over the Rainbow" that Alice had worried he might stop breathing. Now he was outside in the backyard, using a remote control to expertly operate a miniature helicopter.

"He's very cute," said Alice, watching him. She'd gathered that Jasper was in the same class as Olivia. Her daughter. The one with the fat blond pigtails.

"When he's not being a psychotic monster," said Dominick.

Alice laughed. Perhaps too much. She didn't really get parent humor. Maybe he really was a psychotic monster and that wasn't funny.

"So," she said. "How long have you and I been, ummm, seeing each other for?"

Dominick glanced quickly at her and away again. He tied the end of the balloon and watched it float straight up to the ceiling with the others.

Without looking at her, he said, "About a month."

Alice had told Dominick that the doctors had said her memory loss was only temporary. He looked terrified and seemed to be talking to her gently and carefully, as if she had a mild intellectual disability. Unless that was the way he always talked to her, of course.

"And it's, ah, going well?" asked Alice recklessly. It was bizarre. Had she kissed him? *Slept with him?* He was very tall. Not unattractive. Just a stranger. She felt both repelled and mildly titillated by the idea. It reminded her of gurgly, giggly teenage conversations. Oh my God, imagine having sex with *him*.

"Yup," said Dominick. He was doing something funny and nervous with his mouth. He was one of those awkward, geeky types.

He picked up another balloon and hooked it over the nozzle of the helium tank. He looked at her properly, full in the face, and said, almost sternly, "Well, *I* think so, anyway." Actually, he was not unattractive.

"Oh." Alice felt flustered and exposed. "Well, good. I guess."

She longed for Nick to be sitting next to her. His hand warm on her leg. Claiming her. So she could enjoy talking, maybe even flirting, with this perfectly nice man in an appropriate, safe way.

"You seem different," said Dominick.

"In what way?"

"I don't know how to explain it."

He didn't say anything else. Apparently he wasn't a talker, like Nick. She wondered what she saw in him. Did she even like him that much? He seemed sort of dull.

"What do you do for a living?" she asked. The standard dating question. Trying to unfairly slot him into a personality type.

"I'm an accountant," he said.

Fabulous. "Oh, right."

He grinned and said, "Just testing to see if you really had lost your memory. I'm a grocer. A fruit and veg man."

"Really?" She was imagining free mangoes and pineapples.

"Nah!"

Oh, God, this man was a nerd.

"I'm a school principal."

"No, you're not."

"I'm being serious now. I'm principal at the school."

"What school?"

"Where your kids go. That's how we met."

The school principal. *Straight to the principal's office!*

"So you'll be there tonight? At this party?"

"Yes. I'm sort of wearing two hats, because Jasper is in kindergarten, and this party is for parents of kindergarten kids. So I'll be . . ."

He had a habit of not completely finishing his sentences. His voice just drifted away, as if he thought it was so obvious how the sentence finished there was no point saying it out loud.

"And why am I hosting it?" asked Alice. It seemed extraordinary. Why would she even think of doing such a thing?

Dominick raised his eyebrows. "Well, because you and your friend Kate Harper are Class Mums."

"Like classy mothers?"

He smiled uncertainly. "The Class Mums arrange social events for all the other mothers, and communicate with the teachers, organize the reading roster, and, ah, that sort of . . ."

Oh Lord. It sounded horrendous. She'd become one of those volunteer-ing, involved type of people. She was probably really proud and smug; she'd always known she had a tendency toward smugness. She could just imagine herself swanning about in her beautiful clothes.

"You do a lot for the school," said Dominick. "We're very lucky to have you. Speaking of which, it's the big day coming up! Wow! I hope you're going to be well enough for it!"

That man on the treadmill at the gym had mentioned a "big day," too. "What do you mean?" asked Alice with a sense of foreboding.

"You're getting us into the Guinness Book of Records."

She smiled, ready to laugh at his next joke.

"No, really. You don't remember at all? You're baking the world's biggest lemon meringue pie on Mother's Day. It's a big event. All the money raised is going to breast cancer research."

Alice remembered her dream about the giant rolling pin. Ah. The rolling pin wasn't a symbol at all. It was just a giant rolling pin. Her dreams were always so disappointingly obvious.

"I'm baking it?" she said in a panic. "This huge lemon meringue pie?"

"No, no. You've got one hundred mums baking it," said Dominick. "It's going to be amazing." He knotted the end of another balloon together. Alice looked up and saw that the ceiling was now covered with blue and silver balloons.

Tonight she was hosting a party and next weekend she was planning to break a world record. Good Lord. What had she become?

She looked back down and saw that Dominick was staring at her.

"I've worked it out," he said. "What's different about you."

He sat down beside her. Much too close. Alice tried to move unobtru-sively away from him, but it was too hard on the squishy leather sofa with-out making a production of it. So she sat passively with her hands in her lap, schoolgirl style; surely he wasn't going to do anything, with his son just a few feet away.

He was so close, she could see tiny black whiskers on his chin and smell him: toothpaste, washing powder. (Nick smelled of coffee, aftershave, last night's garlic.)

Up close, his eyes were the same liquid chocolate as his son's. (Nick's were either hazel or green, depending on the light, the irises were rimmed with gold, and his eyelashes were so fair, they looked white in the sun.)

Dominick leaned in closer. Oh sweet heavens above, the school principal was going to kiss her, and it would be wrong to slap his face because she might have already kissed him before.

No. He pressed his thumb in between her eyebrows. What was he *doing*? Was it some sort of weird middle-aged-people ritual? Was she meant to do it back to him?

"You've lost your frown," he said. "You always have this little frown right here, as if you're concentrating, or worrying about something, even when you're happy. Now it's . . ."

He took his thumb away. Alice exhaled with relief. She said, "I don't know if you're meant to tell a woman she has a permanent frown." It came out sounding flirtatious.

"Either way, you're still gorgeous," he said, and put his hand to the back of her head and kissed her.

It was not unpleasant.

"I *saw* that!"

Jasper stood in front of them, his helicopter dangling by a rotor from one hand. His eyes were wide and delighted.

Alice put her fingers to her mouth. She'd kissed another man. She hadn't just let him kiss her; she'd kissed him back. Out of nothing more than interest really. Politeness. (Maybe the teeniest flicker of attraction.) Guilt blossomed like heartburn across her chest.

Jasper chortled. "I'm going to tell Olivia that my dad kissed her mum!" He danced on the spot, punching his fists in the air, his face screwed up in an ecstasy of pleasure and disgust. "My dad kissed her mum! My dad kissed her mum!"

Goodness. Were Alice's own children like this? Sort of . . . demented?

Dominick touched Alice gently and respectfully on her arm, and stood up. He grabbed Jasper and held him upside down by his ankles. Jasper shrieked with gasps of laughter and dropped his helicopter.

Alice watched them and felt a weird sense of dissociation. Did she really just kiss that man? That shy school principal? That jolly dad?

Maybe it was her head injury that made her do it. Yes, she had a medical reason. She was not herself.

Then she remembered there was no need to feel guilty, because of Nick's affair with that Gina girl. Right. Now they were even.

Jasper noticed that a part of his helicopter had broken off and he yelled and squirmed as though in terrible agony. Dominick said, "What? What is it, mate?" and turned him upright.

Alice's head began to ache again.

When was Elisabeth coming back? She needed Elisabeth.

Elisabeth's Homework for Dr. Hodges

As I was driving back over to Alice's place, I thought about Gina. I often think about her now. She has acquired an aura of mystery. Once upon a time I just found her irritating.

I'm not sure why I disliked her so much from the beginning. Maybe it was just because it was clear that she and Michael and Alice and Nick had formed such a cozy foursome. They used to be in and out of each other's places all the time. No need to knock. Lots of private jokes. Feeding each other's kids. Gina would walk straight over from her house in her swimming costume—no T-shirt, no towel wrapped under her armpits—just entirely unself-conscious, like a child. She had a softish, round, mocha-colored body. Beautiful jiggly breasts that dragged the men's eyes along with them. I think I remember some story about them all getting drunk and swimming naked in the pool one summer's night. So very seventies of them.

She and Alice were all bright and giggly and swilling champagne, and I was a stiff cardboard cutout. My laugh was forced. It seemed to happen so quickly that she knew my sister better than me.

Gina's kids were IVF pregnancies. She asked lots of expertly interested questions. She would sympathetically rub my hand (very touchy-feely type, soft, sweet-smelling kisses on each cheek every time you saw her; I once heard Roger say to her, "Oh, I do like the way you *European* ladies kiss hello!"). Gina said she understood *exactly* what I was going through. And quite probably she did, except that it was all behind her now. I could tell her memories were rose-colored because of the happy ending. You'd think I would have been inspired by her—she was a success story. She'd traveled across the infertility minefield and got safely to the other side. But I found her patronizing. It's easy to think the minefield wasn't that bad once you're safely watching other people get blown up. She couldn't imagine her children not existing. They were too real, filling up her mind. I felt like I couldn't complain to Alice because Gina was probably in her ear, telling her, with the benefit of experience, that it wasn't that bad and I was just whinging and being melodramatic.

One night I called Alice to tell her that we'd lost another baby.

I had terrible nausea with that pregnancy. I gagged every time I cleaned my teeth. I had to run out of a cinema because the smell of the woman's perfume sitting next to me (Opium) combined with her popcorn made me retch. I'd thought for sure it must be a sign that this one was going to be the lucky one. Ha-ha. It meant nothing.

When I rang Alice, she answered the phone laughing. Gina was in the background, yelling out something about pineapple. They were inventing cocktails for some school function. Of course Alice stopped laughing when I told her the news and put on her sad voice, but she couldn't quite stamp out the leftover laughter. I felt like the boring sister with yet another boring miscarriage, ruining the good times for everybody with her slightly disgusting gynecological bad news. Alice must have signaled to Gina, because her laughter stopped like a switch had been turned off.

I told her not to worry, that we could talk later, and hung up fast. Then I threw the phone across the room and it smashed a beautiful vase that I'd bought in Italy when I was twenty, and I lay on the couch and screamed into a cushion. I still grieve for the vase.

Alice didn't call me the next day. And the day after that was when Madison ran through the French doors. So we were distracted and busy at the hospital worrying about her. My miscarriage got forgotten in between cocktails with Gina and Madison. Alice never even mentioned it. I wondered if she forgot.

I think that's when the coldness started between us.

Yes, I know. Petty and childish, but there you have it.

Chapter 17

Frannie's Letter to Phil

I'm tucked up in bed again, Phil. It's been a long day.

Who should be sitting next to me again in the dining room at dinner tonight? You guessed it. Mr. Mustache.

The man seems to have taken a shine to me. I don't know why because we have absolutely nothing in common and we appear to disagree on everything.

He was talking about his mustache tonight. He said that he'd always wanted a mustache but that his wife had never let him grow one because it would be "too ticklish when she kissed him." (Too much information, as the young people say!) He said that after she died, he'd "cultivated this beautiful specimen."

He asked what I thought of his mustache and I said I thought it was most unattractive.

He roared with laughter.

Then he asked how I'd managed to escape the "shackles of marriage." (Do you mind!)

You will be astonished to hear that I told him about you. Not the whole story. I just said that I was pretty much an old maid when I finally met "Mr. Right." I said that we were engaged to be married, but unfortunately the wedding never took place. It wasn't meant to be.

Mr. Mustache was uncharacteristically quiet. Then he said, "I'm sorry to hear that, Frannie," and touched my hand, and for a moment I couldn't speak.

He had an unexpectedly gentle touch

Of course, only a few minutes after that, he was regaling the whole table with the most tasteless "dirty joke" you have ever heard.

"Nick!"

Alice sat bolt upright, her heart racing, her breath shallow. She felt about the bed with her hand for Nick, to wake him up and tell him about the nightmare, although the details were already slipping away and starting to seem silly. Something to do with a . . . tree?

A huge tree. Branches black against a stormy sky.

"Nick?"

Normally he woke up immediately when she had a nightmare, his voice gruff with sleep, automatically soothing her, "It's okay, it's just a dream, just a bad dream," Part of her mind would always think, He's going to make such a great dad.

She patted at the sheets. He must have gone to get a glass of water. Or had he not come to bed yet?

Nick is not here, Alice. He lives somewhere else. He flew back from Portugal this morning and you weren't there to meet him. Maybe "Gina" picked him up at the airport. Oh, and you kissed that school principal today. Remember? Remember? Can you just please REMEMBER your life, you fool!

She snapped on the bedside lamp, threw back the sheets, and got out of bed. There was no way she was going back to sleep now.

Right.

She ran her palms down her nightie. It was a sleeveless, shimmery oyster-colored silk. It must have cost a fortune. It was just so stupid that she didn't remember buying it. She'd had enough. She wanted to remember everything, right now.

She went into the bathroom and found the bottle of perfume she'd used at the hospital. She sprayed it in big lavish swoops and sniffed deeply. She was going to run and jump straight into that vortex of memory.

The perfume assaulted her nostrils, making her feel a bit sick. She waited for the images of the last ten years to fill her mind, but all she could see were the smiling strange faces from tonight's party, and Dominick's liquid brown eyes, and her mother smiling coyly at Roger, and the disappointed lines around Elisabeth's mouth.

All these recent memories were too fresh and confusing. That was the problem. There was no space for all the old memories.

She sat down on the cold bathroom tiles and hugged her knees in close. All those people tonight, trooping happily into her house, helping themselves to glasses of champagne and tiny canapés from white-aproned caterers (who had turned up at five p.m., taking over the kitchen, blandly efficient), standing around her backyard in little groups, high heels sinking into the grass. "Alice!" they said so familiarly, kissing her on both cheeks. (There was a lot of kissing of both cheeks in 2008.) "How *are* you?" Hairstyles were smoother and flatter than in 1998. It made everyone's heads seem comically smaller.

People talked about petrol prices (how could there be *anything* to say on such a boring topic?), property prices, development applications, and some political scandal. They talked about their children—"Emily," "Harry," "Isabel"—as if Alice knew them intimately. There were hilarious jokes about some school excursion she'd apparently attended where things had gone hilariously wrong. There were serious, lowered voices about some teacher everybody hated. They talked to her about jazz ballet lessons, saxophone lessons, swimming lessons, the school band, the school fête, the tuckshop, the extension class for "gifted and talented" kids. None of it made any sense. The conversations were so detailed—so many names and dates and times and acronyms—the PE-something class, the WE-something teacher. On two occasions different women hissed the unfamiliar word *"Botox"* in Alice's ear as another woman walked by. Alice couldn't be sure if it was a contemptuous insult or an envious compliment.

Dominick hovered unobtrusively close by, explaining to people that she wasn't quite herself after her accident, that she really should be in bed. "Typical Alice to soldier on!" they said. (Was it typical? How strange. Normally she loved the excuse to put herself to bed.) It didn't really seem to matter all that much that she didn't recognize a single person. Nodding and smiling seemed enough to keep the conversations flowing, while Alice kept being distracted by things in her own backyard: Was that a vegetable garden in the corner? There was a swing set creaking gently in the evening breeze—had the Sultana slid down that slippery dip into her arms?

Now Alice traced her fingertips along the grouting of the white bathroom tiles. (She and Nick had done a tiling course together in preparation for this job—number 46 on their Impossible Dream list.) She didn't remember doing it. It was possible she had lost *thousands* of memories.

Was Nick in bed with Gina right now?

Gina's name had come up at the party. It had been awkward. Alice had been talking—or, more accurately, listening—to a woman wearing distractingly large diamond earrings and a man who was obsessively interested in getting another mini-samosa and was watching the caterer's plates with an eagle eye. The topic was homework and how much of a strain it was on the parents.

"It's three a.m. and I'm sticking paddle-pop sticks together to make Erin's early settler's house, and I tell you, something inside me just snaps"— the earring woman clicked her fingers and her diamonds flashed.

"I can imagine," Alice had murmured, although she couldn't. Why hadn't this Erin kid done her own homework? Or why hadn't they done it together? Alice imagined laughing happily with a sweet daughter while they glued together paddle-pop sticks and drank hot chocolate. Also, Alice was *great* at that sort of thing. Her kid's early settler's house would be the best in the class.

"Well, they've got to learn discipline, haven't they? Isn't that the point of homework?" said the man. "Hey! Excuse me! Are they samosas you've got there? Oh, kebabs. Anyway, these days you can just Google anything."

Did he say giggle? Goggle? Alice's head ached.

"You can't Google an early settler's cottage made of paddle-pop sticks into existence! Anyway, I bet *you* don't have to help them with their homework, do you?" The woman had given Alice a womanly "Men!" look, which Alice had tried to return. (She was sure Nick would have helped.) "I'm sure Laura has it all done by the time you get home from work. I remember hearing Gina Boyle say once that she thought homework should be—"

The woman had stopped herself mid-sentence with an exaggerated wince of embarrassment. "Oh, I'm *sorry*, Alice. How insensitive of me."

The man had given Alice a brief, brotherly hug around the shoulders. "It's been so hard for you. Oh, look! Let me get you a samosa."

Alice had been horrified. Did *everyone* know that Nick had cheated on her with Gina? Was it public knowledge in this strange, cliquey circle?

Dominick had appeared from nowhere, gently extricating her. She was starting to rely on him. She even found herself looking for him in the crowd, thinking vaguely to herself, "Where's Dominick?" while at the same time imagining telling Nick the story: "So, this guy acted like my *boyfriend* for the whole night. What do you think of that?"

Elisabeth and Ben had come to the party, too, because Alice had told Elisabeth she would have a panic attack if she didn't come. Ben was even huger and grizzlier than the man Alice had remembered meeting. He looked like a woodchopper who had escaped from a fairytale picture book, and he was particularly conspicuous amongst all the other smooth-faced men with their neat button-down shirts and neat gym-toned shoulders. He seemed fond of Alice. He told her he'd been "thinking a lot about their conversation the other day" and then he said, "Oh, but of course, you probably don't even remember it," and slapped himself lightly on the side of the head. Elisabeth had folded her lips together and looked the other way. "What did we talk about?" Alice had asked. "Not now," Elisabeth had said tersely.

Elisabeth and Ben hadn't circulated much. They talked a lot to Dominick—whom they didn't appear to have met before. It was strange, seeing Elisabeth cradling one drink and sticking to Ben's side. She used to march her way from person to person at parties, as if it were her duty to talk to every single person.

Actually, the funny thing was that she thought she could have managed that party even without Elisabeth or Dominick or even Nick there to help her. Even though it had been surreal and dreamlike, meeting all those strange people who knew her name and intimate details about her health (one woman had tried to drag her into a corner to continue a conversation from a few weeks ago that appeared to be about Alice's *pelvic floor*), she hadn't ever felt that normal feeling of party panic. She seemed to know instinctively how to stand and what to do with her arms and her face. She could feel herself being gracious and vibrant, actually telling people the story of how she'd fallen over at the gym and thought she was ten years younger and pregnant with her first child. The words rolled smoothly. She made eye contact with everyone in the circle. She was *delivering an anecdote*. It appeared she had become very normal and accomplished, now that she was nearly forty.

Maybe it was because she looked so good that she'd felt so confident. She'd chosen a blue dress from her wardrobe with detailed embroidery around the neckline and hem. "Oh, you always have the most *gorgeous* clothes, Alice darling," Kate Harper, the woman from the lift, had said. Kate's rounded vowels had become even rounder the more she drank, so by midnight she sounded like the queen. Alice couldn't stand her.

The party had finished up around one a.m. Dominick had been one of the last to go, kissing her chastely on the cheek and saying he'd call tomorrow. There didn't seem to have been any question about him staying the night, so maybe their relationship hadn't progressed to that point. He was a very nice man, someone she would happily recommend as a single man to a friend, but the thought of taking her clothes off in front of him was laughable.

Then again, maybe he had just been discreet because he knew she had begged Elisabeth and Ben to stay the night. (She hadn't liked the idea of waking up in this strange new world without company.) Maybe they had quite an active sex life.

She shuddered.

Less than twenty-four hours till she saw Nick and the children and everything would finally fall into place.

The bathroom floor was becoming cold. She stood up and surveyed her tired, thin face in the mirror. *Who have you become, Alice Love?*

She walked back into the bedroom and considered trying to go back to sleep but she knew it would be impossible. Hot milk was the answer. Of course it wasn't the answer at all. It never cured her insomnia, but the ritual of it and the feeling that you were doing something that the magazines always recommended for insomnia was soothing and helped pass the time.

The door to the spare bedroom was closed as she crept down the hallway. She had been pleasantly surprised to discover a spare room (previously one of their many junk rooms) all set up with a double bed, chests of drawers and spare towels. "Was I expecting someone to stay?" she'd asked Elisabeth.

"You always keep it like this," Elisabeth had said. "You're very organized, Alice."

That hardness had come back in her voice. Alice didn't know what it meant. She was starting to feel irritated by Elisabeth.

She crept down the carpeted hallway and nearly missed her footing at the top of the stairs, grabbing for the banister. Maybe it would be convenient if she fell and banged her head again. It might bring back all her memories.

She walked down the stairs, clinging to the banister. As she got to the bottom, she saw that there was a light on in the kitchen.

"Hi," she said.

"Oh, hi."

Elisabeth was standing at the microwave.

"Hot milk," she said. "Want some?"

"Yes, please."

"Not that it ever really cures my insomnia."

"No—me neither."

Alice leaned back against the counter and watched Elisabeth pour milk into a second mug. She was wearing a huge man's T-shirt that must belong to Ben. It made Alice feel prissy in her long silk nightie.

"How are you feeling?" asked Elisabeth. "How's your—memory?"

"Nothing new," said Alice. "I still don't remember anything about the children or the divorce. Although I've worked out it's got something to do with Gina."

Elisabeth looked at her with surprise. "What do you mean?"

"It's okay, you don't need to protect me," said Alice. "I've worked out that he had an affair with her."

"*Nick* had an affair with *Gina*?"

"Well, didn't he? Everybody seems to know about it."

"It's news to me." Elisabeth looked genuinely shocked.

Alice said nonchalantly, "He's probably in bed with her now."

The microwave bell dinged but Elisabeth ignored it.

She said, "I really doubt that, Alice."

"Why?"

Elisabeth paused and then looked her in the eye. "Because she's dead," she said.

Chapter 18

G ina was dead?

"Oh," said Alice.

She paused. "I didn't kill her, did I? In a fit of jealous rage? Although I guess I'd be in jail? But maybe I got away with it!"

Elisabeth laughed in a scandalized way. "No, you didn't kill her." She frowned. "Are you saying you *remember* Nick having an affair with Gina?"

"Not exactly," admitted Alice. It had seemed so clear. She brightened. That's why everyone had seemed sympathetic when Gina's name came up—because she was dead! There had been no affair at all! Now she was filled with relief and guilty love for Nick. *Of course you didn't, darling, I never really suspected you, not for a second.*

And if there had been no affair, maybe Gina had been quite nice. So it was sort of terrible that she was dead.

Elisabeth took the mugs of milk out of the microwave and carried them over to the coffee table, switching on a lamp. The helium balloons that Dominick had blown up were still hovering silently. Two half-empty glasses of champagne sat on the windowsill, along with a pile of gnawed sticks from the chicken kebabs.

Alice sat cross-legged on the leather couch, stretching her nightie over her knees.

"How did Gina die?" she asked.

"It was an accident." Elisabeth put her finger in her milk and stirred it around, avoiding Alice's eyes. "A car accident, I guess. About a year ago."

"Was I upset?"

"She was your best friend. I think you were devastated." Elisabeth took a big mouthful of her milk and put the mug down quickly. "Ow! Too hot."

Devastated. Such a big, sweeping word. Alice took a sip of her milk and burned her own tongue. It was so peculiar to think of being "devastated" by this strange woman's death, yet apparently perfectly accepting of her divorce. She had no experience with devastation. Nothing that terrible had ever happened to her. Her dad had died when she was six, but she mostly just remembered a feeling of confusion. Her mother had told her once that Alice had worn an old jumper of her dad's for weeks and weeks after he died and refused to take it off, kicking and screaming when Frannie finally pulled it off over her head. Alice didn't remember that at all. Instead she remembered how at the afternoon tea after the funeral she'd got told off by one of her mum's tennis friends for sticking her fingers in the cheesecake, and how Elisabeth had been doing it, too, even more than she was, but *she didn't get into trouble.* Instead of remembering grief and devastation, she remembered the terrible injustice of the cheesecake.

There had been that night before her wedding when she had found herself crying in bed over the fact that her dad wasn't alive to walk her down the aisle. She had been perplexed by the sudden tears and thought that maybe she was just nervous about the next day. She worried that they were fake tears because she thought she should feel that way, when in fact she couldn't even imagine what it would be like to have a father. And at the same time she'd felt pleased, because maybe it meant part of her *did* remember her dad and did still miss him, and then she'd cried harder, remembering how whenever he was shaving in the bathroom, he'd squeeze a whole lot of delicious, creamy foam into her outstretched hands so she could smear it all over her face and wasn't that *cute* and *touching* and she really hoped the hairdresser got her fringe right the next day because when she messed it up, she looked like a wombat—and there you had it, she was a horribly superficial person, actually more worried about her hair than her dead father. She had finally fallen asleep in a lather of emotion, which she didn't know whether to attribute to her father or her hair.

Now, apparently, she had experienced real grown-up grief, for a woman called Gina.

"You were there," said Elisabeth quietly.

"Pardon? I was where?"

"You saw Gina's accident. You were driving along behind her. It must have been terrible for you. I can't even imagine—"

"On the corner of Rawson and King streets?" interrupted Alice.

"Yes. Do you remember?"

"Not really. I think I just remember the feeling of it. It's happened twice now that I've got all panicky, nightmarish feelings when I see that corner."

Would those feelings stop now that she knew what they meant?

She didn't know if she wanted to remember seeing someone killed in front of her.

They drank their milk in silence for a few seconds. Alice reached up for one of the dangling strings of the balloons and pulled upon it. She watched it bob about and remembered again those pink bouquets of balloons floating angrily about in a stormy sky.

"Pink balloons," she said to Elisabeth. "I remember pink balloons and this terrible feeling of grief. Is that something to do with Gina?"

"That was at her funeral," said Elisabeth. "You and Michael—that's her husband—organized for balloons to be released at the graveyard. It was very beautiful. Very sad."

Alice tried to imagine herself talking about balloons with a bereaved man called Michael.

Michael. That was the name on that business card in her wallet. Michael Boyle—the physiotherapist from Melbourne—must be Gina's husband. That's why he'd written about "happier times" on the back of his business card. It was all very simple.

"Did Gina die before Nick and I separated?" asked Alice.

"Yes. I think about six months before. You've had a pretty hard year."

"Sounds like it."

"I'm sorry," said Elisabeth.

"Don't be." Alice looked up guiltily, worried she'd look like she was filled with self-pity. "I don't even remember Gina. Or the divorce."

"Well, you're going to have to see that neurologist," said Elisabeth, but she spoke without conviction, as if she couldn't be bothered pushing the point.

They sat in silence for a while, except for the intermittent gurgling sounds of the fish tank.

"Am I meant to be feeding those fish?" asked Alice.

"I don't know," said Elisabeth. "Actually, I think they're Tom's responsibility. I think nobody else is allowed to have anything to do with them."

Tom. The fair-haired little boy with the snuffly voice on the phone. She felt torrified at the thought of meeting him. He was in charge of fish. He had responsibilities and opinions. All three children would have opinions. They'd have opinions on Alice. They might not even like her that much. Maybe she was too strict. Or maybe she embarrassed them. Wore the wrong clothes when she picked them up from school. Maybe they preferred Nick. Maybe they blamed her for driving Nick away.

She said, "What are they like?"

"The fish?"

"No, the children."

"Oh—well, they're great."

"But tell me about them properly. Describe their personalities."

Elisabeth opened her mouth and shut it again. "I feel stupid telling you about your children. You know them so much better than me."

"But I don't even remember giving birth to them."

"I know. It's just so hard to believe. You look exactly like yourself. I feel like any second you'll get your memory back and then you'll be saying, oh please, don't tell *me* about *my* children."

"For heaven's sakes," said Alice.

"Okay, okay." Elisabeth held up her hands. "I'll have a go. So, Madison, well, Madison is—" She stopped and said, "Mum would do a much better job of this than me. She sees the children all the time. You should ask her."

"But what do you mean? You know my children, don't you? I thought, well, I thought you'd know them better than anyone. You bought me my very first present for the baby. Tiny socks."

Elisabeth had been the first person Alice had called after she and Nick had laid out all those positive pregnancy tests on the coffee table. She'd been so excited. She'd turned up with champagne ("For Nick and me, not you!"), a copy of *What to Expect When You're Expecting*, and the socks.

Elisabeth said, "Did I? I don't remember that." She put down her mug and picked up a framed photo from the table next to her. "I used to see the children all the time when they were little. I adored them. I still do adore them, of course. It's just that you're all so busy. The children have so many activities. They've all got swimming lessons. Olivia has ballet. Tom plays soccer and Madison plays hockey. And the birthday parties! They're always going to someone's birthday party. Their social lives are amazing. I remember when they were little, I always knew exactly the right thing to get them for their birthdays. They'd rip off the paper in a frenzy. Now I have to ring you, and you tell me exactly where to go and what to ask for. Or else you just buy it yourself and I give you the money. And then you make the children send me a thank-you card. *Dear Auntie Libby. Thank you so much for my blah blah.*"

"A thank-you card," repeated Alice.

"Yes. I know, I know, it's teaching them good manners and everything, but I sort of hate those thank-you cards. I always imagine the kids groaning and having to be forced into writing them. It makes me feel like an elderly aunt."

"Oh. Sorry."

"No! I can't believe I complained about thank-you cards. I've become a bitter old hag. Have you noticed?"

"It sounds more like I've become   —" Alice didn't know how to describe the person it seemed she'd become. Insufferable?

"Anyway," said Elisabeth dismissively. "Your children. Well, Madison is just Madison." She smiled fondly.

Madison is just Madison. There was a whole world of memories in that sentence. If that world were lost to Alice forever, it would be unbearable.

"Mum always says, 'Where did we get her from?'" said Elisabeth.

"Okay," said Alice. This really wasn't helping much.

"Well, ever since she was a baby, she's always been so intense. She feels everything very deeply. On Christmas Eve she'd become almost feverish with excitement, but then she couldn't stand it when Christmas was over. You'd find her sobbing in a corner because she had to wait a whole year for Christmas to come again. What else? She's accident prone. She ran through those French doors last year and had to have forty-two stitches. It was very traumatic. A lot of blood. Apparently, Tom called an ambulance and Olivia fainted. I didn't know it was possible for a five-year-old to faint. But Olivia has a blood phobia. Well, she did. I don't know if she's still got it. Actually, didn't she get all excited about becoming a nurse for a while there? When Mum bought her that nurse's uniform?"

Alice just looked at her.

"I'm sorry," said Elisabeth, flustered. "I can't imagine how weird this must feel—and I keep forgetting."

Alice said, "Tell me more about the Sultana. I mean, Madison."

"Madison likes to cook," said Elisabeth. "Well, I assume she still does.

I believe she's been a bit moody lately. She used to make her own recipes. They were good, too. Except the kitchen always looked like a bomb had exploded and she wasn't so good at the cleaning up part. Also she was a bit of a prima donna about her cooking. If the recipe didn't turn out exactly the way she wanted, she'd cry. I once saw her throw this triple-layer chocolate cake she'd spent hours decorating in the bin. You went *ballistic*."

"I did?" Alice tried to readjust yet again to this new picture of herself. She never got angry. She was more of a sulker.

"Well, apparently you'd gone on some special shopping trip to find exactly the right ingredients for this cake, so I don't really blame you."

"Madison sounds like one of the Flakes," said Alice. It had never occurred to her before that Nick's sisters' genes could infiltrate her child. She had always assumed that if she had a daughter, it would be a miniature version of herself, a fresh new Alice she could improve upon, maybe with Nick's eyes thrown in for interest.

"No, she's not like the Flakes," said Elisabeth definitely. "She's just Madison."

Alice pressed her palms to her stomach and thought about how fiercely she and Nick had loved the Sultana. It had been such clean, simple, almost narcissistic love. Now the Sultana ran through glass doors and threw cakes in the bin and made Alice "ballistic." It was all so much more complex and chaotic than she'd ever imagined.

"And Tom? What's he like?"

"He's smart," said Elisabeth. "And surprisingly witty at times. He's a suspicious kid. You can't put anything over him. He goes and checks it up on the Internet. He gets obsessed with things and learns everything there is to know about them. It was dinosaurs for a while. And then roller coasters. I don't know what he's into at the moment. He does really well at school. He gets awards, and he's class captain. That sort of thing."

"That's good," said Alice.

"It was probably a relief after Madison."

"What do you mean?"

"Oh. Well, it's just that Madison has always had problems at school. 'Behavioral problems' you call them."

"Right."

"But I think you've got it all under control. I haven't heard of any dramas for a while."

Dramas. Alice had a life with "dramas."

"And then there's Olivia," said Elisabeth. "She's just one of those children everyone adores. When we took her out when she was a baby, people used to stop you in the street to compliment you. Even serious middle-aged businessmen rushing along to meetings would smile when they saw Olivia sitting in the stroller. It was like being with a celebrity, heads turning everywhere. And she's still so cute. We keep waiting for her to turn into a monster, but she doesn't. She's very loving—maybe too loving. I remember her squatting down in the kitchen saying, 'Hello, little fella,' and we all looked down and saw she was trying to pat a cockroach. Mum nearly dropped dead on the spot."

Elisabeth stopped talking and yawned enormously.

"You'd probably describe them differently," she said, and her tone was defensive. "You're their mother."

Alice was thinking about the first time she'd set eyes on Nick. She was wearing a striped apron, sitting on a high stool at a long counter, ready to learn Thai cooking. Her friend Sophie was meant to be there but she'd twisted her ankle and missed the first class. Nick came in late with a girl who Alice assumed was his girlfriend but later turned out to be the flakiest of his sisters, Ella. When they walked in, they were both laughing, and Alice, who was newly, sadly single, was immensely irritated. Typical. Here comes another happy, laughing, loving couple. Alice remembered how her eyes had met Nick's as he looked about the class for free spots (while Ella gazed reverently and weirdly at the ceiling, entranced for some reason by the ceiling fan). Nick had raised his bushy eyebrows questioningly and Alice had smiled politely, thinking yes, yes, fine, come and sit here, lovebirds, and let's make boring conversation.

There had been another free spot at the front of the class. If her eyes hadn't met his, if she'd looked down at the fish cakes recipe in front of her, or if Sophie had walked two centimeters to the left and therefore missed twisting her ankle in that pothole, or if they had decided to do the wine tasting course instead, which they very nearly did, then those three children would never have been born. Madison Love. Thomas Love. Olivia Love. Three little individuals who already had their own personalities and quirks and stories.

The moment Nick raised his hairy eyebrows in her direction, they all got their stamps of approval. Yes, yes, yes, you will exist.

Alice was filled with elation. It was amazing. Of course, a billion babies were born every second or something, so it wasn't that amazing, but still. Why weren't they just overcome with joy every time they *looked* at those kids? Why in the world were they divorcing?

She said, "So, Nick and I are fighting over custody of the children?" Such a grown-up, alien concept.

"Nick wants them with him half the time. We don't know how Nick thinks he can do it, when he works such long hours. You've always been their 'primary caregiver,' as they say. But it's all got—well, it's all turned so nasty. I guess it's just the nature of divorce."

"But does Nick think—" Alice was overwhelmed with hurt. "Does he think I'm not a good mother?" *And was she a good mother?*

Elisabeth lifted her chin and her eyes flashed like the old Elisabeth. "Well, if he thinks that, he's wrong, and we'll have a million witnesses ready to stand up in court and say otherwise. You're a *great* mother. Don't worry. He's not going to win. He hasn't got a chance. I don't know what he's trying to prove. It's just a power game for him, I think."

It was confusing because although it gave Alice pleasure to see Elisabeth angry on her behalf, at the same time she felt automatic loyalty for Nick.

Elisabeth had always adored Nick. If Alice and Nick ever had an argument, Elisabeth took Nick's side. He was a "catch," she said.

Elisabeth was getting herself worked up. "I mean, it's just so *stupid*. He doesn't know the first thing about looking after them. He doesn't cook. I doubt he's ever used the washing machine. He's always traveling, anyway. He's just so—"

Alice held up her hand to make her stop. She said, "I expect it's just that he can't stand the idea of being a part-time dad like his own father. He used to hate it when Roger came to take him and his sisters out. He said Roger always tried too hard, you can just imagine, and it was awkward and strange, and the girls squabbled and took advantage of his credit card. Whenever we go out to a restaurant and Nick sees a man alone with his children, he always says, 'Divorced dad,' and shudders. I mean—that's what he did. Ten years ago."

She tried to get control of her voice. "He wanted to be there every night for his children, and hear about what they did at school, and make breakfast with them on the weekend. He talked about that a lot. It was like he was going to make up for his own childhood, and I loved it when he talked like that because it was making up for *our* childhood, too, and not having our dad around. He had such lovely, romantic ideas about how we'd be a family. Well, we both did. I can't believe—I can't *believe*—"

She couldn't talk anymore. Elisabeth came over and sat on the couch beside her. She hugged her awkwardly. "Maybe," she said tentatively. "Maybe this memory loss is sort of a good thing because it will help you see things more objectively without your mind being cluttered with everything that's happened over the last ten years. And once you get your memory back, you'll still have a different perspective and you and Nick will be able to work things out without all the fighting."

"What if it never comes back?"

"Oh, of course it will come back. You're already remembering bits and pieces," said Elisabeth.

"Maybe my old self has been sent from the past to stop the divorce," said Alice only half flippantly. "Maybe I won't get my memory back until I've done that."

"Possibly!" said Elisabeth too brightly. Then she paused and said, "Dominick seemed nice. Really nice."

Alice thought of how she'd let Dominick kiss her on this very couch and felt suffused with guilt. She said, "He is perfectly nice. He's just not Nick."

"No. He's *very* different from Nick."

Now, what exactly did that mean? Should she be offended on Nick's behalf? Anyway, she wasn't going to have a conversation comparing their pros and cons, as if they were competing boyfriends. Nick was her husband. She changed the subject instead. She said, "Well, speaking of men, I liked Ben."

"It's funny to hear you talk about him as if you've only just met him."

"What did Ben mean when he said he'd been thinking about our discussion the other day?" Alice knew there was something controversial about this topic; it was time to get to the bottom of whatever this thing was between her and Elisabeth.

"Ummm." Elisabeth yawned and stretched. "Do you want a glass of water?"

"No thanks."

"I'm really thirsty." She stood up and went into the kitchen. Alice watched her go and wondered if she was pretending not to have heard her.

She came back with the glass of water and sat back down on the single couch in front of Alice.

"It's late," she said.

"Libby."

Elisabeth sighed. "On Thursday—the day before your accident—Ben came over to help you with some problem you were having with your car. Except apparently there wasn't really a problem at all. It was a little setup."

Good grief. What had she done? Alice sat up straight. She could feel her face flushing. Surely she hadn't made a move on her sister's husband? (For one thing, the man was freakishly large.) Had breaking up with Nick sent her over the edge?

"You gave him banana muffins straight out of the oven. He loves your banana muffins."

Oh my Lord.

"With lots of butter. I never let him have butter. He's got high cholesterol, you know. I mean, you're the health-conscious one."

She'd *seduced her brother-in-law with butter,* Alice's heart pounded.

"And then you gave him your little speech "

"Little speech?" said Alice faintly.

"Yes, your little speech about why we should stop IVF and adopt. You had brochures. Application forms. Website addresses. You'd done all this research."

Alice couldn't get her head around it for a few seconds. Her mind had been filled with horrific images of herself going upstairs to "freshen up" and appearing in red lingerie.

"Adoption," she repeated confusedly.

"Yes. You think we should pop over to a Third World country like Angelina and Brad and help ourselves to a cute orphan."

"That was very presumptuous of me," said Alice sternly, weak with relief that she hadn't tried to seduce Ben. "Meddlesome. Nosey!"

Then again, she thought, wasn't adoption actually a pretty good idea?

"Well," said Elisabeth. "I was angry. When Ben came home and told me, I rang you and we got into a big argument about it. You think it's time we 'faced reality.'"

"Did I really say that?"

"Yes."

"I'm sorry."

"I guess you meant well. It's just that you made me feel as if you thought I was stupid. As if you would never have let things get so far. As if you would never be so *messy* as to keep having miscarriage after miscarriage. As if, I don't know, as if I've been overly emotional about the whole thing."

"I'm sorry," said Alice again. "I'm really sorry."

"You don't even remember it," said Elisabeth. "Once you remember it, you'll feel differently. Anyway, I said some pretty nasty things to you."

"Like what?"

"I'm not saying them again! I didn't even mean them. This lets me off the hook."

They were silent for a few seconds. Alice said, "Are Angelina and Brad friends of yours?"

Elisabeth snorted. "Brad Pitt and Angelina Jolie. You've forgotten all your celebrity gossip, too."

"I thought Brad Pitt was engaged to Gwyneth Paltrow."

"Ancient history. He's married and divorced Jennifer Aniston since then, and Gwyneth has had a baby called Apple. I'm not kidding. Apple."

"Oh." Alice felt unaccountably sad for Brad and Gwyneth. "They seemed happy in the photos."

"Everyone looks happy in photos."

"What about Bill and Hillary Clinton?" asked Alice. "Did they stay together?"

"You mean after the Lewinsky thing?" said Elisabeth. "Yes, they did. I don't think anyone even thinks about that much anymore."

Alice looked at Elisabeth. "So," she said with wild abandon, "I take it you don't want to adopt a baby?"

Elisabeth smiled a sick sort of a smile. "I would have considered it years ago, but Ben couldn't stand the idea. He's always been ideologically opposed to adoption because he's adopted himself, and his mother is—difficult. He didn't have a great childhood. My charming mother-in-law told him that his real mother couldn't afford to keep him, so Ben saved up his money. He thought once he had a hundred dollars, he could write to his real mum to tell her he could be self-supporting now, so could she please take him back. On his birthday he always ran to the letterbox, thinking that maybe this year, out of the blue, his real mum might decide to send him a card.

"He thought his baby photos were ugly —he was a funny-looking baby—

and he wondered if maybe his real mother hadn't liked the look of him when he was born. He always felt that his parents wished they had chosen a smaller, smarter son. He'd spent his whole childhood keeping his room tidy, not saying much, feeling like a big clumsy visitor in his own home. It breaks my heart to think of it. When you were saying earlier that Nick wanted to be a good father to make up for his own father leaving, well, Ben was similar. He wanted his own biological child. He wanted to have someone who looked like him, who had the same eyes or whatever. And I was so looking forward to giving him that. I so badly wanted to give him that."

"Of course you did."

"So I was always very respectful of Ben's views on adoption."

"Yes. I can imagine."

Elisabeth gave a wry half-smile.

"What?"

"On Thursday you told Ben that he needed to get over it."

"Get over what?"

"Get over his problem with adoption. You said that plenty of people didn't get on with their biological parents and that it was a lottery, but that any kid who got Ben and me as parents would hit the jackpot. Thank you, by the way. That was a nice thing to say."

" That's okay." At least she'd said one thing right. "But Ben must not have appreciated me saying that."

"Well, that's the thing. Yesterday when I came home from lunch he said he'd been thinking about what you said, and he thinks you're right. We should adopt. He's all excited. He'd done all this research on the Internet. Apparently all I needed to say to him five years ago was 'Get over it.' Silly old me. All that unnecessary tiptoeing around his traumatic childhood."

Alice tried to imagine herself telling that big grizzly man to "get over it" while she fed him banana muffins. (Banana muffins. She wondered what recipe she used. Also, she must own a muffin tray.) She had never had opinions about how Elisabeth should run her life, although Elisabeth had plenty of opinions about how Alice should run hers. That was fine because she was the big sister. It was her job to be the sensible, bossy one who did her tax returns on time, got her car serviced regularly, and had a career, while Alice could be whimsical and hopeless and make fun of Elisabeth for her motivational posters of mountains and sunsets. Actually, now she thought about it, it had been *Elisabeth* who had bullied her into doing that Thai cooking course with Sophie, instead of wasting her life moping over that sneering IT consultant.

Now Alice was the one doing the bullying.

"So if Ben is considering adoption now, isn't that maybe a good thing?" she said hopefully.

"No, it's not." Elisabeth's voice became flinty. She sat up straight. Here we go, thought Alice. "It's not at all. You don't know what you're talking about, Alice."

"But—"

"It's too late now. You don't seem to realize how long adoption takes. What you have to go through. You don't just order a kid online. We're not Brad and Angelina. We've got to jump through hoops and pay thousands of dollars, which we don't have. It takes years and years, and it's stressful and things go wrong, and I don't have the energy for it. I've had enough. We'd be nearly fifty by the time we got a child. I'm too tired to start dealing with bureaucrats and trying to convince them why I'd make a good mother and how much money we earn and blah, blah, blah. I don't know why you're suddenly taking this interest in my life, but you're too late."

"I'm *suddenly* taking an interest?" Alice was wounded, desperate to defend herself, except she had no facts at her disposal. She didn't believe it. She would never have not been interested in Elisabeth's life. "Are you saying I haven't been interested before?"

Elisabeth breathed out noisily, deflating like a balloon, and sank back in her chair.

"Of course you have."

"Well, why did you say it?"

"I don't know. Sometimes I've felt it. Look, I withdraw the comment."

"We're not in court."

"I didn't even mean it. Anyway, you could probably say the same thing about me. I don't see the children as much as I did. I should have done more for you after Gina, and after Nick. But you're always so . . . I don't know. Busy. Self sufficient." She yawned. "Just forget it."

Alice looked down at her strange wrinkled hands. "What's gone wrong between us?" she asked quietly.

There was no answer. Alice looked up and saw that Elisabeth had closed her eyes and put her head back against the couch. She looked exhausted and sad.

Finally she spoke without opening her eyes. "We really should go to bed."

Chapter 19

It was five-thirty p.m., Sunday afternoon. In half an hour Nick would be home with the children.

Alice had a sick, excited feeling in her stomach as if she were going on a first date.

She'd been wearing a pretty floral dress and makeup, her hair all fluffy and motherly, when she decided that she was trying too hard. Presumably she didn't normally dress up like a 1950s mother at a fancy-dress party. So she'd run back upstairs and scrubbed off the makeup, and pulled the dress over her head in mad panic. She'd found jeans and a white T-shirt, and flattened her hair. No jewelry except for Nick's bracelet and her wedding ring, which she'd found at the back of a drawer, together with Granny Love's engagement ring. It had been yet another fresh shock to find these symbols of her marriage carelessly tossed in with her underwear. She remembered when Nick had placed the wedding ring on her finger for the first time. Most grooms were clumsy at this point, grinning goofily, soft chuckles from the guests, but Nick had smoothly, tenderly slid it onto her finger in one go, his eyes locked on hers; she'd been proud. He was so dexterous.

With this ring I thee wed...

... until I thee divorce.

She wondered why she hadn't given the awful engagement ring back. Wasn't the ring normally torn from the finger and thrown at the man's face in a fit of rage at some point during a divorce?

She looked at herself in the bedroom mirror. This was much better, casual, unaffected—although her face looked pale and very old; she resisted an intense longing to go through that amazing dab, dab, slap, slap routine again that transformed her face. Surely she didn't normally wear makeup on a Sunday night at home.

Earlier in the day, after Elisabeth and Ben had gone home, it had suddenly occurred to Alice that it was presumably her responsibility to feed those three children. She had called her mother and asked her what she should cook for dinner, saying she wanted to cook their favorite thing. Barb had spent a full twenty minutes discussing each child's dietary idiosyncrasies throughout their lives. "Remember when Madison went through that vegetarian stage? And of course it would have to be at the same time that Tom was just refusing to eat *any* vegetable. Then Olivia couldn't decide whether she should only eat vegetables, like Madison, or refuse to eat vegetables, like Tom! Oh, you were tearing your hair out every tea time!" At last, after much changing of her mind, she'd finally settled on homemade hamburgers. "I think you found a healthy recipe in your Heart Foundation recipe book. You were saying just the other week that you were sick to death of it but the children can't get enough of it. I'm sure you remember *that*, don't you, darling? Because it was only last *week*."

Alice had found the recipe book and it had opened straight at the right food-splattered page. All the ingredients were in her amazingly well-stocked freezer and pantry. It seemed like there was enough there to feed hundreds of children. As she made the mince for the hamburgers, she realized she wasn't looking at the recipe book anymore. She seemed to know that now she grated in two carrots, one zucchini, now she added two eggs. Once it was ready, she had put the mince back in the fridge, defrosted rolls ready to be toasted, and made a green salad. Would the children eat a green salad? Who knew? She and Nick could eat it. He would stay for dinner, wouldn't he? He wouldn't just drop the children off and *leave*? But she had an awful feeling that was exactly what divorced parents did. She'd just have to ask him to please stay. Beg him, if necessary. She couldn't be left alone with the children. It wasn't safe. She didn't know the procedures. For example, did they bath themselves? Did she read them stories? Sing them songs? When was bedtime? And how was it enforced?

She went back downstairs in her jeans and looked around her gleaming, beautiful house. Two cleaners had turned up at the door at midday, laden with mops and buckets, asking how the party had gone as they plugged in vacuum cleaners. They'd scrubbed and polished while Alice had wandered vaguely about, feeling embarrassed and not sure what she was meant to be doing. Should she help? Get out of the way? Supervise? Hide the valuables? She had her purse ready to give them however much they asked for, but there had been no request for money. They told her they'd see her on Thursday at the usual time and disappeared, waving cheerily. She'd closed the door behind them, breathed in the smell of furniture polish, and thought, "I am a woman with a swimming pool, air-conditioning, and *cleaners*."

Now she looked about the kitchen and her eyes fell on a rack of wine. She should have a bottle open and breathing for Nick. She selected a bottle, went to get a corkscrew, and realized that the bottle didn't have a cork. Instead she unscrewed a normal bottle top. How funny. The smell of the wine hit her nostrils and she found she was pouring herself a glass. She buried her nose in it. Part of her mind thought, "What are you doing, you tosser?" Another part thought, "Mmmm. *Blackberries.*"

The wine slid smoothly down her throat and she wondered if she'd turned into an alcoholic. It wasn't even six o'clock. She'd never been much of a wine drinker. Yet drinking this wine felt right and familiar, even as it felt strange and wrong. Maybe that's why Nick had left her and wanted custody of the children. She'd become a drunk. Nobody knew, except for

Nick and her children. It was a terrible secret. Well, but couldn't she just get help? Join AA and follow those twelve steps? Never touch a drop again? She took another sip and tapped her fingers on the countertop. Soon she would see him and then the mystery of all this would finally be solved. It wasn't logical, but she had a strong feeling that the moment she saw Nick's face her entire memory would land back in her head, fully intact.

Dominick had turned up again this afternoon. He had takeaway hot chocolates in a tray and tiny polenta cakes (she had a feeling they were her favorites and acted accordingly grateful). She'd been surprised by the pleasure she'd felt when she saw him standing at the door. Maybe it was because of his somewhat nervy demeanor. It made her feel like she was adored. Nick adored her, but she adored him back, so it was equal. Talking to Dominick made her feel as if every word she said was somehow amazing.

"How is your, ah, memory today?" he'd asked her politely, while they drank their hot chocolates and ate the cakes on the back veranda.

"Oh, maybe a bit better," she'd said. People liked to think you were making progress when it came to health matters.

Apparently Jasper was with "his mother." She realized that Dominick must be a divorced dad. How strange it all was. Wouldn't it be a lot less messy if everyone just stayed with the people they married in the first place?

That meant divorce was a shared interest. She'd had a moment of inspiration and said to him, "Have we ever talked about Nick—about why we separated?"

He gave her an odd sideways look. "Yes."

Aha!

"Would you mind giving me a quick summary of what I told you?" She said this lightly, trying not to show how desperately she needed to know the answer.

"You don't remember anything about why you and Nick split up?" he'd said slowly.

"No! I couldn't believe it! It was a total shock to me."

The words spilled out of her mouth before she realized that they might be upsetting to someone who was hoping to start a relationship with her.

He'd scratched hard at his nose. "Well. Obviously I don't know every detail, but, ah, it seemed that he—Nick—was pretty much involved with his job. He was away a lot and he worked long hours, and so I guess, I think you said, you just drifted apart. That's the way it happened. And, ummm, I guess, maybe some sexual issues. You mentioned . . ." He coughed loudly and stopped talking.

Sex? She'd talked to this man about sex? It was an unforgivable betrayal of Nick. And besides which, what *issues* could there have been relating to sex? They had a glorious, funny, tender, highly satisfying sex life.

It was so embarrassing to hear the word "sex" coming out of Dominick's mouth. He was too nice. Too grown-up and proper. Even now, when Alice was alone thinking about it, she felt her face become warm.

Dominick had seemed embarrassed, too. He'd cleared his throat so many times, Alice had offered him a glass of water, and then he'd left soon after, telling her to take care of herself. At the front door he'd suddenly wrapped his arms around her in a quick, warm hug. He'd said in her ear, "I care a lot about you," and then he was gone.

So that hadn't helped much at all. "Drifting apart because of Nick's long hours." That was such a cliché. The sort of thing that broke up other marriages. If Nick had to work long hours, they would have just made up for it in the hours they did have.

She looked at her wineglass and saw that the level had gone down considerably. What if her lips and teeth were stained purple and she opened the door to Nick and the children looking like a vampire? She rushed to the mirror in the hallway and checked her reflection. Her lips were fine. Her eyes just looked a bit wild and crazed, and she still looked extremely old.

As she walked back into the kitchen, she stopped by the Green Room, except it wasn't green anymore. It was a small room off the hallway that had originally been painted a bright lime green. Now the walls were painted a tasteful mushroom. Alice leaned against the doorway and found that she missed the green. It had made people laugh and shield their eyes whenever they saw it. Of course, it had to go—but still. The house was literally perfect now. Instead of being thrilling, that suddenly seemed depressing.

The Green Room had been turned into a study, which had always been their plan. There was a computer on a desk and bookshelves lined the walls. She walked in and sat down at the computer. Immediately, without thinking, she leaned down and pushed a round silver button on a black box sitting on the floor. The computer whirred to life and she pressed another button on the monitor. The screen turned blue. White letters ordered her "'To begin, click your user name." There were four icons: Alice, Madison, Tom, and Olivia. (Did that mean the children used this computer? Weren't they too little?) She clicked on her own name and a colorful photo filled the whole screen. It was the three children. They were all rugged up in parkas and scarves, sharing a toboggan that was flying down a snowy incline. Madison was at the back, Tom was in the middle, and the little one, Olivia, was at the front. Madison had hold of the control rope. Their mouths were open as if laughing or shrieking, and their eyes were wide with fear and exhilaration.

Alice put a hand to the base of her throat. They were extraordinarily beautiful. She wanted the memory of that day back so bad. She stared at the photo and for a second she thought she heard the faint sounds of children shouting, the feeling of an icy-cold nose and fingertips   and as soon as she tried too hard to grab hold of it, it slipped deftly away.

Instead, she clicked on an icon that said E-mail. It asked for a password.

Naturally, she didn't know it, but as she held her hands over the keyboard, her fingers went ahead and inexplicably typed out the word OREGANO.

What in the world? But it seemed her body remembered more than her mind because the screen was obediently vanishing, to be replaced by a dancing image of an envelope and a message saying, "You have 7 new messages."

What inspired her to choose an *herb* for her password?

There was an e-mail from Jane Turner with the subject heading:

"How's the head?"; another one from a Dominick Gordon (Who? Oh, of course. Him. Her *boyfriend*) with the subject heading: "Next weekend?" and five from names she didn't recognize, all with the heading: "Mega Meringue Mother's Day."

Mega Meringue Mother's Day. It made her want to snort with derision. It seemed like something Elisabeth—the old energetic Elisabeth—might have arranged. Not her.

There was also an e-mail from Nick Love, with no subject heading, dated Friday, the day of her accident. She clicked on it and read:

> Well a lot of traditions are going to have to change now, aren't they? What a load of crap. XMAS Day WILL be different whatever we do. You can't reasonably expect to have them for the morning AND the night, so I only get them for five fucking minutes in the middle of the day. It makes perfect sense for them to stay at Ella's on XMAS eve. They love being with their cousins. Can't YOU think of THEM for a change? This is all about YOU. As usual.
>
> PS. Please make sure they pack their swimming costumes for the weekend. I'm taking them to the Aquatic Center on Sunday when I get back from Portugal.
>
> PPS. I had two sisters on the phone in tears last night about Granny Love's ring. Can you please be reasonable about this? It's not like you ever wore it that often. If you're thinking of selling it, you've really sunk to a new low. Even for you.

"Even for you." Alice struggled to catch her breath. It was like being winded. The coldness. The viciousness. The dislike.

It was impossible to believe that this was written by the same man who got tears in his eyes when she said she would marry him; who would crash-tackle her onto the bed and lift her hair and kiss the back of her neck; who told her when it was safe to look back at the television because the blood and guts had gone now; who sang all the words to "Living Next Door to Alice" to her in the shower.

And why was she refusing to give back Granny Love's dreadful ring? It was a family heirloom. Of course the Love family should get it back.

She scrolled down and saw that Nick's message was part of a whole conversation that had been going on for days.

There was one from herself dated just three days ago.

> The children should wake up in their own beds on Christmas Day this year. I'm not moving on this matter. Obviously, I want to keep all the same traditions for them—putting out their Santa Sacks at the end of their beds, etc. They've had to go through enough disruption as it is. This is just another power game for you. All you care about is winning. I couldn't care less what points you win over me—just don't win at the expense of the children. By the way, I have asked you at least twice before now not to give the children, especially Olivia, so much junk food over the weekend. I'm sure it makes you feel like a wonderful father to say yes to whatever they want, but they're tired and irritable every Monday after a weekend with you—and I'm the one who has to deal with it.

It was May! Why were they even talking about what would happen on Christmas Day?

Some impostor had been living her life. She was stunned by her sanctimonious, contemptuous tone.

She scrolled down further and bitter words and phrases jumped out at her.

May I remind you . . .

You are so small-minded . . .

You are so sanctimonious . . .

You must be out of your mind if you think . . .

What is WRONG with you?

Can we just try and be rational about this?

You're the one who . . .

There was a scrunch of gravel and a flicker of headlights. A car pulled up in the driveway. Alice stood up, her heart beating like a jackhammer. She pushed a hand back through her hair as she walked down the hallway toward the front door. She was such an idiot for not doing her makeup again. She was about to see a man who hated her.

Car doors were slamming. A child was whining, "But Dad, that's not fair!"

Alice opened the front door. Her legs were shaking so badly, she thought she might collapse. Maybe that would be a good thing.

"*Mummy!*" A little girl came hurtling up the stairs and threw her arms around Alice, her head colliding hard with her stomach. She talked straight into Alice's T-shirt, her voice muffled. "Is your sore head better? Did you get my card? What was it like sleeping in the hospital?"

Alice hugged her back and couldn't speak.

I don't even remember being pregnant with you.

"Olivia?" she croaked and put her hand on top of the little girl's tangled white-blond curls. There was sand in her hair and a crooked line revealing a pink scalp. Her hair was soft and her skull was hard, and when she looked up, she was impossibly beautiful: smooth skin with a cinnamon dusting of freckles and enormous dark-lashed blue eyes.

They were her own eyes staring back at her, but much bigger and definitely much more beautiful. Alice felt dizzy.

"Oh Mum," crooned Olivia. "Are you actually still feeling a bit sick? Poor darling Mum. *I know!* I'll listen to your heart and be your nurse! Yes!"

She was gone, slamming the screen door behind her, pounding down the hallway.

Alice looked up and saw Nick leaning over to pull out stuff from the boot of a swish silver car.

He straightened. Both his arms were filled with backpacks and soggy beach towels.

"Hi," he said.

His hair seemed to have disappeared. As he walked toward her, she saw that it was completely gray and cropped close to his head. His face had got thinner but his body was somehow thicker: his shoulders chunkier, his stomach paunchier. There were spiderwebs of lines around his eyes. He was wearing a green T-shirt and shorts she'd never seen before. Well, of course, but it was still unsettling.

He walked up the stairs toward her and stood in front of her. She looked up at him. He was different and strange but he was still essentially Nick. Alice forgot everything that she'd just read on the computer and the way he'd talked to her on the phone the other day and was filled with the pure simple pleasure of Nick coming home after a long trip away. She smiled joyously at him. "Hi yourself."

She went to step forward toward him and Nick stepped back. It seemed involuntary, as if she were an unpleasant insect. His eyes were blank, and they seemed to be fixed on her forehead.

"How are you?" he said. His tone was the frosty one he used when he was being mucked around by incompetent tradespeople.

"Mum! You should have seen the wave I caught today! It was, like, twenty feet tall. It was, like, as high as the roof there. Look. No, look, Mum, at the roof there. Yeah, there. That's how high it was. Or maybe a few centimeters less. Anyway, Dad took the best photo! Show Mum the photo on your camera, Dad. Can you show her the photo?"

So this was Tom. He was wearing long board shorts and a cap that he pulled off so he could rub the top of his head hard. His hair was the same color as Olivia's—so blond it was almost white. Nick had that color hair when he was a child. Tom's limbs were skinny and tanned and strong. He was like a miniature surfie teenager. Good Lord. He had Roger's nose. It was definitely Roger's nose. It made her want to laugh. Roger's nose in this vibrant little boy's face. She wanted to hug him, but she wasn't sure if that was appropriate.

Instead, she said, "Yeah, let me see the photo, Nick."

Nick and Tom stared at her. Her tone must have been wrong. Too flippant?

Tom said, "You sound a bit funny, Mum. Did you get stitches at the hospital for your head? I asked Auntie Libby if it was a brain tumor and she said it definitely was *not*. I did a lie-detector test on her."

"It definitely was not a brain tumor," said Alice. "I just fell over."

"I'm starved to death," sighed Tom.

"I'm making hamburgers for dinner."

"No, I mean, I'm starved right now."

"Oh."

A girl walked up onto the veranda. She dropped a wet towel on the veranda, put her hands on her hips, and said, "Did you say you're making *hamburgers* for dinner?"

"Yes," said Alice.

Madison. The Sultana. The two blue lines on all those pregnancy tests. The flashing heartbeat on the screen. The mysterious invisible presence listening to Nick's voice through the toilet roll.

Madison had very fair, almost translucent skin. There was a patch of angry red sunburn on her neck with white fingerprints as if someone had given up on putting on the sunscreen too soon. She had lank, dark brown hair that was falling in her eyes and beautiful strong white teeth. Her eyes were the same shape as Nick's but a darker, unusual color, and her eyebrows were someone's—Elisabeth's as a child! They were subtly raised at the corners, like Mr. Spock. She wasn't adorable like Olivia and Tom. Her body was chunky. Her lower lip jutted out sulkily. But one day, thought Alice, one day I think you might be striking, my darling Sultana.

"You *promised*," the Sultana said to Alice. Her eyes were murderous. She was formidable. She filled Alice with awe.

"I promised what?"

"That you would buy the ingredients so I could make lasagna tonight. I *knew* you wouldn't do it. Why do you pretend you're going to do something when you know that you're *not*." She punctuated the last sentence with rhythmic stamps of her foot.

Nick said, "Don't be so rude, Madison. Your mother had an accident. She had to spend the night at the hospital."

Alice wanted to laugh at Nick's stern dad voice. Madison lifted her chin. Her eyes blazed. She stormed into the house, slamming the screen door behind her.

"Don't slam the door!" called out Nick. "And come back and pick up your towel."

Silence. She didn't return.

Nick sucked in his lower lip and his nostrils flared. Alice had never seen him pull a face like that. He said, "Go inside, Tom. I want to speak to your mother. Will you take Madison's towel inside, too?"

Tom was standing at the front wall of the house, tracing the brickwork with his fingertips. He said, "Dad, how many bricks do you reckon there are in this whole house?"

"Tom."

Tom sighed theatrically, picked up Madison's towel, and went inside.

Alice took a deep breath. She couldn't imagine living with those three children twenty-four hours a day. She'd never imagined them actually talking. They fizzed and crackled with energy. Their personalities were right there on the surface without that protective sheen of adulthood.

"The Sultana," began Alice, but words eluded her. Madison could not be put into words.

"I beg your pardon?" said Nick.

"The Sultana. I could never have imagined her growing up to be like that. She's so . . . I don't know."

"Sultana?" He didn't know what she was talking about.

"You remember—when I was pregnant with Madison, we used to call her the Sultana."

He frowned. "I don't remember that. Anyway, I wanted to see if we could work out this thing with Christmas Day."

"Oh, that." She thought of all those nasty e-mails and got a bad taste in her mouth. "Why are we even talking about Christmas now? It's *May*!"

He stared at her as if she were crazy.

"I beg your pardon? You're the one obsessed with your precious spreadsheet. You said you wanted everything in black-and-white for the whole year ahead. Every birthday. Every concert. You said that was best for the kids."

"Did I?" Did she even know how to do a spreadsheet?

"Yes!"

"Right. Well. Whatever you want. You can have them on Christmas Day."

"Whatever I want," he repeated suspiciously, almost nervously. "Is there something I'm missing here?"

"Nope. Hey—how was Portugal?"

"It was fine, thank you," he said formally.

She had to clench her fingernails into her hands to stop herself leaning forward and laying her face against his chest. She wanted to say, "Talk in your normal voice."

"I'd better go," he said.

"What?" She nearly grabbed for him in a panic. "No. You can't go. You have to stay for dinner."

"I don't think that would be appropriate."

"Oh yes! Daddy, stay for dinner!" It was Olivia. She had a red cape tied around her shoulders and a toy stethoscope around her neck. She clung to Nick's arm. Alice was jealous she was allowed to touch him so freely.

"I think I'd better go," said Nick.

"Please stay," said Alice. "We're having hamburgers."

"Yes! See, Mummy wants you to stay." Olivia was doing a tap dance of delight back and forth across the veranda. She yelled, "Tom! Guess what? Dad's staying for dinner!"

"Jesus, Alice," said Nick under his breath, and this time he looked her properly in the eyes.

"I opened some really nice wine for us," said Alice, and smiled at him.

She didn't need lipstick to get her husband back.

Chapter 20

Nick didn't seem to know what to do with himself when he came inside. He shoved his hands in the pockets of his shorts and wandered around the living room, stopping and looking at things, as if he were in somebody else's home.

"You got the pool under control?" he asked, and jutted his chin toward the backyard.

Alice stood in the kitchen, pouring them both a glass of wine. She had no idea what he was talking about. How do you get a pool under control?

"The pool has been very calm," she said. "Very serene. I think I must have it on a tight leash."

Nick turned back from the windows and looked at her sharply.

"Good," he said.

Alice walked out of the kitchen and handed him a glass of wine. She noticed that he took it from her carefully, so that their hands didn't touch. "Thanks," he said. She kept standing in front of him and he backed away again as if she were contagious.

Tom was wandering around the kitchen, opening cupboard doors. He stood in front of the fridge, swinging the door back and forth.

"What can I eat, Mum?" he said.

Alice looked around vaguely for her mother.

"*Mum*," said Tom.

Alice jumped. She was the mum.

"Well," she said, trying to sound cheery and loving. "What do you feel like? Maybe a sandwich?"

"You can wait till dinner, Tom," said Nick.

Oh, so that had been the correct response.

"Yes," she said. She put on a similar voice to Nick's. "Your father is right." Then she giggled. She couldn't help it. She gave Nick a mischievous look. Didn't he find it funny, too? The two of them being the mum and the dad?

Nick just looked back at her nervously. She saw his eyes dart involuntarily to her glass of wine. Did he think she was drunk?

The little boy slammed the fridge door so hard it rattled, and said, "I think if I don't eat soon, I might get malnourished. Look. My stomach is sticking out like a starving person. See?" He thrust out his stomach.

Alice laughed. Nick said sharply, "Stop being silly. Go and get changed out of those wet clothes." Yes, well, it probably wasn't the best idea to encourage your children to laugh at the plight of the starving.

The littlest child appeared. Olivia. She had smeared her lips with bright-red lipstick. It had got on her teeth. Was that allowed? Alice looked over at Nick for guidance, but he was standing at the back door and looking out at the pool. "The color looks a bit green to me," he said. "When was the last time you had the guy around?"

"Okay, Mummy, I'm ready now to be your nurse. Sit down and I'll take your temperature." Olivia grabbed her by the hand. Charmed by the feel of her small, warm palm, Alice let herself be led over to the sofa.

"Lie down, there's a dear," said Olivia.

Alice lay down and Olivia stuck a toy thermometer in her mouth. She stroked back Alice's hair from her forehead and said, "Now I will listen to your heart, patient." She plugged the stethoscope to her ears and pressed the other end against Alice's chest. She frowned professionally. Alice tried not to laugh. This kid was adorable.

"Okay, patient, your heart is beating," she said.

"Phew," said Alice.

Olivia removed the thermometer and looked at it. Her mouth dropped. "You have a terrible fever, patient! You're burning up!"

"Oh no! What should I do?"

"You should watch me do a cartwheel. That will cure you."

Olivia did a perfect cartwheel. Alice applauded and Olivia bowed. She went to do another one.

"Not in the house, Olivia!" snapped Nick. "You know that!"

Olivia stuck her bottom lip out. "Please, Daddy, please. Just one more."

"Should she be wearing your lipstick like that?" asked Nick.

"Oh, well," said Alice, "I'm not exactly sure."

"Let your mother get dinner started." Nick had the same exhausted, defeated look as Elisabeth had the night before. Everyone was so tired and cranky in 2008.

"Sorry, darling Daddy." Olivia threw her arms around Nick's legs.

"Go and get changed out of your swimming costume," said Nick. Olivia danced off, swirling her red cape around her.

They were alone.

"By the way, I didn't get all of Olivia's homework done," said Nick. He sounded defensive, like he was confessing something.

"You mean you do Olivia's homework for her?" asked Alice.

"Of course not! Jesus. You really do think I'm incompetent, don't you."

Alice sat up. "No I don't."

"She's only got eight questions to go. It's obviously more difficult when you're all together in a small apartment. Also we didn't quite finish Tom's reading. And we spent three hours doing Madison's science experiment today. Tom wanted to do it for her."

"Nick."

He stopped talking, took a mouthful of his wine, and looked at her.

"What?"

"Why are we getting a divorce?"

"What sort of question is that?"

"I just want to know."

The longing to stand up and touch him was so strong, she had to press her hands against her thighs to stop herself from leaping up and burying her head under his chin.

"It doesn't matter why we're getting a divorce," said Nick. "I'm not having this conversation. What is the point of it? I'm not interested in playing games tonight, Alice. I'm exhausted. If you're trying to make me say something you can use against me, it's not going to work."

"Oh," said Alice.

Would her capacity for shock ever run out? She realized that ever since Elisabeth had first uttered the word "divorce" at the hospital, she'd been waiting to see Nick so that he could take it away, make it nothing to do with them.

"Maybe I should just go home," said Nick, putting his glass down on the coffee table.

"You told me once that if we were ever having trouble with our relationship, you would move heaven and earth to try and fix it," said Alice. "We were at that new Italian restaurant when you said that. We were peeling the wax off the candlestick. I remember it very, very clearly."

"Alice."

"You said we were going to get old and grumpy together and go on coach tours and play bingo. The garlic bread was cold but we were too hungry to complain."

Nick's lower lip had dropped, so he looked stupid.

"One night, we were standing in Sarah O'Brien's driveway waiting for a taxi and I asked if you thought Sarah looked even more beautiful than usual that night, and you said, 'Alice, I could never love anyone the way I love you,' and I laughed and said, 'That wasn't the question,' but it was the question, because I was feeling insecure, and that's what you said. You said that. It was cold. You were wearing that big woolly jumper that you lost at Katoomba. Don't you remember?"

She could feel her nose starting to block.

Nick was holding his palms up in a panicky fashion, as if there were a fire starting right in front of him but he couldn't see anything handy to extinguish it.

Alice sniffed noisily. "Sorry," she said, and looked at the floor because she couldn't bear to look at his familiar but strange face.

She said, "These tiles are the absolute perfect color. Where did we get them?"

"I don't know," said Nick. "It must have been ten years ago." She looked back up at him. He dropped his hands by his sides and his eyes widened as comprehension swept his face. He said, "Alice, you did get your memory back, didn't you? I just assumed—I mean, you're home from the hospital. You don't still think it's 1998, do you?"

"I know it's 2008. I believe it. It just doesn't feel like it."

"Yes, but you *remember* the last ten years, don't you? That's not why you're asking these bizarre questions, is it?"

Alice said, "Did you have an affair with that woman who lived across the road? The one who died? Gina?"

"An affair? With *Gina*? You are joking."

"Oh. Good."

He said, "You don't remember Gina?"

"No. I remember the balloons at her funeral."

"But Alice . . ." Nick leaned forward urgently. He looked around the room to make sure they were alone and lowered his voice. "You do remember the *kids*, don't you?"

Alice met his eyes and silently shook her head.

"Not at all?"

"The last thing I remember properly is being pregnant with the Sultana. I mean, Madison."

Nick slammed his palms against his knees. (He had all these new grown-up grumpy gestures.) "For God's sake, why aren't you still at the hospital?"

"Did you have an affair with someone *other* than Gina?" asked Alice.

"What? No, of course not."

"Did *I*?"

"Not that I know of. Can we get back to the point?"

"So there were no affairs at all?"

"No! Jesus. We didn't have *time* for affairs. We didn't have the energy. Well, I didn't. Maybe you did, in between your precious aerobics classes and beautician appointments, in which case, good luck to you."

Alice thought about how she'd kissed Dominick.

She said, "Do you have a girlfriend now? Oh, don't answer that. I can't bear it if you've got a girlfriend. Don't answer it." She put her hands over her ears, took them away, and said, "Do you?"

Nick said, "You must have hit your head really hard, Alice."

For a moment it seemed like the real Nick was back. He was shaking his head in comical disbelief, the way he did when he caught her crying over that margarine ad with the ducklings, or hopping around swearing because she'd hurt herself kicking the washing machine, or down on her knees frenziedly pulling everything out of the fridge in the hope of finding a forgotten bar of chocolate.

Then the look vanished as if he'd just recalled something highly irritating and he said, "Anyway, according to Olivia, you've got a boyfriend yourself. Jasper's dad. The school principal, no less. Do you remember *him*?"

Her face became warm. "I didn't remember him, but I met him yesterday."

"Right," said Nick testily. "Well, he sounds very nice. Think I remember him from the school. Tall, lanky bloke. Anyway, so glad everything is working out so well for you. The question is, are you well enough to look after the children tonight? Or should they come back with me?"

Alice said, "If neither of us had an affair, why aren't we still together? What could be bad enough to break us up?"

Nick exhaled noisily. He looked around the room in a flabbergasted way, as if looking for guidance from an equally flabbergasted audience. "It seems to me like this is a pretty serious head injury. I can't believe they let you leave the hospital."

"They did a CT scan. There's nothing physically wrong with me. Also, I sort of told them that I had my memory back."

Nick's eyes rose to the heavens. Another pompous new gesture. "Oh, great. Brilliant. Lie to the doctors. Well done, Alice."

"Why are you being so mean to me?"

"What, are we five now? I'm not being mean to you."

"You are. And you don't even sound like yourself. You've got all sarcastic and clichéd and . . . ordinary."

"Thank you. Thank you so much. Clichéd and ordinary. Yes, it's such a great mystery why our marriage has ended."

He looked around with a triumphant jeer for his invisible audience again, as if to say, "See what I have to put up with?"

"I'm sorry," said Alice. "I didn't mean . . ." She drifted off because she was remembering what it was like when you broke up with someone. Conversations became so hopelessly tangled. You had to be polite and precise. You couldn't safely criticize anymore, because you didn't have the right. You'd lost your immunity.

"Oh, Nick," she said helplessly.

She was experiencing all those familiar symptoms of a relationship breakup. The nausea. The sensation of something huge and hard lodged in the center of her chest. That trembly, teary feeling.

She wasn't supposed to ever have to feel this way again. Breakups were meant to be something from her youth. Painful memories. Actually not that painful, because it was sort of nice to look fondly back at her younger self and think, "Oh you silly thing, crying over that jerk."

This was meant to be her grown-up relationship. The one that lasted forever.

She put her wineglass on the coffee table and turned to face him. "Just tell me why we're getting a divorce. Please."

"That's an impossible question to answer. There are a million reasons. And you'd probably give a million different reasons."

"Well, just sort of . . . sum it up."

"In twenty-five words or less."

"Yes, please."

He smiled slightly and it was the real Nick again. He kept appearing and disappearing.

He said, "Well, I guess—" and then he stopped and bowed his head. "Oh, Alice." An expression of pure misery crossed his face.

It was too much for Alice. Her instinct was to comfort him, and she wanted to be comforted herself, and it was *Nick*, for heaven's sake.

She launched herself across the room and into his arms and buried her face in his chest, breathing in deeply. It was still Nick. He still smelled exactly like himself.

"Whatever went wrong, we'll fix it," she babbled. "We'll get counseling. We'll go on a nice holiday somewhere!" She was inspired. "With the *children*! They can come too! *Our* children! How fun would that be? Or we'll just hang around here. Swim in the pool. The pool! I love the pool! How did we ever afford that? I guess with your new job. Do you like the job? I couldn't believe it! You've got your own personal assistant. She wasn't very nice to me, but that's okay, I don't mind."

"Alice."

He wasn't hugging her back. The words kept tumbling out of her mouth. She could talk her way out of this.

"I'm skinny, aren't I? I might even be too skinny. What do you think?

How did I get so skinny? Did I give up chocolate? I can't find any chocolate in the whole house. My password is 'oregano.' Weird. Hey, why isn't Mrs. Bergen talking to me? Did I offend her? Elisabeth seems mad at me, too. But you still love me, don't you? You must still love me."

"Stop it." He held on to her shoulders and pushed her gently away.

"Because we have three children. And I still love you."

"No, Alice." He shook his head sternly, as if she were a toddler about to touch an electrical socket.

"What are you two fighting about this time?" Alice and Nick turned to see Madison leaning against the door frame. She must have had a shower. She was wearing a dressing gown, her face was scrubbed, and her hair was wet, pulled back from her face.

"Oh, you look so beautiful," said Alice involuntarily.

Madison's face changed, became ugly with rage.

"Why do you always say such stupid, retarded things?"

"Madison!" boomed Nick. "Do not speak to your mother like that."

"Well, she *is*! Anyway, I heard you say to Auntie Ella that Mum was a hard bitch, so why are you pretending to like her? I know you hate her."

Alice caught her breath.

"I do *not* hate your mother," said Nick. Alice could see tension pulling the skin around his mouth tight. He looked so old.

"You do so hate her," said Madison.

"He *does not* hate Mum!" It was Tom. He punched Madison in the arm. "I hate *you*."

"Tom!" snapped Nick.

"Owwww!" Madison clutched her arm, her knees collapsed beneath her, and she fell in a heap on the floor. "He *hit* me. You're not meant to hit girls. That is domestic violence. That is violence against women."

"You're not a woman," sneered Tom. "You're just a stupid girl."

Madison kicked viciously at Tom's leg. Tom threw back his head and howled. He looked at Alice, his face bright red and filled with righteous fury. "Mum, did you see how hard she kicked me? I only punched her a little bit!"

"A little bit?" Madison pulled up the sleeve of her dressing gown. "What's that? That is a mark! There will be a bruise! A huge bruise."

"Goodness," breathed Alice. She picked up her wineglass and looked around for some grown-up to take control.

"I think I should go," said Nick.

"Are you kidding?" said Alice. "You can't leave me with them!"

Madison and Tom now appeared to be trying to kill each other. They were wrestling like rabid cats on the floor. There was kicking, hair-pulling, and ear-piercing screams of rage. It was remarkable.

"Do they do this a lot?" asked Alice. She stuck her fingers in her ears. "Maybe it wouldn't be so much fun going on holidays with them."

Nick laughed, a surprised guffaw that he stopped short.

Alice said, "Did you really tell Ella I was a hard bitch?"

She paused. "Am I a hard bitch?"

Nick walked over to the children and grabbed the back of Tom's T-shirt in one hand. He wrenched him up in the air and carried him over to the couch and dropped him. Then he turned back to Madison and said, "Go to your room."

"Me? But *he* started it! He punched me first! That's not justice! *Mum?*"

Madison sat upright, her back against the wall, and looked at Alice imploringly.

At that moment Olivia came running into the room, wearing only a T-shirt and underpants dotted with pictures of strawberries. "Mummy, where are my shorts? I mean the denim ones. And don't say, 'Have I looked in the drawer?' because yes, I have looked, for ages and ages, and yes, actually, I did use my eyes." She pirouetted on the spot with her arms held gracefully above her head.

"You're very good at that," said Alice, glad of the distraction.

"Yes, I am pretty good," sighed Oliva, as if it were quite a responsibility.

She lifted one skinny brown leg and admired her pointed toe. A thought struck her. "Mum, who is going to take me to the Family Talent Night concert at Frannie's retirement city? You or Daddy? Which house will I be sleeping in?"

"I'm not exactly sure," said Alice.

"We only sleep at Dad's place on weekends." Madison looked sharply at Alice. "Olivia's concert is on Wednesday night, right?"

"Well, that must be right then, Madison," said Alice.

"I'm so hungry," sighed Tom from the couch. "When is dinner? Mum? Excuse me, please, when is dinner? I think my blood sugar has dropped."

"Okay, Tom—"

"Why are you saying our names all the time?" interrupted Madison.

"Oh, sorry, I just—sorry."

Madison said, "You don't remember us, do you?"

Tom sat up straight on the couch and Olivia stopped twirling.

"She doesn't even know who we are," Madison told them.

Chapter 21

A lice pursed her lips together in the manner of a stern, distracted mother and tried not to let the panic show.

"Of course I know who you are," she said to Madison. "Don't be silly."

"How could Mum not remember us?" Olivia put her hands on her hips and stuck her stomach out. "Madison? What does that mean?"

Madison gave her a bored, superior look. "Mum fell over and hit her head at the gym. I heard Auntie Libby telling Uncle Ben she'd lost ten years of her memory. Well, guess what? We weren't born ten years ago!"

"Yes, but so—she still knows who we are! We're her *children*!" Olivia seemed both agitated and excited.

"Okay, why don't you kids watch some TV," said Nick. "Or PlayStation? And maybe it's time you stopped eavesdropping on grown-up conversations, Madison."

"I was not eavesdropping! I was just *there*! In the kitchen! Getting some juice out of the fridge. What am I meant to do? Walk around like this?" She stuck her fingers in her ears.

"Amnesia," said Tom. "That's called amnesia. Is that what you've got, Mum?"

"Your mother is perfectly fine," said Nick.

"Mum?" said Tom.

"We'll do a test," said Madison. "Ask her some questions."

"Like what?" said Olivia.

"I know!" Tom put his hand up as if he were in school. "I know! Okay, Mum, what is my favorite food?"

"French fries," said Nick. "Now that's enough."

"That's wrong!" cried Tom. "It's chicken schnitzel. Sometimes. Or otherwise sushi."

"Well, there you go, I've got amnesia, too. Now that's enough."

"My favorite food is chicken schnitzel, too," commented Olivia.

"It is not," said Tom. "Think of your own thing! You copy every single thing I do."

"What's my teacher's name, Mum?" said Madison.

"Now that's enough," repeated Nick.

"Oh! I know that one!" Alice managed to stop herself from putting her hand up. She'd seen a notice on the fridge door about a Year 5 excursion with a teacher's name on it. "Mrs. Ollaway! I mean Alloway. Ollaway? Something like that."

There was an ominous silence.

"Mrs. *Holloway* is the deputy principal," said Madison quietly, in the tone of one pointing out an incredibly foolish, potentially dangerous mistake.

"Oh, yes, of course, that's what I meant," said Alice humbly.

"You didn't," said Madison.

"When's my birthday, Mum?" asked Tom, and he pointed a warning finger at his father. "Don't you answer for her!"

"Right!" Nick clapped his hands together and made a loud hollow sound. "Your mother had an accident and she's a bit muddled about some things, that's all. She needs you all to be extra helpful and extra quiet. She doesn't need you interrogating her. So I want all three of you setting the table now."

Olivia came and stood beside Alice and slipped a hand in hers. She whispered, "You know that my birthday is twentieth June, don't you?"

"Of course I do, darling," said Alice, and suddenly she felt like a mother. "That's the day you were born. I could never ever forget that."

She looked up and saw Madison standing in the hallway, staring at her with fierce concentration.

"You're lying," she said.

Elisabeth's Homework for Dr. Hodges

Dear Doctor Hodges,

You know what? I'm going to give in and call you by your first name. I was remembering today how you made such a point of it at our first session. "Jeremy," you said firmly each time I said "Dr. Hodges." You probably don't like your name. I don't blame you. Hodges is a plump, greasy name, and you're not plump and greasy. You're actually quite good-looking, which I find distracting. Your nice looks keep reminding me that you're a real person, and I don't want you to be a real person. Real people don't have the answers. They make mistakes. They say things with great authority and they're *wrong*.

But anyway, whatever, I'm officially taking you off your pedestal.

How are you, anyway, Jeremy? What are you doing this Sunday night? Are you drinking red wine with your pretty, fertile wife while she prepares a roast dinner and you help those fair-haired kids with their homework? Is the house warm and toasty and smelling of garlic and rosemary?

There is no roast dinner in the oven here. There is no conversation. There is only the sound of the television. There is always the sound of the television. I can't stand to turn it off. I can't stand the silence. "Couldn't we just play some music?" Ben says. No. I want TV. I want gunshots and canned laughter and dog food commercials. Nothing seems too tragic when the television is blaring. (I lived for two years without a television when I was in my twenties. How did I do that? Now it's like a narcotic.)

So, what did I want to tell you? Oh yes. Ben. We're fighting.

On the way home from Alice's place today, Ben started telling me about some man he'd met at last night's party. I'd seen them talking while I was chatting with Alice's new boyfriend, who, by the by, is sweet and awkward. It made me feel a bit weird. As if I was being unfaithful to Nick. But I liked him. Anyway, I thought, oh good, Ben's found someone to talk about cars.

But no.

They were talking about infertility and adoption. Suddenly Ben is the sort of guy who reveals details of his personal life to strangers at kindergarten cocktail parties. I've had him wrong all these years. He's not the silent, strong, damaged type at all. Oh no.

This guy's sister went through eleven failed IVF cycles before adopting a baby girl from Thailand and the little girl is a talented violin player and they all lived happily ever after.

Ben got this woman's number. He's going to call her. My husband has a zealous new look in his eyes. It's as if he's discovered religion or golf. Mr. Never Ever Adopt has become Mr. I Can't Wait to Adopt.

I asked how many years it took, but Ben didn't know.

I changed the subject.

Then, tonight, we're watching the news and they're showing the cyclone in Burma.

There was a woman wearing a red dress a bit like Alice's. She was standing in front of a pile of rubble that had once been her daughter's school. She had a photo of a solemn-faced girl. She looked about Olivia's age. The mother talked politely in good English to the reporter and explained that the local authorities were doing everything they could. She seemed fine, almost businesslike. The camera moved away. Then it came back and now the mother was writhing on the ground, wailing and biting her knuckles. The reporter explained that she'd just heard that there would be no further rescues from the school because it was too dangerous.

I was eating corn chips and watching a woman experiencing the worst moment of her life.

I have no right to be sad about anything. No right to have therapy from expensive doctors like you for losing children who never existed. There is real grief in the world. There are real mothers losing real children. I make myself sick.

And that's when Ben said, "Lots of children must have lost their parents." He said it solemnly, but also with a definite hint of cheer. As in, hey, how handy! Lots of dead parents! Lots of spare kids up for grabs! Maybe a cute little violin player is crawling out of the rubble right now. Jesus.

I said, "Yes, isn't this cyclone *great!*"

He said, "Don't be like that."

And suddenly I was screaming, "I would have adopted! I would have! I would have! But YOU SAID NO. You said you were psychologically damaged by being adopted, you said—"

And he interrupted and said, "I never EVER used the words 'psychologically damaged.'"

Which is true. But he implied it.

I said, "You did so." I mean he might as well have said it, Jeremy.

He said, "Bullshit."

I really hate that word. He knows that. And it doesn't even make sense. A bull's shit.

Then he said, and this is the kicker, Jeremy, he said, "I thought it was *you* who didn't want to adopt."

After my head stopped exploding, I said, "Why would you think that?"

He said, "Whenever people asked us about it, you'd get so angry with them. You'd say we want our own biological child."

I said, "But I was saying that because of you. Because you'd been so against it in the beginning."

He said, "I was against it, but then after we kept losing the pregnancies, it seemed the obvious thing to do, but I didn't want to bring it up because the idea seemed to upset you so much."

So there you go. How's that for great communication in a marriage?

It reminds me of that television show where they investigate airplane crashes. Sometimes a major disaster happens because of the tiniest, most stupid error.

I said, "Anyway, it's too late now."

He said, "It's not."

I said, "I'm not adopting. I'm too tired."

It's true, Jeremy. It has occurred to me recently that for the last few years I have been in a permanent state of tiredness. I'm so tired of trying and trying and trying. I don't have anything left. I'm done. I would like to go to sleep for a year or two.

I said, "We're not going to be parents. It's over."

And after a while of him munching corn chips (energetically grinding them with his teeth like a guinea pig), he said, "So are we just going to sit around and watch TV for the rest of our lives?"

And I said, "Suits me."

He got up and left the room.

Now we're not talking. I haven't seen him since. But I know

when he comes back, we won't talk. Or if we do, we'll talk very, very politely and coldly—which is the same as not talking.

Right now, I feel . . . nothing.

Nothing at all.

A huge, empty, endless nothing that I am filling up with corn chips and *Australia's Funniest Home Videos*.

Chapter 22

The Love family was sitting around the dinner table. There had been an awkward moment when Alice went to sit in Olivia's place, but Nick saved her by jerking his chin at the place opposite.

The children had become wriggly and giggly, almost as if they were drunk. They seemed unable to sit still. They were sliding off their chairs, constantly knocking cutlery onto the floor, and talking in high-pitched voices over the top of one another. Alice didn't know if this was normal behavior or not. It wasn't exactly relaxing. Nick had his jaw clenched, as if this dinner were a horrible medical procedure he had to endure.

"I *knew* you wouldn't remember that you promised I could make lasagna." Madison poked disgustedly at her hamburger.

"She's got amnesia, stupid," said Tom thickly, his mouth amazingly full.

"Manners," said Alice automatically, and then caught herself. Did she just say, "Manners"? What did that even mean?

"Oh, yeah," said Madison. She turned her dark eyes on Alice. "Sorry."

"That's okay," Alice said, and dropped her eyes first. The kid could be sort of scary.

"What's for dessert, Mummy?" said Olivia. She was kicking the table leg rhythmically as she ate. "Maybe ice cream? Or I know, Chocolate Mush?"

"What's Chocolate Mush?" asked Alice.

"Oh, silly, you know that!" said Olivia.

Tom slapped his hand against his forehead. "You girls! She's got amnesia!"

"Mummy, darling," said Olivia. "Is it gone now? Your am—thing? Because maybe you could take an aspirin? I could get it for you? I could get it for you now!"

She pushed her chair back from the table.

"Eat your dinner, Olivia," said Nick.

"Daddy," groaned Olivia. "I'm trying to *help*."

"As if an aspirin is going to help," said Tom. "She probably needs an operation. Like brain surgery. By a brain surgeon. I saw a brain surgeon on television the other night." He brightened. "Hey! I would like to dissect a mouse and see its brain, as well as its intestines! With a scalpel. That would be excellent."

"Oh my *God*." Madison put down her knife and fork and put her head on the table. "That is making me sick. I am so going to be sick."

"Stop it," said Nick.

"This is a mouse's brain, Madison." Tom squished his fork into his hamburger meat. "Chop, chop, chop, mousie's brain!"

"Make him stop!" wailed Madison.

"Tom," sighed Nick.

"So!" said Alice. "How was the Aquatic Center today?"

Madison lifted her head from the table and said to Alice, "Did you remember that you and Dad were getting a divorce? After you hit your head? Did you remember that?"

Nick made a strangled, helpless sound.

Alice considered the question. "No," she said. "I didn't."

No one spoke. Olivia banged her knife against her plate. Tom twisted his arm over and frowned ferociously at something on his elbow. There were spots of crimson on Madison's cheekbones.

"So do you still love Dad?" said Madison. There was a slight tremor in her voice. She sounded much younger.

"Alice," said Nick warningly, at the same time as Alice said, "Yes, of course I do."

"Can Daddy come home, then?" Olivia looked up, elated. "And sleep in his own bed again!"

"Okay, time for a change of subject," said Nick. He avoided Alice's eyes.

"They'd fight too much," said Tom.

"What do we fight about?" asked Alice, greedy for facts.

"Oh, I don't *know*," said Tom irritably. "You said that's why you couldn't live together anymore. Because you fight too much. Even though I still have to live with my stupid sisters and we fight all the time. So it wasn't even logical."

"You fight about Gina," said Madison.

"Don't talk about Gina!" said Olivia. "It makes me sad. It's an absolute *tragedy*."

"R.I.P. ," said Tom. "That's what you say when you talk about someone who has died. It means rest in peace. You have to say it whenever you hear their name."

"Why did we fight about Gina?" asked Alice.

"R.I.P.!" cried Tom, as if he were saying "snap!"

"So, the Aquatic Center was a lot of fun," said Nick. "Wasn't it, kids?"

"Well," said Madison. "I think Dad thought you liked Gina better than him."

"R.I.P.!" shouted Tom and Olivia.

"Oh shut up!" said Madison. "Someone dying is not funny!"

Alice looked at Nick. His face looked red and raw, like windburn. She couldn't tell whether it meant he was angry or embarrassed. Goodness. Had *she* had some sort of torrid lesbian affair with Gina?

"You fight about the American Expense a lot," said Tom.

"American *Express*," said Madison.

"American Expense works for me." Nick lifted his wineglass in a mocking sort of salute but he still didn't look at Alice.

"Once you had a really extremely big fight about *me*," said Olivia with satisfaction.

"Why?" asked Alice.

"Oh, you remember." Olivia looked wary. "That day. At the beach."

"For the twenty-billionth time, she doesn't remember!" said Tom.

"Olivia got lost," said Madison. "The police came. You were crying." She gave Alice a malicious look "Like this: 'Olivia! Olivia! My daughter! Where is my *daughter*?'" She buried her face in her hands and pretended to sob dramatically.

"Did I?" Alice felt ridiculously hurt by Madison's act.

"Just in case you're wondering," said Madison, "Olivia is your favorite child."

"Your mother doesn't have favorites," said Nick.

Did she? She hoped not.

"When I was pregnant with you, Madison," said Alice, "your Dad and I called you the Sultana. Did you know that? Because you were as tiny as a sultana."

"You never told me that." Madison looked doubtful.

"What did you call *me*?" asked Olivia.

"Really? I never told you that?" said Alice.

Madison turned to Nick. "Is that true? Did you call me the Sultana?"

"Your Dad spoke to you through a toilet roll on my tummy," said Alice. "He said, 'Ahoy there, Sultana! It's me! Your father!'"

Madison smiled. Alice stared. It was the most exquisite smile she had ever seen. She felt a shot of love so powerful, it hurt her chest.

She looked down at her plate and a memory dropped straight into her head.

She was in a car filled with gold, filmy light. There was a smell of salt and seaweed. Her neck hurt. She turned around to check the baby. Miracle. She was asleep. Fat pink cheeks. Long lashes. Her head lolling against the side of the car seat. As Alice watched, a bar of light fell across her face. Her eyes fluttered open and she yawned and stretched sleepily. Then she caught sight of Alice and her whole face lit up with a huge, surprised grin, as if to say, "Hey! I can't believe it! You're here, too!" There was a sudden loud, rumbling snore from the driver's seat and the baby looked startled. "It's okay," said Alice. "It's just Daddy."

"The baby wouldn't sleep." Alice looked at Nick. "She wouldn't sleep unless we were driving."

Nick kept shoveling food into his mouth and looked straight ahead.

Alice stared at Madison and blinked. The angry, strange little girl at the table was the baby. The giggling baby in the car was the Sultana.

"We drove all through the night," said Alice to Madison. "Every time we stopped you screamed."

"I know," said Madison. She was sullen again. "And you drove me all the way to Manly and you stopped in the car park and you and Daddy and me all fell asleep in the car, and then you took me on the beach and I rolled over for the first time. Whatever."

"Yes!" said Alice excitedly—she remembered. "The baby rolled over on the picnic rug! We got takeaway coffees from that place with the blue awning. And toasted ham-and-cheese sandwiches."

It felt like yesterday and it felt like a million years ago.

"I slept through the night when I was eight weeks old," said Olivia. "Didn't I, Mum? I was a gold-star sleeper."

"Just—shhhh," said Alice, holding up her hand, trying to focus. She could see that morning so clearly. The baby's striped suit. Nick's unshaven face and red eyes. A seagull white and squawky against a very blue sky. They were so tired, they were light-headed. The blessed feeling of the caffeine hitting her bloodstream. They were parents. They were filled with the wonder and the horror, the bliss and the exhaustion of being parents.

"Mummy," whined Olivia.

If she remembered that day, she should be able to feel her way back to when Madison was born. And she should be able to feel her way forward to the day that Nick packed his bags and left.

"Mummy," said Olivia again. *Oh, please be QUIET.* She groped about in the dark but there was nothing else.

All she had was that morning.

"But Nick," she began.

"What?" he said grimly, irritably. He really didn't like her. It wasn't just that he didn't love her anymore. He didn't even like her.

"We were so happy."

Elisabeth's Homework for Jeremy

3 a.m.

Hi J. Ben drove off somewhere. I don't know where he is.

I'm so tired.

Hey. You know how if you say a word over and over again, it starts to sound really weird?

Like, let's say the word is, oh, I don't know, INFERTILITY.

Infertility. Infertility. Infertility. Infertility.

It's a twisty, curly, nasty word. Lots of syllables.

Anyway, Jeremy, my darling therapist (as Olivia would say), my point is that things become weird and pointless if you examine them for too long. I've thought about being a mother for so many years the whole concept has started to seem weird. I've wanted it, wanted it, wanted it. Now I'm not even sure if I wanted it in the first place.

Look at Alice and Nick. They were so happy before they had the children. And sure, they love their kids, but let's be honest, they're hard work. And it's not like you get to *keep* those adorable babies. Babies disappear. They grow up. They turn into children who are not necessarily that cute at all.

Madison was the most beautiful baby. We adored her. But the Madison of today doesn't seem to have anything to do with that baby. She's so furious and strange and she can make you feel like an idiot. (Yes, Jeremy, a ten-year-old can make me feel inferior. That shows a lack of emotional maturity or something, doesn't it?)

Tom used to bury his face in my neck and now he wriggles away if I try and touch him. And he tells you the plots of TV shows with a lot of unnecessary detail. It's sort of dull. Sometimes I think of other things while he's talking.

And Olivia is still gorgeous, but actually she can be manipulative. Sometimes it's like she knows she's being cute.

And the FIGHTS. You should see them fight. It's amazing.

See. I'm a terrible auntie. I'm making bitchy remarks about those three beautiful children, whom I hardly see anymore anyway. So what sort of mother would I be? A horrible one. Maybe even an abusive one. They'd probably take my children away and give them to someone else. An infertile woman could adopt them.

You know, Jeremy, once, when Olivia was a toddler, I minded her for a whole day. Alice and Gina were out at some school function. Olivia was perfectly behaved and she was so cute, she would have won an award for the cutest baby, but you know, by the end of the day, I was BORED OUT OF MY SKULL from walking around after her and saying, no don't touch that, ooooh yes, look at the bright light.

Bored. Tired. A bit irritable. I was relieved to hand her over when Alice came home. I felt as light as a feather.

How's that? All this "oh, poor me" obsession with being a mother and I was bored after one day.

I've always secretly thought that Anne-Marie, my friend from the Infertiles, would make a terrible mother. She's so impatient and brittle. But maybe they're all thinking that about me, too. Maybe we'd all make terrible mothers. Ben's mum is probably right when she says that "Nature knows best." Nature knows that I would make a terrible mother. Each time I get pregnant, Nature says, "Actually, this kid would be better off dead than having a mother like her."

After all, Ben's mum couldn't have children either and look at her, she DID make a terrible mother.

The bottom line is, we shouldn't adopt.

I don't want to be a mother anymore, Jeremy.

A mother. A mother. A mother. A mother.

Sounds like smother. It's a weird word.

I don't even know why I'm crying.

Frannie's Letter to Phil

Mr. Mustache turned up at my door this morning just as I was about to leave for Tai Chi.

I almost didn't recognize him. He'd shaved off his mustache.

I said, "I hope you didn't do that for me."

His upper lip looked so naked! He seemed like an entirely different person. Softer and gentler. Although at the same time, more sophisticated and . . . masculine.

He was wearing tracksuit pants and a T-shirt and he said he'd been thinking he might give this "Tai whatchamacallit" a go, but he said he felt "shy" about turning up on his own.

I said, "Oh, yes, because you're such a shy, retiring type."

We went along to the Tai Chi, and he was utterly hopeless. I had to keep trying not to giggle like a naughty schoolchild. Afterward he looked so endearingly rumpled, I invited him back for a cup of tea and some of Alice's banana muffins that she'd given me last week.

We had quite a chat. I told him how I'd recently become quite addicted to "Facebook" after an old student invited me to join. (Little Mattie Marks. Remember him, Phil? He's some sort of IT big shot these days.) Mr. M was impressed. He said he used the Internet a lot but didn't know anything about Facebook. It made me feel quite hip!

He told me about his two sons and how much he misses them. (One lives in the U.K. and the other is in Perth.) He said both his boys were adopted.

"My wife and I couldn't have our own children," he explained. "That's why I felt so sorry for your granddaughter."

(He says "granddaughter" so naturally, even though he knows I'm not really related to Elisabeth. It may be to do with his own children being adopted. Perhaps it's not so presumptuous of him. Perhaps it's rather nice. I can't make up my mind.)

"It's a very lonely feeling when all your friends are having babies," he said. He told me he could still remember the expression on his wife's face while they went to her niece's baptism, even though it was over sixty years ago. "It made me want to punch a wall," he said.

I wonder if he was reprimanding me for my "babies are not the be-all and end-all" comment. I wonder if he thinks I'm being a bit harsh about poor Elisabeth.

Do you know something, Phil? I had always secretly hoped that you and I might have our own little baby. Just the one. Boy or girl. Didn't matter. I was thirty-eight, but I knew it wasn't beyond the realms of possibility. One of the sixth-form mothers at the school had a baby at forty-one. She was almost embarrassed about it. She brought the baby to the school one day and I remember holding out my finger for the baby to clutch and suddenly thinking, I'm younger than her. I felt that sudden rush of disbelief and exhilaration you feel when your *ticket number is called in a raffle. I could still be a mother, I thought, and I felt like dancing.*

It was two weeks before what should have been our wedding day.

One week before the phone call.

It's true I've never been pregnant, but I know what it's like to lose the possibility of a baby. So of course I sympathize with Elisabeth, Phil! Deeply. My heart breaks for her. I've cried and cried for her each time she's lost another baby.

It's just that sometimes I want to say to her, "Darling, maybe you don't get to be a mother, but you still get to be a wife."

Chapter 23

"R ight. Seat belts on?" said Alice. Her hand shook slightly as she turned the key in the ignition. Did she really drive this gigantic car every day of her life? It felt like a semi-trailer. Apparently, it was called an SUV.

"Are you sure you're safe to take them to school tomorrow? Because if you think there is any risk at all to the children, I'd rather drive them myself," Nick had said the night before when he was leaving, and Alice had wanted to say, "Of course I'm not right, you idiot! I don't even know where the school is!" But there had been something about Nick's tone that made the hairs on the back of her neck stand up with a powerful, strangely familiar feeling that was close to . . . fury? He had such a sneery way of talking to her now. That snippy voice spoke up again in her head: *Sanctimonious bastard! Trying to make me look like a bad mother.* "I'll be fine," she'd said. And he'd sighed his huffy new sigh, and as she watched him walk out to his shiny car, she felt something almost like relief at the same time as she thought, "But why don't you just come up to bed with me?"

Now her three children sat in the seat behind her. They were in horrible moods. If they'd been drunk last night, now they were all suffering from terrible hangovers. They were pale and snarly, with purple shadows under their eyes. Had they slept badly because of her? She suspected she'd let them stay up way past their normal bedtimes. There had been a lot of vagueness when she asked them what time they normally went to bed.

Alice adjusted the rear-vision mirror.

"Do you remember how to drive?" asked Tom.

"Yes, of course." Alice's hand hovered nervously over the handbrake.

"We're late," said Tom. "You might have to go quite a bit over the speed limit."

It had been a strange and stressful morning. Tom had appeared at Alice's bedroom door at seven a.m. and said, "Have you got your memory back?" "Not quite," Alice had said, trying to shake her head free of a night of dreams all involving Nick yelling at her. "She hasn't got it back!" she heard Tom cry, and then the sound of the television being switched on. When she got out of bed, she found Madison and Tom lounging around in their pajamas, eating cereal in front of the television. "Do you normally watch television before school?" Alice had asked. "Sometimes," Tom had answered carefully, without removing his eyes from the TV. Twenty minutes later, he was in a frenzy, yelling that they needed to leave in five minutes' time. That's when it emerged that Olivia was still sound asleep in bed. Apparently it was Alice's job to wake her.

"I think Olivia might be sick," Alice had said, as Olivia kept collapsing back against the pillow, her head lolling to one side, saying sleepily, "No thank you, I'll just stay here, thank you, goodbye."

"Mum, she's like this every morning," Tom had said disgustedly.

Finally, after Alice had dragged a half-comatose Olivia into a school uniform and spooned cereal into her mouth, while Madison had spent half an hour with a roaring hair dryer in the bathroom, they had left the house, incredibly late, according to Tom.

Alice put her hand around the handbrake.

"Did you even brush your hair this morning, Mum?" asked Madison. "You look sort of . . . disgusting. No offense."

Alice put a hand to her hair and tried to smooth it down. She had assumed that she didn't need to dress up for dropping the kids off at school. She hadn't bothered with hair or makeup and had pulled on a pair of jeans, a T-shirt, and an old watermelon-colored jumper she'd found at the back of the drawer. The jumper was faded and frayed, and it had given Alice a start when she realized she remembered buying it brand new with Elisabeth just the other week.

Just the other week ten years ago.

"Don't be mean to darling Mummy," Olivia said to Madison.

"Don't be mean to darling Mummy!" mimicked Madison in a sugary-sweet voice.

"Stop copying me!" Alice felt the thud of Olivia's feet against her lower back as she kicked the seat.

"We're so late," moaned Tom.

"Would you three just be quiet for once in your lives!" snapped Alice, in a voice entirely unlike her own, and at the same time, she released the handbrake and reversed out of the driveway and turned left, her hands smooth and capable on the leather-clad steering wheel, as if she'd said exactly those words and done exactly that maneuver a million times before.

She drove toward the lights, her hand already on the indicator to turn right.

There was a sullen silence in the back of the car.

"So, what's happening at school today?" she said.

Madison sighed dramatically as if she'd never heard a more stupid comment.

"Volcanoes," answered Tom. "We're talking about what makes a volcano erupt. I've written down some questions for Mrs. Buckley. Some pret-ty tricky questions."

Poor Mrs. Buckley.

"We're making a Mother's Day surprise," said Olivia.

"Now it's not a surprise, is it?" said Madison.

"It is so!" said Olivia. "Mum, it is, isn't it?"

"Yes, of course it's still a surprise, I don't know what you're making," said Alice.

"We're making special candles," said Olivia.

"Ha!" said Madison.

"Well, I still don't know what color they are," said Alice.

"Pink!" said Olivia.

Alice laughed.

"Idiot," said Madison.

"Don't call her that," said Alice. Had she and Elisabeth spoken to each other in such a horrible way? Well, there was that time Elisabeth threw the nail scissors at her. For the first time, Alice felt sorry for their mother. She didn't remember her ever yelling at them when they fought, just sighing a lot, and saying plaintively, "Be nice, girls."

They were pulled up at a red light. The lights changed and Alice had no idea where to go.

"Umm," she said.

"Straight ahead. Second on the left," said Tom laconically from the back, sounding so much like his father that Alice wanted to laugh.

Alice drove. The car was huge and unfamiliar again.

She saw she was driving behind a similarly huge car with a woman at the wheel and two small heads bobbing about in the back.

Alice was a mother driving her three children to school. She did this every day. It was unbelievable. Hilarious.

"So, compared to the other mums at school," she said, "am I strict?"

"You're like a Nazi," said Madison. "You're like the Gestapo."

"You're about average," said Tom. "Like, for example, Bruno's mum won't even let him go on school excursions, that's how mean she is. But then there's Alistair's mum—she lets him stay up till nine o'clock, and they have KFC whenever they want, and they watch television when they're eating their breakfast."

"Hey!" said Alice.

"Oh, yeah." Tom gave a dry chuckle. "Sorry, Mum."

"When am I like the Gestapo?" asked Alice.

"Don't worry about it," sighed Madison. "You can't help it."

"I don't think you're strict," said Olivia. "Just—sometimes, you get a bit angry."

"What makes me angry?" asked Alice.

"Me," said Madison. "Just looking at me makes you mad."

"Running late for school normally makes you *really* mad," said Tom. "Ummm, let's see, what else. Doors slamming. You can't stand it when a door slams. You have got really delicate ears."

"Daddy makes you angry," said Olivia.

"Oh, yeah," agreed Tom. "Dad makes you the angriest."

"Why?" Alice tried not to sound too interested. "What does he do that makes me so angry?"

"You hate him," said Tom.

"I'm sure that's not true," said Alice.

"You do," said Madison wearily. "You've just forgotten that you do."

Alice looked in the rear-vision mirror at her three extraordinary children. Tom was frowning at a chunky plastic wristwatch, Olivia was staring dreamily ahead, and Madison had her forehead pressed against the car window, her eyes closed. What had she and Nick done to them? This casual talk about hatred. She was filled with shame.

"I'm sorry," she said.

"Sorry for what?" said Olivia, who seemed to be the only one listening.

"I'm sorry about your dad and me."

"Oh, that's okay," said Olivia. "Can we have hot chocolates after school?"

"That's a green arrow," said Tom tersely.

Alice pulled into a street lined with trucklike cars similar to the one she was driving. It looked like a festival. A festival of women and children. The women stood in groups of two or three, sunglasses pushed up on their foreheads, scarves slung around necks. They wore jeans and boots, beautifully cut suede jackets. Were mothers always this attractive and thin? Alice tried to remember the mothers from her own school days. Weren't they sort of chunky and plain? Sort of irrelevant and fading into the background? A few women waved when they saw Alice. She recognized someone who had got quite drunk at the kindergarten cocktail party. Oh Lord, she should have done her hair.

The children whooped and swooped about in their blue school uniforms, like flocks of tiny birds. All those innocent, smooth-skinned faces.

"We're not late," said Alice.

"We're late for *us*," muttered Tom. "I've got a meeting of my spy club. They don't know what to do without me."

They found a parking spot.

"Watch it," winced Tom as Alice backed the car into the curb with a thud.

She breathed a sigh of relief as she pulled the keys from the ignition. The children immediately unclicked seat belts and opened the heavy car doors with a clunk, sliding out of the car, backpacks slung over their shoulders.

"Hey, wait for me!" said Alice, worried about procedures and kisses goodbye.

As she got out of the car, she saw Dominick. He was wearing a tie, his shirtsleeves carefully folded up to his elbows, and he was squatting down to talk to three boys who were explaining something to him that appeared to be about a soccer ball. Dominick was nodding seriously, as if he were in a top-level business negotiation. Two mothers were standing nearby, waiting to talk to him. Dominick caught sight of Alice and winked. Alice smiled self-consciously. He was nice. There was no denying it. He was very, very . . . nice.

"Have you slept with him yet?" said a posh voice in her ear, and the heavy sweet scent of a beauty salon filled Alice's nostrils.

It was that dreadful Kate Harper woman again.

"Oh, hi." Alice reeled back. Kate was wearing a beautifully fitted trench coat, skin polished, lips shimmery. It was a bit much for this time of the morning.

Kate didn't wait for an answer. "God, I'm jealous. It's been a year for us."

"A year?"

"A year since we've done the deed. I must have cobwebs down there."

The things strangers told you.

Kate was still looking at Dominick. "The claws are out, by the way. Miriam Dane has had her eye on him for ages. Apparently, she told Felicity that she thought it was rather poor form for you to go after him only three months after you and Nick separated. I promised I wouldn't pass it on, but of course I knew you'd want to know!" She lowered her voice. Her beautiful face turned nasty. "You'll die laughing when you hear this. Apparently, after she'd had a few drinks at the party the other night, Miriam called you the S-word."

Alice looked at her without comprehension.

Kate lowered her voice and whispered, *"Slut!"* Then she raised it again and screeched, "Isn't that *hilarious*? Isn't that just so *eighties*! I thought, I must tell Alice, she'll *love* that! The woman is pea green with jealousy! And of course she hated it when Tom kicked that goal at soccer, when, you know, she's been getting all that extra training for Harry, because he's supposedly so *talented*, ha, ha, that little piglet!"

Alice felt sick. She looked around for her children, wanting an excuse to get away from Kate. Tom was sitting on a bench, lecturing two other boys, who were listening intently; one even appeared to be taking notes. Olivia was doing a cartwheel while a group of girls applauded. She couldn't see Madison.

"Well," she said, "you can tell that Miriam not to worry. Nick and I are getting back together."

Kate grabbed Alice's arm so hard, it hurt. "You're joking."

"No." She thought of Nick's cold face last night as he said goodbye. "Well, anyway, we're working on it."

"But what *happened*? I mean, the things you were saying, just last week— I mean, gosh, it just seemed completely irretrievable! You said you couldn't stand the sight of him, he made you physically *ill*! You said you could never forgive him! You said—"

"Forgive him for what?" interrupted Alice.

"This is such a surprise!" Kate pulled at a strand of gold hair that had got caught in her sticky, shimmery lips. She'd lost some of her posh accent in her excitement.

"What did I need to forgive him for?" Alice repressed an urge to put her hands around Kate Harper's perfect neck and squeeze.

"Hey there."

Someone's hand settled gently on her shoulder.

Alice looked up and saw Dominick standing next to her.

"How are you, Kate?" said Dominick. His hand was still on Alice's shoulder, invisibly caressing her. It was nice, but *Nick* did that in public. "Congratulations, you two. Saturday night was great."

He was such a strange mix of authority and shyness.

"How are *you*, Dominick?" asked Kate. Her face was shiny with sympathy and fresh new gossip.

"Fighting fit for a Monday." Dominick removed his hand from Alice's shoulder (she missed it) and shuffled his feet while doing an absurd little boxing move.

He smiled at Alice and touched her arm again. "I'll talk to you later."

She smiled back. He was looking at her the way Nick looked at her when they first started going out. It was a look that made her feel highly desirable and extremely interesting. She thought of how Nick looked at her now.

"Yes, okay," she said.

"Oh, Dominick, we need you over here!" trilled a woman.

He loped off obediently.

"So I'm assuming you haven't told him, then? About you and Nick?" asked Kate avidly.

"Oh. No. Not yet."

"But it's definite?"

"Oh, well, yes. I think so. I hope so. It's sort of a secret."

"Got it! My lips are sealed." Kate mimed the zipping up of her lips.

"What did I need to forgive Nick for?"

"Mmmm. Pardon?" Kate looked distracted. "Oh, well, you know, we were talking about Gina."

"What about Gina?" In her head she had Kate by the shoulders and was shaking her until her teeth chattered.

"You know, you were saying how he didn't even make the effort to go to the funeral. You seemed so . . . well, that's why this is so out of the blue."

So Nick didn't go to Alice's best friend's funeral. Why not? There must have been a good reason. Surely they weren't getting divorced over that.

"Can I just say one thing?" said Kate. She fiddled with a button on her jacket and looked up, her face awkward. "Just, look, don't get back together if it's just for the kids. My parents stayed together for the children." She hooked her fingers in the air to form quotation marks around "for the children." "And let me tell you, children know when their parents despise each other. It's not nice. It's not a nice way to grow up. And you know, Dominick is a catch. He really is. So, anyway, that's Kate's two cents' worth for the day, my dear! I must go! Busy, busy, busy!"

Kate clip-clopped off in her high heels, swinging her handbag over her shoulder and tightening the belt of her trench coat.

Maybe she wasn't so dreadful after all.

Elisabeth's Homework for Jeremy

I really thought about not bothering with this morning's blood test. Just not showing up. Playing truant.

But of course I was there right on eight a.m. Writing my name on the clipboard. Presenting my forearm to the nurse. Checking the spelling of my name and my date of birth on the test tube. Pressing the cotton-wool ball to the speck of blood.

"Good luck," said the nurse as I left.

She's the one who always says "Good luck." In a sort of patronizing way.

"Oh, fuck off with your good luck," I said, and punched her in the nose.

Got you, J! I never said that. Of course I didn't. I said, "Thanks!" Then I went into the office and Layla was there all bright-eyed and bushy-tailed and telling me about how well the rest of Friday's seminars went after I left, and how all the evaluations were positive and she got twelve bookings for the advanced seminar.

I said, "Are you even going to ask about the reason I had to leave early? You know, my sister? The one who was in hospital?"

And Jeremy, her earnest face crumpled. She looked so embarrassed, I felt like I'd kicked a kitten. She was falling all over herself to apologize. She said she thought I didn't like to discuss personal stuff.

I don't! I never have! Poor woman.

This is the final confirmation that I am a horrible person.

Alice sat on her front veranda steps in the autumn sunshine, eating the leftover custard tart her mother had left behind and wondering whether she was meant to be somewhere soon. Her diary for today said: "L—10 a.m." Was "L" a person who was waiting for her somewhere? Was "L" important? She supposed she should call Elisabeth or her mother and find out, but she couldn't seem to make the effort. Maybe she would have a nap.

A nap! Are you kidding? You have got a million and one things to do.

There was that snippy voice again.

"Go away," said Alice out loud. "I can't remember what those million and one things are."

She closed her eyes and enjoyed the feeling of sun on her face. There was no sound except for the far-off roar of a motorbike. The amazing silence of the suburbs in the middle of the day. She normally only experienced this feeling if she was sick and took the day off work.

She opened her eyes again and yawned. She might as well eat the rest of the custard tart now. There was only a sliver left. From where she was sitting she could see the For Sale sign on the house opposite. So that's where Gina had lived. Alice had probably been inside that "stunning renovated character home" many times, borrowing sugar, or whatever. If Alice had thought about it at all, she would have assumed she wouldn't have made any new friends in her thirties. She had quite sufficient. Besides which, she really just wanted to hang around with Nick and Elisabeth, and she was going to become a mother. She thought that would have been enough of a distraction.

Yet it seemed as though her friendship with Gina had been a significant part of her life.

And then Gina had died and she'd been "devastated." It made Alice feel sort of silly. As if she'd made too big a fuss over something.

The sound of the motorbike got closer.

Goodness. It was coming up her driveway. Was this "L"?

Alice wiped a hand across her mouth and put the plate down on the step next to her.

A man in a black leather jacket, his face invisible behind his opaque black helmet, lifted a casual gloved hand in greeting as he pulled up in front of her. He stopped the bike and turned off the ignition.

"Hey there," he said, as he pulled off his helmet and unzipped his jacket.

"Hey," said Alice, and coughed because she'd never said "Hey" to anyone before. He was so handsome, it was like a joke. He was all broad shoulders, biceps, piercing eyes, and stubbled jaw. Alice found herself looking around for another woman. There was no point in such a gorgeous man without a friend or sister there so you could exchange glances.

Surely, she wasn't *dating* him as well? It wouldn't be possible. He was way out of her league. He was a cartoon character. She felt a wave of giggles rising in her chest.

"What are you doing eating just before a session?" asked the sex god.

"A session?" asked Alice. Her mind raced. Oh, my Lord, maybe he was a *gigolo* and he was here to *service her*. After all, she was a middle-aged woman with a swimming pool.

"That's not like you."

He pulled off his leather jacket and his white T-shirt rode up to reveal his stomach.

Well, it wouldn't be the end of the world.

No sirrreee. If she'd paid in *advance*, for example . . .

Alice began to giggle helplessly.

He smiled warily. "What's the joke?" He rested his helmet on the front of his bike and walked over toward her. What could she say? *You're so good-looking, I find it hilarious.*

She was giggling so hard her legs felt weak. He looked frightened. For heaven's sake. Attractive people were still real. They had feelings. Alice took a hold of herself.

"I had an accident," she said, looking up at him. "Last week. At the gym. Hit my head. I'm suffering a bit of memory loss. So, I'm sorry, I don't know who you are, or, ah, why you're here."

"You're kidding." He looked down at her suspiciously. "It's not April Fools' Day, is it?"

"No," sighed Alice. Her giggles drifted away. She had a bit of a headache actually. Damned head. "I don't know who you are."

"It's me," he said. "Luke."

"I'm sorry, Luke. I need more information."

He laughed a bit, and his eyes darted around nervously as if someone might be watching him make a fool of himself. "I'm your personal trainer. I come every Monday morning to give you a training session."

Oh, for heaven's sake. No wonder she was so skinny.

"So, we exercise, is that right? What do we do exactly?"

"Well, we vary it. A bit of cardio, some weights. We've been doing well with the interval training lately."

Alice had no idea what he was talking about.

"I just had three pieces of custard tart," she said, holding up the plate.

Luke sat down next to her and helped himself to the last piece of tart. "Yeah, I won't tell you how many calories you just consumed."

"Oh, thousands!" said Alice. "Thousands of divinely delicious calories."

He gave her an odd look, and said, "Well if you've got a head injury, I suppose we shouldn't be training today."

"No," said Alice. She didn't want to exercise in front of him. The very thought made her feel self-conscious. "I'll still pay, of course."

"That's okay."

"No, no, I insist."

"Well, let's just make it a hundred."

Geez. What did he normally charge?

"So, this memory thing is just temporary, I assume?" he said. "What do the doctors say?"

Alice waved him away irritably. She didn't want to talk to him about that. *One hundred dollars!* "How long have you been my personal trainer?"

Luke stretched out his long legs and leaned back on his elbows. "Oh, wow, it must be coming up to three years now. You and Gina were, like, maybe my second-ever clients. Bloody hell, she made me laugh in the beginning. Remember the fuss she made whenever we did the stairs down at the park? *Not the stairs, Luke, anything but the stairs.* She got pretty good, though. You both got so fit." He stopped talking and Alice realized with a start that he was trying not to cry.

"Sorry," he said in a muffled voice. "It's just that I never knew anyone who died before. It sort of freaks me out. Every time I come over to train you, I think of her. I mean, obviously you miss her so much more than me. Probably sounds stupid."

"I don't remember her," said Alice.

Luke looked at her, shocked. "You don't remember *Gina*?"

"No. I mean—I know she used to be my friend. And I know she's dead."

"Wow." He seemed lost for words. Finally he came up with one. "Freaky."

Alice stretched her neck from side to side. She felt a strong desire to eat or drink something quite specific, except she couldn't work out what it was. Frankly, it was making her feel quite irritable.

"Luke," she said snappishly. "Did I ever talk to you about Nick?"

If she was paying him one hundred dollars for a chat, she might as well gather some useful information.

He smiled, revealing chunky white teeth. He was a walking multivitamin advertisement. "You and Gina were always trying to get the male perspective from me on your marriage problems. I'd say, 'Hey, girls, I'm outnumbered here!'"

"Yes," said Alice. She was surprised at just how very, very irritable she was feeling. "It's just that I don't remember why Nick and I are splitting up."

"Oh," said Luke. He flipped over on his stomach and started doing push-ups on the top veranda step. "I remember once you said that in the end your divorce all came down to one thing. I went home and told my girlfriend that night. I knew she'd be interested."

He put one arm behind his back and started doing his push-ups on one hand. Was that really necessary?

"So . . ." said Alice, as he switched arms with a grunt. "What was that one thing?"

"I can't remember." He flipped back over and grinned at the expression on Alice's face. "You want me to call her?"

"Could you?"

He pulled out a mobile phone from his pocket and pushed a button.

"Hey, babe. Yeah, no, nothing's wrong. I'm just with a client. Do you remember I told you that lady said her divorce was caused by one thing? Yeah, no, I just want to know, what was that one thing?"

He listened.

"Really? You're sure? Okay. Love ya."

He hung up and looked at Alice. "Lack of sleep."

"Lack of sleep," repeated Alice. "That doesn't make much sense."

"No, that's what my girlfriend said, but I remember Gina seemed to understand."

Alice sighed and scratched the side of her face. She was sick of hearing about Gina. "I'm feeling really grumpy. I need chocolate or . . . something."

"You probably need to see your dealer," said Luke.

"My dealer?" What next? Was she a drug addict? Did she drop the kids off at school and then go home and snort a few lines of cocaine? She must be! How else did she know this drug-addict sort of terminology, like "snort a few lines"?

"The coffee shop. Your body is screaming for a flat white."

"But I don't drink coffee," said Alice.

"You're a caffeine junkie," said Luke. "I never see you without a take-away coffee in your hand."

"I haven't had a coffee since my accident."

"Have you had a headache?"

"Well, yes, but I thought that was the injury."

"It was probably the caffeine withdrawal as well. This might be a good opportunity to give it up. I've been trying to get you to cut back for ages."

"No," said Alice, because now the desire she'd been feeling had a label. She could smell coffee beans. She could taste it. She wanted it right now. "Do you know where I get my coffee?"

"Sure. Dino's. According to you, they do the best coffee in Sydney."

Alice looked at him blankly.

"Next to the cinema. On the highway."

"Right." Alice stood up. "Well, thanks."

"Oh. We're done? Okay." Luke stood up, towering over her. He seemed to be waiting for something.

Alice realized with a start that he wanted his money. She went inside and found her purse. It was physically painful to hand over two fifty-dollar notes. He actually wasn't that good-looking at all.

Luke's huge hand closed cheerfully around the cash. "Well, I hope you're back to yourself next week, eh? We'll do a killer session to make up!"

"Great!" beamed Alice. She *paid* this man over a hundred dollars to tell her how to exercise each week?

She watched him roar out of the driveway and shook her head. Right. Coffee. She looked at the step where Luke had done his push-ups and suddenly she was down on her hands and knees, palms flat, body horizontal, stomach muscles pulled in hard, and she was bending her elbows and bringing her chest smoothly down toward the step.

One, two, three, four . . .

Good Lord, she was doing push-ups.

She counted to thirty before she collapsed, her chest burning, arms aching, and yelled, "Beat that!" as she looked around triumphantly for someone who wasn't there.

There was silence.

Alice hugged her knees to her chest and looked at the For Sale sign across the road.

She had a feeling the person she'd been looking for was Gina.

Gina.

It was very strange to miss a person she didn't even know.

Chapter 24

Elisabeth's Homework for Jeremy

Well, I don't know, you seemed a bit grumpy this morning. Is that allowed? Are therapists allowed to have feelings? I don't think so, J. Save them for your own therapy sessions. Not on my time, buddy.

I really wanted a bit more praise when I showed you how many pages I'd written for my homework. Couldn't you tell that, as a therapist? I mean, I know you're not meant to read it, but the reason I brought along my notebook was so you could say something like "Wow! I wish all my clients were as committed to this process as you!" Or you could have said what nice handwriting I had. Just a suggestion. You're the one who is meant to be good with people. Instead you just looked a bit taken aback, as if you didn't even remember asking me to do the homework. It always bugged me when teachers forgot to ask for the homework they'd set. It made the world seem undependable.

Anyway, today, you wanted to talk about the coffee shop incident.

Personally, I think you were just curious about it. You were feeling a bit bored for a Monday morning and thought it might spice things up.

You seemed quite testy when I said I preferred to talk about Ben and the adoption issue. The customer is always right, Jeremy.

This is what happened in the coffee shop, if you must know.

It was a Friday morning and I'd stopped in at Dino's on the way to work. I was having a large skim cappuccino because I wasn't pregnant or in the middle of the cycle. There was a woman at the table next to me with a baby and a toddler about two years old.

A little girl. With brown curly hair. Ben has brown curly hair. Well, actually, he doesn't because he gets it cut really close to his head like a car thief but I've seen photos from before we met. When I used to imagine our children I always gave them brown curly hair like Ben's.

So, there was that, but she wasn't particularly cute or anything. She had a dirty face and she was being sort of whiny.

The mother was talking on her mobile phone and smoking a cigarette.

Well, she wasn't smoking a cigarette at all.

But she *looked* like a smoker. That sort of thin, edgy face. She was telling someone a story on the mobile phone that was all about how she put someone in their place and she kept saying, "It was just *too* funny." How can something be too funny, Jeremy?

Anyway, she wasn't watching the little girl. It's like she forgot the child even existed.

Dino's is on the Pacific Highway. The door is always being opened and closed as people come in and out.

So I was watching the little girl. Not in a weird, obsessive infertile way. Just watching her, idly.

The door opened to let in a Mothers' Group. Prams. And mothers.

I thought, Time to go.

I stood up and the mothers came crashing through with their giant prams, sending chairs and tables skidding, and I watched the little girl slip out the door and onto the street.

The woman on the phone kept talking. I said, "Excuse me!" and nobody heard me. Two mothers had already sat down and were busy unbuttoning shirts and pulling out breasts to feed babies (this relaxed attitude to breast-feeding has got a bit too relaxed if you ask me) while they shrieked coffee orders across the room.

As I walked out of the coffee shop, the little girl was toddling straight toward the curb. Semi-trailers and four-wheel-drives were thundering down the highway. I had to run to get to her. I scooped her into the air just as she was about to step down into the gutter.

I saved the kid's life.

And I looked back to the coffee shop and the thin-faced mother was still on her mobile phone and the Mothers' Group was deep in conversation and the little girl was in my arms, smelling of sugar and maybe a touch of cigarette smoke. One fat little hand resting so trustingly on my shoulder.

And I kept walking. I just walked off with her.

I wasn't thinking. It wasn't like I was planning to dye her hair blond and drive off to the Northern Territory to live with her in a caravan by the sea, where we would both become nut brown in the sun and live on seafood and fresh fruit and I could home-school her and . . . Kidding! I wasn't thinking any of that.

I was just walking.

The little girl was giggling as if it was a game. If she'd cried, I would have taken her straight back, but she was giggling. She liked me. Maybe she was grateful that I saved her life.

And then, pounding feet behind me, and the thin-faced woman grabbing at my shoulder, screaming, "Hey!" Her face filled with terror, her nails scratching my skin as she dragged the little girl out of my arms, and then the little girl did cry because she got a fright, and the mother was saying, "It's okay, sweetie, it's okay," and looking at me with such revulsion.

Oh God, the shame and the horror.

Some of the mothers had come out of the coffee shop and were standing silently, cupping their babies' heads and staring, as if I was a traffic accident. The owner of the coffee shop, Dino himself, I guess, had come out, too. I'd only ever seen the top half of him over the counter. He was shorter than I expected. It was a surprise: like seeing a newsreader in full length. It's the only time I've seen him serious. He's normally one of those permanent chucklers.

All those people watching me and judging. It was like I was bleeding in public. I felt something come loose in my mind. I really did. It was an actual physical sensation of going crazy. Maybe there is a word for it, Jeremy?

I collapsed to my knees on the footpath, which was so unnecessary, and also excruciatingly painful. The grazes took weeks to heal.

That's when Alice turned up. She was wearing a new jacket I'd never seen before, hurrying into Dino's, handbag swinging, frowning. I saw the expression on her face when she recognized me. She actually recoiled, as if she'd seen a rat. She must have been mortified. I had to pick her local coffee shop for my public meltdown.

She was nice, though. I have to admit she was nice. She came and knelt down beside me and when our eyes met, it reminded me of when we were children and we'd run into each other in the school playground and I would suddenly feel as if I'd been performing on a stage all day, because only Alice knew my real self.

"What happened?" she whispered.

I was crying too hard to talk.

She fixed everything. It turned out she knew the mother of the child, as well as some of the Mothers' Group women. There was a lot of intense mother-to-mother talk while I stayed kneeling on the footpath. She made their faces soften. The crowd melted away.

She helped me up off the footpath and took me to her car and strapped me into the passenger seat.

"Do you want to talk about it?" she said.

I said I didn't.

"Where do you want to go?" she said.

I said I didn't know.

Then she did exactly the right thing and drove me to Frannie. We sat on Frannie's tiny balcony, drinking tea and eating buttered arrowroot biscuits, and we didn't talk about what had happened.

In fact, we talked about something quite interesting. I could see some new stationery on Frannie's desk, and it prompted me to ask her about the time I found her writing a mysterious letter when I was a teenager. I told her that Alice and I had been convinced that she had a secret lover.

Frannie didn't look embarrassed, just dismissive. She waved her hand impatiently as if it wasn't an important subject. She said she had once been briefly engaged when she was in her late thirties, and she still wrote occasionally to her ex-fiancé, and she probably just hadn't wanted to talk about it at the time.

"So you're still friends?" said Alice, all agog.

"I guess you could say that," Frannie had said. There was a peculiar quizzical expression on her face.

"And he writes back?" I asked.

And she said, "Well, no."

So that was odd. And it seemed like she was about to say more but then we had to rush off because Alice had to pick up the children from school, so I never got to hear more about this man, this "Phil" who never answers her letters. Did she leave him at the altar all those years ago? Why has she never mentioned him before?

I've been meaning to call Frannie to ask her about it, but I haven't even got the energy to be nosy these days. Also I've been avoiding her because I know she thinks I should stop trying to have a baby. She said it at least two years ago. She said that sometimes you had to be brave enough to "point your life in a new direction." I was a bit snappy at the time. I said a baby wasn't a "direction." Besides which, as far as I can see, *she* never pointed her life in a new direction. We just fell into her life after Dad died.

Thank goodness we did, of course. And who knows, maybe there will be a convenient death in our local area! Think positive! That father two doors down always looks like he's about to drop dead when he mows the lawn.

Anyway, the day after my psychotic episode I went to my GP and asked for a referral to see a good psychiatrist. I wonder if you pay her a spotter's fee.

So that's how I came into your life, Jeremy.

When Alice walked into Dino's Coffee Shop her senses were flooded with familiarity. The aroma of coffee and pastries. The rhythmic thud and hiss of the espresso machine.

"Alice, my love!" said a small, dark-haired man behind the counter. He was working the coffee machine with two hands, expertly and elegantly, as if it were a musical instrument. "I heard on the grapevine you had an accident! Lost your memory! But you never forget Dino, do you?"

"Well," said Alice carefully, "I think I remember your coffee."

Dino laughed as if she'd made a hilarious joke. "Of course you do, my love! Of course you do! I won't be one moment. I know you're in a hurry. Busy lady. Here you go."

Without waiting for an order, he handed her a takeaway cup. "How you feeling, anyway? You all better? You remember everything? You ready for the big day on Sunday? Mega Meringue Day at last! My daughter is so excited! All she talks about is '*Daddy, Daddy, this pie will be the biggest in the world!*'"

"Mmmm," said Alice. She was assuming that by Sunday she would have her memory back, because she really had no idea how to bake the world's biggest lemon pie.

She peeled off the lid of the cup and took a sip. Ewww. No sugar, and extremely strong. She took another sip. Actually very good. She didn't need sugar. She took another sip, and another and another. She wanted to tip back her head and pour it straight down her throat. The caffeine was zipping through her veins, clearing her head, making her heart beat faster and her vision sharpen.

"Maybe you need two today?" chortled Dino.

"Maybe I do," agreed Alice.

"How is your sister, by the way?" said Dino, still chuckling. He appeared to be a jolly fellow. He stopped and clicked his fingers. "Ah, my mind! I keep forgetting, my wife gave me something to give to her."

"My sister?" Alice ran her finger around the edge of the cup and licked the froth while she wondered how well Dino knew Elisabeth. "She's okay, I guess." She is an entirely different person. She appears to be desperately unhappy. I'm not sure how I've wronged her.

"I went home and told my wife the whole story, about how this lady walks off with a child, and then when she collapsed like that, crying, and none of us knew what to do! I was making her coffee! That's no help, is it? Even Dino's coffee! Those stupid women wanting to call the police."

Good Lord. Had Elisabeth tried to kidnap a child? Alice felt pity (Her poor darling Elisabeth, how bad must she be feeling to so publicly break a rule!), a horrified shame (How *embarrassing*! How illegal!) and guilt (How could she be worried about what people thought when her sister was obviously suffering so badly?).

Dino continued, "I said to those women, 'No harm done!' It was so lucky you showed up and made them see sense, and when you told me her story, so sad! Anyway, my wife gave me this. It's an African fertility figurine. If you have one of these dolls, you give birth to a beautiful baby. That's the legend."

He handed her a small dark wooden doll with a Post-it note stuck to it saying "Alice." The doll seemed to be an African woman in tribal dress with an oversized head.

"That's so sweet of your wife." Alice handled the doll reverently. Was his wife African perhaps and this was some sort of mystical tribal heirloom?

"She bought it off the Internet," confided Dino. "For her cousin, who couldn't get pregnant. Nine months later—baby! Although to be honest, not such a beautiful baby." He slapped his knee, his face creased with mirth. "I say to my wife, That's one ugly baby! Got a big head, like the doll!" He could hardly speak, he was laughing so hard now. "Big head, I said. Like the doll!"

Alice smiled. Dino handed her another coffee and he became serious again.

"Nick came in the other day," he said. "He didn't look too good. I said, You should get back together with your wife. I said, It's not right. I remember when I first opened the shop and you came in every weekend with little Madison. All three of you in overalls. She used to help you with the painting. You two were so proud of her. Never saw prouder parents! Remember?"

"Hmmmm," said Alice.

"I told Nick that you two should get back together, be a family again," said Dino. "I said, What went so wrong you can't fix? None of my business, right? My wife says, Dino, it's not your business! I say, I don't care, I say what I think, that's just me."

"What did Nick say?" asked Alice. She was already halfway through the next cup of coffee.

"He said, 'I would fix it if I could, mate.'"

Alice drove home chanting Nick's words in her head. He would if he could, so therefore . . . why not!

She had the takeaway cup of coffee in a handy cup holder close to the steering wheel. She found she could steer this enormous car with one hand and take sips of coffee with the other. So many useful new skills! The caffeine was making her tremble with energy. She felt like her eyes were protruding. When the light changed to green and the car in front didn't move straightaway, she shoved it along with a bossy beep of her horn.

That sharp voice was back in her head, working out everything she had to do before she picked the children up at 3:30 p.m. "You need to be on time, Mum," Tom had told her. "Monday afternoons are a pretty tight schedule."

Well, you can't spend your day lounging around eating custard tart. You won't fit into those beautiful clothes for long, will you? Speaking of which, what about laundry? You probably should do laundry when you get home. Mothers are always complaining about washing.

What else do they complain about? Groceries! When do you shop? Check pantry. Do list. You probably have a list somewhere. You seem like the sort of person who has a list. What about dinner tonight? Snacks when they come from school? Were the children used to freshly baked cookies on arrival?

Ring Sophie. She's your best friend! You must have told her something about what's going on.

Your diary says you've got a Mega Meringue meeting at 1 p.m. Presumably you've got to run it. Great! That should be a hoot. Find out where it is! How? Ring someone. Ring that Kate Harper if you must. Or your "boyfriend."

Would fix it if he could. Would fix it if he could.

Laundry.

Yes, you already said that.

Laundry!

Yes, calm down.

She shouldn't have had the two cups of coffee. Her heart was beating much too fast. She took a few deep, shaky breaths to steady herself. She couldn't keep up with her own body. She felt as if she needed to run crazily across a huge expanse of grass, flinging her body about like a puppy let off its leash.

When she got home she ran through the house as if she were in some sort of weird competition, gathering piles of clothes from laundry hampers and the floors of the children's bedrooms and bathrooms. There was a lot. She pounded down the stairs to the laundry. No surprise to see a huge, shiny-white washing machine taking up half the room. She lifted the lid ready to toss in the clothes when she felt a rush of feelings. Embarrassed. Betrayed. Shocked.

What did it mean? The memory flipped to the front of her brain like a neat index card. Of course. Something had happened right here. Right here in this extraordinarily clean laundry. Something horrible.

That's right. It was a party.

In the summer. Still warm late in the evening. There were tubs of ice on the laundry floor. Bottles of beer and wine and champagne poking out of the melting ice cubes. She went to get a new bottle of champagne and she was laughing as she pushed open the door and when she saw them, she automatically said, "Hi!" like an idiot, before her brain caught up with what they were doing, what she was seeing. A tiny graceful woman with closely cropped red hair sitting up on the washing machine, her legs apart, and Nick standing in front of her, his hands flat on the machine on either side of her legs, his head bent. Her husband was kissing another woman in the laundry.

Alice stared down at the pile of clothes in the machine. She could see the woman's face so clearly. The delicate bones of her face. She could even hear her voice. Sugar-sweet and childlike to match her tiny body. It made her teeth ache.

She poured in a scoop of washing powder and slammed down the machine lid. How dare Nick guffaw when she asked if he'd had an affair? That kiss was worse than catching them in bed together. It was worse because it was so obviously a kiss at the beginning. Early kisses were so much more erotic than early sex. Sex at the beginning of a relationship was fumbly and silly and vaguely gynecological, like a doctor's appointment. But fully clothed kisses, before you'd slept together, were delicious and mysterious.

Nick had kissed her for the first time up against the car after they'd just seen *Lethal Weapon 3* at the movies. He tasted of popcorn, with a hint of chocolate. He was wearing a black jumper over a white T-shirt and jeans, and he was a bit stubbly under his lower lip and even as he was kissing her, she was already carefully saving it up as a memory, knowing that she'd be sitting at her computer screen the next day, reliving it. She'd pulled it out and replayed it like an old movie so many times. She had described it in minute detail to her friend Sophie, who had been in a relationship for five years and had therefore moaned with jealousy, even though Jack was the love of her life.

Sophie. Her oldest friend. Bridesmaid at her wedding.

She would ring Sophie right now. There was no way she hadn't called Sophie and told her about the horror of that kiss in the laundry. First she would have called Elisabeth. Then Sophie. She would have skewed the story for each of them. For Elisabeth she would have concentrated on her own feelings. "How could he do that to me?" she would have asked and her voice would have quivered. For Sophie she would have spun out the story for maximum shock: "So I walked into the laundry to get some champagne and you will never in a million years guess what I saw. Go on, guess." From Elisabeth she would have got sympathy and very clear instructions on what to do next. From Sophie she would have got shock and fury and an invitation to go out right now and get very drunk.

She found her address book and Sophie's mobile number. It seemed that Sophie was living in Dee Why. The northern beaches. Good for her. She'd always wanted to live by the beach, but Jack preferred to live close to the city. She must have won out in the end. They must be married with children by now, although of course Alice had to remember not to take that for granted. She hoped Sophie hadn't had fertility problems like Elisabeth. Or she and Jack could have broken up? No. Not possible.

"Sophie Drew."

Goodness. Everyone had become so professional and grown-up.

"Sophie, hi, it's me, Alice."

There was a slight pause. "Oh, hi, Alice. How are you?"

"Well, you're not going to *believe* what happened to me," said Alice, and she realized she was feeling strangely silly. Almost nervous. Why? It was only Sophie.

There was another pause. "What happened to you?"

There was something not quite right. Sophie's voice was too polite. Alice wanted to cry. Oh, for heaven's sake, I can't have lost you as well, can I? Who do I *talk* to?

She didn't bother spinning out the story. She said, "I had an accident. Hit my head. I've lost my memory."

This time there was an even longer pause. Then she heard Sophie say to someone in the background, "I won't be long. Just tell them to hold on."

Her voice came back. Louder. Maybe a touch impatient. "Sorry, Alice. So, umm, you had an accident?"

"Are we still friends?" said Alice desperately. "We are still friends, aren't we, Soph?"

"Of course we are," said Sophie immediately, warmly, except now her voice had an undercurrent of *"Something weird is going on here. Must tread carefully!"*

"It's just that my last proper memory is of being pregnant with Madison. And now I find I've got three children, and Nick and I aren't together anymore, and I can't work out why, and Elisabeth—"

"No, no, not that one! The green one!" Sophie spoke sharply. "Sorry. I'm in the middle of a shoot for the new line. It's a madhouse around here."

"Oh. What do you do?"

Another pause. "Does that look green to you? Because it sure doesn't look green to me. Alice, I'm sorry, but can I call you back?"

"Oh. Sure."

"Look. I know we keep saying it but we must catch up!"

"Okay." So they weren't friends anymore. Not proper friends. They were "must catch up" friends.

"I mean, the last time I saw you was when we had that drinks thing with that friend of yours. The neighbor? Gina. How's she?"

Gina, Gina, Gina. It occurred to Alice that she wouldn't have called Elisabeth or Sophie about the kiss in the laundry. She would have called Gina.

"She's dead."

"Sorry, she's what? Green! Green! Are you color-blind? Look, Alice, I've got to go. I'll call! Soon!"

"Just tell me one thing," said Alice, but the phone was beeping at her. Sophie had gone.

Just like everyone, it seemed.

The phone rang in her hand and Alice jumped as if it had come alive.

"Hello?"

"Oh, you sound much better." It was her mother. Alice relaxed. Barb might now be the salsa-dancing, cleavage-baring wife of Roger, but she was still her mother.

"I've just been speaking to Sophie," said Alice.

"Oh, that's nice. She's so famous these days, isn't she? After that article? I was just talking to someone about her the other day. Who was it? Oh, I know! It was the lady who comes to do Roger's feet. The chiropractor. No, no, that's not it. The podiatrist. She said her daughter wanted one of those 'Sophie Drew' handbags for her birthday. I said, well, I've known Sophie since she was eleven years old, and I was nearly going to offer to try and get a discount for her, because it has to be said, Roger has awful hairy feet, so I do feel a bit sorry for her, but then I thought, you and Sophie don't really see much of each other these days, do you? Just Christmas cards, isn't it? So I changed the subject quick smart in case she asked, because she's that sort of person, I think, who likes to try and use connections to get bargains. Gina was a bit like that, wasn't she? Not that there's anything wrong with it, I guess. It's quite a clever way to live your life really, oh dear, what an absolute tragedy, it really is, anyway, what made me think of Gina? Oh yes, ah, connections. Anyway, I've got three reasons why I rang, I've actually written them down, my memory is just shocking these days—now speaking of which, how *are* you, darling?"

"I'm fine," began Alice.

"Oh good, I'm so pleased. Frannie was making such a fuss about it. I said, 'You watch, she'll have her memory back by Monday.'"

"I'm remembering some things," began Alice. Should she ask her mother about Nick and the kiss in the laundry?

"Wonderful!" Her mother wavered and then obviously decided to take the optimistic approach. "Wonderful! Now, darling, I wondered, when you said at the hospital that you and Nick might be getting back together, is that something that I possibly shouldn't have mentioned to anyone? Because I happened to run into Jennifer Turner today at the shops."

"Jennifer Turner?" The name didn't mean anything to her.

"Yes, you know. That fierce sort of girl. The lawyer."

"Oh, you mean *Jane* Turner." Mmmm. The first face she saw when she woke up in this strange new life. Jane who was helping her divorce Nick.

"Yes, Jane. She wanted to know how you were. She said you hadn't been answering her texts."

Texts. What did that mean?

"Anyway, I said you were fine, and then I mentioned that you and Nick were getting back together. Well, she seemed quite taken aback. She said to tell you that you must not, under any circumstances, sign anything. Went on and on about it. I wondered if maybe I shouldn't have said anything? Have I messed up?"

"Of course not, Mum," said Alice automatically.

"Thank goodness, because Roger and I are just thrilled. Thrilled! We were thinking we could take the children for a weekend and you and Nick could go somewhere romantic. That was the second thing on my list. I'll just cross it off. You say the word. We'd love to have them. Roger said he'd even foot the bill for a meal at somewhere fancy-schmancy. He's so generous like that."

"That sounds great."

"Really? Oh, I'm so pleased because I mentioned it to Elisabeth and she said she thought once you got your memory back that you would be 'singing a different tune.' But you know, she takes the pessimistic approach to things these days, poor thing, and that was my third reason for calling. Have you heard from her by any chance? I'm desperate to know if she's got the results yet. I've been ringing and ringing and no answer."

"What results?"

"Today was the blood test. You know, for the last egg. Oh, wait a minute, I always get that word wrong. Embryo." Her mother's voice broke. "Oh, Alice, I've been praying and praying and sometimes I have to admit I get a bit *cross* with God. Elisabeth and Ben have tried so hard. Just one little baby isn't too much to ask for, is it?"

"No," said Alice. She looked at Dino's fertility doll sitting on the counter. Why didn't Elisabeth tell her there was a blood test today?

Her mother sighed. "I said to Roger, I'm so happy myself now, why can't my girls be happy, too?"

Elisabeth's Homework for Jeremy

A lot of people have left messages for me today.

Mum has called five times.

I just saw a missed call from Alice.

Oh, and the nurse has called twice trying to give me the results of today's blood test.

Layla has called, probably wondering where I am, because I went out at lunchtime and for some reason I just never got the energy to go back to the office. She probably thinks it's because she offended me by not asking about Alice.

Ben has called three times.

I don't seem to be able to call anyone back. I'm just sitting here behind the wheel of my car outside your office, writing to you.

Now the phone is ringing again. Ring, ring! Ring, ring! Engage
with the world, Elisabeth! Go away, all of you.

Alice was hanging clothes on the line (it was taking forever) when the
phone rang again. She had to run to answer it.

"Hello?" she said breathlessly.

"Oh, hi, it's me," said Nick. He paused. "Nick."

"Yes, I recognized your voice actually."

You kissed another woman in the laundry! I can't believe you did that!
Should she mention the kiss? No. She should think about the right way to
approach it first.

He said, "I just thought I should call and see how you, how your ah,
your head, your injury, is today. Were you okay driving the children to
school?"

"It's a bit late if I wasn't," said Alice tartly. Last night she'd had to *iron*
all their school uniforms, do all the cleaning up, and make very specific
lunches for each of them (after Tom had politely pointed out that was what
she normally did on a Sunday night).

"Oh, good," said Nick. "So, I assume, you've got that memory thing all
sorted out?"

"Well, I've got one memory back," burst out Alice. It appeared she was
going to mention the kiss after all. It was physically impossible not to mention it. "I remember you kissing that woman in the laundry."

"Kissing a woman in the laundry?"

"Yes. At a party. I came in to get a drink."

There was silence and then Nick laughed sharply.

"Sitting on the washing machine, right?"

"Yes," said Alice, wondering how he could sound so smug, as if this point
went to him, when it so clearly went to her.

"You remember *me* kissing a woman sitting on our washing machine?"

"Yes!"

"You know what? I never even looked at another woman while we were together. I never kissed another woman. I never slept with another woman."

"But I remember—"

"Yeah. I know exactly what you remember, and I find that very interesting."

Alice was baffled. "But—"

"Very interesting. Look, I've got to go, but clearly you haven't got your memory back properly yet and you need to see a doctor. If you're not capable of looking after the children, you need to let me know. You've got a responsibility to them."

Oh, but it was fine to leave her with them last night when he knew perfectly well that she didn't even recognize them, let alone know how to look after them. It wasn't logical, and yet, he was speaking in that pompous, I'm-so-rational-you're-so-irrational voice, each word stuffed with his own rightness. She could remember that voice from arguments in the past, like that morning when they didn't have milk for breakfast, and the night when they ran late for his sister's first baby's christening, and the time neither of them had enough cash for the ferry tickets, and each time he had put on that voice. That superior, crisp, businesslike voice, with a hint of a sigh. It drove her bananas.

Each time he used that voice it brought back the other occasions he'd used it before and she would think, That's right, I can't stand it when you talk like that.

"You know what?" she said. "I'm *glad* we're getting a divorce!"

As she slammed the phone down, she could hear him laughing.

Chapter 25

The Mega Meringue Committee turned up at Alice's door at 1:00 p.m. She'd forgotten all about them.

When the doorbell rang she was sitting on the living room floor surrounded by photo albums. She'd been there for hours, flipping pages, peeling photos off so she could hold them close to her and study for clues.

There were photos of picnics and bushwalks and days at the beach, birthday parties and Easters and Christmases. She'd lost so many Christmas memories! It gave her a pain in the center of her chest oooing the photos of tangle-haired children in their pajamas, their faces solemn with concentration as they unwrapped presents under a huge, gorgeously decorated tree.

Maybe she could go to the doctor and ask if she could please have all her happy memories returned, minus the sad ones.

The photos were mostly of the children and Nick. Alice would have been the one behind the camera. Nick always looked so capable when he was taking a photo, a grave, professional look on his face, but actually he was hopeless, skimming off the tops of people's heads.

Alice had discovered she could take good photos when she was a child.

After their father died nobody had taken photos of them. He had been the photographer and their mother would no more think about trying to use his camera than she would have tried to change a light globe. It was Alice who picked up his camera one day and worked out how to use it. In those years when their mother disappeared into herself and "old Miss Jeffrey" next door turned into "Frannie," their honorary grandmother, Alice also taught herself how to change light globes, fix running toilets, and cook chops and veggies, while Elisabeth learned how to demand refunds, pay bills, fill in forms, and talk to strangers.

Whenever she came upon another rare photo of Nick she tried to read the expression in his eyes. Was it possible to track the decline of their marriage? No. She could track the decline of his *hair* over the years, but his smile at the person behind the camera seemed unchangingly genuine and happy.

In the ones where they were together, they always had their arms around each other, their bodies curved together. If a body-language expert were asked to objectively judge their marriage on the basis of these photo albums they would surely say, "This is a happy, loving, good-humored family and the likelihood of that couple breaking up is nil."

She didn't bother much with the photos of people she didn't recognize but one face kept appearing again and again, and it dawned on her that this must surely be Gina. She was a busty, big-toothed woman with a heap of dark curly hair. She and Alice always seemed to be photographed holding champagne or cocktail glasses up to the camera like trophies. They seemed to be very physical together, which was unusual for Alice. She had never had those sorts of lavish friendships where you threw your arms around each other, but Alice and this woman always seemed to have their heads angled together so their cheeks were touching, big wide lipsticky smiles for the camera. Alice felt embarrassed by these photos. "Oh stop it, you don't even *know* her," she said out loud at a photo of herself actually planting a big, smoochy kiss on Gina's cheek.

Alice stared at the photos of Gina for ages, waiting for the recognition—

and the grief? But nothing. She looked sort of fun, she guessed, although not really the sort of woman Alice would have picked as a friend. She looked like she had the potential to be a bit overbearing. A loud, zany, tiring type.

But maybe not. Actually, Alice looked a bit loud and zany herself in some of those photos. Maybe she *was* loud and zany now that she was so slim and drank so much coffee.

There were photos of Alice and Nick together with Gina and a man who must be her husband Mike Boyle. That physiotherapist who had moved to Melbourne. So these were the "happier times" he'd mentioned on his business card. There were a lot of BBQs and dinner parties (lots of empty wine bottles on the table in an unfamiliar room that must have been Gina and Mike's house). She worked out from the pictures that Gina and Mike had two pretty dark-haired daughters—twins, perhaps?—about the same age as Tom. There were photos of the children playing together, eating giant slices of watermelon, splashing about in the pool, curled up asleep on couches.

The two families had gone on camping trips together. It looked like they'd been back regularly to some beach house with stunning ocean views.

Friendship and holidays. A swimming pool. Champagne and sunshine and laughter. It seemed like a dream life.

But maybe every life looked wonderful if all you saw was the photo albums. People always obediently smiled and tilted their heads when a camera was put in front of them. Perhaps seconds after the shutter clicked, she and Nick sprang apart, avoiding each other's eyes, their smiles replaced by snarls.

She was just studying the photos of Elisabeth's wedding (she and Ben looked so young and unguarded, their faces rosy, Elisabeth slender and luminous) when the doorbell rang. She jumped to her feet and left the albums with all those days and days of forgotten memories on the floor.

There were two women at the door, and another three were walking up the driveway. A couple were complete strangers but she recognized the rest from the party and from dropping off the children at school that morning.

"Mega Meringue meeting?" guessed Alice as she held open the door for them. They were carrying folders and notebooks and looked terrifyingly efficient.

"Only six days to go!" said a tall, elegant, gray-haired woman, making her eyebrows pop up and down above her square-framed glasses.

"How are you?" said another one with dimples who kissed her warmly on the cheek. "I've been meaning to call all weekend. Bill said he couldn't believe it when he was on the treadmill and he saw you go past on the stretcher. He said he never expected to see Alice Love flat on her back. Oh dear, that doesn't sound quite right."

Alice remembered the red-faced man on the treadmill saying he would get "Maggie" to call.

"Maggie?" she tried.

The woman squeezed her arm. "Sorry! I'm in a silly mood today!"

Without being asked, the women all trooped into the dining room and sat themselves around the table, placing their notebooks in front of them.

"Tea, coffee?" said Alice faintly, wondering if she fed them.

"I've been hanging out for your muffins all morning," said the eyebrow popper.

"I'll come and help you bring it all in," said Maggie. Oh dear. It appeared they were used to a spread.

Alice registered Maggie's look of surprise when she saw the state of the kitchen. Last night's dinner plates and the children's breakfast dishes were still lying around. Alice had meant to clean up after she had the laundry on but the photo albums had distracted her. There were splashes of milk and hamburger mince all over the counters.

As Alice hurriedly checked through the freezer for muffins, Maggie put the kettle on and said, "I saw Kate Harper this morning. She said you and Nick were getting back together."

"*Yes!*" Alice pulled from the freezer a container labeled "Banana Muffins" and dated two weeks earlier, feeling quite fond of herself. Oh, you're a trouper, Alice.

"Well, I was a bit surprised," said Maggie.

Alice looked up at the tone of her voice. She sounded wounded.

"It's just that I know Dominick is pretty keen," continued Maggie, sounding as if she were trying to be diplomatic.

"Are you and Dominick friends?" asked Alice.

Maggie jerked her head in surprise. "I'm just saying, he's my big brother, and he's sort of vulnerable. If it's not going anywhere, maybe you should tell him?"

Oh Lord, she was his *sister*. Now that Alice looked, she could see a slight resemblance about the eyes. That Kate Harper was a real piece of work.

"And I don't know, Alice," continued Maggie. "All that stuff you were saying the other day, about how Nick never respected your opinion, and made you feel like you were stupid, and how you and Dominick had a much more equal relationship, and you loved the way he talked to you about the school, because Nick never talked to you about his work. What was that all about, then? And I don't mean to be rude, but I wondered, could this possibly be related to your head injury? I mean, I know that sounds like, 'Oh, you must be nuts not to want my brother!' But I just think that, well, you know, don't rush . . ."

Her voice drifted away, just like Dominick's did.

Nick didn't respect her opinion? But of course he did! Sometimes he thought she was a bit foolish about current affairs, but only in an adorable way.

Alice went to open her mouth, without knowing what she would say, when the doorbell rang again.

"Just a sec," she said, holding up her hand.

She ran down the hallway past the babble of female voices from her dining room and opened the door.

"So sorry I'm late," said a tiny red-haired woman with a sweet, childlike voice.

It was the woman who kissed Nick on the washing machine.

Elisabeth's Homework for Jeremy
So I called and got the blood-test results.

"Come in!" said Alice.

Her body definitely remembered this woman. The sound of her sugar-sweet voice actually made her feel slightly sick, like the way avocado always made her feel, because of that time she got violently ill after eating guacamole.

"I heard you fell over at the gym," said the woman. "Told you exercise was bad for you." Oh Lord, she was leaning in to kiss her on the cheek. This cheek-kissing thing was out of control. It was a Mega Meringue meeting! Shouldn't they keep things a bit more professional?

The woman was unraveling a scarf from her neck, casually looping it over Alice's hat stand and looking at Alice artlessly, without a shred of guilt. Could she do this if she had kissed Alice's husband in the laundry of this very house? *"I never looked at another woman. I never kissed another woman,"* Nick had said. So why did she remember it so clearly? And how did he know what she meant when she talked about it happening on the washing machine?

"You're late, Mrs. Holloway!" a voice called out from the dining room.

Holloway. Holloway. Alice mentally snapped her fingers. This was the deputy principal. She was far too tiny and pretty and sugary to be a deputy principal.

Mrs. Holloway waltzed into the dining room as if she owned the place while Alice went back into the kitchen. Dominick's sister had put Alice's muffins into the microwave and the smell of banana filled the kitchen.

"Mrs. Holloway," said Alice.

"Bleh," said Maggie, making a face without looking up from the boiling water she was pouring into a row of coffee mugs. She put down the kettle and winked at Alice. "You make sure you keep Mrs. H. in line if she tries to take over again. It's your meeting. You're in charge."

"About that," said Alice. "I can't run this meeting."

"Why not?"

"Dominick obviously didn't tell you—"

"Dominick doesn't tell me anything. You know brothers. Oh, right, you don't. Well, they're not like sisters."

Alice explained yet again about her memory loss, and how, yes, she would be seeing a doctor, and no, she didn't think she should be in bed, and no, she wasn't joking, and yes, it must have been quite a thump on the head.

Someone called out from the dining room, "What's going on in there? We can smell muffins!"

"Hold your horses!" called out Maggie. She turned back to Alice and said happily, "So *that's* why you've been talking about getting back together with Nick! You've forgotten the last ten years! Gosh. It must be the weirdest feeling. I'm trying to imagine it. What was I doing when I was twenty-six?"

Alice realized with a start that Maggie, who seemed so *middle-aged*, was actually four years younger than she was. In fact, all these grown-up women here today were probably in her age group.

Maggie chortled. "I'd say, 'Oh my God, how did you end up marrying the chubby guy who services your car!' And then I'd look down at my hips and think, 'What happened there?'"

She slapped herself on what looked to Alice like perfectly slim hips.

"It's getting boring in there." The tall, gray-haired woman with the glasses came into the kitchen and swung herself up onto the counter, swinging long, slim, blue-jeaned legs.

She lowered her voice. "You need to get in there fast, Alice, before Mrs. H. plans a coup. Don't worry, I've been subtly undermining everything she says." She lowered her voice even further. "If she thinks we'll ever let her live down the shame of the laundry incident, she's very much mistaken. The evil little troll."

"You know about the laundry incident?" Alice gripped the knife she was holding to cut the muffins.

"Alice has lost her memory," said Maggie. "She probably doesn't even know who you are. Alice, meet Nora." She paused. "Actually, you mustn't even know who I am! I'm Maggie! Did you even know that?" She had that disbelieving, self-conscious expression on her face that Alice had seen so many times now. People couldn't quite believe you could forget *them*.

"There's a rumor going around you lost your memory," said Nora. "I didn't believe it. I heard someone in Dino's Coffee Shop talking about it, but I thought it was just the village grapevine gone haywire. Geez. What do the doctors say?"

"Did Nick kiss that Mrs. Holloway in the laundry?" asked Alice, feeling juvenile to be discussing kissing with this elegant gray-haired woman.

"Nick?" said Nora. "No, honey. It was Michael. Gina's husband. Gina walked in on them." She looked at Maggie. "She really has lost her memory."

"She doesn't remember *anything*," said Maggie, excitedly taking a huge bite of muffin. "It's like she's Rumpelstiltskin in the fairy tale."

"I think you mean Rip Van Winkle."

"Do I?"

"But I remember it so clearly," said Alice slowly. "I remember it as if it was me."

"Well, you were so upset for Gina," said Maggie. "Oh God, I just still cannot believe Gina isn't about to walk in here right this minute, carrying another bottle of champagne. Whenever I hear the pop of a champagne cork I think of her. I don't think I've accepted it yet."

"Unless, of course, the troll kissed Nick as well," said Nora thoughtfully.

"Can I take something in?" chimed a childlike voice.

"Mrs. H.!" said Nora calmly. "We were just talking about you."

"All good, I hope?"

"Of course! I'm sure our fine deputy principal doesn't have any *dirty laundry* that needs airing," said Nora.

Maggie choked on her muffin.

"Here you go," said Nora. "You can take those mugs in for Alice."

"Sure thing." Mrs. Holloway seemed unruffled. "Will we be getting started soon, Alice?" She looked at her watch. "It's just that I've got to be back at the school."

"Won't be long," said Nora briskly, her eyes hard.

Mrs. Holloway took the mugs and left.

As soon as the deputy principal walked out the door, Maggie slapped Nora on the back of her head, ruffling her smooth hair. "You're a shocker."

It was just like being with girls at school, except with wrinkles and gray hair and talk of children. Alice felt comforted by this. It seemed you still got to be silly when you grew up.

"But I don't understand," she said. "How can this Mrs. Holloway be deputy principal if she's . . ."

"Kissing dads in the laundry?" finished Nora. "We're the only ones who know about it. Gina made us promise not to tell anyone. Mrs. H. has got children herself at the school. Gina said she didn't want to be responsible for breaking up another marriage."

"You don't know how often I've had to bite my tongue whenever Dominick talks about her," said Maggie. "He thinks she's so professional. But anyway, I guess she just had too much to drink that night. We all make mistakes."

"Don't go all forgiving on us, Maggie," said Nora. "She doesn't deserve forgiveness. The bitch didn't even flinch when I said 'dirty laundry.'"

"She might have forgotten about it," said Maggie. "It's been three years."

"Were Mrs. Holloway and Mike having an affair?" asked Alice, and realized she was steeling herself for the answer. Even though she knew it hadn't been Nick, that raw, betrayed feeling remained.

"As far as we know, it was just that one drunken kiss," said Maggie. "But it seemed to trigger all of Gina and Mike's problems. It never seemed fair. Gina and Mike break up, and meanwhile the Holloways still look like the golden couple. I saw them holding hands, do you mind, at the Trivia Night the other week and I thought, 'Someone please bring me a bucket.'"

"Maybe they've got an *arrangement*," mused Nora. "It could be an open marriage."

"Do you think?" said Maggie with wide eyes. Then she shook herself. "We'd really better go do this meeting."

"Maybe I should stay here," said Alice. "Tell them I'm sick." She had no idea how to "do a meeting."

"I'll run through the agenda," said Nora. "Just nod along. Anyway, you've had everything organized so well in advance, we all know exactly what we've got to do. You're the most efficient person I know, Alice."

"I wonder how that happened," sighed Alice. She licked her finger and pressed it against the muffin crumbs on the plate in front of her. She saw the two women were studying her, as if she were behaving oddly.

Instead of sucking her finger, she let it drop by her side and said, "Why are we making the world's biggest lemon meringue pie, anyway? Why not a cheesecake or something?"

"It was Gina's signature dish," said Maggie. "Remember? You're dedicating the day to Gina."

Of course she was. In the end, everything circled back to Gina.

Once she remembered Gina, she would remember everything.

Elisabeth's Homework for Jeremy

I feel like I could easily do one of two things.

I could drive out of Sydney. Maybe down that long winding ribbon of highway on the South Coast with the lush green hills and the flashes of turquoise sea. That would be cheerful.

And then I could find a long empty stretch of road with an appropriate telephone pole. One that's begging for a memorial cross.

And I could drive at it very fast.

Alternatively!

I could drive back to the office. And I could ask Layla to buy me a Caesar salad, yes, with anchovies, and a Diet Coke, or perhaps a banana smoothie, and I could eat my lunch while I prepare my keynote address for next month's Australian Direct Marketing Association conference.

I could do one. Or I could do the other.

The telephone pole or the office.

It seems no more important a decision than whether or not I will have the Diet Coke or the banana smoothie.

"Oh, Alice, glad I caught you, I was wondering, the weekend after this I've got that thing I was telling you about, so I was thinking, what if I picked up Tom for you from Harry's party, because I know you said you had that thing, so I could keep the boys before soccer and then you could pick them both up after the game?"

"Excuse me please, Mummy. Excuse me please, Mummy. *Excuse* me *please*, Mummy."

"Alice! Has Olivia decided what she's wearing to Amelia's fancy-dress party? Have you heard? There's a drama. *Seven* kids want to go as Hannah Montana, and apparently *Amelia* wants to go as Hannah Montana, and after all, she is the birthday girl, so apparently all other Hannahs are banned!"

"Big day coming up, Alice!"

"Mum, I *said* excuse me and you just keep ignoring me!"

"Mum, can Clara come over this afternoon? Please, please, please, please? Her mum said it was okay!"

"Mummy?"

"Mum?"

"Not long now, Alice!"

"Mrs. Love?"

"Can I talk to you, Alice?"

———

Alice stood in the school playground and the world of canteen duty and playdates and birthday parties whirled around her like a spinning top.

She didn't remember any of it.

Yet it all seemed oddly familiar.

Elisabeth's Homework for Jeremy

Just in case you're wondering, I decided to go to the office today.

The Caesar salad wasn't very nice. A lackluster attempt. Wilted lettuce. Stale croutons. Very disappointing. Like life.

I wasn't really serious about the telephone pole.

I would never do that. I'm far too sensible and dull.

By the way, I have canceled our next session. I do apologize for the inconvenience.

Frannie's Letter to Phil

Mr. Mustache has a name, and I guess I should use it now that he no longer has a mustache.

It's Xavier. It doesn't suit him at all, does it? What was his mother thinking? Xavier is far too elegant a name for a man who "places bets on the doggies" and loves beer and "the footie season" and tomato sauce and dreadful right-wing talkback radio.

We have nothing in common, obviously. Not like you and I! Remember the plays we saw, the books we shared, the—well.

Did we like the same books? I might be making that part up. Sometimes the details become a little hazy. I couldn't tell you, for example, whether you liked tomato sauce or not. Did you?

While I was having my shower this morning, I was thinking about how just last week Alice said to me, "Frannie, when will I stop being shocked that Gina isn't alive?"

I was full of grandmotherly wisdom about how "time heals," but I understood.

It was the same when my dear, silly Barb lost their father. She must have said it a million times: "But Frannie, he ate a mandarin that morning. He was fine."

Because how is it possible for your husband to eat a mandarin at eight a.m. and be dead by ten a.m.?

And how is it possible to watch your best friend hop into a car and then for you to never hear her voice again? (And goodness, that Gina had a loud voice!)

And how is it possible to believe your lovely fiancé isn't still gallivanting around Queensland when a letter full of love and jokes and a pile of snapshots arrives the day after his coffin is lowered into the ground?

Your mind resists death with all its might.

Oh, Phil, it's completely foolish that I've kept writing back to you all these years. It's become one of those habits I can't seem to break. Writing to a memory

Someone was screaming.

"Mum! Stop it! Make it stop! *Mummy!*"

Alice was catapulted up and out of her bed and was walking rapidly, blindly, down the hallway, before she woke up properly, her mouth dry, her head fuzzy with interrupted dreams.

Who was it? Olivia?

The hysterical screams were coming from Madison's room. Alice pushed open the door. In the dark, she could just make out a figure on the bed thrashing about and screaming, "Get it off! Get it off!"

Alice's eyes adjusted enough to make out the lamp on the bookshelf next to Madison's bed. She switched it on.

Madison's eyes were shut, her face screwed up tight. She was tangled up in her sheets and her pillow was on her chest. She batted it away.

"Get it off!"

Alice took away the pillow and sat down on the bed next to her.

"It's only a dream, darling," she said. "It's only a dream." She knew from her own nightmares how Madison's heart would be racing, how the words from the real world would slowly infiltrate the dream world and make it fade away.

Madison's eyes opened and she threw herself at Alice, pushing her head painfully into Alice's ribs and clutching her tightly.

"Mummy, get it off Gina! Get it off her!" she sobbed.

"It's only a dream," said Alice, stroking back sweaty strands of hair from Madison's forehead. "I promise you, it's only a bad dream."

"But Mummy, you need to get it off her! Get it off Gina."

"Get what off her?"

Madison didn't answer. Her hands loosened and her breathing began to slow. She burrowed herself more comfortably into Alice's lap.

Was she falling back asleep?

"Get what off her?" whispered Alice.

"It's only a dream," said Madison sleepily.

Chapter 26

"Auntie Alice! Auntie Alice!"

A boy of about three came running into Alice's arms.

She automatically lifted his compact body up and whirled him around, while his legs gripped around her hips like a koala. She buried her nose in his dark hair and breathed in the yeasty scent. It was intensely, deliciously familiar. She breathed in again. Was she remembering this little boy? Or some other little boy? Sometimes she thought it might be easier to block her nose to stop these sudden frustrating rushes of memories that evaporated before she could pin down what exactly it was she remembered.

The little boy pressed fat palms on either side of Alice's face and babbled something incomprehensible, his eyes serious.

"He's asking if you brought Smarties," said Olivia. "You always bring him Smarties."

"Oh, dear," said Alice.

"You don't know who he is, do you?" said Madison with happy contempt.

"She does so," said Olivia.

"It's our cousin Billy," said Tom. "Auntie Ella is his mum."

Nick's youngest sister had got pregnant! What a scandal! She was fifteen—still at school!

You're really not the sharpest knife in the drawer, are you, Alice? It's 2008! She's twenty-five! She's probably an entirely different person by now.

Although, actually, not that different, because here she came now, unsmilingly pushing her way past people. Ella still had a gothic look about her. White skin, brooding eyes with a lot of black eyeliner, black hair parted in the middle and cut in a sharp-edged bob. She was dressed in a long black skirt, black tights, black ballet flats, and a turtlenecked black jersey with what looked like four or five strings of pearls of varying lengths around her neck. Only Ella could pull off such a look.

"Billy! Come back here," she said sharply, trying unsuccessfully to peel her son off Alice.

"Ella," said Alice, while Billy's legs gripped harder and he buried his head in her neck. "I didn't expect to see you here." If she really *had* to pick a favorite Flake, it would have been Ella. She had been an intense, teary teenager who could dissolve into hysterical giggles, and she liked talking to Alice about clothes and showing her the vintage dresses she'd bought at secondhand shops that cost more to dry-clean than what she'd paid.

"Have you got a problem with me being here?" said Ella.

"What? No, of course not."

It was the Family Talent Night at Frannie's retirement village. They were in a wooden-floored hall with glowing red heaters mounted up high along the sides of the room, radiating an intense heat that was making all the visitors peel off cardigans and coats. There were rows of plastic chairs set up in a semicircle in front of a stage with a single microphone looking somehow pathetic in front of fraying red velvet curtains. Underneath the stage was a neat line of walkers of varying sizes, some with ribbons around them to differentiate them, like luggage at the airport.

Along the side of the hall were long trestle tables with white tablecloths laid with urns, tall stacks of Styrofoam cups, and paper plates of egg sandwiches, lamingtons, and pikelets with jam and blobs of cream melting in the heat.

The front rows of chairs were already occupied by village residents. Tiny wizened old ladies with brooches pinned to their best dresses, bent old men with hair carefully combed across spotted scalps, ties knotted beneath V-necked jumpers. The old people didn't seem to feel the heat.

Alice could see Frannie sitting right in the center row, engaged in what looked like a rather heated conversation with a grinning white-haired man who stood out because he was wearing a shiny polka-dot vest over a white shirt.

"Actually," said Ella, finally managing to wrench Billy out of Alice's arms, "it was your mother who rang and asked us to come. She said Dad had stage fright about this performance, which I find hard to believe, but still. The others all refused to come."

How strange for Barb to ring up Nick's sisters and actually ask them to do something, as if they were equals.

Alice caught herself.

Well, of *course* they were equals. What a strange thing to think.

But then, really, deep down (or maybe not even that deep down) she'd always thought of her own family as inferior to Nick's.

The Love family was from the eastern suburbs. "I rarely cross the Bridge," Nick's mother had once told Alice. She sometimes went to the opera on a Friday night, in the same way that Alice's mother might pop along to Trivia Night at the church hall on a Friday night (and maybe win a meat tray or a fruit box!). The Love family knew people. Important people, like MPs and actresses, doctors and lawyers, and people with names you felt you should know. They were Anglicans and went to church only at Christmas, languidly, as if it were a rather charming little event. Nick and his sisters went to private schools and Sydney Uni. They knew the best bars and the right restaurants. It was sort of like they owned Sydney.

Whereas Alice's family was from the stodgy northwest, home to happy clappy Christians, middle managers, CPAs, and conveyancers. Alice's mother rarely crossed the Bridge either, but that was because she didn't know her way around the city. Catching the train into town was a big event. Alice and Elisabeth went to local Catholic girls' schools, where the students were expected to become nurses and teachers, not doctors and lawyers. They went to church every Sunday, and local kids played the guitar while the congregation sang along in thin, reedy voices, following the words projected up on the wall above Father's bald head while the light from the stained-glass windows reflected off his glasses. Alice had often thought it would have been preferable to come from the proper western suburbs. That way she could have been a gritty, tough-talking westie chick. Maybe she would have had a tattoo on her ankle. Or, if only her parents could have been im-migrants, with accents. Alice could have been bilingual and her mother could have made her own pasta. Instead, they were just the plain old sub-urban Jones family. As bland as Weet-Bix.

Until Nick came along and made her feel interesting and exotic.

"So what do you actually *confess* at confession?" he'd asked once. "Are you allowed to tell?" He'd looked at pictures of Alice in her pleated Catholic-school uniform hanging well past her knees and said into her ear, "I am crazy with lust right now." He'd sat on Alice's mother's floral couch, with a square brown coffee table next to him (the biggest one from the "nest" of coffee tables) with an embroidered doily on top, eating a thickly buttered piece of bun with bright-pink icing and drinking his tea, and said, "When was this house built?" As if their red-brick bungalow deserved such a re-spectful question! "Nineteen sixty-five," said Barb. "We paid twelve thou-sand pounds for it." Alice had never known that! Nick had given their house a *history*. He'd nodded along, making some comment about the light fit-tings, and he was exactly the same as when he was sitting at his mother's antique dining room table, eating fresh figs and goat cheese and drinking champagne. Alice had felt faint with adoration.

"Will we sit with Daddy when he gets here?" Olivia tugged at Alice's sleeve. "Will you two sit together? So when I'm dancing, you can say to each other, 'Oh, that's our darling daughter. How proud we are!'"

Olivia was dressed in a leotard with a frothy tulle skirt and ballet slippers, ready for her performance. Alice had done her makeup for her, although according to Olivia she hadn't applied nearly enough.

"Of course we'll sit together," said Alice.

"You are the most embarrassing person alive, Olivia," said Madison.

"No, she's not," said Ella, hugging Olivia to her, and then she pulled at the hem of Madison's long-sleeved dark red top. "That top looks gorgeous on you. I knew it would."

"It's my favorite," said Madison fiercely. "Except Mum always takes *ages* washing it."

Alice watched Ella watching Madison and saw how her face softened. It seemed that Nick's sister loved Alice's children, and judging by the way Billy was still hopefully trying to grab at Alice's bag, searching for Smarties, Alice loved her little boy. They were aunties to each other's children. Even if they hadn't become stepsisters, they were family. Alice was filled with affection for her.

"You've grown up so beautiful and elegant," said Alice to Ella.

"Is that a joke?" Ella stiffened and her jaw set.

"You might find Mum a bit weird tonight, Auntie Ella," said Tom. "She's had a traumatic head injury. I've printed some stuff out from the Internet if you want to read it FYI. That means *for your information*. You say it when you want to tell somebody something. FYI."

"Darling Daddy!" cried Olivia.

Nick had just walked in the door of the hall and was scanning the crowd. He was dressed in an expensive-looking suit, his collar unbuttoned, and no tie. He looked like a successful, sexy, older man. A man who made important decisions, who knew his place in the world and no longer dropped toast on his shirt before a presentation.

Nick saw the children first and his face lit up. A second later he saw Alice and his face closed down. He walked toward them and Olivia threw herself into his arms.

"Oh, I've missed you three roosters," said Nick into Olivia's neck, his voice muffled, while he reached out with one hand to ruffle Tom's hair and the other to pat Madison on the shoulder.

"Hey, Dad, guess how many kilometers it was from our place to here," said Tom. "Guess. Go on guess."

"Umm, fifteen k."

"Close! Thirteen kilometers. FYI."

"Hey kid," said Nick to Ella, using the nickname he'd always given Ella. Ella looked at him adoringly. Nothing had changed there. "And the kid's kid!" He scooped up Billy into his arms, so he was holding both Olivia and Billy. Billy chortled and repeated, "Kid's kid! Kid's kid!"

"How are you, Alice?" His eyes were on the children. He didn't look at her. Alice was last to be greeted. She was the least-favorite person. He used his polite voice for her.

"I'm well, thank you." *Do not under any circumstances cry.* She found herself longing, bizarrely, for Dominick. For someone who liked her best. How horrible it was to be despised. To feel yourself to be despicable.

A familiar quavery voice came over the microphone. "Ladies and gentlemen, girls and boys, it's my very great pleasure to welcome you all to the Tranquillity Wood Retirement Village Family Talent Night. Could I ask you all to take your seats?"

"Frannie!" said Olivia.

It was Frannie up onstage, looking rather beautiful in a royal-blue dress and speaking calmly into the microphone, although she was putting on a posh voice.

"She doesn't look nervous," said Madison. "If it was me, I would be so nervous talking to all these people, I would probably faint."

"Me too," agreed Alice.

Madison curled her lip. "No, you wouldn't."

"I would!" protested Alice.

There was some confusion as they all settled into their seats. Madison, Tom, and Olivia all wanted to sit next to their father, and Olivia needed to be at the end of the row so she could be ready to go up when her name was called, and she also wanted Nick and Alice to sit together, while Billy wanted to sit on Alice's lap, which Ella clearly did not want. She finally gave in and Alice found herself with Madison on one side and Nick on the other, and Billy's warm little body snuggled into hers. At least *he* liked her.

Where was Elisabeth? Alice twisted around in her seat to look for her. She was meant to be coming tonight, but maybe she'd changed her mind. Mum had called to say that the blood-test results had been negative and Elisabeth seemed fine, although a little peculiar. "I actually wondered if she was drunk," Barb had said. Alice still had Dino's fertility doll in her handbag to give her. Would it just upset her now? But what if she was depriving Elisabeth of its magical powers? She would ask Nick what he thought.

She glanced over at Nick's stern profile. Could she still ask his opinion on things like that? Maybe not. Maybe he didn't care.

When the crowd had settled down, Frannie tapped the microphone and said, "Our first act is Mary Barber's great-granddaughter performing 'Somewhere over the Rainbow.'"

A little girl in a glittery sequined dress, plastered with makeup ("See, Mummy?" hissed Olivia, leaning forward across Nick to look reproachfully at Alice), strode out onto the stage, shimmying her chest like an aging cabaret singer. "Jesus," said Nick under his breath. She clasped the microphone with both hands and began to sing, her voice filled with exaggerated emotion, making the audience flinch in unison each time she hit the high notes.

She was followed by tap-dancing grandchildren in top hats and canes, a great-nephew's magic show ("FYI, I know exactly how he did that," Tom whispered loudly), and a niece's gymnastic routine. Ella's little boy got bored and started a game where he clambered from lap to lap, touching each person on the nose, saying, "Chin," or touching them on the chin and saying, "Nose," and then falling about laughing at his own wit.

Finally Frannie said, "Next up, Olivia Love, my own great-granddaughter, performing a routine she choreographed herself called 'The Butterfly.'"

Alice was terrified. Choreographed it *herself*? She'd assumed Olivia would be performing something she'd learned at ballet school. Good Lord, it would probably be dreadful. Her hands were sweaty. It was as if she were going up there herself.

"Hmmmm," said Olivia without moving.

"Olivia," said Tom. "It's your *turn*."

"I actually feel a bit sick," said Olivia.

Nick said, "All the best performers feel sick, sweetie. It's a sign. It means you're going to be great."

"You don't have to—" began Alice.

Nick put a hand on her arm and Alice stopped.

"As soon as you start, the sick feeling will go away," he said to Olivia.

"Promise?" Olivia looked up at him trustingly.

"Cross my heart and hope to be killed by a rabid dog."

Olivia rolled her eyes. "You're so silly, Dad." She slid down from the chair and marched down the aisle toward the stage, her tulle skirt bobbing. Alice's heart twisted. She was so *little*. So alone.

"Have you seen this routine?" whispered Nick, as he adjusted the focus on a tiny silver camera.

"No. Have you?"

"No." They watched as Olivia climbed the stairs of the stage. Nick said, "I actually feel a bit sick myself."

"Me too," said Alice.

Oliva stood in the center of the stage with her head bowed and her arms wrapped around herself, her eyes closed.

Alice massaged her stomach. She could feel the tension emanating from Nick.

The music started. Olivia slowly opened one eye, then the other. She yawned enormously, wriggled and squirmed. She was a caterpillar sleepily emerging from its cocoon. She looked over her shoulder, pretended to catch sight of a wing and her mouth dropped comically.

The audience laughed.

They *laughed.*

Alice's daughter was funny! Publicly funny!

Olivia looked over her other shoulder and staggered with delight. She was a butterfly! She fluttered this way and that, trying out her new wings, falling over at first and then finally getting the hang of it.

It was true that she probably wasn't quite in time with the music, and some of her dance moves were, well, unusual, but her facial expressions were priceless. In Alice's opinion, and she felt she was being quite objective, there had never been a funnier, cuter performance of a butterfly.

By the time the music had stopped Alice was suffused with pride, her face aching from smiling so much. She looked about at the audience and saw that people were smiling and clapping, clearly charmed, although they were perhaps holding themselves back so as not to make the other performers feel bad (why not a standing ovation, for example?), and she was shocked to see a woman in the middle of checking her mobile phone. How could she have dragged her eyes away from the stage?

"She's a comic genius," she whispered to Nick.

Nick lowered the camera, and his face, when he turned to look at her, was filled with identical awe and pleasure.

"Mum. I helped her a bit," said Madison tentatively.

"Did you?" Alice put her arm around Madison's shoulder and pulled her close. She lowered her voice. "I bet you helped her a lot. You're a great big sister. Just like your Auntie Libby was to me."

Madison looked amazed for a second, and then she smiled that exquisite smile that transformed her face.

"How did I get such talented children?" said Alice, and her voice shook. Why had Madison looked so surprised?

"Comes from their father," said Nick.

Olivia came dancing back down the aisle and sat up on the chair next to Nick, grinning self-consciously. "Was I good? Was I excellent?"

"You were the best!" said Nick. "Everybody is saying we may as well just pack up our bags and go, now that Olivia Love has performed."

"Silly," giggled Olivia.

They sat through another four acts, including a comedy act by someone's middle-aged daughter that was so incredibly unfunny it was sort of funny, and a little boy who lost his nerve and got stage fright halfway through reciting a Banjo Paterson poem until his grandfather came unsteadily up onstage and held his hand, and they read it together, which made Alice cry.

. Frannie walked up to the microphone again. "Ladies and gentlemen, boys and girls, this has been such a special night and in a moment you can enjoy supper, but we have just one final act for you and I hope you'll forgive me, but it's another one of my own family members. Please put your hands together for Barb and Roger performing the salsa!"

The stage went dark. A single spotlight revealed Alice's mother and Nick's father in full Latin costumes, standing completely still. Roger had one knee thrust between Barb's legs, his arm around her waist. Barb was leaning back, exposing her neck. Roger's head was bowed toward hers, his face dramatic, frowning tremendously.

Nick made a sound like something was stuck in his throat. Ella made a sympathetic choking sound back.

"Grandma and Grandpa look like people on TV," said Tom happily. "They look *famous*."

"They do not," said Madison.

"They do so."

"Shhhh," said Alice and Nick together.

The music started and their parents began to move. They were good in a horrendous sort of way. Swiveling their hips proficiently. Moving in and out of each other's arms. It was just so mortifyingly *sexual*—and in front of all these *old* people!

After five agonizing minutes of dancing, Roger stopped at the micro-phone while Barb danced around him, flicking up the sides of her skirt and stamping her feet provocatively. Alice could feel an attack of giggles about to sweep over her. What on earth are you *doing*, Mum?

"Folks!" said Roger in his best plummy radio-announcer voice. The spot-light lit up the beads of sweat on his yellow-tanned forehead. "You may have heard that my lovely wife and I will be offering salsa-dance lessons every second Tuesday. It's great exercise, and a lot of fun to boot! Now, anybody can do the salsa, and to prove it, I want to invite two people out of the audi-ence who have never salsa-danced before up onto the stage. Let's see now . . ."

The spotlight began bouncing around the audience. Alice watched the light, hoping Roger had the sense to choose a couple who could actu-ally walk.

The spotlight stopped on Alice and Nick and they both held up their hands to shield their eyes.

"Yes, those two blinking like rabbits in the headlights look like the per-fect victims, don't you think, Barb?" said Roger.

Olivia, Tom, and Madison jumped from their seats like lottery winners. They began pulling at their parents' arms, shrieking, "Yes, yes! Mum and Dad dance! Come on!"

"No, no! Pick somebody else!" Alice swatted away their hands in a panic. She never, ever volunteered for this sort of thing.

"I think they'd be perfect, Roger," said Barb from the stage, with a big game-show-hostess smile.

"I'm going to kill them," said Nick quietly. Then he yelled, "Sorry! Bad back!"

The old people weren't buying that. They were the ones with arthritis.

"Bad back, my foot!" cried out an old lady.

"Have a go, you mug!"

"Don't be party poopers!"

"Don't worry, the sick feeling will go away, Daddy," said Olivia sweetly.

"Dance, dance, dance!" shouted the old people, stamping their feet with surprising energy.

Nick sighed and stood up. He looked down at Alice. "Let's just get it over with."

They walked up onto the stage, Alice pulling self-consciously at her skirt, worried it was riding up at the back. Frannie shrugged from her place in the front row and held up her hands in a "nothing to do with me" gesture.

"Facing each other, please," said Roger.

Roger stood behind Nick and Barb stood behind Alice. Their parents maneuvered them so that Alice's hand was on Nick's shoulder, his around her waist.

"Closer now," boomed Roger. "Don't be shy. Now look into each other's eyes."

Alice looked miserably up at Nick. His face was blankly polite, as if they were two strangers who had been pulled out of the audience. This was excruciating.

"Come on now, are you a man or a mouse?" Roger clapped his son on the shoulder. "The man has got to take charge! You're the leader. She's the follower!"

Nick's nostril twitched, which meant he was highly irritated.

In a sudden movement, he put his hand on Alice's lower back and pulled her close to him, frowning masterfully in an over-the-top imitation of his father.

The audience erupted.

"I think we've got a natural here, folks!" said Roger. His eyes met Alice's and seemed to be sending her some sort of kindly message. He was a pompous old twit, but he meant well.

"Okay, light on your toes!" said Barb, demonstrating to Nick. "And forward on your *right* foot, back with your *left* foot, rock back onto your *right* foot, step back with your *left* foot. Shift your weight to your *left* foot, step back with your *right* foot. That's it! That's it!"

"And let's get those hips moving!" cried Roger.

Alice and Nick didn't dance much in public. Alice was always too self-conscious, and Nick wasn't fussed either way, but sometimes at home, if they'd had wine with dinner and they had the right sort of CD on while they were packing the dishwasher, they danced in the kitchen. A silly, hamming-it-up dance. It was always Alice who initiated it, because actually, she quite liked to dance, and actually, she wasn't bad.

She began to move her hips in imitation of her mother, while trying to keep the top half of her body still. The crowd roared its approval and she heard a child, probably Olivia, shout, "Go, *Mummy!*" Nick laughed. He was stepping on her toes. Barb and Roger were grinning like Cheshire cats. She could hear their children shouting out from the audience.

There was still chemistry. She could feel it in their hands. She could see it in his eyes. Even if it was just a memory of chemistry. There was still something. Alice's head was dizzy with hope.

The music stopped. "See! Anyone can learn to salsa!" cried Roger as Nick dropped his hands from her waist and turned away.

Elisabeth's Homework for Jeremy

We were driving to the Family Talent Night when I had a sudden craving for television.

House was on. I needed to see Dr. House being nasty and sarcastic while he diagnosed impossible medical conditions. What would Dr. House say about me? I wish you were more like Dr. House, Jeremy. You're so nice and polite. It's annoying. Niceness doesn't cure anyone. Why don't you just bring me face-to-face with a few home truths?

"You're infertile. Get over it," House would sneer, brandishing his cane, and I'd be shocked and invigorated.

"Can we turn around?" I told Ben.

He didn't try to change my mind. He is being very gentle and careful at the moment. The adoption application forms have disappeared from the kitchen counter. He's put them away. Temporarily. I can see the idea still shining in his eyes. He still has hope. Which is exactly the problem. I cannot afford any more hope.

I rang him after I got the blood-test results and when I went to speak, I found no words came out of my mouth, and when he didn't say anything, I knew he was trying not to cry. You can always tell when he's trying not to cry. Like he's fighting off something invisible trying to take over his head.

"We'll be okay," he finally said.

No we won't, I thought. "Yes," I said.

I almost told him the truth.

Actually, no I didn't. Not even close.

After *House* I watched *Medium*, and then *Boston Legal* and then *Cheaters*! That's the show where they spy on real people cheating on their spouses and then confront them with television cameras. It's seedy and gray and trashy. We sure do live in a seedy, gray, trashy world, Jeremy.

It's possible my mental health is poorly at the moment.

The show was over and the adults were standing around, drinking tea and coffee from paper cups and balancing pikelets on serviettes in the palms of their hands.

A huge gang of grandchildren and great-grandchildren were whooping with joy, racing on wheelchairs down the front of the hall.

"Should they be playing on those?" Alice asked Frannie, trying to be a responsible grown-up, as she saw Madison pushing a chair with Olivia and Tom squished in side by side, their legs stuck straight out in front of them.

"Of course not," sighed Frannie. "But I think it might be one of our residents running the race." She pointed to the white-haired man she'd been arguing with earlier who was wearing the shiny polka-dot waistcoat.

He was racing along in a wheelchair, spinning the wheels with his hands, yelling, "You can't catch me!"

Frannie's lips twitched. "He's eighty-five going on five." She paused. "Actually, I might just take some photos for the newsletter." She hurried off. Nick, Alice, and Ella were left together.

"Well, that was quite a performance." Ella was carrying Billy, who had his thumb in his mouth, his head draped over her shoulder. She squinted over his head at Nick and Alice as if they were scientific specimens. "That was the last thing I expected to see."

"Just wanted to show Dad up," said Nick. He picked up a scone and put the whole thing in his mouth.

"Are you hungry?" asked Alice. She scanned the tables. "Do you want a sandwich? They've got curried egg." Nick liked curried egg sandwiches.

He cleared his throat uncomfortably and glanced at Ella. "No, that's okay, thanks."

Ella was now openly staring.

"So how come you're the only one of the sisters here tonight, Ella?" asked Alice. Normally the Flakes traveled in a pack.

"Well, to be frank, Alice," said Ella, "they sort of refuse to be in the same room as you."

Alice flinched. "Goodness." She wasn't used to provoking such violent reactions in people, although, then again, she didn't mind the idea of having such power over the Flakes. It was sort of delicious.

"Ella," remonstrated Nick.

"I'm just saying it like it is," said Ella. "I'm trying to stay neutral. Of course, it would help if you gave back Granny Love's ring, Alice."

"Oh! That reminds me." Alice unzipped her handbag, pulled out a jewelry box. "I brought it to give to you tonight. Here it is."

Nick took the ring slowly. "Thank you." He held the jewelry case in his palm as if he didn't know what to do with it and finally stuffed it into the pocket of his suit jacket.

"Well, if it's that easy," said Ella, "maybe I should bring up another few issues, like, I don't know, the financial situation."

"Ella, this is really none of your business," said Nick.

"And why are you being such a *cow* over the custody?"

"Ella, this is not acceptable," said Nick.

"Moo," said Alice.

Ella and Nick stared.

Alice recited, "Who says 'moo'? A *cow* says 'moo'!" She smiled. "Sorry. It just came into my head when you said 'cow.'"

Billy lifted his head from Ella's shoulder, removed his thumb from his mouth, and said, "Moo!" He grinned appreciatively at Alice before replacing his thumb and putting his head back down on Ella's shoulder again. Ella and Nick seemed lost for words.

"I guess it must come from a book we used to read the children," said Alice.

It had been happening a lot. Strange words and phrases and lines from songs kept appearing in her head. It seemed that those ten years' worth of memories had been stuffed in a too-small cupboard at the back of her mind, and every now and then a fragment of nonsense would escape.

Any second now that cupboard door was going to burst open and her head was going to overflow with memories of grief and joy and who knew what else. She didn't know if she was looking forward to that moment or not.

"I dropped something the other day," said Alice, "and I said, 'Oh my dosh.' And it just sounded so familiar. Oh my dosh."

"Olivia used to say it when she was little," said Nick. He smiled. "We all said it for a while. Oh my dosh. I'd forgotten that. Oh my dosh."

"Am I missing something here?" said Ella.

"Maybe it's time you got Billy home to bed," said Nick.

"Right," said Ella. "Fine. I'll see you on Sunday." She kissed Nick on the cheek.

"Sunday?"

"Mother's Day? Lunch with Mum? She said you were coming."

"Oh, right. Yes, of course."

How did Nick handle his social life without Alice? That was *her* job, telling Nick what he was meant to be doing on the weekend. He must be missing things all over the place.

"Bye, Alice," said Ella, without making a move to kiss her. The only person in 2008 who didn't seem intent on plastering her with kisses. She paused. "Thanks for giving back the ring. It means a lot to our family."

In other words, *You are not our family any longer.*

"No problem," said Alice. *You're perfectly welcome to that horrendous ring.*

When Ella had gone, Nick looked at Alice and said, "Still haven't got your memory back, then?"

"Not quite. Any minute now."

"How are you coping with the children?"

"Fine," said Alice. No need to mention her daily failures with lost permission notes, unwashed school uniforms, and forgotten homework, or how she didn't know what to do when they fought with each other over the computer or the PlayStation. "They're lovely. We made lovely children."

"I know we did," said Nick, and his face seemed to collapse. "I know we did." He paused, as if not sure whether he should speak, and then said, "That's why the thought of only seeing them on weekends kills me."

"Oh, that," said Alice. "Well, if we don't get back together, then of course we should do the fifty-fifty thing. One week for you. One week for me. Why not?"

"You don't mean that," said Nick.

"Of course I do," said Alice. "I'll sign something!"

"Fine," said Nick. "I'll get my lawyer to draft something. I'll have it couriered over to you tomorrow."

"No problem."

"Once you get your memory back, you're going to change your mind," said Nick. He laughed harshly. "And you're not going to want to get back together, I'd put money on that."

"Twenty bucks," said Alice, holding out her hand.

Nick shook her hand. "Done."

She still loved the feel of his hand holding hers. Wouldn't her body tell her if she hated him?

"I found out it was Gina's husband who kissed the woman in the laundry," said Alice. "Not you."

"Oh yes, the infamous laundry incident." Nick smiled at an old lady with a walking stick in one hand attempting to hand around a sagging plate of sandwiches. "Oh, all right, you twisted my arm!" He took a sandwich. Alice noted it was curried egg.

"What did you mean when you said you found it interesting that I thought that was you?" asked Alice, taking a sandwich herself to save it from sliding onto the floor.

"Because I was always saying to you, 'I'm not Mike Boyle,'" said Nick. Even with his mouth full of sandwich, she could hear the leftover anger in his voice. "You identified so strongly with Gina, it was as if it was happening to you. I said to you, 'But it wasn't me.' You got so caught up in that 'all men are bastards' thing."

"I'm sorry," said Alice. Her sandwich was ham and mustard, and the taste of mustard was reminding her of something. This constant feeling of fleeting memories was like having a mosquito buzzing in your ear when you're asleep, and you know that when you turn out the light, it will have vanished, until you lie back down, close your eyes, and then . . . *bzzzzzzz.*

Nick wiped his serviette across his mouth. "You don't need to be sorry. It's all water under the bridge now." He paused and his eyes went blank, looking back on a shared past that Alice couldn't see.

He said, "I often think the four of us were too close. We got all tangled up in Mike and Gina's marriage problems. We caught their divorce. Like a virus."

"Well, let's just get better from it," said Alice. How dare this stupid Mike and Gina come into their lives, spreading their germy marriage problems?

Nick smiled and shook his head. "You sound so . . ." He couldn't find the right word. Finally he said, "Young."

After a pause, he continued: "Anyway, it wasn't *just* Mike and Gina. That's too simplistic. Maybe we were too young when we got together. Mmmm. Do you think fame might have gone to Olivia's head?"

Alice followed his gaze to see Olivia back onstage. She had the microphone held close to her mouth and was doing a grandiose performance of some song they couldn't hear because the sound was turned off. Tom was on his hands and knees next to her, following the microphone lead back to the power plug. Madison was sitting in the front row of the empty chairs in the audience, next to the white-haired wheelchair-race organizer. They were deep in conversation.

"Tell me a happy memory from the last ten years," said Alice.

"Alice."

"Come on. What's the first thing that comes into your head?"

"Ummm. God. I don't know. I suppose when the children were born. Is that too obvious an answer? Although not the actual births. I didn't like the actual births."

"Didn't you?" said Alice, disappointed. She'd imagined herself and Nick sobbing and laughing and holding each other while a movie soundtrack played in the background. "Why not?"

"I guess I was in a crazy panic the whole time, and I couldn't control anything, and I couldn't help you. I kept doing the wrong thing."

"I'm sure you didn't."

Nick glanced at Alice, then looked away again quickly.

"And all the blood, and you screaming your head off, and that incompetent obstetrician who didn't turn up until it was all over with Madison, I was going to knock him out. If it wasn't for that midwife—she was great, the one we said could have been Melanie Barker's twin sister."

He looked distractedly down at his hands. Alice wondered if he knew he was twisting the skin beneath the knuckle on his finger where his wedding ring should have been. It had become a habit of his, fiddling with his ring when he was thinking. Now he was still doing it, even though he wasn't wearing the ring.

"And when they had to do the emergency cesarean with Olivia"—Nick shoved his hands in his pockets—"I genuinely thought I was having a heart attack."

"How horrible for you," said Alice. Although she guessed maybe it hadn't been a barrel of laughs for her either.

Nick smiled and shook his head in wonder. "I remember, I didn't want to distract them from you and the baby, you know, like some man in a movie who faints. I thought, I'll just die discreetly in this corner. I thought you were going to die, too, and the children were going to be orphans. Have I ever told you that before? I must have."

"I thought we were talking happy memories." Alice was appalled. Without those memories, it felt like all that blood and screaming were still ahead of her, still to be endured.

"The happy part was when it was all over and quiet, and they left us alone, with the baby all wrapped up, and we could talk about which doctors and nurses we hated, and have a cup of tea, and just look at the baby for the first time. Count their tiny fingers. That new little person. That was— special." He cleared his throat.

"What's your saddest memory of the last ten years?" said Alice.

"Oh, I've got lots of contenders." Nick smiled strangely. She couldn't tell if it was a nasty smile or a sad one. "Take your pick. The day we told the children we were separating. The day I moved out. The night Madison rang me up, sobbing her heart out and begging me to come home."

All around them people talked and laughed and drank their cups of tea. Alice could feel the warmth from the heaters beating down upon her head. She felt as though the top of her head were melting, softening like chocolate. She imagined Madison on the phone, crying for her dad to come home.

He should have put down the phone and come right home that second, and they should have watched a family video together, snuggled on the couch, eating fish-and-chips. It should have been *easy* to be happy. There were poor Elisabeth and Ben, desperately trying to have a family, while Nick and Alice had just let theirs fall apart.

She stepped closer to Nick.

"Don't you think we should try again? For them? For the children? Actually, not just for them. For us. For the old us."

"Excuse me!" It was another old lady, with a blue-gray perm and a wrinkled, happy face. "You're Nick and Alice, aren't you!" She leaned toward them confidentially. "I recognize you from Frannie's Facebook page. She mentioned that you were separated now, and I just want you to know that I think you two belong together. I could tell it was true love by the way you danced just then!"

"Frannie has *photos* of us on the Internet?" said Nick

The old lady turned to Alice. "Have you got your memory back yet, love? You know, a similar thing happened to a friend of mine in 1954. We could not convince her that the war was over. Of course, she ended up forgetting her own name, which I'm sure won't happen to you."

"No," said Alice. "It's Alice. Alice, Alice."

"Tell me she doesn't post photos of the children on the Internet," said Nick.

"Oh, your children are just beautiful," said the old lady.

"Great. An open invitation to murderers and pedophiles," said Nick.

"I'm sure she doesn't actually *invite* people to murder the children," said Alice. "'Murderers, check out our delicious little victims here!'"

"This is serious. Why do you always think bad things can't happen to us? It's just like that time you let Olivia go missing at the beach. You're so blasé."

"Am I?" said Alice, bemused. Had she really let Olivia go missing?

"We're not immune from tragedy."

"I'll keep that in mind," said Alice, and Nick's face gave an actual spasm of irritation, as if he'd just been bitten by a mosquito.

"What?" said Alice. "What did I say?"

"Is your sister here?" said the old lady to Alice. "I wanted to tell her that I think she should adopt a baby. There must be lots of lovely babies up for adoption after that cyclone in Burma. Of course, in my day a lot more babies were left on church doorsteps, but that doesn't seem to happen so much anymore, which is a pity. Oh, there's your mother!" The old lady spotted Barb, still in her outfit and makeup, holding a clipboard and surrounded by eager old ladies. "I'm going to sign up for salsa! You two have inspired me!"

She tottered off.

"Will you please tell Frannie that I don't appreciate her putting photos of my children on the Net," said Nick. That detached, pompous voice was back.

"Tell her yourself!" said Alice. Nick adored Frannie. The old Nick would have been off to accost Frannie for a spirited debate. At family functions they argued about politics and played cards together.

Nick sighed heavily. He massaged his cheeks as if he had a toothache, pushing the flesh up around his eyes, causing them to crease oddly, so that his face looked like a gargoyle.

"Don't do that," said Alice, pulling on his arm.

"What?" said Nick. "Jesus, what?"

"Oh my goodness," said Alice. "How did our relationship get so *prickly*?"

"I should go," said Nick.

"What happened to George and Mildred?" said Alice.

Nick just looked at her blankly.

"The sandstone lions," Alice reminded him.

"I have no idea," said Nick.

Chapter 27

O h, *Alice*," said Alice to herself.

It was the morning after the Family Talent Night. The children had been safely delivered to school and she was sitting at the desk in the study, searching for things to help jog her memory. She'd just stumbled upon the reason why Mrs. Bergen wasn't speaking to her.

She sat back in her chair, put her feet up on the desk, and leaned right back on the chair so she was staring up at the ceiling. "What were you *thinking?*"

It seemed that Alice was an active member of a residents' committee lobbying the local council to have their street rezoned to allow the building of five-story apartment blocks. Mrs. Bergen was heading up the committee of residents fighting the rezoning proposal.

She took her feet off the desk and pulled out the next piece of paper in the file, biting into a Twix bar to fortify herself. (She had stocked the pantry with essential chocolate. The children were delirious about this, even while they pretended this was nothing out of the ordinary.)

It was a clipping from the local paper with the headline KING STREET

RESIDENTS CLASH, showing pictures of Mrs. Bergen and Alice. They had photographed Mrs. Bergen in her front garden, next to her rosebushes, wearing her gardening hat, holding a mug and looking sad and sweet.

> "This proposal is an outrage. It will ruin the character and heritage of this beautiful street," said Mrs. Beryl Bergen, who has lived in her King Street home for the past forty years and raised five children there.

"Of course it will," said Alice out loud.

The photo of Alice showed her sitting in the very chair she was sitting in now, looking grim and officious and definitely forty.

She groaned out loud as she read her own words.

> "It's inevitable," said Mrs. Alice Love, who moved into the area ten years ago. "Sydney needs high density housing close to public transport. When we purchased this home, we were told the rezoning would happen in the next five years. We took that into account as part of the property's investment potential. The council can't go back on its word and leave people out of pocket."

What? What was she talking about? They had no idea that rezoning was a possibility. They had talked about growing old in this house. They had not talked about selling it to a developer to knock it down and build some horrendous modern apartment block.

She read on, and somehow she wasn't surprised when she came to the final paragraph.

> Alice Love has taken over as president of the Residents for Rezoning Committee following the tragic death of its founder, Gina Boyle.

Of course. Gina. Bloody Gina.

She stood up decisively and went into the kitchen, where a tray of freshly baked chocolate brownies was cooling.

"Have I ever made these for you?" she had asked the children the night before, showing them the photo in the recipe book. "I asked you once," said Olivia, "but you said they were full of sugar." "Well, yes, but, so what?" Alice had asked, while Olivia giggled and Tom and Madison shot each other worried, grown-up glances.

She got a Tupperware container, filled it with chocolate brownies, and, without stopping to think about it, marched next door and rang the doorbell.

Mrs. Bergen's welcoming smile vanished when she saw Alice and she dropped the hand that was about to open the screen door by her side.

"Mrs. Bergen," said Alice. She pressed her hand to the screen door as if she were visiting her in jail. "I am so, so sorry. I've made a terrible mistake."

Elisabeth's Homework for Jeremy

I was delivering a one-day seminar today called "Using Direct Mail to Beef Up Your Sales!" to the Retail Butchers Association.

No, I'm not kidding. Any businessperson or professional can use direct mail to their advantage. Even you could, Jeremy.

Feel like driving your car into the nearest telephone pole?
Therapist Jeremy Hodges can steer you in a better direction.
FREE bottle of antidepressants for the first 10 appointments.

Or something like that. I'm a bit off my game.

Anyway, the butchers were a friendly, interested lot. There was much industry banter going across the room, and some surprisingly astute questions. (I thought the butchers were going to be sort of simple, red-faced, and jolly, but I think that's an act they put on to sell more sausages.) The seminar was going well. It is impossible to feel suicidal when you're explaining how to inject personality into a letter about lamb cutlets.

Then I saw someone sitting in the audience with a very un-butcherlike appearance.

It was Alice. She looks different these days. Less makeup, I think. Her hair is messier. She's wearing the same clothes but in a different way, and she's pulled out old things I haven't seen in years. Today she was wearing a long skirt, a faded cream jersey pulled in at the waist with a big belt, and a glittery tasseled scarf that I recognized from Olivia's dress-up box. She looked lovely, Jeremy, and for once I didn't resent her for having the time and the money to always keep her body in such perfect shape and for not having to stick needles in her stomach every night. When I saw her, she smiled and waved and held a palm in front of her face meaning, pretend I'm not here.

For some reason, the sight of her made me feel strangely emotional. My voice quivered as I went to answer a question about postage costs from Bill of Ryde Fresh Meats.

She came up to me in the morning tea break and said breathlessly, "I feel nervous, like I'm talking to a celebrity!" I don't think she was being sarcastic. It was sort of nice.

She said, "Why didn't you come to Frannie's thing last night?"

And I really did nearly tell her the truth. It was dancing away on the tip of my tongue, ready to jump off. Except that it didn't answer her question, and, anyway, I knew she'd react exactly the wrong way.

Which isn't her fault. Anyone would.

But seeing her reaction would push me right over the abyss

into crazy-land, and I'm only just managing to stay on this side of sanity.

I guess I could tell you, Jeremy, at our next appointment.

But no. I'm not saying it out loud. I'm just going to . . . wait it out, I guess.

Pretend it's not happening and wait for the inevitable, and not let it touch me.

Frannie's Letter to Phil

The Family Talent Night was a triumph, if I do say so myself.

Olivia did the most beautiful silly funny dance. I nearly burst with pride. And Barb and Roger performed one of their salsa dances, which wasn't unbearable. In point of fact, it was probably the most popular act of the night. All the ladies are desperately in love with Roger. There is no accounting for taste.

Alice and Nick even got up to dance, and for a moment there, I thought I might have seen a spark of something between them. However, at the end of the night I saw Nick stomping out to the car park, obviously in a terrible mood. They take their lives so seriously, these young people. "Just appreciate the fact that you can stomp so energetically," I wanted to say to him. I'd pay a million dollars to be Alice and Elisabeth's age again for just one day. I'd dance like Olivia's butterfly and bite into crisp green apples and run across hot sand into the surf, and I'd walk, as far as I wanted, wherever I wanted, in big loping, leaping strides, with my head held high and my lungs filling with air.

And I'd probably have sex!

Wasn't sex nice, Phil?

It was extremely nice.

For some reason I've been thinking about it lately, and the nights we spent in your cramped little flat in Neutral Bay with the lights winking on the harbor.

I'd pay two million for just one more night with you in that flat.

Not that I have two million. Or even a million. I'd have to take out a loan.

My apologies, Phil. I'm in a peculiarly flippant mood. Goodness, I'm going to have to make sure I don't leave this letter lying around for anyone to read. (Actually I might have to destroy it. What if I should drop dead in the middle of the night? What if Barb should find it and show it to the girls. Or far worse, Roger?)

Elisabeth didn't turn up at the Family Talent Night. I've been trying to call her, but without success.

Mr. M. (I can't seem to call him Xavier*) spent a long time talking with Madison. He said, "She's a very complex, intelligent little girl with a lot on her mind," and I was filled with affection for him. (I wonder what's on Madison's mind?)*

I do believe I might have found a new friend, which is a fine and wonderful thing at my age.

He's asked me out to dinner at the local Chinese restaurant.

I automatically went to decline, and then I thought, For heaven's sake, Frannie, why not?

"Look, Tom, police car!" cried Alice, as a police car with its siren flashing blue streaked by. "Nee nar, nee nar!"

She turned her head, ready to see an excited little face in the backseat, then realized she was alone in the car, and that Tom was too old to be excited by police cars anyway, and also, she actually didn't remember him as a baby.

These involuntary flashes of memory, or whatever they were, were happening almost every few minutes now. It was like a weird nervous tic. Just then, at the morning tea break at Elisabeth's seminar, she'd seen one of the butchers taking two chocolate biscuits at once and she only just managed to stop herself from grabbing his hairy wrist and saying, "One is plenty!"

She constantly found herself heading purposefully somewhere, into the study, the kitchen, or the laundry, and then realizing she didn't know why she was heading there. Once, she was all the way across the road, walking up the driveway of Gina's old house, when she stopped and said out loud, "Uh." She picked up the phone and dialed numbers, before quickly dropping the phone with no idea who she was calling. One time, while waiting outside the school for the children, she caught herself rocking her handbag, patting it, and humming a song she didn't recognize. "Yummy, yummy, yummy in your tummy, tummy!" she'd said at dinner the other night, zooming a spoonful of food toward Olivia's mouth. "I think you might be going a bit crazy, darling Mummy," Oliva had said, with wide eyes.

Her memory was coming back any moment now. She could feel it creeping up on her, like the fuzzy head and ticklish throat that heralded a cold. She just couldn't decide if she should resist it or encourage it.

Now she was on her way from Elisabeth's seminar to "help in the library" at the school. This was something she apparently did every third Thursday, which seemed excessively generous of her.

As she drove, she thought about Elisabeth, and how smooth she'd been up onstage, talking to all those butchers, making them laugh, telling them what to do. She'd seemed so natural talking into the microphone. So herself. The same way celebrities casually chatted away in interviews to journalists, as if there weren't cameras right in front of them. But then when Elisabeth had talked to her in the break, she had the strangest feeling that Elisabeth wasn't really there, that she was just pretending to be Elisabeth. That she was more herself up onstage than right now.

Alice still hadn't even got to talk to her yet about the unsuccessful IVF cycle. She'd called the night before when she got home from the Family Talent Night, but Ben had said Elisabeth was watching a favorite TV show and could she call back once it was over? She never called back, and of course she could hardly talk to her about it when she was working. It was ridiculous that she had no idea what was going on in her own sister's mind. She couldn't even take an educated guess as to how Elisabeth was feeling right now. Angry? Devastated? Sick of the whole thing?

She would try to call her again tonight, but it was weirdly hard to find time once she'd driven the children to all their activities, helped with homework (so much homework! It gave Alice a headache. She'd actually groaned when she saw the number of worksheets Tom had pulled out from his bag the other night, which wasn't very parental of her), cooked their dinner, cleaned up, made their lunches, tried to convince them to stop fighting over the computer and the television. By the end of it, she was exhausted.

There just wasn't enough time in 2008. It had become a limited resource. Back in 1998, the days were so much more spacious. When she woke up in the morning, the day rolled out in front of her like a long hallway for her to meander down, free to linger over the best parts. Days were so stingy now. Mean slivers of time. They flew by like speeding cars. *Whoosh!* When she was pulling back the blankets to hop into bed each night, it felt as if only seconds ago she'd been throwing them off to get up.

Maybe it was just because she wasn't used to this life. This life as a separated mother of three children.

She was doing things differently, trying to slow down time. She had a feeling the new Alice, the one with that snippy voice, wouldn't approve of some of the changes.

When she'd picked the children up from school yesterday, Olivia had whined, "I don't want to go to violin," and Alice, who had no idea that she was meant to be "going to violin," had said, "Okay, fine," and taken the three children to Dino's, where they'd done their homework sitting at a round table, drinking hot chocolates, and Dino had been quite helpful with Tom's maths homework.

There had been a very cranky call from someone about the violin lesson who had told Alice that she would still have to pay, seeing as twenty-four hours' notice hadn't been given. "Oh, well," Alice had said, and was met by a shocked silence.

After they had got home from the Family Talent Night, she'd let Madison stay up past eleven baking an enormous Black Forest cake for a "Food from Different Cultures Day" they were having at the school.

"I don't want your help," Madison had insisted before Alice even offered to help "I want to do it myself."

"That's fine," said Alice.

"You always say that," Madison said. "And then you end up helping."

"I bet you a thousand dollars that I will not lift a finger to help," Alice had said, and held out her hand.

Madison stared, before giving her that sudden beautiful smile and shaking her hand.

"*I* want to bet you something for a thousand dollars," Tom said. "Bet me something!"

"*Me too!*" shouted Olivia. "Bet me something, Mum!"

"No, I'm doing the next bet," said Tom. "Mum, I bet you . . . ummm, I bet you, ummm, just hold on, while I think of something really good."

"I bet you I can do a handstand for five minutes!" cried Olivia. "No, two! No, let's maybe just make it one minute."

"I bet you a thousand dollars I can't count to one million!" said Tom. "I mean that I *can*! The way it works is that you give me a thousand dollars if I *can*."

"Nobody can count to one million," said Olivia solemnly. "That would take, like, a week."

"No it wouldn't," said Tom. "Okay, so let's say that it takes you sixty seconds to count to sixty. Or, wait. Okay, maybe you could count, like, to ninety in sixty seconds. So, ummm, where's the calculator? Mum? Do you know where the calculator is? Mum, are you listening?"

"Are you children always this *tiring*?" Alice had asked. Sometimes it felt like they sucked every thought out of her brain.

"Pretty much," said Tom.

Elisabeth's Homework for Jeremy

While the butchers were in groups brainstorming ideas on butcher paper (ha ha), I sat and thought about the transfer of the last embryo two weeks ago.

It had been frozen for a year.

A tiny, ice-encrusted potential person.

When we first started IVF, I would stand at the freezer door and take a sparkly fragment of ice on the tip of my finger and think about my frozen potential children. All those possible people. We had seven frozen at one time. Such a treasure trove of possibility. This one could be a swimmer. This one could be musical. This one could be tall. This one could be short. This one could be sweet and shy. This one could be funny. This one could be like Ben. This one could be like me.

Ben and I talked about it all the time. We sent them telepathic messages of support. "Hang in there," we said. "Hope you're not too chilly."

But as the years went by, we stopped talking like that. We became detached from the process. It was just science. It was just unpleasant medical procedures. We weren't even amazed by the science anymore. Yeah, yeah, they make babies in test tubes. Incredible. But it just doesn't work out for us.

This last time, we'd run late, and we got a ticket for doing an illegal right-hand turn. It was my idea to do the illegal turn to get there faster, and Ben was so cranky with himself for listening to me, because as a result we were even later. "How could you not see that sign?" the policeman had said, and Ben's mouth twisted with everything he probably wanted to say. "It was *her*!" The policeman took an incredible amount of time writing out the ticket, as if he knew we were running late and this was part of our punishment.

"Let's just go home," I'd said to Ben. "It's not going to work anyway. This is a sign. Let's not waste our money on the parking."

I wanted him to say something positive and comforting, but he was in a bad mood by now. He said, "That's a great attitude. Really great." He's not normally sarcastic.

Anyway, I know now that he didn't think it was going to work either. A week later he was eating Alice's banana muffins and getting all excited about adoption, before we even knew if this one had worked or not.

The embryologist was a young girl who didn't look all that much older than Madison. She tripped on something when we were walking into the treatment room, which I didn't think was a very good sign. Oops. There goes your embryo!

When I was in the chair, with my legs elegantly spread, waiting for the gigantic needle, she muttered something and none of us heard her.

"There's your embryo," she said again, embarrassed. Maybe it was her first time. We looked, and there, projected on the lit-up screen, was our potential baby.

It looked just like its non-brothers and non-sisters. A froth of bubbles. A magnified drop of water.

I didn't bother to marvel. I didn't bother to say anything like, "Oh, isn't it amazing." I didn't bother to keep the memory in my head, in case I one day had to describe it to my child. "I saw you when you were just a pretty little blastocyst, sweetie."

I didn't know the doctor who was doing the transfer. My lovely doctor is away in Paris at the moment because her daughter is getting married to a French lawyer. This doctor was a man, with a long somber face, and he reminded me of our tax accountant. An especially ominous sign. (We never get refunds.) My doctor normally chats away about whatever comes into her head, but this man didn't say anything until it was done. Then he showed us the embryo on the ultrasound.

"Good. It's in the right spot," he said blandly, as if my uterus was a piece of industrial equipment.

It looked like the others did on the ultrasound. A tremulously blinking star.

I knew it wouldn't blink for long.

I looked away from the ultrasound screen to Ben, and he was studying his hands.

Bad signs all around.

Breathe in. Breathe out. Breathe in. Breathe out.

After the butchers had finished their brainstorming I went up onstage and told them that my assistant Layla would be taking the remainder of the day, as if that was always the plan.

The butchers clapped her amiably when she stood up, a confused look on her face.

I walked out. I just couldn't get that blinking star out of my damned head.

Alice was walking toward the library at the school (her body seemed to know that it was through that double red door at the corner of the schoolyard) when Dominick appeared. He looked ruffled, his face creased with worry.

"Alice," he said. "I saw you through my office window. I've been trying to phone you."

"Sorry," said Alice. "I keep forgetting to charge my phone. Memory!"

He didn't smile. "I called Nick, too," he said. "He's on his way."

"You called Nick? Why?" Was he going to fight him for her hand? Challenge him to a duel? (Except Nick didn't want her hand anymore. So, you know, maybe not much of a fight. *Sure, mate, have her.*)

"We've got a problem," said Dominick. "A serious problem with Madison."

Elisabeth's Homework for Jeremy

After I left the seminar I got a phone call from Ben. His voice sounded like sandpaper.

"Why didn't you tell me?" he said.

I hung up.

I didn't like his tone.

Chapter 28

"Is she all right?" Terror flooded Alice's bloodstream, making her legs wobble so badly she had to hold on to Dominick's arm to steady herself.

"Oh, yes, sorry." Dominick smiled distractedly and patted Alice on the arm. "Physically, she's fine. It's just that we've had another incident, and I don't think we can ignore this one."

"Another incident?"

"Another bullying incident."

"Someone is bullying Madison?" She would throttle the kid. She would demand to see the parents. She was light-headed with rage. Someone had hurt the Sultana and she was going to have the brat for breakfast.

"Alice," said Dominick. He looked a little stern. School-principal stern. "It's Madison who is the bully."

"Madison wouldn't bully anyone." She knew her daughter. She'd only known her for five days, but she knew her.

And sure, maybe she could be moody and a little, well, *aggressive*, toward her brother and sister when she was riled, but that was just normal sibling rivalry (she hoped). Her heart was in the right place. Look at the way she helped Olivia choreograph her butterfly dance. Look at the way she helped Tom with his geography homework the other day. Okay, Tom said she was being annoying, and it had ended up with Madison stomping off in floods of tears and Tom slapping his hand to his forehead and rolling his eyes like a miniature version of his father, but, well . . . Alice's daughter would not, could not, be a bully.

"Are you still—not yourself?" asked Dominick carefully.

"Not quite," said Alice.

"Well, this isn't the first time we've had problems with Madison. A little boy had to have stitches a few weeks ago after an altercation with Madison."

Ah, thought Alice. That was the "little incident" that Kate Harper had mentioned at the gym.

"I know she's having problems, after Gina's death, and with the divorce," continued Dominick, his forehead puckered with school principal-ish concern. "Alice, I'm so sorry, but this is really—oh." His voice changed as he saw someone over Alice's shoulder. "Here's your, ah—your . . ."

Alice turned around and saw Nick coming toward them. He was wearing his suit and tie and talking into his mobile phone. His aura of business and decisions and important mustn't be-disturbed meetings looked alien in the sunlit playground, with the sounds of children chanting something from the open window of a nearby classroom.

Dominick caught her eye. "Hope this isn't too awkward."

"Yes," said Alice awkwardly.

As he got closer, they heard him say, "Well, let's say two mil. Does that sound okay? Excellent. Bye." He snapped the phone shut with one hand and Alice wanted to say, *Oh, Nick, honey, stop being such a wanker.*

"Dominick, isn't it?" said Nick, holding out his hand, as if Dominick were there to sell them something.

"Yes, hi. How are you?" said Dominick. He was about a head taller than Nick and looked like a gangly schoolboy next to him. Alice wanted to hug him, but she wanted to hug Nick, too. They seemed like boys dressed up in grown-up bodies.

"This must be pretty important for you to call us both down," said Nick, an edge to his voice.

"Yes," said Dominick, and there was an answering edge in his voice. "Madison threatened to stab Chloe Harper with a pair of scissors. She also cut off a huge chunk of her hair and pushed her face into a cake. I'm going to have to suspend her at least until the school holidays. I think she needs to see a counselor."

"I see," said Nick, and he seemed to deflate and sag. All the power had gone to Dominick.

"There must be more to the story," said Alice. "She must have had a reason."

"It doesn't matter about her reason," said Dominick (a bit snootily, Alice thought, for someone who was trying to be her boyfriend). "It's unacceptable. And you can imagine how Kate Harper is going to react to this. She's on her way to the school, too."

So Chloe was the horrendous Kate Harper's little girl. Well, there you go. That explained everything.

"We'll have to—I don't know—offer some sort of compensation," sighed Nick.

"I don't think money is the answer in this particular case," said Dominick. *Ke-pow.*

"I didn't mean—"

"Anyway, I've got both girls waiting for us in my office," interrupted Dominick.

Alice and Nick followed behind him like naughty children. Alice made an "Isn't this appalling" face at Nick, and he grimaced.

In Dominick's office, Madison and another little girl were sitting on chairs in front of his desk. The little girl was sobbing in an outraged "I *so* deserve to cry" way, cradling something in her arms, and Alice saw with sick horror that it was a long, blond plait. She had bits of chocolate cake and cream and cherries smeared all over her face and school uniform and the shocking, hacked-off line of her blond hair stuck up over the back collar of her uniform.

"Oh, Madison," said Alice involuntarily. "How *could* you?"

Madison's face was dead white, her eyes shining with fury. She was sitting very still and straight with her hands in fists on her lap, the image of a little psychopathic killer brought into the police station for questioning.

"You've got some explaining to do, young lady," said Nick, and Alice nearly laughed. He sounded like a man playing the angry dad in a bad amateur play.

Madison didn't say anything.

"Do you want to tell your parents what happened?" said Dominick, sounding much more authentic.

Madison shook her head passionately, as if she were refusing to reveal state secrets to her torturers.

"She hasn't said a word," said Dominick to Alice.

The little girl dangled the blond plait in front of her, tears continuing to roll down her face. "Look at my *hair*. My mum is going to *kill* you, Madison Love. My hair is *beautiful*. It will take me years and years and years to grow it back. I will be, like, forty. You just did it because you're *jealous*, and you haven't even said . . ." Her voice quavered, as if she were overcome with the horror of it, "You haven't even said *sorry*."

"Okay, Chloe," said Dominick. "Let's calm down."

"Madison, apologize to Chloe," said Alice, in a grim, forbidding voice she didn't recognize. "Right now."

"Sorry," muttered Madison.

"She *isn't*!" wailed Chloe, looking up at Alice and Nick. "She's just saying that! Just wait till my mum gets here!"

"Actually," said Dominick. "I don't think we will wait. I think Mr. and Mrs. Love can take Madison with them now."

He squatted down in front of Madison so they were face-to-face.

"Madison, I'm suspending you from school as of now," he said. "You can't be a part of this school and behave like that, do you understand? This is very, very serious."

Madison nodded. Her face had now gone from white to flaming red.

"Right then." Dominick stood up. "Go and get your bag and meet your parents at the gate."

Madison shot from the room, and Chloe burst into a fresh flood of tears.

"Okay, Chloe," said Dominick wearily. "Your mum will be here soon. Just wait here."

He ushered Nick and Alice out of the room, closing the door behind him.

"There's probably not much point you having to see Kate now, while everyone is in such a state," he said. "I think you should take Madison home and try and talk to her and get an idea of what's going on in her head. I would seriously recommend counseling. I can give you some names." There was a sound of hurriedly clicking heels in the distance. "I bet that's Kate. Go." He waved them away, as if he were saving them from the secret police. "Disappear!"

Nick and Alice fled through the playground. They stopped at the school gates. Nick was panting. Alice wasn't. She was much fitter than he was.

"That was awful," said Alice. "I feel like I cut off that child's hair myself. And the cake! She spent so long making that cake. Poor little thing."

"Chloe?" said Nick.

"No, Madison," said Alice. "Who cares about Chloe?"

"Alice, our child threatened to stab her with a pair of scissors."

"Well, I know that," said Alice.

Nick pulled out his mobile phone from his pocket, flipped it open. "I don't see how suspending her helps anything," he said, while frowning at something on the screen of his phone. "It's like they're putting their hands in the air and saying, 'We don't know what to do with her.' Absolving themselves of responsibility." He looked up at Alice. "Not to criticize your boyfriend or anything."

"I guess it's school policy," said Alice, feeling both defensive of Dominick and betrayed by him. Didn't kissing the school principal give you a free pass when it came to suspending your daughter?

"Anyway"— Nick looked at his watch—"I'll get back to the office. I guess we'd better talk about this later. I don't know what sort of punishment you're thinking, but obviously it has to be severe—"

"What do you mean?" said Alice. "I think we should talk to her now. Right now. Both of us."

Nick seemed startled. "Now? You want me to be there, too?"

"Of course I do," said Alice. "I think we should take her for a drive. And we're not going to jump in and start *punishing* her. I hate that word. Punishment."

"Oh, sorry. I guess we should reward her. Say 'Well done, honey, maybe you should consider a career in hairdressing.'"

Alice giggled. Nick smiled. The sunlight was shining directly onto his face. He shielded his eyes with one hand and said, "I'll know when you get your memory back."

"How?"

"The way you look at me. As soon as you remember, I'll see it in your eyes."

"Will they shoot death rays at you?" said Alice.

Nick smiled sadly. "Something like that." He looked again at his watch. "I've got a meeting at midday. I guess I could move it." He seemed uncertain. "So you mean both of us take her for a drive somewhere?"

Alice said, "Is this really so unusual?"

"Normally you'd take charge and make it clear that my assistance was not required."

"There's a new Alice in town," said Alice.

"You're not wrong about that." Nick seemed about to say something. He stopped and looked over her shoulder. "Here comes our little thug."

Madison was walking toward them, her school backpack held loosely in one hand so it was almost dragging along the ground, her head hanging.

"Who am I going with?" she said when she got to them, not meeting their eyes.

"Both of us," said Alice.

"Both of you?" Madison looked up and frowned. She seemed frightened.

"Come here," said Alice.

Madison stomped over to her, still staring at the ground, and Alice pulled her close and hugged her.

"We're going to work this out," said Alice quietly into her hair. "You, your dad, and me are going to sit on the beach, eat ice creams, and work out whatever the problem is."

Madison gave a tiny gasp of surprise and burst into tears.

Elisabeth's Homework for Jeremy

He keeps saying, "Turn the television off."

And I keep saying, "Not yet."

He turned it off himself a while ago, and as soon as he did, I screamed over and over, as if he was hurting me.

A tiny bit dramatic. I will feel embarrassed later.

But it did hurt me. That loud buzzing silence after the TV was switched off was actually painful to my eardrums.

He was probably worried the neighbors would call the police. After all, he looks exactly like the sort of man you expect to see dragged away in handcuffs for domestic violence. So he shrugged and turned it back on.

I am watching Oprah now. She's talking about an exciting new diet. The audience is excited. I'm excited, J. I might try it. I'm taking notes.

They sat on the harbor-side beach at Manly, near the ferry stop, in the same spot where they'd had coffee that early morning after they drove Madison through the night when she was a baby.

They even had the same blue-and-white-checked picnic rug. It was in the boot of Nick's car. The blue wasn't as bright as it was in Alice's memory, but her palms remembered its nubbly feel.

"Where did we get this rug?" asked Alice as they sat down.

"I don't know," said Nick. He sounded defensive. "You can have it if you want. I didn't realize it was in my car."

Oh, for heaven's sake. She hadn't meant she wanted it. It was yet another glimpse of how stupid their lives had become. Would she really have wanted to make a point about who got the picnic rug?

Madison plonked herself down and sat with her arms wrapped around her knees, chin down, lank hair falling down on either side of her face. (Alice itched to snip it off. She would look so much prettier with short hair. Actually that could be the perfect "punishment"! *You cut her hair, kid, so I'm going to cut yours.*)

After her tears in the schoolyard, Madison hadn't said a word. Nick had driven in his shiny car, and he'd spent a lot of time talking on his hands-free mobile. He laughed. He listened. He gave short, sharp instructions. He said, "Let me think about it." He said, "Well, that's a disaster," while glancing over his shoulder to switch lanes. He said, "Well done. That's great news." He was such a boss.

"Do you enjoy work at the moment?" Alice asked him at one point in between calls.

Nick glanced over at her. "Yes," he said, after a few seconds. "I love it."

"That's great," said Alice, happy for him.

Nick raised an eyebrow. "You really think so?"

"Of course," said Alice. "Why wouldn't I?"

"Nothing," said Nick, and Alice could sense Madison listening carefully from the backseat.

Nick had turned his phone off now and had left his jacket and tie in the car. Now he was taking off his shoes and socks. Alice looked at his bare feet digging into the sand. His feet were as familiar as her own. How could she not be with someone forever when even their *feet*—his huge, not especially attractive feet, with their long hairy toes—felt like home?

"Beautiful," said Nick, gesturing at the smooth, hard, yellow sand, the huge turquoise sky, the ferry chugging its way across the harbor to the city. *"Beautiful."* He said it in the same satisfied tone that he would use to describe a good meal at a restaurant, as if the weather and the beach had been prepared especially for him, and presented on a plate, and yes, thank you, it was all up to his high standards and there would be a generous tip as a result. It was so typical Nick. He held up his face to the sun and closed his eyes.

Alice took off her own boots (beautiful—her taste was impeccable, if she did say so herself) and pulled off her socks.

"They're Tom's soccer socks," said Madison, looking up from her knees.

"I was in a rush," said Alice.

Madison gave her a look. "And that scarf you're wearing is from Olivia's *dress-up box.*"

"I know, but it's so beautiful." Alice lifted up the gauzy material.

Madison gave her an inscrutable look and lowered her chin again.

Nick opened his eyes. "Well, Madison—"

"You *promised* ice creams," said Madison, glaring at Alice, as if this was to be yet another in a long line of broken promises.

"That's right, I did," said Alice.

Nick sighed. "I'll go." He put his shoes back on and looked down at Madison. "Don't you be telling your brother and sister that you got ice cream on the beach, will you? Or next thing, we'll have all the Love children suspended from school."

Madison giggled. "Okay."

As Nick walked off, Madison said, "I don't want to say what happened in front of Daddy."

It must be girl stuff. "All right. Just tell me."

Madison dropped her chin back to her knees and said in a muffled voice, "Chloe said that you and Mr. Gordon had—"

Alice didn't catch the last word.

"Pardon?" she said.

"Sex!" Madison choked out. "She said that you and Mr. Gordon probably did sex in his office. Like, a hundred times."

Mr. Gordon. Oh. *Dominick.*

"Darling," began Alice, wondering where to start. For one thing she wasn't sure if it was true. Surely they wouldn't have had sex in his office? Would they?

"I nearly threw up. I had to take sort of deep breaths and put my hand over my mouth. You *didn't,* did you? You never took off your clothes in front of Mr. Gordon, did you?"

Well, if she had, surely Chloe wasn't privy to the information. Presumably Dominick hadn't made an announcement about it at school assembly.

"Chloe Harper is a horrible liar," said Alice decisively.

"I *know,*" said Madison with relief. "That's what I said!" She looked out at the water and pushed her hair back behind her ears. "Then she said that I was the ugliest girl in the whole school, but that part wasn't a lie, that part was true."

Alice's heart broke for her. "It certainly was not true."

"I got this feeling," said Madison. "A feeling like my head was going to explode. She was standing in front of me and I got out my scissors for art and I cut off her plait. I just went, snip! And it fell straight to the ground. And then when she turned around, I threw my cake at her. It wrecked the cake. Nobody even got to taste it. It was the best cake I ever made."

"Did you threaten to stab her with the scissors?"

"No! She just made that bit up so I would get into more trouble."

"Is that the truth?"

"Yes," said Madison.

"Okay," said Alice. Well, that was something.

Alice said, "You know, Madison, people are going to say mean things to you all through your life, and if you keep reacting like that, you're going to end up in jail."

Madison seemed to consider that. Alice wondered whether her wise, tough-love words were sinking in.

"Actually, I'm too young for jail," said Madison.

"Well, *now* you are, but when you're grown up—"

"When I'm a grown-up it won't matter."

"You mean, you won't care if you go to jail? I think you will."

Madison rolled her eyes. "No. I won't care if people say mean things to me, because I'll be grown up. I can just say, 'Who cares? I'm going to France.'"

Ah. Of course. Alice could remember thinking something similar when she was a child. Once you were a grown-up nobody could hurt your feelings because how could your feelings possibly be hurt when you could *drive a car wherever you wanted.*

Before she could think of a way to answer without disillusioning her (what was there to look forward to otherwise?), a shadow fell over them.

"Ice cream delivery." Nick was standing above them, holding three ice cream cones.

"I assume you still like rum and raisin," he said to Alice.

"Of course." Fancy having to ask her that.

They sat and ate their ice creams, looking out at the water.

"Madison has just told me what Chloe said to her," said Alice. "And it was something nasty and untrue."

"Okay," said Nick carefully. He licked his ice cream and looked at them both.

"So, I guess we need to help Madison find some better ways to react when she feels angry."

"I always take ten deep breaths before I say anything when I'm angry," said Nick.

"No you don't," said Madison. "You just yell straightaway. So does Mum. And what about that time Mum threw that pizza box at you?"

Oh my, they'd been setting fine examples for their children.

Alice cleared her throat. "Well, the thing is——"

"Are you going to come home, please, Dad?" said Madison. "I think you should come home now and be Mum's husband again. I'm pretty sure then I would stop being angry. Then I would never do another bad thing in my whole entire life. I could write that in a *contract* for you. So that means you could, like, *sue* me if I was ever bad, which I would not ever be."

She looked at her father with desperate entreaty.

"Sweetheart," began Nick, his face screwed tight as if he had a toothache. Then he stopped, distracted by some sort of disturbance on the beach. There were shouts and people running. Alice could see a small crowd of people forming up on the cliff above the aquarium, pointing at something in the water.

"Humpback whales in the harbor!" a man cried at them, running along with a camera bouncing on his chest.

Nick immediately leapt to his feet, still holding his ice cream. Madison and Alice looked up at him.

"What are you waiting for?" he said, and next thing the three of them were running breathlessly along the beach, up onto the foreshore, and running around the walkway, their ice creams held precariously in front of them.

They had to run a steep set of concrete steps and Alice drew ahead, one hand holding her ice cream, the other holding up her skirt as she effortlessly leapt up the steps, two at a time.

As she reached the top, she was in time to see a massive plume of water shoot up from the water below them.

"It's a mother and her calf," said a woman to Alice. "Watch. Just there. You'll see them again."

Nick and Madison pounded up the stairs behind her. Nick was breathing heavily. (How did he get so unfit?)

"Where? Where?" said Madison. Her face was pink and anxious.

"Just watch," said Alice.

For a few seconds there was nothing but silence. The surface of the harbor rippled in the breeze and a seagull squawked plaintively.

"They've gone," said Madison. "We've missed them. Typical."

Nick looked at his watch.

Come on, whale, thought Alice. *Give us a break.*

The water erupted as a massive creature shot straight into the air. It was like something prehistoric had crashed through an invisible barrier into ordinary life. Alice caught a glimpse of a barnacle-encrusted white front. It seemed to hover in the air before slamming back into the water, with a flurry of icy, salty raindrops against their faces.

Madison grabbed hold of Alice's arm. Her face was radiant with joy, speckled with droplets of water. "Look, Mum! Look!"

The whale rolled luxuriously about, revealing huge curves of velvety black skin, its tail slapping the water, as if enjoying a hot bath.

"Madison, Alice, over there—it's the baby!" shouted Nick, and he sounded like a sixteen-year-old boy.

The calf was splashing about in miniature imitation of its mother. Alice could almost imagine it gurgling with laughter.

"Ha!" said Nick idiotically. "Ha!"

All around them were faces full of joy and wonder. The sea air was cool on their faces, the sun warm on their backs.

"Do it again!" said Madison. "Jump up again, mother whale!"

"Yeah!" agreed the man with the camera. "One more time."

And right on cue, she did.

Elisabeth's Homework for Jeremy

Ben is threatening to ring you up. He thinks I'm behaving like a crazy person.

Frannie's Letter to Phil

Something quite extraordinary has happened, Phil.

As they walked back to the picnic rug, Madison danced around them. She was euphoric. Skipping. Jumping. Swinging on Nick's hand, then Alice's, then both. People walking by smiled at her.

"That was the best thing I've ever seen!" she kept saying. "I'm going to blow that photo up into a poster and put it over my bed!"

The man with the camera had taken Nick's e-mail address and was going to send him the photo he'd taken.

"Let's hope he didn't miss it," said Nick.

"No, he got it," said Madison. "He definitely got it. Can I go paddle? Just to feel the water?"

She looked at Alice, and Alice looked at Nick. He shrugged.

"Sure," said Alice. "Why not?"

They watched her run down toward the water.

"Do you think she needs counseling?" said Alice.

"She's been through a lot," said Nick. "Gina's accident. You and me. And she always feels things so deeply."

"What do you mean, Gina's accident?" Alice thought about Madison's nightmare. *Get it off her.*

"Madison was with you," said Nick. "She saw it happen. You don't remember it, do you?"

"No," said Alice. "Just the feeling of it." Although that feeling of sick horror seemed impossible here today, with the sun and sea, ice creams and whales.

"There was a storm," said Nick. "A tree fell on Gina's car. You and Madison were driving behind."

A tree. So that horrible image of a black leafless tree swaying against a stormy sky was real.

"It must have been horrendous for both of you," said Nick quietly. He lifted a handful of sand and let the grains fall through his fingers. "And I didn't—I wasn't—"

"What?"

"I wasn't as supportive as I should have been," said Nick.

"Why weren't you?" asked Alice curiously.

"Honestly, I don't know," said Nick. "I just felt detached. I felt like you wouldn't want my sympathy. I felt like—I felt that if you'd had the choice, you would have preferred that I'd died rather than Gina. I remember I tried to hug you and you pushed me away as if I made you sick. I should have tried harder. I'm sorry."

"But why would you think I'd prefer you to die?" asked Alice. It seemed such a silly, childish, wrong thing to think.

"We weren't getting on that well at the time. And you two were such good friends," said Nick. "I mean—that was great—that was fine—but . . ." His lips did something funny. "You told Gina that you were pregnant with Olivia before you told me."

"Really?" Why would she have done that? "I'm sorry."

"Oh, well, it was only a small thing." He stopped. "Also, once I overheard you saying something about our sex life. Or lack thereof. I mean, I know women always talk about sex together. It was just the tone in your voice. It was such *contempt* for me. And then, when she and Mike broke up, and you were going out to bars with her, trying to help her pick up men, I got the feeling that you were jealous. You wanted to be a single woman with her. I was in the way. Cramping your style."

"I'm so sorry," said Alice. She felt like some other woman had been horrible to Nick. As if he were describing an awful ex-girlfriend who had broken his heart.

"And then Gina died. And that was it. You froze up. That's how it felt. You were like ice."

"I don't understand why I did that," said Alice. If *Sophie* had died, she would have cried for hours in the safe, comforting circle of Nick's arms.

"Is that why you didn't come to the funeral?" she asked.

Nick shrugged.

"I had to be in New York. It was a huge meeting. Something we'd been planning for months, but I told you a million bloody times I was happy to cancel. I kept asking if you wanted me at the funeral, and you said, 'Do what you want.' So, I thought, maybe you'd actually prefer it if I *wasn't* there. I wanted to go. She was my friend, too, once upon a time. You always seem to forget that. She drove me crazy the way she bossed you around, but I still cared about her. It just got so confusing after she and Mike split up. I wanted to stay friends with him, too, and you saw that as a betrayal of Gina. So did she. She was so mad with me. Each time I saw Gina, she'd say, 'Seen Mike lately?' and you'd both be shooting me evil looks as if I was the villain. I didn't see why I had to dump a good mate just because of one drunken—anyway, we've been over it a million times. I'm just trying to say that I felt so, I don't know, *awkward*, when she died. I didn't know how I was meant to act. I just wanted you to say, 'Of course you should cancel the trip. Of course you should come to the funeral.' I felt like I needed your permission."

"So all our problems were because of Gina and Mike," said Alice. These two *strangers* had destroyed their marriage.

"I don't think we can blame them for everything," said Nick. "We argued. We argued over the most trivial things."

"Like what?"

"Like, I don't know, cherries. One day we were going over to Mum's place for dinner and I ate some cherries we were meant to be taking. It was the crime of the century. You would not let it go. You were talking about those cherries for months."

"Cherries," pondered Alice.

"I'd be at work, where people respected my opinions," said Nick. "And then I'd come home and it was like I was the village idiot. I'd pack the dishwasher the wrong way. I'd pick the wrong clothes for the children. I stopped offering to help. It wasn't worth the criticism."

They didn't say anything for a few moments. Next to them, a family with a toddler and a baby laid out a rug. The toddler picked up a handful of sand with a determined expression on his face and went to drop it all over his baby sister's face. They heard the mother say, "Watch him!" and the father pulled him away just in time. The mother rolled her eyes, and the father muttered something they didn't catch.

"I'm not saying I was perfect," said Nick, his eyes on the father. "I was too caught up in work. You'd say I was obsessed with it. You always talk about the year I was working on the Goodman project. I was traveling a lot. You had to cope on your own with three children. You said once that I 'deserted you.' I always think that year made my career, but maybe . . ." He stopped and squinted out at the harbor. "Maybe that was the year that broke our marriage."

The Goodman project. The words put a bad taste in her mouth. *The bloody Goodman project.* The word "bloody" seemed to belong naturally before "Goodman."

Alice leaned back and pushed the heels of her boots deep into the sand. It all seemed so complicated. Her mistakes. Nick's mistakes. For the first time it occurred to her that maybe their marriage couldn't be put back together.

She looked over at the family with the two small children. Now the father was spinning the little boy around and the mother was laughing, taking photos of them with a digital camera.

Madison walked up from the water toward them, carrying something in her cupped-together hands, her face radiant.

Nick's hand was next to Alice's on the picnic rug.

She felt the tip of his finger lightly touch hers.

"Maybe we should try again," he said.

Chapter 29

George and Mildred turned up on Friday.

Alice found them at the back of the garage. George was lying on his side, as if he'd been kicked over. His once dignified lion's face was now stained a moldy green, which made him look ashamed, as if he were an old man with food all over his face. Mildred was sitting in the middle of a pile of old pots. There was a huge chip out of one paw, and she looked sad and resigned. They were both filthy.

Alice had dragged them both onto the back veranda and was scrubbing them with a mixture of bleach and water, as recommended by Mrs. Bergen next door, who was thrilled that Alice had swapped sides on the development issue, and who was once again waving and smiling when she saw her and asking Alice to send the children over to play on her piano anytime they wanted. "We're not *five* anymore," said Tom wearily. "Doesn't she know we have a PlayStation?"

Barb had offered to take Madison for a shopping trip on the first day of her suspension. "Don't worry, I won't spoil her," she'd told Alice. "No new clothes or anything. Unless she sees something really *special*, of course, in which case I'll put it away for her next birthday."

As Alice scrubbed, she wondered if George and Mildred would ever look the same again. Was it too late? Were they too scarred by the years of neglect?

And would it be the same for her and Nick? Had each argument, each betrayal and nasty word built up into an ugly rock-hard layer covering what was once so tender and true?

Well, if it had, they would just chip away at it until it was gone. It would be fine. Good as new! She scrubbed so vigorously at Mildred's mane that her teeth chattered.

The phone rang and Alice put down the scrubbing brush with relief.

It was Ben. His voice on the phone was deep and slow and very Australian, as if someone from the outback were calling. He said that Elisabeth had been sitting in bed watching television for the last forty-eight hours and screaming if he tried to turn it off, and he wasn't sure how long he should let this go on for.

"It must be because she's so upset about the last IVF cycle failing," said Alice, looking at her fridge with the photos of the children and the school newsletters, and wishing she could somehow share this life with her sister.

There was a slight pause and then Ben said, "Yeah, well, that's the other thing. I found out that it didn't fail. I got a call from the clinic about her first ultrasound. She's pregnant."

Elisabeth's Homework for Jeremy

I can hear him in the next room calling Alice. I made him promise not to tell anyone I was pregnant.

I knew he would. Liar.

You have no idea of the fury I feel. Against him. His mother. My mother. Alice. You, Jeremy. I hate you all. For no particular reason.

I guess it's for the sympathy, the pity and understanding, but most of all, for the hope. For the comments I'm about to hear. "This one could be the one!" "I have a good feeling about this one!"

Waves of red-hot fury keep rising up inside me. I'm trying to ride them like I imagine you might do with labor pains. I feel sick, and my breasts ache, and there is a funny taste in my mouth, and we've been here so many times before, and I can't go through it again, I can't.

And the thing that infuriates me the most, Jeremy, is that even though I'm saying it and I'm believing it and I know with all my heart that I'm going to lose this baby like all the others, I also know that underneath it all, that inanely positive, pathetic voice is still chirping, "But maybe . . . ?"

Alice drove over to Elisabeth's place.

She had to get directions from Ben, and none of the streets or the area seemed remotely familiar. Perhaps she didn't visit Elisabeth much? Because she was so busy. Busy, busy, busy.

They lived in a red-brick cottage with a neatly mowed front lawn. It was a family neighborhood. There was a children's swing set in the front yard of the house next door, and a woman across the road was leaning into her car and unstrapping her baby from a car seat. It reminded Alice of her own street ten years ago.

She could hear the clamor of the television as soon as Ben opened the door. "She wants it up really loud," said Ben. "Be ready. If you try and turn it off, she sounds like a trapped animal. It's freaking me out. I had to go sleep in the spare room last night. I don't know if she even slept at all."

"So, what do you think is going on?" asked Alice.

Ben shrugged his massive bear shoulders. "I guess she's scared she's going to lose it again. So am I. I mean, in a way, I was almost relieved when I thought the blood-test results were negative."

Alice followed Ben through the house (very clean, neat, and bare; no clutter) into the bedroom, where Elisabeth was sitting up in bed with the remote in one hand and an exercise book and pen resting on her lap.

She was still wearing the same outfit she wore at the seminar for the butchers on Wednesday, except her hair was a tangled mess and her mascara had smudged so she had thick black shadows under her eyes.

Alice didn't say anything. She just kicked off her shoes and hopped into bed beside Elisabeth, pulling the covers up and putting a pillow behind her back.

Ben hovered uncertainly at the door. "Okay," he said, "I'll be working on the car."

"Okay." Alice smiled at him.

Alice glanced at Elisabeth's profile. Her face was set, her eyes fixed on the television.

Alice stayed silent. She couldn't think of the right thing to say. Maybe just being there would be enough.

An old episode of *M*A*S*H* was on the television. The familiar characters and the sudden bursts of canned laughter took Alice straight back to 1975. She and Elisabeth sitting on that old beige couch after school, waiting for their mother to come home from work, eating ham-and-tomato-sauce sandwiches on white bread.

Alice's mind drifted. She thought about this strange little period of time in her life that began when she woke up in the gym last Friday morning. It was like this past week had been a holiday in an exotic destination that required the learning of unusual new skills. So many things had happened. Meeting the children. Seeing Mum and Roger together. The Family Talent Night.

Finally, she felt Elisabeth stir next to her. Alice held her breath.

Elisabeth said irritably, "Don't you have things to do?"

"Nothing more important than this."

Elisabeth grimaced and pulled at the blanket so it came away from Alice's legs. Alice pulled it back over her.

M*A*S*H finished and Elisabeth changed the channel. Audrey Hepburn's delicate features filled the screen. Elisabeth switched it again to a cooking show.

Alice felt like coffee. She wondered if it would break the moment, whatever this moment was, if she went into the kitchen and made herself a cup to bring back to bed. Oh, for a Dino's large double-shot skim latte.

Dino.

She dived for her handbag, which she'd left on the floor next to the bed and rummaged through it. She pulled out the fertility doll and carefully placed it on the sheets between herself and Elisabeth. It looked back at them with inscrutable boggle-eyes. Alice angled it so it was facing Elisabeth.

More time passed and Elisabeth said, "Okay, what is that thing?"

"It's a fertility doll," said Alice. "Dino from the coffee shop gave it to me to give to you."

Elisabeth picked it up and examined it. "I guess he's trying to insure against me kidnapping more of his customers' children."

"Probably," agreed Alice.

"What am I meant to do with it?"

"I don't know," said Alice. "You could bring it sacrificial offerings?" Elisabeth rolled her eyes. There was a glimmer of a smile.

Elisabeth put the doll on the bedside table next to her.

"It would be due in January," she said. "If it . . ."

"Well, that seems like a good time to have a baby," said Alice. "It wouldn't be too cold when you got up in the night to feed."

"There won't be any *baby*," said Elisabeth viciously.

"We could ask Dad to put in a good word for you," said Alice. "He must be able to pull some strings up there."

"Do you think I didn't ask Dad with the other pregnancies?" said Elisabeth. "I prayed to the lot of them. Jesus. Mary. Saint Gerard. He's meant to be the patron saint of fertility. None of them listened. They're ignoring me."

"Dad wouldn't be ignoring you," said Alice, and her father's face was suddenly clear in her mind. So often she could only remember the face that appeared in photos, not the face from her own memory. "Maybe he's got to deal with a lot of bureaucrats in Heaven."

"I don't think I believe in life after death anyway," said Elisabeth. "I used to have all these romantic ideas about Dad taking care of my lost babies, but then it got out of hand. He'd be running a whole bloody day care center."

"At least it would take his mind off the sight of Mum and Roger salsa-dancing," said Alice.

This time Elisabeth definitely smiled.

She said, "Mum remembers all my due dates. She calls first thing in the morning and chats, doesn't say anything about the date, just chats away."

"She seems good with the children," said Alice. "They adore her."

"She's a good grandma," sighed Elisabeth.

"I guess we've forgiven her," said Alice.

Elisabeth turned to look at her sharply, but she didn't say "Forgiven her for what?"

It was something they'd never really talked about (well, as far as Alice knew they'd never talked about it); the way Barb had stopped being a mother after their dad died. She'd just given up. It had been shocking. Overnight, she became a mother who couldn't care less if they left the house without warm clothes, or if they cleaned their teeth, or if they ate vegetables—and did that mean she'd only been *pretending* to care before? Even months afterward, she just wanted to drift around all day, holding their hands while she cried over photo albums. That's when Frannie had stepped in and given their lives structure and rules again.

Alice and Elisabeth had stopped thinking of Barb as their mother and more as a slightly simple older sister. Even when she eventually recovered and started trying to exert her authority, they didn't really let her be the mother again. It was a subtle but definite form of revenge.

"Yes," said Elisabeth after a while. "I guess we did eventually forgive her. I don't know when exactly, but we did."

"It's strange how things work out."

"Yes."

They watched an ad for a carpet sale, and Elisabeth spoke again. "I feel really angry. I can't tell you how angry I feel."

"Okay," said Alice.

More silence.

"We've wasted the last seven years trying to create a life for ourselves, just a standard suburban life with two-point-one kids. That's all we've been doing—we haven't been actually *living*—and now this will put everything on hold for a few months longer until I lose it, and then I'll have to get over that, and then Ben will be at me to fill in the adoption papers, and everybody will be all enthusiastic and supportive. 'Oh, yes, adoption, how lovely, how *multicultural!*' And they'll expect me to forget this baby."

"You might not lose it," said Alice. "You might actually have this baby."

"Of course I'm going to lose it."

The cooking show host drizzled honey into a pan. "You must use nonsalt butter. That's the secret."

Elisabeth said, "All I need to do is pretend I'm not pregnant, so that if I lose it, it won't hurt so much, but I can't seem to do that. And then I think, Okay, just be hopeful! Assume it will work. But then every moment I'm scared. Every time I go to the bathroom I'm scared of seeing the blood. Every time I go for an ultrasound I'm scared of seeing their faces change. You're not meant to worry, because stress is bad for the baby, but how can I not worry?"

"Maybe you could delegate the worrying to me," said Alice. "I could worry all day long for you! I'm an excellent worrier, you know that."

Elisabeth smiled and looked back at the television. The cooking show host pulled something out of the oven and sniffed rapturously. "Voilà!"

Elisabeth said, "I should have driven over straightaway when Gina died, and I didn't. I'm sorry."

How strange, thought Alice. Everyone had to apologize for something to do with Gina's death.

"Why didn't you?"

"I didn't know if you'd want me there," said Elisabeth. "I felt as if I'd say the wrong thing. You and Gina were such a pair, and you and I, we've . . . drifted."

Alice moved closer to Elisabeth, so their thighs were touching. "Well, let's drift back."

The credits were rolling on the cooking show.

"I'm going to lose this baby," said Elisabeth.

Alice put a hand over onto Elisabeth's stomach.

"I'm going to lose this baby," said Elisabeth again.

Alice put her face down close. She said, "Come on, little niece or nephew. Why don't you just stick around this time? Your mum has been through so much for you."

Elisabeth picked up the remote, turned off the television, and began to cry.

Frannie's Letter to Phil

> *He kissed me. Mr. Mustache, I mean. Xavier. In the backseat of a cab.*
> *And I kissed him back.*
> *You could knock me down with a feather, Phil.*

"I like the lions," said Dominick.

It was nine o'clock at night and he was standing at the front door, holding a packet of chocolate biscuits, a bottle of liqueur, and a bunch of tulips. He was wearing jeans and a faded checked shirt, and he needed a shave.

Alice looked at George and Mildred, back in their old places, guarding the house. It had been an exhausting effort, cleaning them up, and then she'd had to use a wheelbarrow to get them out to the front of the house. Now she couldn't decide if they looked quirky and fun, or grubby and tacky. "I just thought I'd drop by on the off chance you felt like some company," he said. "If you're too busy planning for tomorrow . . ."

Alice hadn't been doing anything, except lying on the couch, staring at the ceiling, and thinking vague thoughts about Elisabeth's baby, and Nick: "trying again." Nick seemed to think they should start out with a "date." "Maybe a movie," he'd said, and Alice had wondered how hard they would have to "try" as they sat in the movie. Would they have to eat their popcorn really enthusiastically? Have an especially animated conversation afterward? Score each other on how many times they'd been funny, their levels of affection? Would they have to *try* to kiss as romantically as possible? No, she didn't want any of this "trying." She just wanted Nick to move back home and for everything to be the way it should be. She was tired of all this nonsense.

It had been an exhausting day. All the children had sports, one after the other. Olivia played netball (lots of histrionic leaping about but not much actual contact with the ball), Tom played soccer (excellently—scored two goals!), and Madison played hockey (abysmally, miserably). "Do you enjoy it?" Alice had asked her as she came off the field. "You know I hate it," Madison had answered. "So why do you play it?" "Because *you* say I have to play a team sport," she'd answered. Alice had gone straight up to the coach and pulled Madison from the team. Both the coach and Madison were thrilled.

Alice had various duties at each game that she had somehow fulfilled smoothly, almost as if she wasn't an impostor in her own life. She'd kept score at Madison's hockey game. She'd helped cook the sausage sizzle at Tom's soccer game. Incredibly, she'd even *umpired* Olivia's netball. Someone had handed her a whistle, and even as Alice was saying, "No, no, I couldn't possibly," the cool shape of the whistle felt right in her hand. Next thing she was striding up and down the sideline, blowing sharply on the whistle, while strange words and phrases flew from her mouth. "Step!" "Held ball!" "Goal attack, you were off side." The children obeyed without question.

Nick had been there at all the games. There had been no time to talk. He had duties, too. He had to be the referee for Tom's soccer game. We're such *parents*, Alice had thought with a mixture of pride and fear—because, was that the problem? Was that why they would have to "try"? Because she was a "mum" and he was a "dad," and mums and dads were generic, boring, and not very sexy. (That's why kissing still went on in laundries at parties? To remind them that they were once randy teenagers?)

Tomorrow was Mother's Day. Mega Meringue Day. The "big day." Probably Alice should have been preparing things—finishing off paperwork, making last-minute phone calls to check people had done what they were meant to do, but she wasn't especially interested in Mega Meringue Day. Anyway, the committee had seemed to have things under control the other day.

"Come in," she said to Dominick, her eyes on the chocolate biscuits.

"The children asleep?" he asked.

"Yes, although—" She was about to say something lighthearted about Tom probably still playing with his Nintendo under the covers, but the hair-cutting experience with Madison made her stop. It would be like ratting on her son to the school principal.

"How was Kate about Chloe's hair?" she asked.

"Predictably hysterical," said Dominick.

"I left a message apologizing," said Alice. "She never called back."

"You understand that I didn't have any choice but to suspend Madison?" said Dominick, as Alice took the flowers out of his hands. "I didn't want . . ."

"Oh, yes, of course, don't worry about it. These are beautiful, by the way. Thank you."

Dominick put down the biscuits on the counter and twisted the bottle of liqueur around and around in his hands.

He said, "I'll know when you get your memory back."

"How?" said Alice.

"By the way you look at me. Now you have this friendly, polite way of looking at me, as if you don't really know me, as if we never even . . ."

Oh God, little Chloe Harper was right. They had "done sex."

He put down the bottle of liqueur and moved closer to her.

No, no, no. Not another kiss. That would be wrong. That would not be within the spirit of "trying."

"Dominick," she said.

The doorbell rang.

"Excuse me," said Alice.

It was Nick at the front door.

He was holding a bottle of wine, cheese, biscuits, and a bunch of tulips identical to the ones Dominick had brought over. They must be on special at some local shop.

"You've fixed the lions," said Nick, delighted. He bent down and patted George on the head. "Gidday, old mate."

"I should be going." Dominick had come to the front door. Alice saw his gaze take in the flowers and wine.

"Oh, hi." Nick straightened, his smile disappearing. "I didn't realize, I won't stop—"

"No, no. I was just going," said Dominick firmly. "I'll see you tomorrow." He touched Alice on the arm and ran lightly down the steps.

"Was I interrupting something?" Nick followed her down the hallway and saw Dominick's bunch of tulips. "Oh. Everyone is bringing offerings tonight."

Alice yawned. She longed for her life to be normal again. A Saturday night at home. She wanted to say, "I'm tired. I think I'll go to bed," and for Nick to say, without turning his head from the television, "Okay, I'll just finish watching this movie and I'll be up." And then she wanted them to read their books together and switch off the lamps and fall asleep. Who have thought that a Saturday night at home would ever seem so impossibly exotic?

Instead, she opened Dominick's chocolate biscuits and ate one and watched Nick standing awkwardly in his own kitchen.

"Shall I open this?" he said.

"Sure."

He opened the wine and poured them both glasses. Alice put the cheese on a plate and they sat down on opposite sides of the long table.

"Are you coming tomorrow?" asked Alice, eating another chocolate biscuit. "To Mega Meringue Day?"

"Oh, no, I wasn't. Do you want me to go?"

"Of course!"

Nick laughed, in that slightly flabbergasted way. "All right, then."

"I think it will all be over by lunchtime," said Alice. "So you'll be able to make it to your mother's place."

Nick looked blankly at her.

"For the Mother's Day lunch," said Alice. "Remember? You told Ella you were going at the Family Talent Night."

"Oh. Yeah. Right."

"How do you cope without me?" said Alice lightly.

Nick's face closed up. "I cope fine. I'm not totally useless."

Alice flinched at his tone. "I never said you were." She took a piece of cheese. "Or have I said that?"

"You don't believe I'm capable of looking after the children for half the time. According to you, I wouldn't remember all their after-school activities, sign their permission notes, or whatever. I'd forget to read the all-important school newsletter. Not sure how I manage to run a company."

Well, you have a secretary to handle all the pesky details.

She wasn't sure which Alice said that: Snippy Alice from the future or real Alice. Nick had always been a big-picture man.

He refilled their wineglasses. "I can't stand only seeing them on weekends. I can't be natural with them. Sometimes I hear my father's voice come out of my mouth when I see them. Fake jolly. I'm driving over to pick them up and I find myself preparing jokes for them. And I think—how did I end up here?"

"Did you spend a lot of time with them during the week?"

"Yeah, I know the point you're trying to make. Yes, I work long hours, but you never seem to remember the times I *did* come home early. I went bike riding with Madison that time, and Friday nights in summer I played cricket for hours with Tom—well, you always say it was just one Friday night, but I know it happened at least twice, and I—"

"I wasn't trying to make a point."

Nick twirled the stem of his wineglass and looked up at Alice with an "I'm going to come clean" expression. "I haven't been very good at achieving a life-work balance. I need to work on that. If we work things out, I'll get better at that. I'm committed to that."

"Okay," said Alice. She wanted to make fun of him for saying "I'm committed to that," but Nick was acting as though it was some sort of breakthrough moment. It just didn't seem that big a deal to her. So he had to work long hours sometimes. If that's what he had to do for his career, then fair enough.

"I guess my competition doesn't work such long hours," said Nick.

"Competition?" The wine was going to Alice's head. Her mind was filled with hazy half-thoughts, glimpses of people's faces she didn't know, and vague memories of intense feelings she couldn't describe.

"Dominick."

"Oh, him. He's nice, but the thing is, I'm married to you."

"We're separated."

"Yes, but we're *trying*." Alice giggled. "Sorry. I don't know why I find it funny. It's not funny. It's not at all funny. I might actually need a glass of water."

She stood up, and as she walked by Nick, she suddenly plonked herself down on his lap like a flirty girl at a party.

"Are you going to *try*, Nick?" she gurgled into his neck. "Are you going to try really, really hard?"

"You're tipsy," he said, and then he kissed her, and at last everything was as it should be. Her body melted against his with exquisite relief. It was like sinking into a hot bath after being caught in the rain, like sliding under crisp cotton sheets after an exhausting day.

"Daddy?" said a voice from behind them. "What are you doing here?"

Nick's legs jerked up so that Alice was catapulted onto her feet.

Olivia stood in the kitchen in her pajamas, rubbing her eyes with her knuckles, her cheeks flushed with sleep. She yawned hugely, stretching her arms above her head. She frowned, perplexed, and then an expression of pure delight crossed her face.

"Do you love Mummy again?"

Frannie's Letter to Phil

Kissing! At my age! Is it allowed? Is it unseemly? I feel as though I've broken a rule. I've gone full circle and I'm fourteen again.

We had a lovely night at the Chinese restaurant. It's been so long since I've eaten Chinese. (I used to take Elisabeth and Alice when they were little for a special treat. They adored it. Of course now they would be horrified at the thought. Too many calories. Or "carbs" or something.)

We shared a nice bottle of white wine and the steamed dim sums were fabulous. Mr. M. was his ridiculous self. After we paid the bill, he asked the waitress if we could go to the kitchen and "pay our compliments to the chef"!

The little girl looked alarmed. (She probably thought we were undercover health inspectors.) I was saying to her, "Just ignore him, darling," but next thing, Mr. M. marched out to the kitchen and dragged out three young Chinese men dressed in white. There he was, clapping them on the shoulders, loudly telling them a long story about a meal he'd eaten at a fancy hotel in Hong Kong in 1954, and how this was even better than that meal, while all the other diners put down their chopsticks and stared.

I got such an attack of the giggles watching those poor young chefs with their polite, bemused smiles, nervously bobbing their heads up and down, obviously thinking this man was quite deranged. In the end,

Mr. M. convinced the whole restaurant to give them a round of applause. (The food wasn't that good!)

I giggled in the cab the whole way home until finally Mr. M. said, "I think there's only one way to shut you up," and next thing he was kissing me.

I'm very sorry, Phil.

Do you mind?

Well, bad luck if you do. It's your fault anyway! Why did you need a camping trip "with the fellows" just before our wedding? You were forty years old! You shouldn't have had any wild oats left to sow. And then you happily, idiotically, dive headfirst into a river without checking the depth first. You silly fool.

Tonight a handsome man (I may not have referred to his handsomeness previously) kissed me and it was heavenly.

Do you hear that, Phil? HEAVENLY.

Am going to bed, my dear. May have drunk a little too much sauvignon blanc at dinner.

Chapter 30

It was the "big day." Alice felt like a small piece of clothing, a sock perhaps, in a large load of washing, on the spin cycle. People pulled her this way and that. At one point she literally had a person on each arm (neither of whom she recognized), trying to pull her in different directions. Worried faces, excited faces, smiley "ooh, this is it!" faces floated by and vanished. People gathered around her in worried clumps, firing questions, telling her about problems, about things that should have been delivered by now. "Where are the eggs meant to go?" "Where are the pastry ladies meant to be standing?" "The news crew wants to confirm they'll be here by twelve. They want to interview you at twelve-thirty. Is that still okay? Are we on schedule?"

News crew? Interviewing her?

Cameras flashed like strobe lights. She should have listened more at the Mega Meringue meeting. She hadn't fully grasped the immense scale of this production. It was . . . mega.

They were in a giant colorful marquee that had been erected on the school oval with a banner proclaiming: "Mega Meringue Day: Watch 100

Mums Bake the World's Biggest Lemon Meringue Pie! $10 Entry. (Children Free.) All Proceeds to Breast Cancer Research."

Inside, the marquee had been set up auditorium style, with raised benches around the sides where people could sit and watch. All around the sides of the tent were placards with the names of companies that were "proud to sponsor Mega Meringue Day." Alice saw one for Dino's Coffee Shop. In the middle was all the equipment for making the pie. It looked like a construction site. There was huge industrial equipment: a forklift, a concrete mixer, a *crane*, and a specially created pie dish and oven where the pie would be baked. A large round conference table had been set up with mixing bowls placed at intervals. Next to each mixing bowl was a neat selection of ingredients: eggs, flour, butter, lemons, and sugar. Maggie's husband, the red-faced man on the treadmill, who appeared to run some sort of manufacturing company, was in charge of the equipment and was ordering around bemused workmen.

"Now, let me get this straight, we bake the pastry *without* the filling first, is that right?" he said to Alice.

Well, at least she knew the answer to that question. "Yes," she said, and then more firmly: "Yes. That's right."

"Righto, boss," he said, and hurried off.

People were filing into the tent, handing over their cash to two women from the Mega Meringue Committee sitting at the entryway. The benches were filling up fast. A group of children with brass instruments struck up a tune.

A corner of the tent had been devoted to activities for the children. All the activities had a "mega" theme. They could blow giant soap bubbles, toss around a giant foam ball, and paint on a massive canvas with oversized paintbrushes. Alice had left Madison, Tom, and Olivia to enjoy themselves.

"All coming together?" said someone.

It was Dominick. Jasper was with him, swinging on his father's hand. Alice looked up, met Dominick's eyes, and looked away guiltily. She felt like she'd cheated on him, which . . . well, maybe she had.

"I'm sorry about last night," she said.

"Don't even think about that today," he answered. "Oh—but, ah, I wondered if you'd remember about tonight? *Phantom of the Opera?*"

Nick had taken Olivia back up to bed the night before and then left. They had agreed that their first "date" would be the following night. They were going back to their old favorite Italian restaurant. Nick had sent a text message saying he'd got the reservations.

"Um, well, I had actually forgotten," began Alice. She really needed to break up with this kind, but essentially irrelevant, man. "The thing is, Dominick—"

"Alice, my *dear!*" It was Kate Harper, looking especially glossy in the morning sunlight streaming through the tent. An unhappy-faced man trailed behind her, along with a sullen Chloe. Chloe's shorn hair had been cut into a stylish bob, but, it had to be said, she wasn't nearly as pretty without her flowing locks.

"That's all right, we'll talk later," said Dominick. "Let me know if you need me for anything. I'm right here for you."

"I'm right here for you too, Alice!" piped up Jasper.

"I was surprised to see Madison here," said Kate, her voice steely. "I thought you might have kept her at home, in light of . . . the incident."

"Yes, well . . ." began Alice. It really would have been more comfortable if she'd been in the right in this situation, instead of the indisputable, shameful wrong.

"Madison is being very severely punished," she said. Well, she would be, eventually, once Alice got around to thinking of something appropriate. She glanced over and saw Madison looking entranced as she had a turn blowing the giant soap bubbles. It was just that Madison was in such a lovely mood these days. It seemed a pity to spoil it.

"I hope so," said Kate. She lowered her voice. "Because Chloe is *traumatized.* She's not eating or sleeping properly. This will be something that will mark her for life."

"Kate, give the poor woman a break," said Kate's husband. "She's got her hands full at the moment."

Kate's nostrils flared, as if it had been Alice asking for the break for herself. "I realize you're busy, but I'm not sure you fully appreciate the seriousness of this. Your phone message sounded almost flippant. What Madison did was outrageous."

"Sorry! I'm afraid we need to steal Alice away from you."

It was Maggie and Nora, her friends from the Mega Meringue Committee, scooping up Alice by the elbows and smoothly dragging her away.

"You're not one of our Mega Meringue Mums, are you, Kate?" said Nora. "You might want to take a seat."

As Alice looked back over her shoulder, she saw Kate talking furiously into her husband's ear, her hand like a claw on his arm.

"I don't know what I'm meant to be doing," she admitted to Nora and Maggie. "I'm just nodding when people ask me questions." This wasn't like the netball umpiring, when her mind had somehow switched to autopilot.

"It's all right," said Maggie. "Everything is running like clockwork thanks to you."

She waved a sheet of paper in Alice's face with a running sheet for the day and notations in her own handwriting that she didn't remember writing. She could see she'd written, "STICK TO SCHEDULE!!" in full capitals and underlined it twice.

A disgusted expression crossed Maggie's face. "Oh dear, your *ex* is here. What's he doing here? Trying to look like an involved father, I suppose."

Ex. At the word "ex" Alice immediately visualized her most recent exboyfriend before Nick. Peter Bourke. The patronizing one who broke her heart. But when she turned around, it was Nick coming through the marquee entrance, looking gorgeous in a blue shirt. She'd told him once he should always wear blue.

"I invited him," she said to Maggie.

Maggie studied her. "Oh. Well, all right."

"By the way, we're assuming one of us should take over as MC?" said Nora. "We could say you haven't been well. Of course, our resident troll, Mrs. H., would love to get her hands on the microphone and take credit for the whole event if we don't stop her."

"Microphone?" said Alice, confused.

Nora gestured toward a microphone on a stand in the center of the marquee.

Good lord. The idea had been for *Alice* to get up in front of all those people.

"Oh, no, absolutely not, I mean absolutely *yes*, one of you can do it," she said.

"No problem," said Nora. Her face became neutral as Nick reached them. "Hi, Nick."

"Hi, Nora, Maggie. How are you both?" Nick nodded uncomfortably at the two women. It made Alice feel protective of him to see poor Nick in the unpopular ex-husband role. Just like she'd been the "cow" of an ex-wife with his sister at the Family Talent Night.

"Happy Mother's Day," said Nick, as Nora and Maggie disappeared into the crowd. "Did you get breakfast in bed?"

Alice nodded. "Pancakes. I think they started cooking them at five a.m. There were bangs and crashes and yells. You should see the kitchen now. But I have to say, the pancakes were outstanding. I think Madison is going to be a chef one day. A really messy, bossy, noisy one."

"Sorry I wasn't there to supervise," said Nick. "Your first Mother's Day without me."

"Hopefully my last," said Alice.

"Definitely," said Nick. His eyes held hers. "I think definitely."

"Well, well, well, what have we here, Barb? Methinks it's our fine young salsa students!" Nick's father and Alice's mother were upon them. Roger clapped them on the shoulders car-salesman style, the familiar scent of his aftershave drifting across their faces like a filmy scarf, while Barb stood to the side, shiny with pride, as if Roger were once again performing a rather tricky feat.

"How are you, darling?" said Barb to Alice. "You look lovely, of course, but you're so pale. And shadows under your eyes. There must be something going around at the moment, because Elisabeth is pea *green*."

"Is Libby here?" said Alice with surprise.

"She's there with Frannie," said Barb, pointing up to one of the bench seats, where Elisabeth was sitting with Ben. She did look quite ill. Nausea. That must be a good sign. At least she wasn't watching television.

Sitting next to Ben was Frannie, and next to her the white-haired man from the Family Talent Night who had organized the wheelchair races. Frannie was sitting very upright, glancing around self-consciously, but as Alice looked at her, the man said something in her ear and she clapped her hands together and burst out laughing.

"That's Frannie's *gentleman friend*," said Barb. "Xavier. Isn't it lovely! After all these years of holding a candle for her silly dead fiancé!"

"Her what?" said Alice. She pressed a fingertip to her forehead. She didn't think her head could handle any fresh new surprises today.

"Her fiancé died just two weeks before their wedding. It wasn't all that long before your father died," said Barb calmly, as if this weren't a huge revelation. "He went away with some mates on a camping trip and he broke his neck diving into a river. That's why I was always telling you girls to never, ever dive *anywhere* without checking the depth."

"Are you saying you knew about this all these years?" said Alice. She looked up at Frannie smiling at Xavier and tried to incorporate this sad new information about her grandmother. "And *you* kept it a secret?"

"No need to look so surprised," said Barb crisply. "I can keep secrets. Frannie didn't like to talk about it. She's so private! She admitted to me once that she had kept on writing to him all these years, as if he was still away on holiday. She said she felt silly about it, because she knew perfectly well that he'd died, but that it was nice to keep writing to him. She'd seal the letters up and put them in a drawer. She told me she'd address them but she didn't go so far as to waste her money putting stamps on them. So we agreed that proved she wasn't completely deluded! It was just a funny little quirk of hers."

"And you never said a word," marveled Alice. The fact that her mother had kept a secret was more surprising than the secret itself.

"Although she has let the cat out of the bag now," chortled Roger.

"Only because Frannie told me she intended to tell the girls now!" retorted Barb. "Apparently she started to tell you and Elisabeth the whole story just a few weeks ago, but then you had to go pick up the children."

"I don't remember," said Alice. Her catchcry.

"Anyway, she's finally found love again!" Barb sighed and shook her head regretfully. "If only it hadn't taken so *long*!"

"She's probably just fussy," said Roger. "Needed to find the right fellow. Like you."

"Oh, you!" said Barb flirtatiously, and she gleamed with happiness. "I was lucky to find you!"

"Dad was lucky to find you," said Nick, suddenly serious. Alice's mother looked up at him with surprise, her cheeks pink with pleasure. "Well, that's a lovely thing to say, Nick."

Maggie appeared again wearing a long apron that said *Mega Meringue Day* on the front, with a picture of a huge lemon meringue pie. Underneath it said, *Mother's Day, Sydney, 2008*. She was holding another one for Alice.

"The aprons turned out beautifully, Alice!" she said as she slid the apron over Alice's neck and tied it at her waist.

Alice looked around and saw rows of pink-aproned women lining up around the big table with the mixing bowls.

"It looks like we're about ready to start," said Maggie. "Is that okay with you?"

"Sure thing," said Alice recklessly.

"You're over here," said Maggie. "Next to me."

"Good luck, darling," said Barb. "I do hope they're careful with that oven.

It's very easy to burn the meringue on a lemon meringue pie. I remember once I was making one when your father's boss was coming for dinner. I was terribly upset, I remember looking in the oven and thinking—"

"Come on, Barbie," said Roger, pulling on her arm. "You can tell me the rest of the story while we're sitting down."

He winked at Alice as he guided her still-chattering mother into the audience, and Alice was filled with affection for him. He loved Barb—in his own self satisfied way, he loved her.

"I'll get the kids to come and sit down," said Nick, and he headed off to the children's area.

Alice went to stand beside Maggie behind the tables.

"What an event," said the woman standing next to Alice. She had a birthmark like a burn across the bottom half of her face. "You're a bloody marvel, Alice."

I'm a bloody marvel, thought Alice. Her head was feeling fuzzy.

Nora stood at the microphone. "Can everybody take their seats, please? The baking is about to commence!"

Alice found Nick in the audience. He had Olivia on his lap. The fairy wings she'd insisted on wearing that day were brushing against his face. Tom was on Nick's left, taking photos with a digital camera, and Madison was on his right, seemingly intensely interested in the proceedings. Nick said something and pointed at Alice, and all three children beamed and waved in her direction.

Alice waved back, and as she did, Dominick and Jasper caught her eye. They were sitting just two rows behind Nick and the children, and waving enthusiastically, as if they'd thought Alice had been waving at them.

Oh dear. Now she could see Libby and Ben waving at her, along with Frannie, Xavier, Barb, and Roger.

Alice tried to make her smile and wave seem all encompassing and personal to each of them.

Nora was speaking again.

"I'm stepping in on behalf of Alice Love to be your host today. As many of you know, Alice had an accident at the gym last week and still isn't feeling a hundred percent. You know, I can still remember the day Alice said to me that she wanted to get one hundred mums together to bake the world's largest lemon meringue pie. I thought she was nuts!"

The audience chuckled.

"But you all know Alice. She's like a bull terrier when she gets an idea in her head." There was appreciative laughter. *A bull terrier?* How had she changed so much in just ten years? She was more like a Labrador. Anxious to please and overexcited.

"But just a few months later, no surprise, here we are! Let's put our hands together for *Alice!*"

There was a burst of enthusiastic applause. Alice nodded and smiled fraudulently.

"We're dedicating this day to a very dear friend and member of the school community who we tragically lost last year," said Nora. "We're using her lemon meringue pie recipe and we're sure she's with us in spirit today. I'm referring, of course, to Gina Boyle. We miss you, Gina. A minute's silence, please, for Gina."

Alice watched as people reverently bowed their heads and remembered the woman who had apparently been such a significant part of Alice's life. Her own mind was blank. This morning's pancakes sat uncomfortably in her stomach. After what seemed much longer than a minute, Nora lifted her head.

"Ladies," she said. "Pick up your whisks."

Chapter 31

The women picked up their whisks solemnly as if they were musicians in an orchestra.

"Whisk the eggs, cream, sugar, lemon rind, and juice until combined," read out Nora.

There was a pause and then everyone put their whisks back down and began to select ingredients.

Alice cracked her eggs one after the other into her bowl. All around her, women were doing the same thing. There were nervous giggles and whispers.

"Don't get any eggshell in there!" called out someone from the audience, to much hilarity.

After a few minutes, the sound of brisk whisking filled the marquee.

Under Nora's instructions, once they were all finished, they stood in line to pour their mixture into a huge yellow industrial vat.

This is going to be an absolute disaster, thought Alice.

"Place the flour, almond meal, icing sugar, and butter into a food processor and process until it resembles fine bread crumbs," read out Nora. "Instead of using a food processor, we're going to use a concrete mixer. Don't worry, it's clean! So could each mum please place her combined ingredients into the mixer."

"I can't believe we're doing this," whispered Alice to Maggie, as the mothers lined up with their bowls of ingredients. "It's madness."

Maggie laughed. "It's all your doing, Alice!"

One of the bemused workmen operated the concrete mixer while the mothers separated yolks from whites.

"Add the egg yolk and process," ordered Nora.

Once again the woman lined up to add their egg yolks. A few minutes later a massive glob of yellow dough was upended from the concrete mixer and onto the floury surface of the center table.

"Knead until smooth."

The women gathered around the table, kneading and pulling at the dough. *This pastry is going to be inedible,* thought Alice, watching inexpert hands pushing and pulling. Cameras flashed.

"Now we really should be putting the pastry into the fridge for half an hour, but today is all about quantity, rather than quality," said Nora. "So we're going to go straight to rolling out the pastry."

The workmen carried over the giant rolling pin.

Alice stood back and watched as three women stood on each side of the rolling pin, took a firm grip of the handles, and began to push forward, as if they were pushing along a broken-down car.

There was giggling and shrieking and yelled suggestions from the audience as the women went off in different directions, but, incredibly, after a few minutes, the dough began to flatten. It was working. It was actually working. A huge sheet of pastry, the size of a king-size bed, was emerging.

"Now, the hard bit," said Nora. "Line the pie dish."

We'll never do it, thought Alice, as the women gathered around the sheet of pastry and lifted it into the air, with their palms flat, as though they were carrying some sort of precious canvas. Every woman had the exact same expression of terrified concentration on her face.

"Shit, shit, shit, shit," said the woman with the birthmark, as the pastry began to sag in the middle. Another woman rushed to try and save it. They were treading on each other's toes, calling out sharp orders like "Be careful there!" and "Watch that part there!"

No one smiled or laughed until the delicate sheet of pastry was safely placed in the massive pie dish. They'd done it. No serious tears or cracks. It was a miracle.

"Hooray!" cried the crowd, and the women shared ecstatic grins as they used their thumbs to push the pastry against the sides of the dish. Next they covered it with sheet after sheet of baking paper and weighted it down with rice, and the workmen lifted the dish and placed it into the oven.

"We'll bake that for ten minutes," said Nora smoothly, as if it weren't at all surprising that they had got this far, "And in the meantime our clever mums will make the meringue."

The ladies went back to their tables and began to whisk egg whites, gradually adding the sugar as they did so.

The tent filled with heat from the giant oven. Alice could feel her face flushing and beads of perspiration forming at her hairline. The fragrance of cooking pastry filled the air. Her head ached. She wondered if she was coming down with the flu.

The smell of the pastry was making her want to remember something. Except it was somehow too large to remember. It was like the huge sheet of pastry. Too big for one person. She couldn't find an edge to grasp so she could pull it in front of her. But there was definitely something there.

"Are you okay?" Maggie's face loomed in front of Alice.

"Fine. I'm fine."

The pastry shell was pulled from the oven to a round of applause. It was golden brown. The baking paper and rice were removed and the vat of lemon-colored filling was poured into the pastry. Next came the meringue. The women seemed tipsy with relief. They danced around the pie like schoolgirls, pouring their frothy white meringue mixtures over the filling and using wooden spoons to create snowy peaks.

More cameras flashed.

"Alice?" said Nora into the microphone. "Do we have your approval?"

Alice felt like the world had been wrapped in some sort of gauzy material. Her vision was slightly blurred, her mouth felt full of cotton wool. It was as though she'd just woken up and was trying to clear her head of the previous night's dreams. She blinked and considered the pie. "Can someone just smooth the meringue over in that corner?" she said, and was surprised that her voice came out sounding quite normal. A woman rushed to obey her.

Alice nodded at Nora.

"And now, ladies and gentlemen, we *bake*," said Nora.

Maggie's husband gave the thumbs-up signal to the forklift driver. Everyone's eyes were fixed on the magnificent pie as it was lifted by the forklift and slid into the oven. There was a round of applause.

"Year 4 has kindly offered to keep us entertained while the lemon meringue pie is baking," said Nora. "As many of you will remember, our dear friend Gina loved Elvis. Whenever she was cooking, she always had Elvis playing. You couldn't get her to play anything else. So Year 4 is going to perform a medley of Elvis hits for us. Gina, honey, this is for you."

There was a burst of laughter and cheers as thirty miniature Elvises swaggered into the center of the marquee. They were wearing dark glasses and white satin jumpsuits complete with sparkly rhinestones. A teacher pressed a button on a stereo and the children began to dance, Elvis style, to "Hound Dog."

There was nowhere for the Mega Meringue mums to sit, so they all leaned back against the long tables. Some of them took off their pink aprons. Alice's legs ached. Actually, everything ached.

Oh, this song is so . . . familiar.

Yes, that's because it's Elvis. Elvis is familiar to everyone.

The song switched to "Love Me Tender."

The sweet lemony smell of the baking pie was overpowering. It was impossible to think of anything else but lemon . . . meringue . . . pie . . .

That smell is so . . . familiar.

Yes, that's because it's a lemon meringue pie. You know what a lemon meringue pie smells like.

But there was something more than that. It meant something.

Alice's face had been feeling flushed and hot. Now she felt cold, as if she'd stepped into an icy wind.

Oh, dear, she wasn't well. She really wasn't well.

She looked desperately into the audience for someone to help.

She saw Nick suddenly lift Olivia off his lap and stand up.

She saw Dominick bounce to his feet, frowning with concern.

Both men were making their way past people's knees, trying to get to her.

Now the song was "Jailhouse Rock."

The scent of lemon meringue was becoming stronger and stronger. It was going straight up her nostrils and trickling into her brain, filling it with memory.

Oh, God, of course, of course, of course.

Alice's legs buckled.

Elisabeth's Homework for Jeremy

I missed seeing Alice collapse because I'd gone outside to the toilet.

They had a row of those blue plastic Port-a-loos.

I was bleeding.

I thought, How fitting. That I should be losing my last baby in a Port-a-loo.

Trashy and slightly laughable. Like my life.

Chapter 32

"*Hi!*"

The woman who opened the door was smiling delightedly, wiping her hands on a floury apron, as if Alice were a very dear friend.

Alice hadn't wanted to come. She hadn't been at all thrilled when this "Gina" had moved into the house across the road and turned up the very next day, knocking on their door to invite Alice for "high tea." For one thing, shouldn't Alice have been the one doing the asking—seeing as she was the one already living there? That made her feel guilty, as if this woman already had some sort of etiquette point over her. And she could tell just by looking at Gina that she wasn't her sort of person. Too loud. Too many teeth. Too much makeup for the middle of the day. Too much perfume. Too much everything. She was one of those women who drained Alice of her personality. And "high tea"? What was wrong with just ordinary old afternoon tea?

This was going to be awful.

"HELLO there, sweetie!" Gina bent down to say hello to Madison.

Madison clung to Alice's leg in an agony of shyness, burying her face in

Alice's crotch. Alice hated it when she did that. She always worried people might think the kid had inherited her poor social skills from her mother.

"I'm terrible with children," said Gina. "Terrible. That's probably why I'm having so much trouble getting pregnant."

Alice followed Gina through the house, trying to dislodge Madison, who was still clinging to her leg. There were boxes everywhere waiting to be unpacked.

"I should have invited you to my place," said Alice.

"It's okay, I'm the one desperate to make friends," said Gina. "I'm going to try and seduce you with my lemon meringue pie." She turned around quickly and then walked into a box. "Not literally seduce you."

"Oh, that's a pity," said Alice. And then she said quickly, idiotically, "That was a joke."

Gina laughed and led her into the kitchen. It was warm and filled with the sweet smell of lemon meringue pie. Elvis was playing on the stereo.

"I thought I'd say 'high tea' instead of 'afternoon tea,'" said Gina, "so we could have champagne. Would you like champagne?"

"Oh, sure," said Alice, although she normally wouldn't drink in the day.

Gina danced a jig on the spot. "Thank God! If you'd said no, I wouldn't have been able to drink on my own, and you know, it just makes it a bit easier when you're talking to new people." She popped the cork and produced two glasses she had waiting. "Mike and I are from Melbourne. I don't know a soul here in Sydney. That's why I'm on the prowl for friends. And Mike is working such long hours at the moment, I get lonely during the week."

Alice held out her glass to be filled.

"Nick has started working pretty long hours, too."

"Alice?"

"Alice."

Nick was supporting one side of her and Dominick was supporting the other. Her legs had turned to jelly.

"Back," said Alice.

"You've hurt your back?" said Dominick.

No, I meant it's all coming back. My memory is coming back.

It was as if a dam wall had burst in her brain, releasing a raging torrent of memories.

"Get her some water," said someone.

Alice had needed a new friend. When Madison was about one, Sophie had broken up with Jack (such a shock) and she found a new circle of single, glossy, stiletto-heeled friends who shrieked a lot and started their nights at nine p.m., catching taxis into elegant bars in the city. She and Alice grew apart.

And Elisabeth was distracted, sad, never really listening.

So Alice's friendship with Gina grew fast. It was like falling in love. And Nick and Mike got on, too! Camping trips. Impromptu dinners that went on late into the night, while the kids slept on sofas. It was wonderful.

Gina's twin girls, Eloise and Rose, were born a few months before Olivia. Big brown eyes and snub freckled noses and Gina's bouncing hair. They all played so well together.

One year, the two families hired houseboats together on the Hawkesbury River. They moored their boats next to each other. Rowed the dinghies across in the moonlight for BBQs on the top deck. Olivia and the twins painted Alice's and Gina's toenails different colors. Gina and Alice went for a swim after breakfast, floating on their backs, admiring their toenails, while Nick and Mike and the kids played Marco Polo. They all agreed, it was the best holiday they'd ever had.

Of course she'd told Gina she was pregnant with Olivia before she told Nick.

Nick was in the UK for two weeks. He only called twice.

Twice in two weeks.

He was too busy, he said. He was distracted.

But they won the account! He got the bonus! We can afford a swimming pool!

———————

"There," she said to Nick.

"What did you say?"

She was trying to say, *You were never there.*

The year of the Goodman project Nick was never there. Never there. When he came home, he smelled of the office. Corporate sweat. Even when he was talking to her, he was still thinking about the office.

Olivia had three ear infections in three months.

Tom was throwing terrifying tantrums.

Overnight, Madison became so nervous about school she was vomiting every morning. That's not normal, Nick. We've got to do something about it. I can't sleep I'm so worried about it.

Nick said, It's just a stage. I can't talk about it now. I've got an early flight tomorrow morning.

Gina said, I've found a child psychologist who might be able to help. Should you talk to the school principal about it? What does her teacher say? Could I look after the kids for you while you have some special time with her? What a worry for you.

Gina was the sort who got involved with things at the school. Volunteered for everything. Alice became that sort of person, too. She liked it. She was good at it.

Mike and Gina were having problems. Gina told Alice every cruel remark, every thoughtless gesture. Mike told Nick he wasn't happy with his life. Alice and Nick had a Christmas party one hot December night. Mike got drunk and kissed that horrendous Jackie Holloway in the laundry. Gina went in to get champagne and found them.

Nick and Alice were in bed one night talking in the darkness.

Mike is my friend.

Are you saying you approve of him kissing another woman in our laundry?
Of course not, but there are two sides to every story. Let's just stay out of it.
There are not two sides! It's not excusable. He shouldn't have kissed her.
Well, maybe if Gina stopped trying to turn him into something he's not.
She is not! What do you mean? Because she's encouraging him to get a different job? But that's because he's not happy there!
Look. Is there any point in us playing out another version of their fights? You playing Gina and me playing Mike?
They turned away from each other, carefully not touching.

It was not "cherries." It was half a fruit platter. A beautifully presented fruit platter she'd spent the morning making to take to his mother's place. She was rushing around trying to get the children dressed and instead of helping, he was reading the paper and happily eating his way through the fruit platter, as if Alice were the hired help.

After Mike moved out, Gina wanted to lose weight. So Alice and Gina decided to get a personal trainer. They joined a gym. They started doing spin classes. The weight fell off them. They got fitter and fitter. Alice loved it. She dropped two dress sizes. She had no idea exercise could be so exhilarating.

Gina went on a date with a guy she'd met on the Internet. Alice minded the kids. Nick was working late.
When Gina came home, she was all glittery and flushed. Alice, lying on the couch in her tracksuit pants, felt envious. First dates. How wonderful to experience a first date again.
When Nick came home that night he said, You're getting too thin.

When Nick heard that his dad was dating Alice's mother, he laughed out loud.
She's not his type. He goes for eastern suburbs women with fake boobs and big divorce settlements. Women who read all the right books and see all the right plays.

Are you saying my mother isn't cultured enough for your father?

I hate the sort of woman my father normally dates!

So your dad's slumming it, then? With my poor simple Hills District mother?

It is impossible to talk to you. It's like you want me to say the wrong thing. Fine. Dad is slumming it. Is that what you want me to say? Satisfied?

Elisabeth had disappeared. Her sister turned into this bitter, angry person, with a hard, sarcastic laugh. Nothing as bad had ever happened to anyone else as was happening to Elisabeth. Alice couldn't say the right thing to her. Once she asked if she'd had another embryo implanted and Elisabeth's lip curled contemptuously. The embryo is "transferred," she sneered, it's not implanted. If only it were that easy. How the hell was Alice meant to know all the right terminology? If she invited her to one of the kids' birthday parties, Elisabeth sighed, in a way that meant it would be excruciating for her, but she would still come, and she'd look like a martyr the whole time. Didn't offer to help, just stood there with her lips folded together. Don't do me any favors, Alice wanted to say. After the fourth miscarriage, she tried to talk to Elisabeth. She offered to donate her eggs. Your eggs are too old, Elisabeth had said. You really don't know what you're talking about.

When Roger proposed to Alice's mother, Nick was angry.

Well that's just fabulous. Wonderful. How is that going to make my mother feel?

As if it were somehow Alice's fault. As if her mother had somehow trapped Roger into marrying her.

They stopped having sex. It just stopped. They didn't even talk about it.

"Let's get her outside into the fresh air."

She was dimly aware that she was being half carried, half dragged out of the marquee. People were staring, but she couldn't focus on anything but the memories rushing through her brain.

—————

When she felt her first labor pain with Madison, she thought to herself, They must be joking. They can't expect me to put up with this. But it seemed they did. Seven hours later, when the baby was born, neither she nor Nick could believe it was a girl. They'd both been so ridiculously convinced it was a boy. It's a girl, they kept saying to each other. The surprise made them euphoric. She was extraordinary. As if a baby girl had never been born before.

Tom was in the posterior position. She kept screaming at that midwife with the soft, worn face—it's my back, the pain is in my back. And the whole time she was promising herself, I will never, ever go through this again.

Olivia was the worst. Your baby is in distress. We need to do an emergency cesarean, they told her, and suddenly the room filled with people, and she was being wheeled down a long corridor, watching the ceiling lights flash rhythmically by, and wondering what she'd done to distress her poor baby before it was even born. When she woke up from the anesthetic, a nurse said, You have the most beautiful baby girl.

Madison got her first tooth when she was eight months old. She kept touching it with her finger and frowning.

Tom refused point blank to ever sit in the high chair. Never ever sat in it.

Olivia didn't walk until she was eighteen months old.

Madison's little red hooded jacket with the white flowers.

Tom's filthy blue elephant that had to come everywhere with him. Where's Elephant? Have you seen his damned elephant?

Olivia ran into the schoolyard on her first day of school shrieking with joy. Madison had to be dragged out of Alice's arms.

Alice walked into the kitchen one day and found Tom carefully stuffing his nose with frozen peas. I wanted to see if the peas would come out of my eyeballs, he told the doctor.

They lost Olivia at Newport Beach. The panic made Alice hyperventilate. You were meant to be watching her, Nick kept saying. As if that were the point. That Alice had made a mistake. Not that Olivia was missing, but that it was Alice's fault.

"Alice? Take big deep breaths."

She ignored their voices. She was busy remembering.

It was a really cold August day. She and Gina were driving in separate cars home from the gym. Normally, they would have driven together, but Alice had taken Madison to the dentist beforehand. The dentist said there was nothing wrong with Madison's teeth. He didn't know what was causing that ache in her jaw. He'd sent Madison to the waiting room and asked Alice quietly, Could it be stress?

Alice had looked at her watch impatiently, desperate to get to the gym. She didn't want to miss the beginning of the spin class. She'd already missed a class yesterday because Olivia had some school presentation. Stress? What did Madison have to be stressed about? She was just impossible. She probably just wanted to get out of school.

As they were driving home Madison was whining about having to stay in the gym day-care while Alice and Gina did their class.

I am too old for the crèche. It is just stupid crying babies.

Well, you should have gone to school today instead of making up stories about toothaches.

I didn't make it up.

It was a black stormy day. Lightning cracked across the sky. It started to rain. Heavy drops splattering on the windscreen like pebbles.

Mum. I didn't make it up.

Be quiet. I'm trying to concentrate on the road.

Alice hated driving in the rain.

The wind was howling. The trees were swaying about as if they were per-forming some sort of ghostly dance.

They pulled into Rawson Street. Alice saw Gina's brake lights turn red.

Gina was driving her wildly impractical fortieth-birthday present to her-self. A little red Mini with white stripes along the side and personalized num-ber plates. Not a family car. It makes me feel young and crazy, said Gina. She drove it with the sunroof open and Elvis on full blast.

Alice watched the Mini in the rain and knew that Gina would be singing along lustily to Elvis.

That tree looks like it's going to fall right over, said Madison.

Alice looked up.

It was the liquid amber on the corner. Beautiful in the autumn. It was rock-ing back and forth, making a horrible creaking sound.

It won't fall.

It fell.

It was so fast and violent and unexpected. Like a dear friend suddenly punching you in the face. Like some cruel god had done it on purpose. To be nasty. Picked up the tree and slammed it across the Mini in a fit of temper. The sound was tremendous. An explosion of terrifying sound. Alice's foot jammed on the brake. Her arm flew sideways protectively across Madison's chest, as if to save her from the tree. Madison screamed—Mummy! Mummy! Mummy!

And then silence, except for the sound of the rain. The beeps for the one-o'clock news came on the radio.

There was a massive tree trunk lying on the road in front of them. Gina's little red Mini looked like a squashed tin can.

A woman came running out from her house. She stopped when she saw the tree, her hands pressed to her mouth.

Alice pulled over to the side of the road. She put the hazard lights on. Stay here, she said to Madison. She opened the car door and ran. She was still wear-

ing her shorts and T-shirt from the gym. She slipped and fell, hard on one knee, stood up and kept running, her arms flailed uselessly at the air, trying to pull back time to just two minutes ago.

"Get her a blanket. She's shivering."

Nick didn't come to the funeral. He didn't come to the funeral.
    He didn't come to the funeral.

The school principal was at the funeral. Mr. Gordon. Dominick. He said, I'm so sorry, Alice. I know you were such close friends. And he hugged her. She cried into his shirt. He stood close by her while they released pink balloons into the gray sky.

She didn't know how to live her life without Gina. She was part of her daily routine. Gym. Coffee. Taking the kids to swimming lessons. Personal training. Minding each other's kids. Movie nights. Laughing at stupid things. Sure she knew lots and lots of other mums at the school, but not like Gina. She was her one true friend now that Nick was too busy with work.
    All the joy had gone.
    Everything seemed pointless. Each morning in the shower she cried, her forehead against the bathroom tiles, the shampoo sliding into her eyes.
    She fought with Nick. Sometimes she deliberately picked fights because it was a good distraction from the grief. She had to stop herself from hitting him. She wanted to scratch and bite and hurt him.

Nick said one day, I think I should move out. She said, I think you should, too. And she thought, As soon as he goes, I'll phone Gina. Gina will help me.

The nastiness seemed to begin so quickly and easily, as if they'd always hated each other, and here at last was their opportunity to stop pretending and let each other know how they really felt. Nick wanted the children to be with him fifty percent of the time. It was a joke. How could he possibly take care of them on his own with the hours he worked? It would be so disruptive for them. He didn't even really want them. He just wanted to reduce the amount of maintenance he would have to pay. Luckily, she remembered that her old work friend Jane had become a family lawyer. Jane was going to take him on.

Four months after Nick moved out, Dominick asked her out on a date. They went for a bushwalk in the National Park and got caught in the rain. He was easy and kind and unaffected. He didn't know the right restaurants. He liked unpretentious cafés. They talked a lot about the school. He respected her opinions. He seemed so much more real than Nick.

They had made love for the first time just the other night at his place. The children were with her mother.

(The night before she hit her head.)

It was beautiful.

Well, okay, it was awkward. (For example, he seemed to think he should lick her toes. Where had he got such an idea? It tickled unbearably, and she accidentally kicked him in the nose.)

But still, it had been so, so lovely to have a man appreciating her body again. Right down to her toes.

Dominick was the right sort of man for her. Nick had been a mistake. How can you pick the right man when you're in your twenties and stupid?

The grief started to ease a little. It was still there, but it wasn't an impossible weight crushing her chest. She kept herself very busy.

She stopped by at Dino's one afternoon for a coffee and found a small crowd of solemn-faced people surrounding a woman having some sort of attack on the footpath. Even Dino was out there. Alice went to avert her eyes—it seemed like the poor woman might be mentally ill—when she saw to her horror that it was her sister. It was Elisabeth, and when Dino told her what had happened, her first feeling was shame. How could she not have seen that it had got so bad? As she was explaining to Dino what Elisabeth had been going through, she felt a growing anger at herself. It was like she'd just come to accept Elisabeth's miscarriages as part of life. She'd led Elisabeth to her car and left her sitting in the passenger seat, staring straight ahead, and then she'd gone back and managed to soothe the mother of the child Elisabeth had apparently tried to kidnap. (It was Judy Clarke. Judy had a son in Madison's class.) On the way home Elisabeth said, "Thanks," and nothing else.

Well, enough was enough. This endless cycle of miscarriages had to stop. They were just beating their heads against a brick wall, and Elisabeth was losing her mind. Alice had lost her best friend and her marriage had fallen apart but she was still getting on with things. Someone needed to talk sense to Elisabeth. As soon as she got home, Alice got on the Internet to research adoption. Last Thursday she made a fresh batch of banana muffins and then she rang up Ben and told him she was having trouble with her car. He said he'd be right over.

"I wonder if we should call a doctor?"

"No," said Alice out loud, her eyes shut. "I'm all right. Just give me a minute."

Now she was remembering the past week. It was as if she'd been permanently drunk. She was mortified.

She hadn't had time for breakfast the morning of the spin class with Jane, and actually, now she thought about it, she hadn't even had any water, which was stupid, no wonder she'd fainted. Her last memory was pedaling hard, sweat dripping, listing off in her head everything she had to do for Mega Meringue Day, only half listening to Narelle (the annoying instructor: Spin Crazy Girl) going on about "the finish line" and "the semi-trailer holding you up." Instead, she was watching the television screen playing soundlessly above Narelle's head. There was a commercial on that always irked Alice, featuring a woman looking flirtatiously at the camera while licking a glob of cream cheese off the tip of her finger (she looked a bit like Jackie Holloway) and Alice was feeling sick at the very thought of eating cream cheese.

That's why her mixed-up brain had been thinking about cream cheese when she regained consciousness.

Being carried out of the spin class like that. How completely bizarre that she didn't recognize the gym, or Maggie's husband on the treadmill, or Kate Harper coming out of the lift.

The shock of finding she and Nick were divorcing.

Talking to Nick's PA on the phone. That awful woman had never liked her (Alice suspected a crush) and since the separation she'd become quite breathtakingly rude.

Dancing the salsa at the Family Talent Night. That "chemistry" she imagined she felt. Good Lord, she'd given back Granny Love's ring. She'd been determined to keep that ring for Madison. Now it might go to Nick's new wife if he ever remarried. It was part of Madison's heritage.

He'd bet her twenty dollars that she wouldn't want to get back together when she got her memory back. He must have been laughing at her the whole time.

She had kissed Nick. It made her sick to the stomach. He was using her memory loss to get her to agree to the fifty-percent care arrangement. Thank God she'd never signed anything.

For heaven's sake, they'd taken Madison for ice creams and whale watching after she'd cut off Chloe's hair. Talk about the right way to bring up a delinquent.

She'd told Mrs. Bergen that she'd switched sides on the development issue. Well, she'd just have to tell her that she'd switched right back. She didn't want to stay living in the house. Too many memories. The developers could knock it to the ground and put up the tackiest, most sterile high-rise apartment block for all she cared.

Tom was meant to have been one of the Elvis dancers today! She had his suit already. He'd deliberately not reminded her.

Nora hadn't mentioned the sponsors in her speech!

She needed to check all the paperwork for the Guinness Book of Records. Everything had to be done properly or it wouldn't be an official record. Maggie and Nora meant well but they didn't really know what they were doing.

The mum standing next to her with the birthmark was Anne Russell, mother of little Kerrie, in Tom's class. They helped together at the library on the same day. How could she have forgotten Anne Russell?

How could she have forgotten any of it?

Alice opened her eyes.

She was sitting on the grass of the school oval.

Nick and Dominick were both squatting down uncomfortably in front of her.

"Are you all right?" said Nick.

Alice looked at him. He flinched, as if she'd hit him.

"You've got your memory back," he said. It wasn't a question. He stood up. It was as if he were folding up his face, making it bland and cold. "I'll go let the kids know you're okay." He started to turn away and then looked back at her and said, "You owe me twenty bucks."

Alice turned to Dominick.

He smiled, hugged her to him, and said, "Everything is all right now, darling."

Chapter 33

Alice was running with her mobile in her hand, so she wouldn't miss the call when it came.

She was running the route that Luke used to take her and Gina on. She'd let Luke go. She couldn't justify spending one hundred and fifty dollars on a personal-training session. Not when she and Nick were still trying to work out the money settlement. She'd also dropped the gym membership. These days she just liked to run and remember.

Since she'd lost her memory and got it back again, she was obsessed with remembering her life. She kept a daily journal, and whenever she went running she let memories drift through her head. When she got home she would write them down. It was hard to know whether she'd fully recovered her memory of the ten years she'd lost, or if there were still gaps. She understood that even before the accident she wouldn't have had perfect recall of the previous decade, but she kept scouring her mind, searching for any missing pieces.

Today she was remembering a night when Tom was a baby. Everyone had told her that her second child would be a wonderful sleeper after her problems with Madison. Everyone was wrong. Tom was a "cluster feeder." He didn't like having a proper feed every three to four hours, thanks anyway. He much preferred a snack every hour. Every *single hour*. That meant Alice slept for only forty minutes at a time before she was wrenched awake again by the sound of his cry through the baby monitor. And Madison was a toddler but she *still* had never slept through a single night in her life.

It was a time in her life when Alice was obsessed with sleep. She lusted for it. She saw television ads for sleeping pills or beds with people sleeping and they made her want to spit with envy. After feeding Tom, she would half stumble, half run back to the bedroom and dive into the bed. Her sleep would be full of dreams about the baby: she'd fallen asleep on the baby and suffocated him; she'd left him on the change table halfway through changing his nappy and he'd rolled onto the floor. And then, just at the moment she was sleeping the deepest, most exquisite sleep, the sound of the monitor would wake her again. It was like being desperately thirsty and having somebody hand you a tall glass of ice water and then tear it away from your mouth just as you took a sip. Better not to have any water at all.

On this particular night, Nick was leaving early the following morning for an important business trip. She'd just got back into bed after convincing Madison to go back to sleep (*Why* can't I play outside now? *Why* is it the middle of the night?) when Tom began wailing. Her head swam as she bent over the crib to pick him up. She felt a wave of pure rage at this person who refused to let her sleep. *Just what do you expect of me?* Her arms tightened around the baby. *You . . . need . . . to . . . be . . . quiet.*

She laid him back down with elaborate care. Tom was enraged, and screamed as though she'd just put him down on a bed of knives. Alice went back to the bedroom, switched on the light, and said to Nick, "You need to lock me up. I wanted to hurt the baby."

Nick sat up in bed, his eyes bleary and confused. "You hurt the baby?"

Alice was trembling all over. "No. I *wanted* to. I wanted to squeeze him until he stopped crying."

"Right, then," said Nick calmly, as if she'd just reported something perfectly normal. He got up and led her by the hand back to bed. "You need sleep."

"But I need to feed him."

"I'll give him the expressed milk you've got in the freezer. Just go to sleep. I'm canceling tomorrow. Sleep."

"But—"

"Sleep. Just sleep."

It was the most erotic thing he'd ever said to her. He pulled the covers up under her chin, unplugged the monitor, and left, switching off the light and closing the door behind him. The room became divinely silent and dark.

She slept.

When she woke, her breasts rock hard and leaking, the room was filled with sunlight, and the house was quiet. She looked at the clock and saw that it was nine o'clock. He'd done it. He actually canceled his trip. She'd slept for six straight glorious hours. Her vision was brighter, her brain sharper. She went downstairs and found Nick giving Madison her breakfast, while Tom cooed and kicked in his bouncer.

"Thank you," said Alice, almost delirious with gratitude and relief.

"No problem." Nick smiled.

She could still see the pride on his face, because he'd saved her. He'd fixed things. He'd always loved to fix things for her.

So it wasn't strictly true that he was never there, or that he always put work first.

Maybe if she'd just asked him for help more? If she'd fallen apart more often so he could be the knight in shining armor (but how sexist and wrong was that?); if she hadn't made herself the expert on everything to do with the children; if she hadn't been so condescending when he dressed the children in weirdly inappropriate combinations. He couldn't stand being made to feel stupid, so then he just stopped offering to dress them. His stupid pride.

Her stupid pride about being the best, most professional mother. *I might not have made it in your world, Nick, like Elisabeth, and all those career women in suits, but I've made it in my world.*

She'd come to the steepest part of the route, the part that always made Gina use terrible language. Her calf muscles tightened.

It was good to remember that for every horrible memory from her marriage, there was also a happy one. She wanted to see it clearly, to understand that it wasn't all black, or all white. It was a million colors. And yes, ultimately it hadn't worked out, but that was okay. Just because a marriage ended didn't mean that it hadn't been happy at times.

She thought about that strange period of time straight after she'd got her memory back. At first, images, words, emotions crashed over her in violent waves. She could hardly breathe for the chaos. Then, after a few days, her mind had calmed, the memories had fallen into their correct places, and she felt a kind of beautiful relief. Without her memory, she'd been swimming through cloudy water, half blind: now she had clarity of vision again. And what she saw was this: her marriage was over and she was in love with Dominick. That was that. With Dominick she felt the sweet, soothing comfort of being with a man who was besotted by her, fascinated by her, and wanted to find out who she was. With Nick, all she felt was bitterness, fury, and hurt. He was a man who had already decided who she was, who could list all her flaws, annoying tendencies, and mistakes. She could hardly stand to be in the same room with him. The idea that she'd planned to get back together with him was terrifying and shocking. As if someone had drugged her, hypnotized her, duped and deceived her.

It wasn't just that her memories of the last ten years were back. It was that her true self, *as formed by those ten years,* was back. As seductive as it might have been to erase the grief and pain of the last ten years, it was also a lie. Young Alice was a fool. A sweet, innocent fool. Young Alice hadn't experienced ten years of living.

But even as she tried to reason with her, scolded her, and grieved for her, young Alice stubbornly refused to go away.

Over the months that followed she kept popping up. She'd be paying for petrol at the service station and find her hand reaching out for a bar of heavenly Lindt chocolate. She'd be talking seriously to Nick about complicated logistical arrangements with the children and she'd find herself asking him something flippant and entirely unrelated to the conversation, like what he'd had for breakfast that morning. She'd be rushing to the beautician and find herself calling Elisabeth to suggest they meet for a coffee instead. She'd be hurrying between appointments and a voice would whisper in her head: *Relax.*

Finally she stopped resisting and called a truce. Young Alice was allowed to stay as long as she didn't eat too much chocolate.

Now it seemed like she could twist the lens on her life and see it from two entirely different perspectives. The perspective of her younger self. Her younger, sillier, innocent self. And her older, wiser, more cynical and sensible self.

And maybe sometimes Young Alice had a point.

Like with Madison, for example. Before she'd lost her memory, Alice had been going through a bad stage with Madison. She'd been so tough on her, so frustrated by her behavior, and in the deepest, most shamefully childish part of her mind, she had blamed Madison for Gina's accident. If she hadn't had to take her to the dentist that morning, Gina wouldn't have been pulling up at the corner at that time. They would have stopped to have coffee instead.

And of course Madison would have been smart enough to pick up on Alice's resentment. She was already a child who felt everything far too deeply. She'd seen her mother's friend killed in an accident and then her parents separated.

No wonder she'd been playing up. Elisabeth recommended a psychiatrist she'd heard about. A Dr. Jeremy Hodges. Madison had been going to see him twice a week, and it seemed to be helping. At least she hadn't assaulted anyone lately at school; and Kate Harper's husband had been transferred to somewhere in Europe, so the Harper family was now thankfully out of their lives.

There was a friendly toot of a horn and Alice looked up to see Mrs. Bergen driving by in her little blue Honda. It was strange, but after she got her memory back Alice found she'd lost interest in the development issue. The idea of selling up for a nice profit and moving to a fresh, new house without memories no longer seemed that important. She knew the bad memories would come with her anyway, and she didn't want to leave the good ones behind.

On the other hand, if the developers won—well, that was life. Things changed. Oh, things sure did change.

She came to the corner where Gina had died and remembered yet again the terror and disbelief of that moment. Her grief had changed since she lost and regained her memory. It was simpler, calmer, sadder. Before, she had somehow channeled her grief into a whole lot of different directions: fury toward Nick (*He should have taken Gina's side when she was splitting up with Mike*), coldness toward Elisabeth (*She never really liked Gina all that much*), and irritation toward Madison (*Gina would still be alive if they'd driven in the same car*). Hearing the facts of her life—"Your friend died"—without the memories, had untangled her feelings. Now she just missed her.

The phone rang in her hand. She stopped to answer it without looking at the name on the screen.

"Heard anything yet?" It was Dominick.

"No!" she said. "Stop taking up the phone line."

"Sorry." He laughed. "I'll see you tonight. I'm bringing a chicken, right?"

"Yes, yes! Go away!"

He liked to check things. And double-check. And triple-check. Just to be sure. It could potentially become an annoying habit, but then, everyone had annoying habits. And she wouldn't have even considered asking Nick to do something so menial as buy a barbecue chicken on a weeknight! Nick was too busy and important. When Dominick came over after a day's work, he was totally present. Not like Nick, who would sometimes act as if Alice and the children weren't quite real, as if his real life was at the office. It wasn't as if Dominick didn't have a stressful job, too. Nick might run a company but Dominick ran a school. And which one was contributing more to the community?

She just wished she would stop comparing Dominick to Nick, as if all the reasons she loved Dominick were simply because he was so different from Nick. It sometimes seemed as if the whole *point* of her relationship with Dominick was how it compared to her relationship with Nick.

The other day she and Dominick had been at Tom's soccer game and Nick was there, too. She'd been so aware of his eyes on them from the other side of the field as she laughed extra hard at Dominick's jokes. She'd made herself a bit sick, to be honest.

The awful thing was that even when Nick *wasn't* there, she was always imagining him watching. *Look at us snuggled up on the couch together watching TV, Nick. He's rubbing my feet. You never did that. Look at us walking hand in hand into this café. No fuss about finding the "perfect" table—we just sit down! Look, Nick, look!*

So did that make her relationship with Dominick nothing more than a performance?

She slowed down to a brisk walk, panting hard, and remembered how she'd sat in the kitchen drinking wine with Nick and the blissful relief she'd felt kissing him.

Stupid. So mortifying. He'd kissed her back, though. He'd been willing to "try again."

She had absolutely no desire to try again. None whatsoever. Been there, done that. Time to move on with her life. She had made the right decision. The children loved Dominick. He'd probably spent more time with them than they'd ever spent with their father.

And she and Nick were so civil and grown-up nowadays! They had finally worked out a "shared parenting arrangement" that suited them both. Nick wasn't having them fifty percent of the time, but he was seeing them a lot more than just on weekends. He was actually taking Friday afternoons off from work so he could pick them up from school.

Recently, she had found she was actually looking forward to seeing him when he dropped off the children. It was going to be one of those "amicable" divorces.

Yes, a good marriage (if you averaged it all out) followed by a good divorce. According to the children, Nick had a girlfriend. Megan.

Alice wasn't exactly sure how she felt about *Megan*.

The phone rang again.

At last. It was him. She sat down on somebody's red-brick garden wall.

"Tell me," she said. "Hurry up and tell me!"

At first she couldn't understand him. He seemed to be in the middle of blowing his nose.

"What? What did you say?"

"A little girl," said Ben, loud and clear. "A beautiful little baby girl."

Chapter 34

Elisabeth's Homework for Jeremy

I never believed I was going to have a baby until I heard her cry. Sorry to admit that, Jeremy, because I know you worked your heart out trying to stop me from being a basket case.

But I never believed it. That day in the Port-a-loo, while the world's largest lemon meringue pie baked, I was convinced I was having my last miscarriage.

But then the bleeding stopped. It was just "spotting," as the medical world cheerily calls it. A spot of rain. A spot of bother.

But even when the spotting finally stopped, I didn't believe I was having a baby. Even when every ultrasound was normal. Even when I could feel the baby kicking and rolling, even when I was going to prenatal classes, choosing a crib, washing the baby clothes, and even when they were telling me, Okay, you can push now, I still didn't believe I was having a baby. Not an actual baby.

Until she cried. And I thought, *That sounds like a real newborn baby.*

And now she's here. Little Francesca Rose.

Through all those horrible years I hardly ever saw Ben cry. Now he can't stop crying. It seems like he had gigantic drums of tears stockpiled that he can finally release. I look over at him holding her asleep in his arms, and he has tears running silently down his face. We'll be bathing her together and I'll ask him to pass me a towel, and I'll discover he's crying again. I say, Ben, *please*. Darling.

I don't cry as much. I'm concentrating too hard on doing it all right. Ringing Alice up to ask questions about breast-feeding. How do you know if she's getting enough? Worrying about her crying. What is it this time? Wind? Worrying about her weight. Her skin. (It seems a bit dry.)

But sometimes, in the middle of the night, when it's a good breast-feed and she's attached properly and sucking well, suddenly the reality of her, the actuality of her, the aliveness of her, the exquisiteness of her, hits me so hard, wham, and the happiness is so huge, so amazing, it explodes like fireworks through my brain. I don't know how to describe it. Maybe it's like your first hit of heroin.

(How will I get her to just say no to drugs? Could I put her in some sort of early preventative therapy? What do you think, J? So much to worry about.)

Anyway, I wanted to tell you that we did finally have a ceremony for the lost babies, like you suggested. We took a bunch of roses to the beach one calm sunny winter's day, and we walked around the rocks and dropped one in the water for each lost little astronaut. I'm glad we did that. I didn't cry. But as I watched each rose float off, I felt something loosen, as if I'd been wearing something too tight around my chest for a very long time. As we walked back to the car, I found myself taking very deep breaths of air, and the air felt good.

(We were going to read a poem as well, but I thought the baby's ears might have been cold. She hasn't had a cold yet. She was a bit sniffly the other day, but it seemed to go away, so that was a relief. I'm thinking about giving her a multivitamin. Alice says it's not necessary but—anyway, I digress.)

I also wanted to apologize for thinking that you were a smug dad with a perfect life. When you told me at our last session that you and your wife were actually going through fertility treatments too, and that photo on your desk wasn't your children, but your nephews, I was ashamed of all my self-centered thoughts.

So, here is my homework, Jeremy. I know you never wanted to read it, but I thought I'd submit it anyway. Maybe it will help you with other patients. Or maybe it will help you when your wife is acting crazy, as she will sometimes do.

The Infertiles came to visit yesterday, laden with expensive gifts. It was sort of horrible. I knew exactly how they were feeling. I knew how they would be trying to hold it together, promising themselves they would only stay for twenty minutes and they could cry in the car, keeping their voices light and bright, their poor, tired, bloated bodies aching with need when they each dutifully held the baby. I complained about the lack of sleep (we'd had a really bad night) and I knew I was overdoing it, even though I *knew* there is nothing more patronizing to an Infertile than to hear a new mother complaining, as if that will make you feel better for not having your own baby. It's like telling a blind person, "Oh, sure, you get to see mountains and sunsets, but there are also rubbish dumps and pollution! Terrible!" I don't know why I did it, except that I understand now that desperate, clumsy desire to make people feel better—even when you know perfectly well that nothing will. The Infertiles will probably bitch about me at the next lunch. I won't see them again—the distance between us is just too great—unless, I guess, one of them gets to join me here on the other side.

I don't know if this is presumptuous of me, Jeremy, but I was wondering if you and your wife might be struggling with the problem of when is the right time to give up.

And if so, I want to say something that will make no sense.

We should have given up years ago. It's so clear now. We should have "explored other options." We should have adopted. We gave up years of our lives and we very nearly destroyed our marriage. Our happy ending could have and should have arrived so much sooner. And even though I adore the fact that Francesca has Ben's eyes, I also see now that her biological connection to us is irrelevant. She is her own little person. She is Francesca. If we weren't her "natural" parents, we would still have loved her just as much. I mean, for heaven's sake, I named Francesca after her great-grandmother, who has no genetic connection to us at all and wasn't even part of our lives until I was eight years old. I couldn't love Frannie any more than I do.

So there's that.

But now, to be completely honest, I have to contradict myself.

Because if your wife were to ask me if I would go through it all again, then this is how I would answer.

Yes. Absolutely. Of course I would. No question. I would go through it all again, every needle, every loss, every raging hormone, every heartbreaking second, to be here right now, with my beautiful daughter sleeping beside me.

PS. I'm enclosing a strange, rather ugly doll. It might just do the trick. Good luck, Jeremy. I think you'll make a wonderful dad. However long it takes and whichever way you choose to get there.

Chapter 35

Frannie's Letter to Phil

Hello again, Phil.

I've had this unfinished letter in my desk for months now.

My days are so full at the moment, I don't seem to have time to write to you. (Or to your memory, or your ghost, or to myself, or to whoever it was I've been writing all these years!)

I've just returned home from seeing Madison compete in an oratory competition and I'm still on cloud nine.

SHE WON FIRST PLACE!

It was a competition against the best children from other primary schools, so it was quite a big deal. She gave an extremely informative and entertaining speech about world records. (Did you know that the world record for the most live rattlesnakes held in the mouth at the same time is . . . eight!)

We were all so nervous beforehand. Xavier was pale and perspiring, and Alice was snapping at everyone. When they announced Madison's name, we went quite crazy. Olivia danced in the aisle. Roger leapt to

his feet, knocking his elbow into some poor woman's eye. (Somewhat
embarrassing.) Barb burst into tears. I could hear Xavier telling the
man next to him, "That's my great-granddaughter you just heard. Gets
all her talent from me!" He has appropriated my family in typical
Xavier fashion. They don't seem to mind.

Elisabeth and Ben were there with the baby. You know what
I love? Secretly watching Barb when she's secretly watching Elisabeth.
The bliss on Elisabeth's face every time she looks at her baby is
mirrored on Barb's face—and maybe it's mirrored on mine, too,

(Sometimes Barb comes across as a bit of a silly thing, but there's
more to her than people think. That Roger knows he's on to a good
thing. And I'm not just saying that because she's my daughter.
A daughter I wouldn't swap for the world.)

Of course, little Francesca gets prettier every day. Tom kept her
amused by rattling Ben's keys. He's good with babies. He finds them
scientifically interesting.

Alice and Dominick seemed quite happy together. Alice is so much
more relaxed since her accident. She's lost that tense, gaunt look.
Perhaps we all need a good thump on the head from time to time?
There is talk of them moving in together.

I hear Nick has a new girlfriend too, although she wasn't there,
thankfully. Nick was kept busy with his sisters and his mother. I
believe the modern term for these women is "high maintenance."

Everyone keeps telling me there is no chance of reconciliation
between Alice and Nick. "No chance at all," they tell me, as if I'm a
deluded old woman. And yet . . .

Xavier and I happened to be sitting next to Nick, directly behind
Alice and Dominick. When they announced Madison was the winner,
Alice didn't even look at Dominick. She turned straight around to look
for Nick. She reached out her hand to him almost involuntarily. He
took it. Just her fingertips. Just for a fleeting second. I saw the
expressions on their faces. That's all I'm saying.

Well, I think perhaps it's time I signed off, Phil, and I hope you don't mind, but I think this may be my last letter.

Xavier is waiting for me to come to bed.

Love,

and goodbye,

Frannie

Epilogue

She was floating, arms outspread, water lapping her body, breathing in a summery fragrance of salt and coconut. There was a pleasantly satisfied breakfast taste in her mouth of bacon and coffee and possibly croissants. She lifted her chin and the morning sun shone so brightly on the water, she had to squint through spangles of light to see her feet in front of her. Her toenails were each painted a different color. Red. Gold. Purple. Funny. The nail polish hadn't been applied very well. Blobby and messy. Someone else was floating in the water right next to her. Someone she liked a lot, who made her laugh, with toenails painted the same way. The other person waggled multicolored toes at her companionably, and she was filled with sleepy contentment. Somewhere in the distance, a man's voice shouted, "Marco?" and a chorus of children's voices cried back, "Polo!" The man called out again, "Marco, Marco, Marco?" and the voices answered, "Polo, Polo, Polo!" A child laughed; a long, gurgling giggle, like a stream of soap bubbles.

We're on the Hawkesbury River. This is our magical houseboat holiday.

Alice lifted her head from the water and looked at Gina. She had her eyes shut; her long curly hair was floating out from her head like seaweed.

"Gina! You're not dead, are you?"

Gina opened one eye and said, "Do I look dead?"

Alice was filled with exquisite relief. "Let's have champagne to celebrate!"

"Oh, definitely," said Gina sleepily. "Definitely."

There was someone swimming toward them. Bobbing up and down in a clumsy breaststroke. Brown shoulders rising in and out of the water. It was Dominick. His hair plastered close to his head. Drops of water sparkling on his eyelashes.

"Hi, girls," he said, treading water next to them.

Gina kept quiet.

Alice felt embarrassed in front of Gina. For some reason it was wrong. It wasn't right that Dominick was here.

Gina rolled over onto her stomach and swam away.

"No, no, come back!" shouted Alice.

"She's gone," said Dominick sadly.

"You shouldn't be here," said Alice to Dominick. She splashed him and he looked hurt. "This isn't your holiday."

The radio alarm went off. An eighties song, loud and jarring in the morning silence.

There was a flurry of movement and the quilt slid off her shoulders. "Sorry." The radio was switched off again.

She turned over and pulled the quilt back up again.

A Gina dream. She hadn't dreamed of her for so long. She loved those dreams that felt so real, it was almost like she was seeing her again, spending another day with her. Except Dominick shouldn't have popped up like that. It felt like a betrayal of Nick to let Dominick into her houseboat holiday memory. Nick had loved that holiday. She could see him standing on the top deck of the boat, loping about, pretending to be a pirate. "Arg! Arg!" He would grab Tom around the waist and say, "Time to walk the plank, my boy!" and throw him high, so high in the air. She could see Tom's exhilarated face so clearly, his little brown boy's body suspended forever against a bright blue sky.

Tom.

She opened her eyes.

Had Tom come home last night?

He'd promised to be home by midnight and they'd gone to bed early. She'd meant to get up and check on him, but for some reason she'd fallen asleep so soundly.

Was that a memory of his key in the door? The car scraping in the driveway, music hastily switched off, the explosive sounds of teenage boys trying to be quiet. Huge feet thumping up the stairs.

Or was that another night?

Maybe she'd better go and check, but it was so early, and she was sleepy, and it was Sunday. Her one sleep-in day. She would get up, push open his bedroom door, and he'd be there, sprawled out fully dressed on top of his bed. The room dank and musty with the smell of aftershave and unwashed socks. Then she'd be wide awake with no chance of getting back to sleep. She'd have to spend the next two hours sitting in the kitchen, waiting for someone to wake up.

And it was Mother's Day! They were meant to bring her breakfast and presents in bed. If they remembered. Last year they forgot entirely. They were teenagers, full of the tragedies and the ecstasies of their own lives.

But what if Tom hadn't come home? And she didn't report him missing until ten a.m.? "I was asleep," she'd have to explain to the police officers when they asked why it had taken her so long to report that her eighteen-year-old son was missing. The police officers would exchange glances. Bad, lazy mother. Bad, lazy mother who deserves to have her son killed on Mother's Day.

She pushed back the covers.

"Tom came home," said a sleepy voice beside her. "I checked earlier."

She pulled the covers back up.

Tom would always come home. He was reliable. Did what he said he would. He didn't like being asked too many questions about his life (no more than three in a row was his rule), but he was a good kid. Studying hard for his exams, playing his soccer, and going out with his friends, bringing home pretty, eager-faced girls, who all seemed to think that if they just sold themselves to Alice they'd be in with a chance. (How wrong they were! If Alice showed too much interest in a girl, she was never seen again.)

It would be Olivia who wouldn't come home one night.

Alice couldn't stop being surprised at the transformation of Olivia from sweet, angelic little girl to surly, furious, secretive teenager. She'd dyed her beautiful blond curls black and pulled her hair dead straight, so she looked like Morticia from *The Addams Family*. "Who?" Olivia had sneered. You couldn't talk to her. Anything you said was likely to give offense. The slamming of her bedroom door reverberated throughout the house on a regular basis. "I hate my life!" she would scream, and Alice would be researching teenage suicide on the Net, when next thing she'd hear her shrieking with laughter with her friends on the phone. Drugs. Teenage pregnancy. Tattoos. It all seemed possible with Olivia. Alice was pretty sure she was going to need intense therapy when Olivia was studying for her HSC in two years' time. For herself.

It's just a stage, Madison told her. Just ride it out, Mum.

Madison had got all her teenage angst over and done with by the time she was fourteen. Now she was a joy. So beautiful to look at that it sometimes made Alice catch her breath in the morning when she saw her come down to breakfast, her hair tousled, her skin translucent. She was studying economics at uni and had a besotted boyfriend called Pete, whom Alice had begun to think of as a bonus son (which was unfortunate, because she had an awful feeling that Madison would be breaking his heart in the not too distant future). It had all gone so fast. One minute they were driving her home from the hospital, a tiny, wrinkled, squalling baby. The next she was all legs and cheekbones and opinions. *Whoosh.* It made Alice's head spin.

"It goes so fast," she told Elisabeth, but Elisabeth didn't really believe her. Anyway, she was the expert on all things mothering now. Even if she didn't have teenagers yet, she still knew best. Alice wanted to say, *Just you wait until your beautiful little Francesca is sleeping until noon and then slumps about the house, flying into a rage when you suggest she might want to get dressed before it's bedtime again.*

But Elisabeth was too busy to hear it. Busy, busy, busy.

She and Ben had ended up adopting three little boys from Vietnam after Francesca was born.

Two were brothers. The youngest was a severe asthmatic and was constantly in and out of hospital. One was in speech therapy for a stammer. Francesca was into swimming, which required early-morning training sessions. Elisabeth was involved with the Vietnamese expatriate community, a support group for adoptive parents, and of course she was treasurer of her school's Parents and Friends Committee. She'd also got back into rowing and was as thin as a rake.

She and Ben also had two dogs, a cat, three guinea pigs, and a fish tank. That quiet, neat little house Alice had visited all those years ago when Elisabeth was refusing to get out of the bed was now an absolute madhouse. Alice got a headache after five minutes.

Luckily they were all coming here today for a Mother's Day lunch, rather than Elisabeth's crazy house, and Madison, the precious girl, was going to cook.

Sleep, Alice. In a few hours the house will be filled with people.

Mum and Roger would be early. They'd be desperate to show them their photos from their recent holiday to the Latin Dance Convention in Las Vegas. Salsa dancing was still their passion.

As Frannie once said, "They've created a whole life around salsa dancing." Xavier had added, "Not like us. We've created a whole life around sex." Frannie hadn't spoken to him for a week, she had been so humiliated to hear him speak like that in front of the grandchildren.

Frannie and Xavier would be there today, together with Jess, one of Xavier's granddaughters, who had moved to Sydney a few years ago and made contact with her grandfather, to his everlasting joy. She was an extremely hip young Web designer who was also the lead singer in a band. Frannie and Xavier enjoyed going along to Jess's "gigs" and making knowledgeable comments afterward about the "crowd" and the "acoustics."

Alice worried sometimes that Frannie was overtiring herself, keeping up with all of Xavier's activities, but there was no denying her happiness.

She shifted in her bed. Sleep. As Frannie would certainly point out, she was quite old enough to take care of herself!

Hurry up and sleep.

She slept, and dreamed of Gina again.

She, Mike, Nick, and Alice were sitting around the dinner table after a long night of eating and drinking.

"I wonder what we'll all be doing in ten years' time," said Gina.

"We'll be grayer and fatter and wrinklier," said Nick, who was a bit drunk. "But hopefully the four of us will still be friends sitting around a table like this, talking about our memories."

"Awwww," said Gina, raising her glass. "You're so sweet, Nick."

"Preferably on a yacht," said Mike.

Was it a dream or a memory?

"Alice," said a voice in her ear.

Alice opened her eyes.

Nick's face was creased with sleep. "Were you dreaming about Gina?"

"Did I say her name?"

"Yes. And Mike's name."

Thankfully she hadn't said Dominick's name. He was still a bit strange about Dominick. Did Nick sometimes dream of that Megan? She looked at him suspiciously.

"What?" he said.

"Nothing."

"Happy Mother's Day."

"Thank you."

He said, "I'll go bring us up some coffee in a minute."

"Okay."

Nick closed his eyes and fell immediately back asleep.

Alice put her hands behind her head and considered her dream. Dominick had made an appearance because she'd seen him at the IGA yesterday. He was studying a packet of floss as if his life depended upon it. She had a feeling he'd seen her first and wasn't in the mood for one of their overly hearty, let's-pretend-this-isn't-awkward chats and so she'd obligingly darted into the next aisle.

It was so strange to think that she'd seriously considered spending her life with him. (He was married now to one of the other mothers from school; he probably thought the same thing about her.)

Madison had been asking Alice a lot of questions lately about the year they separated.

"If you hadn't lost your memory that time, do you think you and Dad would have still got back together?" she'd asked just yesterday.

It made Alice sick with guilt when she thought about what they had put the children through that year. She and Nick had been so *young*, so full of the earth-shattering importance of their own feelings.

"Do you think we damaged you?" she asked Madison anxiously.

"No need to get hysterical, Mum," Madison had sighed, worldly-wise.

Would they have got back together if she hadn't lost her memory?

Yes. No. Probably not.

She remembered that hot summer's afternoon a few months after Francesca was born. Nick had stopped by the house to return a schoolbag Tom had left in his car. The children were out back, in the pool, and Alice, Dominick, and Nick were on the front lawn, reminiscing about their own childhood summers playing with water sprinklers on front lawns, before the days of water restrictions. Alice and Dominick were standing together, and Nick was standing a little way apart.

The conversation had led to Alice and Nick telling Dominick about how they'd painted the front veranda on a sweltering hot day. It had been a disaster. The paint had dried too quickly; it had all cracked and peeled.

"You were in such a bad mood that day," Nick said to Alice. "Stomping around. Blaming me." He imitated her stomping.

Alice gave him a shove. "You were in a bad mood, too."

"I poured a bucket of water over you to calm you down."

"And then I threw the tin of paint at you and you went *crazy*. You were running after me. You looked like Frankenstein."

They laughed at the memory. They couldn't stop laughing. Each time their eyes met they laughed harder.

Dominick smiled uneasily. "Guess you had to be there."

That just made them laugh harder.

When they finally stopped and wiped the tears from their eyes, the shadows on the lawn had lengthened and Alice saw that she was standing next to Nick and Dominick was standing apart, as if she and Nick were the couple and Dominick was the visitor. She looked at Dominick and his eyes were flat and sad. They all knew. Maybe they'd all known for the last few months.

Three weeks later, Nick moved back in.

The funny thing was that Nick didn't even remember that moment on the lawn. He thought she imagined it. For him, the significant moment had been at Madison's oratory competition.

"You turned around and looked at me and I thought, Yep, she wants me back."

Alice didn't remember that at all.

"What are you thinking about?"

Alice blinked. Nick stood at the foot of the bed, looking down at her. "Your face has gone all serious."

"Pancakes," said Alice. "I'm hoping they're seriously good pancakes."

"Ah. Well, they will be. Madison is cooking."

She watched him pull back the curtains and examine the day outside. He lifted the window and breathed in luxuriously. Obviously the weather had met with his approval. Then he went into the en suite bathroom, pulling up his T-shirt to scratch his stomach and yawning.

Alice closed her eyes and remembered those first few months after Nick moved back in.

Sometimes it was exhilaratingly easy to be happy again. Other times they found that they did have to "try," and the trying seemed stupid and pointless and Alice would wake up in the middle of the night thinking of all the times Nick had hurt her and wondering why she hadn't stayed with Dominick. But then there were the other times, unexpected quiet moments, where they'd catch each other's eyes, and all the years of hurt and joy, bad times and good times, seemed to fuse into a feeling that she knew was so much stronger, more complex and real, than any of those fledgling feelings for Dominick, or even the love she'd first felt for Nick in those early years.

She had always thought that exquisitely happy time at the beginning of her relationship with Nick was the ultimate, the feeling they'd always be trying to replicate, to get back, but now she realized that was wrong. That was like comparing sparkling mineral water to French champagne. Early love is exciting and exhilarating. It's light and bubbly. Anyone can love like that. But love after three children, after a separation and a near-divorce, after you've hurt each other and forgiven each other, bored each other and surprised each other, after you've seen the worst and the best—well, that sort of a love is ineffable. It deserves its own word.

And quite possibly she could have achieved that feeling with Dominick one day. It was never so much that Dominick was wrong for her and that Nick was right. She may have had a perfectly happy life with Dominick.

But Nick was Nick. He knew what she meant when she said, "Oh my dosh." They could look at an old photo together and travel back in time to the same place; they could begin a million conversations with "Do you remember when . . ."; they could hear the first chords of an old song on the radio and exchange glances that said everything without words. Each memory, good and bad, was another invisible thread that bound them together, even when they were foolishly thinking they could lead separate lives. It was as simple and complicated as that.

When Olivia started high school, Alice had begun work as a consultant for fund-raising events. Working seemed to give her relationship with Nick a new edge. Sometimes they would go out to dinner after they'd both been working, and she felt an entirely new attraction for him. Two professionals flirting across the table. It had the frisson of an affair. It was so good to find that their relationship could keep on changing, finding new edges.

Nick stopped suddenly beside the bed and looked down at her, his hand pressed to his chest.

"What?" Alice sat upright. "Chest pain? Are you feeling chest pain?"

She was obsessed with chest pain.

He removed his hand and smiled. "Sorry. No. I was just thinking."

"God," she said irritably, lying back down again. "You nearly gave *me* a heart attack."

He knelt on the bed next to her. She swatted him away. "I haven't cleaned my teeth."

"Oh, for heaven's sakes," he said. "I'm trying to say something profound."

"I prefer you to be profound when I've cleaned my teeth."

"I was just thinking," he said, "how grateful I am that you hit your head that day. Every day I say a little prayer thanking God for creating the spin class."

She smiled. "That's very profound. Very romantic."

"Thank you. I do my best."

He lowered his head, and she went to give him a friendly, perfunctory kiss (she hadn't cleaned her teeth; she was impatient for her coffee) but the kiss turned unexpectedly lovely and she felt that ticklish, teary feeling behind her eyes as a lifetime of kisses filled her head: from the very first brand-new-boyfriend kiss, to *"You may kiss the bride,"* to the unshaven, shell-shocked, red-eyed kiss after Madison was born, to that aching, beautiful kiss after she broke up with Dominick and told Nick (standing in the car park of McDonald's, the kids arguing in the backseat of the car), *"Will you please come back home now?"*

The bedroom door burst open and Nick jumped back to his side of the bed, grinning. Madison was balancing a tray set for breakfast, Tom was holding a huge bunch of sunflowers, and Olivia had a present.

"Happy Mother's Day to you," they sang, to the tune of "Happy Birthday."

"We're trying to redeem ourselves for last year," explained Madison as she placed the tray on Alice's lap.

"I should think so," said Alice. She picked up the fork, took a mouthful of pancake, and closed her eyes.

"Mmmmm."

They would think she was savoring the taste (blueberries, cinnamon, cream—excellent), but she was actually savoring the whole morning, trying to catch it, pin it down, keep it safe before all those precious moments became yet another memory.

Acknowledgments

A special thank-you to my lovely sisters, Jaclyn and Nicola Moriarty, for reading and commenting on my first drafts.

Thank you to my cousin, Penelope Lowe, for advice on medical matters, and my friend Rachel Gordon for patiently answering questions about life as a mother to school-aged children.

Thank you to my U.S. agent, Faye Bender, for all her support in finding the right home for this book.

Thank you to my wonderful editors around the world: Amy Einhorn in the United States, Cate Paterson and Julia Stiles in Australia, Melanie Blank-Schroeder in Germany, and Lydia Newhouse in the UK. You all helped make *What Alice Forgot* a better book.

About the Author

Liane Moriarty is the author of two novels, *Three Wishes* and *The Last Anniversary*, both of which were published around the world and translated into seven languages. She is also the author of the Nicola Berry series for children. Liane lives in Sydney with her husband and two small, noisy children.